OVER THE WINE-DARK SEA

By H. N. Turteltaub from Tom Doherty Associates

Justinian
Over the Wine-Dark Sea

OVER THE WINE-DARK SEA

H. N. TURTELTAUB

A TOM DOHERTY ASSOCIATES BOOK  NEW YORK

Turteltaub

OVER THE WINE-DARK SEA

This book is printed on acid-free paper.

Edited by Patrick Nielsen Hayden

Design by Jane Adele Regina

Map by Mark Stein Studios

A Forge Book
Published by Tom Doherty Associates, LLC
175 Fifth Avenue
New York, NY 10010

www.tor.com

Forge® is a registered trademark of Tom Doherty Associates, LLC.

Library of Congress Cataloging-in-Publication Data

Turteltaub, H. N.
    Over the wine-dark sea / H. N. Turteltaub.—1st ed.
        p.   cm
    "A Tom Doherty Associates book."
    ISBN 0-312-87660-2 (acid-free paper)
    1. Greece—History—Macedonian Hegemony, 323–281 B.C.—Fiction. 2. Mediterranean Region—Fiction. 3. Merchant mariners—Fiction. 4. Rhodes (Greece)—Fiction. 5. Ship captains—Fiction. 6. Brothers—Fiction. I. Title.

PS3570.U758 O94 2001
813'.54—dc21

                                                                2001023201

First Edition: July 2001

Printed in the United States of America

0 9 8 7 6 5 4 3 2 1

This book is for Professor Stanley Burstein
of California State University, Los Angeles, and for Noreen Doyle,
with many thanks for their friendship and for their help with my research.

A NOTE ON
WEIGHTS, MEASURES, AND MONEY

I have, as best I could, used in this novel the weights, measures, and coinages my characters would have used and encountered in their journey. Here are some approximate equivalents (precise values would have varied from city to city, further complicating things):

1 digit = ¾ inch
4 digits = 1 palm (3 IN)
6 palms = 1 cubit (18 IN)
1 cubit = 1½ feet
1 plethron = 100 feet
1 stadion = 600 feet (200 YDS)

12 khalkoi = 1 obolos
6 oboloi = 1 drakhma
100 drakhmai = 1 mina
    (about 1 pound of silver)
60 minai = 1 talent (60 LBS)

As noted, these are all approximate. As a measure of how widely they could vary, the talent in Athens was about 57 pounds, while that of Aigina, less than thirty miles away, was about 83 pounds.

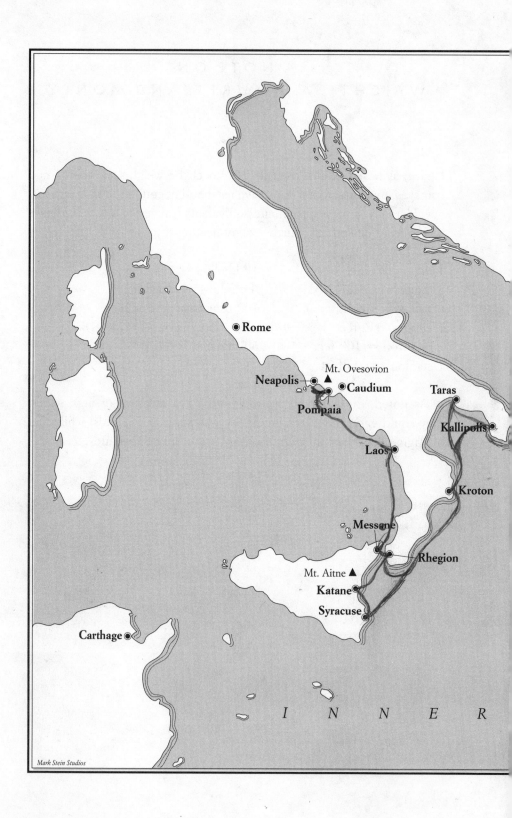

Rome

Mt. Ovesovion ▲
Neapolis
Caudium
Pompaia
Taras
Kallipolis
Laos
Kroton
Messane
Rhegion
Mt. Aitne ▲
Katane
Syracuse
Carthage

I N N E R

Mark Stein Studios

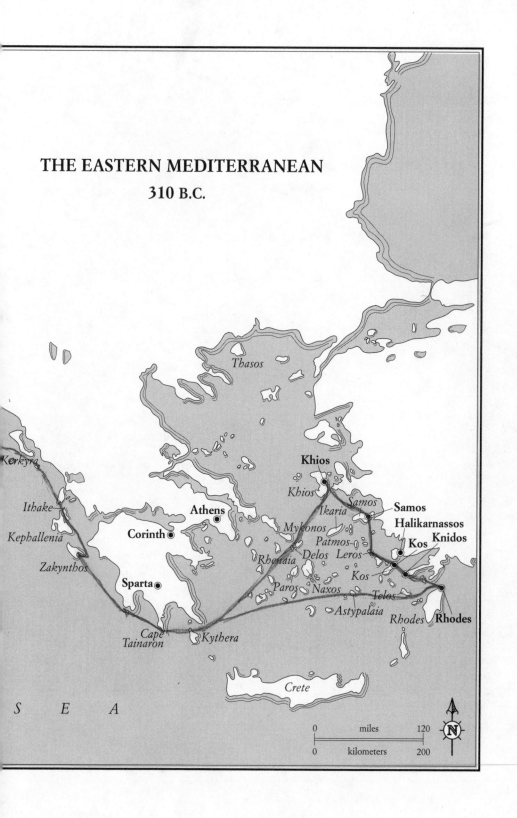

THE EASTERN MEDITERRANEAN
310 B.C.

Thasos

Khios

Khios

Athens

Ikaria

Samos

Samos

Halikarnassos

Corinth

Mykonos

Patmos

Kos

Knidos

Rhenaia

Delos

Leros

Kerkyra

Ithake

Kephallenia

Zakynthos

Sparta

Paros

Naxos

Kos

Telos

Astypalaia

Rhodes

Rhodes

Cape
Tainaron

Kythera

Crete

S E A

| 0 | miles | 120 |

| 0 | kilometers | 200 |

N

1

MENEDEMOS AND HIS COUSIN SOSTRATOS WALKED DOWN
toward the *Aphrodite* in the main harbor of Rhodes. Both young men
wore thigh-length wool chitons. Sostratos had a wool chlamys on over
his tunic. He didn't really need the cloak, though; it was still late in
the month of Anthesterion, before the vernal equinox, but the sun
shone warm out of a clear blue sky. Like any men who often went
to sea, the two cousins went barefoot even on dry land.

A mild breeze blew down from the north. Tasting it, Menedemos
dipped his head in anticipation. "Good sailing weather coming
soon," he said. He was little and lithe and very handsome, his face
clean-shaven in the style Alexander the Great had made popular
twenty years before.

"Sure enough," Sostratos agreed. He'd spent enough years studying in Athens to have a sharper accent than the Doric drawl usual in
Rhodes. Careless of fashion, he'd let his beard grow out. He towered
more than half a head above his cousin. "Some traders have already
put to sea, I hear."

"I've heard the same, but Father says it's too early," Menedemos
answered.

"He's probably right." Sostratos, as far as Menedemos was concerned, showed altogether too much self-restraint for someone only
a few months older than he was.

"I want to be *out* there," Menedemos said. "I want to be *doing*
things. Whenever we sit idle over the winter, I feel like a hare caught
in a net."

"Plenty to do during the winter," Sostratos said. "It's what you do
then that lets you succeed when you can sail."

"Yes, Grandfather," Menedemos said. "No wonder I command
the *Aphrodite* and you keep track of what goes aboard her."

Sostratos shrugged. "The gods give one man one thing, another
man another. You're always ready to seize the moment. You always

have been, as long as I can remember. As for me . . ." He shrugged again. Even though slightly the older and much the larger of the two of them, he'd had to get used to living in Menedemos' shadow. "As you said, I keep track of things. I'm good at it."

"Well, nobody can quarrel with you there," Menedemos said generously. He raised his voice to a shout and hailed the akatos ahead: "Ahoy, the *Aphrodite*!"

Carpenters in chitons and naked sailors aboard the merchant galley waved to Menedemos and Sostratos. "When do we go out, skipper?" one of the sailors called. "We've been stuck in port so long, my hands have got soft."

"We'll fix *that,* don't you worry," Menedemos said with a laugh. "It won't be long now, I promise." His sharp, dark-eyed gaze swung to a carpenter at the poop of the forty-cubit vessel. "Hail, Khremes. How are those new steering oars coming?"

"They're just about ready, captain," the carpenter answered. "I think they'll be even smoother than the pair you had before. A little old bald man sitting in a chair with a cushion under his backside could swing your ship any way you wanted her to go." He waved in invitation. "Come on up and get the feel of 'em for yourself."

Menedemos tossed his head to show he declined. "Can't really do that till she's in the water, not hauled out to keep her timbers dry." Sostratos following him, he walked toward the bow of the ship. The *Aphrodite* had twenty oars on either side, giving her almost as many rowers as a pentekonter, but she was beamier than the fifty-oared galleys so beloved by pirates: unlike them, she had to carry cargo.

Sostratos tapped the lead sheathing the *Aphrodite* below the waterline with a fingernail. "Still good and sound."

"It had better be," Menedemos said. "We just replaced it year before last." He tapped, too, at one of the copper nails holding the lead and the tarred wool fabric below it to the oak planking of the hull.

Up at the bow, another carpenter was replacing a lost nail that helped hold the three-finned bronze ram to the bow timbers inside it. He must have heard Menedemos' remark, for he looked up and said, "And I'll bet you were glad you finally could do it year before last, too."

"He's got you there," Sostratos said.

"No, we finally got him and his pals back," Menedemos answered. "For a while there, ordinary Rhodians had a cursed hard time getting carpenters to work for them—everybody was building ships for Antigonos to use against Ptolemaios."

"That was a mistake—helping Antigonos, I mean," Sostratos said. "Rhodes does too much business with Egypt for us to get on Ptolemaios' wrong side."

"You can say that—you were studying up in Athens. You don't know what things were like here." Menedemos scowled at the memory. "Nobody had the nerve to try crossing One-Eyed Antigonos, believe you me."

As terns screeched overhead, Sostratos made a placating gesture. "All right. I wouldn't want to try crossing him myself, since you put it that way." Another screech rang out, this one louder, more raucous, and much closer than the high-flying sea birds. Sostratos jumped. "By the dog of Egypt, what was that?"

"I don't know." Menedemos trotted away from the *Aphrodite*. "Come on. Let's go find out."

Sostratos flipped his hands in protest. "Our fathers sent us down here to see if the ship is ready to take out."

"We'll do that," Menedemos said over his shoulder. "But whatever's making that noise may be something the Hellenes in Italy haven't seen before. I know I've never heard it before."

The horrible screech rang out again. It sounded more like a bugle than anything else, but it didn't really sound like a bugle, either. "I hope I never hear it again," Sostratos said, but, as he did so often, he followed where Menedemos led.

Since the screeches, once begun, resounded at pretty regular intervals, tracking them didn't require dogs. They came from a ramshackle pierside warehouse about a plethron from the *Aphrodite*. The owner of the building, a fat Phoenician named Himilkon, came running out, hands clapped over his ears, just as Menedemos and Sostratos trotted up.

"Hail," Menedemos said. "Is that the noise a leopard makes?"

"Or has some Egyptian wizard summoned up a kakodaimon from the depths of Tartaros?" Sostratos added.

Himilkon shook his head from side to side, as Phoenicians did when they meant no. "Neither, my masters," he answered in gutturally accented Greek. Gold gleamed from hoops that pierced his ears. He plucked at his curled black beard, much longer and thicker than Sostratos', to show distress. "That accursed fowl is pretty, but it will drive me mad."

"Fowl?" Menedemos raised an eyebrow at yet another screech. "What kind of fowl? A pigeon with a brazen throat?"

"A fowl," Himilkon repeated. "I do not recall the name in Greek." He shouted back into the warehouse: "Hyssaldomos! Bring out the cage, to show the miserable creature to these fine gentlemen."

"He wants you to buy it, whatever it is," Sostratos whispered to Menedemos. The captain of the *Aphrodite* dipped his head in impatient agreement.

Hyssaldomos' voice came from within: "Be right there, boss." Grunting under the weight, the Karian slave carried out a large, heavy wooden cage and set it down on the ground by Himilkon. "Here you go."

Menedemos and Sostratos crouched to peer through the slats of the cage. A very large bird with shiny blue feathers and a curious crest or topknot stared back at them with beady black eyes. It opened its pale beak and gave forth with another screech, all the more appalling for coming from closer range.

Rubbing his ear, Menedemos looked up at Himilkon. "Whatever it is, I've never seen one before."

Hyssaldomos supplied the Greek word: "It's a peacock."

"That's right, a peacock," Himilkon said with pride that would have been greater if he hadn't had to talk around a screech.

"A peacock!" Menedemos and Sostratos exclaimed, in excitement and disbelief. Menedemos wagged a finger at the creature and quoted Aristophanes, his favorite playwright: " 'Which are you, bird or peacock?' "

"My slave and I told you it was a peacock," said the Phoenician merchant, who'd probably never heard of the *Birds*. "And be careful with your hands around it. It bites."

"Where does it come from?" Sostratos asked.

"India," Himilkon replied. "Since the divine Alexander went there with an army of you Hellenes, more of these birds have come back to the Inner Sea than ever before. I have the peacock here, and five peahens still caged in the warehouse. They're quieter than he is, Baal be praised."

"From India?" Sostratos scratched his head in bewilderment. "But Herodotos doesn't talk about peafowl in India in his history. He talks about the clothes made from tree-wool, and the enormous ants that mine gold, and the Indians themselves, with their black hides and their black semen. But not a word about peacocks. If they came from India, you'd think he'd say so."

Himilkon shrugged. "I don't know anything about this Hellene, whoever he is. But I know where peacocks come from. And if he didn't talk about them, my bet is he didn't know about them."

With a chuckle, Menedemos said, "You can't argue with that, Sostratos." He enjoyed teasing his cousin, who, he sometimes thought, would sooner read about life than live it. He took another look at the peacock, then asked Himilkon, "What are those feathers piled up on top of it? They don't look like they're growing out of its back."

"No, no, no." The Phoenician made little pushing motions, as if to deny the very idea. "Those are tail feathers. The cage is too small, too crowded."

"All that mess? Its tail?" Menedemos raised that eyebrow again. "You're having me on."

"No such thing." Himilkon drew himself up, the picture of affronted dignity. "I'll show you." He turned to Hyssaldomos. "Open the door and let it out, to show the gentlemen. They may be customers, eh?"

His slave plainly didn't care whether Menedemos and Sostratos were customers or not. "Oh, boss, have a heart!" the Karian wailed. "I'm the one who'll have to herd it back in there afterwards."

"And what else have you got to do?" Himilkon retorted. "It's not going to fly away; its wing is clipped. Go on, you lazy good-for-nothing."

Muttering under his breath, Hyssaldomos squatted and undid the two bronze hooks and eyes that held the cage door closed. Even after he opened the door, the peacock didn't come out right away. "He's stupid," Hyssaldomos said, looking up at the two Hellenes. "I mean to tell you, he's really stupid."

But then, with another screech, the peacock finally seemed to realize what had happened and rushed out of the cage. Menedemos exclaimed in astonishment. He'd seen it was big, but hadn't realized just how big: its body was almost swan-sized, and the tail—Himilkon hadn't lied—at least doubled its apparent size.

"He's beautiful," Sostratos breathed. The sun gleamed metallically from the blue and green feathers of the peacock's body and tail.

Menedemos dipped his head in agreement. "He certainly is. They've never—" He'd started to say they'd never seen the like in Italy, but bit down on the words before they escaped. If Himilkon knew he badly wanted the bird, the price was bound to go up.

"Oh, there he goes!" Hyssaldomos wailed as the peacock started to run. "Get in front of him, young sirs, and head him off!"

Both Menedemos and Sostratos tried to get in front of the peacock, but it dodged them like a flutegirl dodging a drunken, groping reveler at a symposion. And then it was off, running like a racehorse and screeching as it ran. Its legs weren't goose- or swanlike; they put Menedemos more in mind of those of a bustard or pheasant. He and Sostratos pounded after it. Urged on by Himilkon's curses, Hyssaldomos ran after them.

The peacock kept trying to take to the air. It couldn't fly; as Himilkon had said, its wings were clipped. But every flapping, fluttering burst lent it extra speed. "It's—faster—than we are," Sostratos panted.

"I know." Menedemos was panting, too. "We could enter it at the next Olympics, and it'd win the dash." He raised his voice to a shout: "Two oboloi to whoever catches the bird unhurt!"

Sailors and workmen and passersby were already staring at the peacock, or perhaps at the spectacle of three men chasing a peacock. The prospect of a reward sent a double handful of them after the bird, too, converging on it from every angle at once.

A naked sailor grabbed for the peacock. "I've got you!" he cried in triumph. A moment later, he cried out once more, this time in dismay: "*Oimoi!* Help!" The peacock kicked and raked him with its big clawed feet. It buffeted him with its wings. And it pecked, hard. "*Oimoi!*" he yelled again, and let go.

"Himilkon told you it could bite off a finger," Sostratos said to Menedemos.

"That wasn't his finger," Menedemos answered. "And he's lucky it didn't bite it off."

From then on, nobody seemed nearly so eager to close with the peacock. From the doorway to his warehouse, Himilkon shouted, "Herd it back over here." People were more willing to try that. Yelling and waving their arms and shying pebbles—and staying at a respectful distance—they managed to turn the peacock so it was running toward the Phoenician merchant instead of away from him.

"It'll trample him if he tries to catch it by himself," Menedemos said, still running after the bird.

"He's brought something else out of the building," Sostratos said. "Looks like another cage."

When they got a little closer, Menedemos asked, "Is that another peacock in there?"

"Not a pea*cock*." Sostratos replied. "See how much plainer it is?"

The peacock had seen the same thing as Sostratos, and more quickly, too. It skidded to a stop, sand and gravel flying up from between its toes. All at once, it might have forgotten the mob of men pursuing it. Noting as much, Menedemos slowed down, too, and waved his comrades to a halt with him.

"What's it doing?" somebody asked.

"Showing off for the peahen," Sostratos answered.

And then everyone, even Himilkon, said, "Ahhh!" as the peacock raised its long tail and spread it wide. The blue spots on the green and yellow plumes caught and held the light. The peacock slowly backed toward the caged peahen, then turned to give her the full magnificent display.

"Argos' eyes," Sostratos said softly.

"There's no myth about Argos and the peacock," Menedemos said.

"Of course not," Sostratos said. "Back in the days when the myths were made, who'd ever seen a peacock? But if people had, that's the myth they would have made."

While they spoke, Himilkon, a practical man, tossed a net over the distracted peacock. It let out a horrified squawk and tried to get away again, but couldn't. Despite its struggles, Himilkon and Hyssaldomos wrestled it back into its cage without incurring more than minor flesh wounds.

"*Please* don't let it out again any time soon, boss," the Karian slave pleaded, fastening the hooks and eyes that kept the peacock imprisoned.

"Oh, shut up." The merchant drew back his foot as if to kick Hyssaldomos, but relented. "If I have a customer, I'll put the bird through his paces."

"And me through mine, by Zeus Labraundeus," Hyssaldomos grumbled. He scowled at Menedemos and Sostratos. "Besides, who says they're customers? Just a couple of gawkers, if you ask me."

"Oh, we might be interested . . . if the price is right," Menedemos allowed.

In the fight with Himilkon and Hyssaldomos, the peacock had shed one of those astonishing tail feathers. Menedemos plucked it off the ground and admired it. "Three oboloi if you want to keep it," Himilkon said briskly.

"Half a drakhma?" Menedemos yelped. "For a *feather*?" A drakhma a day could feed and house a man and his family—not in any style, but it would put a roof over their heads and keep them from starving. "That's robbery!"

Himilkon smiled. "I'll deduct it from the price of the bird . . . if you're a customer."

Like any Hellene going out where he might spend some money, Menedemos had a couple of oboloi tucked between his cheek and his teeth. He spat the little silver coins into the palm of his hand and dried them on his tunic. Then he nudged his cousin, who produced another one. Menedemos handed Himilkon the coins. The Phoenician popped them into his own mouth. Menedemos asked, "Well, what do you want for him—and for the peahens, too?"

Some of the men who'd chased the peacock went back to what they had been doing now that it was back in its cage. Others hung around to watch the haggling, which might also prove entertaining.

Himilkon plucked at his fancy curled beard, considering. He put so much into it, he might have been an actor in a comedy using his body to get across what his mask couldn't. At last, elaborately artless, he said, "Oh, I don't know. A mina a bird sounds about right."

"A pound of silver? A hundred drakhmai?" As Himilkon had worked to sound casual, Menedemos worked to sound horrified. Actually, he'd been braced for worse. Peafowl were obviously for the luxury trade. Nobody would raise them in the courtyard like ducks. Like any merchant galley, the *Aphrodite* specialized in carrying luxuries. She didn't have the capacity to make a profit hauling wheat or cheap wine, the way a tubby sailing ship could.

Menedemos shot Sostratos a glance. A little slower than he should have, his cousin chimed in, "It's an outrage, Himilkon—pure hubris. Half that much would be an outrage, and you know it."

Himilkon shook his head back and forth again, then tossed it as a Hellene would to show disagreement. "No such thing, O best ones. I know you both. I know your fathers. If you buy my birds, you'll take them somewhere far away, and you'll sell them for plenty more than you pay. Tell me I'm wrong." He set his hands on his hips and looked defiantly at the younger men.

"We'll try to do that, no doubt," Menedemos said. "But what if the peacock dies while we're at sea? What do we sell then? I saw the peahen in her cage; she's not pretty enough to bring much by herself."

"Breed her to the cock. Breed all the hens you buy—if you buy any; if you don't go on trying to cheat me—to the cock," Himilkon replied. "Once they lay, you'll have plenty of birds to sell."

Sostratos said, "But only the one peacock shows what anyone who buys a bird from us would want."

Himilkon's smile might have shown off a shark's teeth, not his own, which were square and rather yellow. "In that case, you should pay me more for him, eh, not less."

The hangers-on laughed and clapped their hands at that. Menedemos shot Sostratos another glance, an angry one this time. But Sostratos tossed his head as calmly as if his opponent hadn't landed a telling blow. "Not at all," he said. "A mina is too much for the peacock, and much too much for the peahens."

"Without the peahens, you'll get no more peacocks," Himilkon said. "That's the value in them."

"We'll give you a mina and a half for the peacock and the five peahens," Menedemos said, wondering how loudly his father—and Sostratos' father, too—would scream at him for plunging into this dicker.

No louder than Himilkon screamed now; he was sure of that. "Twenty-five drakhmai a bird?" the Phoenician merchant bellowed.

"You're no trader—you're a pirate, robbing honest men. I'd sooner roast the fowl myself than sell them for that."

"Invite us to the banquet," Sostratos said coolly. "A white wine from Thasos would go well with them, don't you think? Come on, cousin." He set a hand on Menedemos' shoulder.

Menedemos didn't want to leave. He wanted to stay and haggle with Himilkon, or possibly punch the Phoenician in the face. But when he angrily rounded on Sostratos, he saw something in his cousin's eyes that gave him pause. He dipped his head in agreement. Sometimes the only way to get a better bargain was to pretend one didn't matter. "Let's go," he said.

They started to walk away. If Himilkon kept quiet, they would have to keep walking. Menedemos didn't want that. What would the rich Hellenes in Taras or Syracuse pay for a peacock? A lot more than a mina, or he wildly missed his guess.

From behind them, Himilkon said, "Because I've dealt with your families before, I might—just might, mind you—let you have six birds for five minai, though I'd not do it for any other men born of woman."

With the best appearance of reluctance they could manage, Menedemos and Sostratos turned back. The little crowd of hangers-on sighed and shifted their feet and made themselves comfortable, ready to enjoy a long, vituperative dicker.

They got one, too. After much shouting and many invocations of gods both Greek and Phoenician, the two cousins settled with Himilkon on fifty drakhmai for each of the peahens and seventy-five for the peacock. Just when everything seemed agreed, Menedemos suddenly tossed his head and said, "No, it won't do."

Himilkon eyed him apprehensively. "What now?"

Holding up the fancy tail feather he'd bought, Menedemos said, "Seventy-four drakhmai, three oboloi for the peacock."

The Phoenician dug his tongue into his cheek, feeling for the silver coins he'd already got from Menedemos. "All right," he said. "Seventy-four drakhmai, three oboloi it is."

"WE'LL HAVE OURSELVES an interesting cargo when the *Aphrodite* sails," Sostratos said, as he and Menedemos walked back from the harbor to their homes, which sat side by side near Demeter's temple in the northern part of the city.

"Father's got those jars of ink in the warehouse," Menedemos agreed, "and the rolls of papyrus with them, and the vials of Egyptian poppy-juice, too. And we'll put in at Khios and pick up some wine." He ran his tongue over his lips. "Nothing finer than Khian. It's thick as honey, and even sweeter."

"Khian's a lot stronger than honey, too," Sostratos observed. "Those are vintages you need to drink well-watered."

With a snort, Menedemos said, "Those are vintages *you* can drink well-watered, my dear cousin. Me, I like to have some fun every so often."

Sostratos sighed. "I like drinking wine. I don't like swilling it down neat like a barbarian. I don't like getting drunk and breaking things and getting into fights." He was, or at least tried to be, moderate. All the philosophers maintained that moderation was a virtue. By the look on Menedemos' face, he reckoned it not only a vice but a nasty vice at that. Sostratos sighed again. His cousin had all the noteworthy good traits: he was handsome, outgoing, strong, nimble. He could as easily sing a song as guide a ship through a gale without showing fear.

And what about you? Sostratos asked himself. He shrugged. Nobody'd ever written *Sostratos is beautiful* on the walls when he was a youth. He wasn't a bad haggler, but he got what bargains he got with reason and patience, not by making people like him and go easy or by persuading them black was white. He towered over Menedemos, but his cousin always threw him when they stripped off their clothes and wrestled in the gymnasion.

I have a good prose style. Theophrastos told me that himself, up in Athens, and he doles out even less praise than Aristoteles did when he headed the Lykeion. *Everyone says so. I remember what I read, too. And I've always been clever—better than clever, really—with numbers.*

It didn't seem enough. Even with moderation and reliability thrown in, it didn't seem enough. Sostratos shrugged again. *I can't be Menedemos. I am what the gods made me. I have to make the most of what they gave me.*

His cousin laughed and pointed. "Look, Sostratos. It really is getting on toward spring. There's a gecko on a wall."

Sure enough, a gray-brown lizard clung to the gray-brown mud brick of a poor man's house. It walked up the wall as easily as a fly might have done, and snapped up a bug before the insect knew it was there.

Half a block past the house with the gecko, they turned right so as to go north. That was the only turn they'd have to make till they got to their homes. Sostratos said, "Gods be praised, Rhodes is laid out on a grid, the way Peiraieus is up in Attica. Anyone can find his way around here or in Athens' harbor. Athens itself?" He tossed his head. "You have to be born there to know where you're going, and even the Athenians aren't sure half the time. Hippodamos of Miletos was a man of godlike wit."

"I never much thought about it," Menedemos confessed. "But most towns are pretty bad, aren't they? You can't get from the harbor to an inn a bowshot away without asking directions three different times, on account of the streets go wherever they please, not where you need 'em to."

"Of course," Sostratos said musingly, "Peiraieus and Rhodes are new cities; they *could* be planned. It's what, two years shy of a century since Rhodes was founded? A town that's been there since before the fall of Troy, the streets probably follow the way the cows used to wander."

"Homer doesn't say anything about whether Troy was laid out in a grid," Menedemos said. He paused to eye a slave woman carrying a jar of water back to her house. "Hello, sweetheart!" he called. The slave kept walking, but she smiled back at Menedemos.

Sostratos sighed. If he'd done that, the slave woman might have ignored him—if he was lucky. If he wasn't lucky, she'd have showered him with curses. That had happened to him once, up in Athens. Like a puppy that once stuck its nose into the fire, he hadn't taken the chance of its happening again.

Potters and jewelers and shoemakers and smiths and millers and tavernkeepers and all the other artisans whose work helped keep Rhodes prosperous had their shops in the front part of the buildings in which they and their households also lived. Some of them steadily kept whatever they did for a living. Others made periodic forays out into the street in search of customers.

"Here—look at my fine terracottas!" cried a potter—or would he think of himself as a sculptor? Sostratos didn't know. He didn't much care, either. He hoped the fellow made better pots than burnt-clay images. If he didn't, his wife and children would starve.

"Coming out!" somebody else shouted, this time from a second-story window. Sostratos and Menedemos sprang back in a hurry. So did everyone else close by. The odorous contents of a slops jar splashed down in the middle of the street. Somebody who didn't spring back fast enough—and who got his mantle splattered as a result—shook his fist at the window, whose wooden shutters were now closed again.

More men than women strode the streets. Respectable wives and maidens spent most of the time in the women's quarters of their houses. They sent slaves out to shop and run errands for them. Poor men's wives—the women in families that had no slaves of their own—had to go out by and for themselves. Some were brazen, or simply resigned to it. Others wore shawls and veils to protect themselves from prying eyes.

"Don't you wonder what they look like?—under all that stuff, I mean," Menedemos said after such a woman walked past. "Puts charcoal on my brazier just thinking about it."

"If you did see her, you'd probably think she was ugly," Sostratos said. "For all you know, she's a grandmother."

"Maybe," his cousin admitted. "But for all I *know,* she could be Helen of Troy come back to earth again, or Aphrodite slumming among us poor mortals. In my imagination, she is."

"Your imagination needs cold water poured on it, like a couple of dogs mating in the street," Sostratos said. Menedemos mimed taking an arrow in the chest. He staggered around so convincingly, he alarmed a donkey with four big amphorai of olive oil lashed onto its back with a web of leather straps. The fellow leading the donkey had several pointed things to say about that. Menedemos took no notice of him.

And Sostratos felt a little guilty, for he too sometimes tried to imagine what women looked like under their wraps and tunics, under their shawls and veils. What man didn't, every now and then? Why did women conceal themselves, if not to spur men's imaginings?

Musing thus, he almost walked past his own doorway. Menedemos laughed and said, "Don't come along with me yet. You need to go in and let your father know what we've done, while I tell mine. Merchants' supper at our house tonight, you know."

Sostratos dipped his head to show he remembered. "I expect we'll have plenty to talk about, too—if our fathers haven't skinned us by then and sold our hides to the tanners."

"We'll make money with those birds," Menedemos said stoutly.

"We'd better," Sostratos said. His cousin winced, then waved and went on to his own house. Nothing got Menedemos down for long. Sostratos wished he could say the same. He knocked on the door and waited for his father or a house slave to let him in.

Gyges, the majordomo, unbarred the doors and threw the two panels wide. "Hail, young master," the Lydian slave said. "How is the *Aphrodite* shaping?" He knew almost as much about the business as Sostratos and his father.

"Well enough," Sostratos answered. "Is Father home? Menedemos and I bought some goods to take west when we sail, and I want to tell him about them."

"Yes, he's here," Gyges said. "He'll be glad to see you; Xanthos just left."

"He'd be glad to see anybody else, if Xanthos just left," Sostratos said with a laugh. The other merchant was honest and reliable, but deadly dull.

Sostratos walked through the courtyard on the way to the andron—the men's room—where he expected to find his father. His sister Erinna was out there, watering some of the plants in the herb garden with a jar. "Hail," she said. "What's the news out in the city? I think Xanthos had some, but I stayed in till he left."

"Some business I want to tell Father first," Sostratos said. "Other than that, I didn't hear much. The *Aphrodite* will be ready to sail whenever we decide the weather's good enough."

Erinna sighed. "And then you and Menedemos will be gone till fall." She was eighteen; she'd been married for three years, but had returned to her father's household after her husband died. The dark, curly hair she'd cut short in mourning had finally grown out to close to its proper length.

With a sly smile, Sostratos said, "You know we're only leaving to annoy you."

"I believe it," Erinna said, and went back to watering the herbs. "Well, go on and tell Father whatever you've got to tell him. I suppose I'll hear about it eventually." She made a point of looking put-upon.

If Father reacts the way I'm afraid he will, you'll hear about it right away, when he starts bellowing, Sostratos thought. Taking a deep breath, he went into the andron.

Lysistratos was sitting in a chair, flicking pebbles back and forth on a counting board and muttering to himself. Sostratos' father looked up when the light changed as the younger man came in. Lysistratos was more than a palm shorter than his gangling son, but otherwise looked much like him. His hair had been darker brown than Sostratos'—almost black, in fact—but gray streaked it these days, for he'd seen more than fifty years.

He smiled. His teeth were still good, which helped give him the appearance of a younger man despite the gray. "Hail, son," he said, and waved Sostratos to another chair. "I have news."

"Erinna said you might," Sostratos answered. "So do I, as a matter of fact."

"You go first." They said it together, and both laughed.

"Go on, Father," Sostratos insisted. That was both respect for his father's years and genuine liking; Lysistratos hadn't beaten him more than he deserved when he was a boy, and more than once hadn't beaten him at all when he knew he deserved it.

His father dipped his head in assent. "Xanthos was here a little while ago," he began.

"Yes, I know—Gyges told me when I came in," Sostratos said.

"All right, then. You know how Xanthos is. You have to hear about the state of his bowels, and the speech he made in the last Assembly meeting—which must have been as boring as all the rest he's ever made—and how much worse we are these days than the heroes of the Trojan War." Lysistratos rolled his eyes. "But there's usually a little wheat mixed in with all the chaff, and there was to-day, too."

"Tell me," Sostratos urged.

"I will. You know the town of Amphipolis, next door to Mace-donia?"

"Oh, yes." Sostratos dipped his head. "The historian Thoukydides talks about the place in his fifth book. Brasidas the Spartan beat Kleon of Athens there, though they both died in the battle."

His father looked impatient. "I don't mean Amphipolis in the old days, son. I'm talking about now. You know how Kassandros, the commander in Europe, has been holding Roxane and Alexandros, her son by Alexander the Great, in the fortress there."

"Oh, yes," Sostratos repeated. "Alexandros would be—what, twelve now? I know he was born after Alexander died. He'll be old enough to make a proper king of Macedonia before too long."

Lysistratos tossed his head. "Oh, no, he won't. That was Xanthos' news: some time this past winter, when word would travel slow, Kassandros killed Alexandros—and Roxane, too, for good measure."

Sostratos whistled softly and shivered, as if the andron had suddenly got colder. "Then it's just the generals now, to quarrel over the bones of Alexander's empire. Kassandros in Macedonia, Lysimakhos in Thrace, Antigonos in Anatolia and farther Asia, and Ptolemaios down in Egypt."

"And Polyperkhon over in the Pelopennesos, and that Seleukos fellow who's squabbling with Antigonos in inner Asia," Lysistratos said. "I wonder how long the peace your four made last summer will last. No longer than one of them sees an advantage in breaking it, or I miss my guess."

"You're bound to be right." Sostratos shivered again. He wondered what Thoukydides would have thought of the world as it was nowadays. Nothing good; he was sure of that. In the historian's day, each polis in Hellas had been free to go its own way. Now almost all the Greek city-states danced to the tune of one Macedonian warlord or another. Rhodes remained free and independent, but even his own polis had had to throw out a Macedonian garrison after Alexander died.

Lysistratos might have been thinking along similar lines, for he said, "Being a polis these days is a lot like being a sardine in a school of tunny. But what's your news, son? I hope it's cheerier than mine."

"So do I," Sostratos said, wondering how his father would react. Well, he'd soon know. He brought it out in a rush: "Menedemos and I bought a peacock and five peahens from Himilkon the Phoenician, to take to Italy in the *Aphrodite*."

"A *peacock*!" Lysistratos exclaimed. "Do you know, I've never seen a peacock in all my life. I don't blame you and your cousin one bit. If *I* haven't seen a peacock, you can bet none of the Hellenes in Italy has, either. They'll pay through the nose." His gaze sharpened. "And what did *you* pay?"

Sostratos told him. He waited for his father to burst like a lidded pot left too long on the fire, to thunder like Zeus of the aegis.

But Lysistratos only stroked his gray beard, a gesture Sostratos had copied from him. "Truth to tell, I haven't the faintest idea what a peacock's worth, or a peahen, either," he confessed. "I suspect nobody else does, either. What you lads paid doesn't sound too bad, not unless the birds die on the way and you have to throw them into the sea—the peacock especially."

"That's what we thought, too," Sostratos said. "It's one of the reasons we were able to beat Himilkon down as far as we did."

"He's a man to be reckoned with in a dicker." Lysistratos stroked his beard again. "Tell me . . . Is the peacock as splendid as everyone imagines?"

"He's more splendid than I imagined," Sostratos answered, almost stammering in his relief that things had gone so much smoother than he'd expected. "When he spread his tail to show off for the peahen, I'd never seen anything like it."

"All right," his father said. "When we go next door to supper tonight, we'll find out what your uncle Philodemos has to say about it."

"Yes, that will tell the tale," Sostratos agreed. Philodemos was Lysistratos' older brother, and the senior partner in their trading operation. He was also a man of less certain temper than Lysistratos, just as Menedemos was touchier than Sostratos. Now Sostratos dipped his head to his father. "If you'll excuse me . . ."

He went up the wooden stairs to his bedroom on the second story. One of the house slaves, a redheaded girl about Erinna's age called Threissa, was coming downstairs. By her looks and the name she'd been given—it simply meant *the Thracian*—she'd probably been captured not too far from Amphipolis. Sostratos smiled at her. He'd summoned her to his bed a couple of times. As a bachelor, he could get away with such things, where his father would have had trouble: keeping a wife and a mistress under the same roof was a recipe for trouble and scandal.

Threissa nodded back, polite but no more than that. She'd pleased him; he feared the reverse wasn't so true. Of course, he had to worry about her opinion only if he chose to.

The bedroom was sparsely furnished: a bedstead with a wool-stuffed mattress, a chamber pot under it, a chair beside it, and two cypresswood chests, a smaller atop a larger. The larger one held Sostratos' tunics and mantles. The smaller held his books. While in Athens, he'd had complete sets of Herodotos and Thoukydides copied out for him.

When he opened the smaller chest, he smiled at the spicy scent of cypress. Like the more expensive cedar, it helped keep insects away from wool and linen and papyrus. He went through the rolls of papyrus till he found the one that held the fifth book of Thoukydides' masterful narrative of the Peloponnesian War. The battle of Amphipolis began the book.

Like most literate Hellenes, Sostratos murmured the words on the papyrus to himself as he read. Halfway through the account of the battle, he paused, shaking his head in wonder. No matter how often he read Thoukydides, his admiration never flagged. *Father Zeus, if you are kind, one day let me write half as well as that man did. Let me think half as well as that man did.* It was, he supposed, a peculiar sort of prayer, but no less sincere for that.

MENEDEMOS HURRIED into the kitchen. "I trust we'll have something specially luscious tonight, Sikon," he said.

"Well, I hope so, young master," the cook answered. "I do my best, no matter how hard things are." He complained all the time.

From everything Menedemos had seen, that and petty thievery were diseases of cooks. Even the comic poets agreed with him. Trying to soothe Sikon's ruffled feathers, he said, "I know the sitos will be splendid. It always is. Nobody in Rhodes bakes better bread with wheat or barley than you do. But what have you got for the opson?" The relish course of a supper wasn't so thoroughly under the cook's control as the staple. If the fishermen had had an unlucky day, the opson would suffer.

"Well, there's always salt-fish. We've got plenty of that, on account of it keeps," Sikon said. "And I did manage to get my hands on some sprats—a few, anyhow. I'll fry 'em in olive oil and serve 'em slathered with cheese. Add in some pickled olives, and it shouldn't be too bad."

"Salt-fish? Sprats? *Olives?*" Menedemos' voice grew more horrified at every word. "For opson? For a proper supper? With *guests?*" He clapped a hand to his forehead. "We're ruined. Father will kill me, and then I'll kill you." Sostratos would have pointed out the logical flaw in that; Menedemos was sure of it. He didn't care. This was disaster, nothing less.

Only when the cook brought a hand up to his mouth to try to stifle laugher did Menedemos realize he'd been had. Sikon said, "Well, maybe these will do better, then," and swept the damp cloth off the seafood lying on the slate countertop.

"What have we here?" Menedemos murmured, and then answered his own question: "Prawns. Some lovely squid. Eels. And . . . a Rhodian dogfish. Oh, lovely, lovely!" He might almost have been talking about a hetaira who'd finally doffed her undertunic of silk from Kos and let him see her naked. "The gods will envy us tonight. All we feed them is thighbones wrapped in fat—and there's no telling what sort of meat people will bring home from a sacrifice, either. But fish, now—with fish, you know what you're getting ahead of time."

"And you pay for it, too," Sikon grumbled, for all the world as if he'd spent his own money and not the household's. Menedemos also had no doubt that he'd squirreled away for his own enjoyment some of the seafood he'd bought. Who in the history of the world had ever seen a skinny cook?

But all that was by the way. Menedemos clapped Sikon on the shoulder. "You have what you need. I know you'll do us proud tonight."

"I'll do *me* proud tonight," Sikon said. "Maybe somebody won't be happy with his own cook, and he'll hire me to do up some feast of his. Every obolos I stick in my mouth brings me that much closer to buying back my freedom."

"If you ever should, I'm afraid everyone in the house would starve," Menedemos said. He let it go at that; like most slaves, Sikon worked better in the hope of eventual liberty.

Satisfied the supper wouldn't suffer on account of the food, Menedemos went back to the andron to let his father know. "A dog-fish?" Philodemos said once he'd heard the report. "Out to bankrupt us, is he? You can eat it once and die happy, but who could afford to eat it twice?" Still, he didn't sound altogether displeased. He wasn't an opsophagos, someone who ate the relish at a feast as if it were bread, but he enjoyed a fine opson as well as any man.

So did Menedemos. "And the eels . . ." His mouth watered in an-ticipation.

"Out to bankrupt us," Philodemos repeated. Like his son, he'd been a handsome youth, but the years had left his mouth narrow, his nose sharp, and his eyes cool and hard. When he turned that embit-tered gaze on Menedemos, his son braced himself for a beating, though it had been several years since his father hit him. "Sikon won't get the chance to bankrupt us," Philodemos said. "You and your cousin will beat him to the punch. Peafowl!"

"If they live, we'll make a good profit," Menedemos said.

"And if they don't, you might as well have pissed away better than three minai of silver on wine and women and . . . and dogfish," his father said. "You act as if we were made of money, not as if we had to go out and make it."

"Shall I go tell Himilkon he can keep the miserable birds, then?" Menedemos asked.

As he'd known his father would, Philodemos tossed his head. "No, no. You made the bargain. You can't go back on it." He was a canny merchant, but one of stern rectitude. "You made the bargain. I only wish you hadn't."

"Wait till you *see* the peacock, Father," Menedemos said. "Wait till you see him fan his tail out. Then you'll understand."

"I saw the feather you brought home. I can imagine the bird," Philodemos said. His attitude was so cut-and-dried, Menedemos was convinced he missed a lot of the juice of life. For his part, Philodemos was at least half convinced he'd raised a wastrel. He went on. "I wonder how the birds would do boiled and stuffed with olives."

"I don't know," Menedemos said. "I'll tell you this, though, sir: finding out would make dogfish look cheap."

"Heh." His father got to his feet. He was lean and leathery and still strong for a man of his years. "We'd best clear out and let the slaves get the andron ready for tonight."

Sure enough, the slaves started bringing in the couches on which Lysistratos, Sostratos, and the other guests would recline, two to a couch. They set them up around the edge of the andron. Philodemos didn't clear out; he fussed at them till they got the couches exactly as he wanted them. Menedemos had to work to keep from scowling as he listened to those orders. His father had treated him just the same way till he finally grew to manhood—and still did, in absent-minded moments or when he thought he could get away with it.

Once all seven couches were placed, Philodemos rounded on Menedemos. "You *did* arrange for the flutegirls and the acrobat?" he said anxiously. "It wouldn't be much of a symposion after the feast if we had no entertainers."

"Yes, Father," Menedemos assured him. "Gyllis is sending over Eunoa and Artemeis. They both play well, and they're both supposed to be lively in bed."

His father sniffed. "That's why I left *those* details to you. I was sure you would know all about them."

"And why not?" Menedemos said with a smile. "I'd rather laugh at Aristophanes and drink some wine and boff a flutegirl than sit around moping and wishing I'd get sent into exile so I could have the time to write history, the way my cousin does." He snapped his fingers. "Where was I? Oh, the acrobat. Her name is Phylainis, and I saw her perform before I told Gyllis to send her. She can twist herself up like a braided loaf of bread. You could probably find ways to do it with her that'd break a regular woman in half."

"Gods preserve an estate from a cockproud son," Philodemos said. "You'll spend it all on flutegirls and acrobats, and leave *your* son nothing but debts to call his own."

"May you live many years, Father," Menedemos said. "I'm in no hurry to inherit anything. And I'm still years younger than you were when you married the first time, so I'm going to enjoy myself a little."

Philodemos raised his eyes to the heavens. "What is this new generation coming to? It's not worth half of mine."

His generation included Alexander the Great. He was, no doubt, about to say as much. Menedemos forestalled him: "Nestor complained about the new generation in the *Iliad,* too, but they were heroes even so."

"The older I get, the more sense I think Nestor makes," his father answered. "And as for you, it's a wonder you're not singing the praises of Thersites."

"Homer makes Thersites a loudmouthed fool," Menedemos said. Then, seeing the gleam in his father's eye, he retreated in a hurry.

SOSTRATOS WRAPPED HIS himation around himself and over his left shoulder. He peered down, trying to study the effect. He was hoping for philosophical; his beard would help there. But a true philosopher wouldn't have worn a tunic under the himation, or else wouldn't have put the wrap on over a chiton. Sokrates had gone about in nothing but his tunic in all kinds of weather. Sostratos shrugged. He wasn't Sokrates. He felt the chill.

Someone knocked on the door. His father: Lysistratos said, "Are you ready?"

"Yes, Father." Sostratos opened the door. His father inspected him like an officer looking over a soldier in his phalanx. Sostratos flushed. "I won't disgrace us."

"No, of course not," Lysistratos said, though he didn't sound completely convinced. "Come on, it's sundown. Let's grab a torch and go on over to my brother's."

They needed the torch; this late in the month, the moon wouldn't rise until a little before sunup. More guests, also carrying torches, were rapping on Philodemos' door as they walked up. One of the men turned to Sostratos and Lysistratos and said, "Hail, best ones. Is it you that bought peafowl from Himilkon the Phoenician?"

"I didn't, Lykon," Lysistratos answered. "My son made the bargain, along with his cousin Menedemos."

Lykon shot questions at Sostratos as if he were a slinger shooting lead bullets. As Sostratos was answering them, another merchant, a plump fellow named Telephos, came up to the doorway and started asking some of the same ones over again.

To Sostratos' relief, he didn't have to answer them twice, for the door opened and Philodemos said, "Welcome, my friends. Hail, Lysistratos. Hail, Sostratos. Come in, all of you." He sniffed. "By all means, come in. You can already smell the opson cooking, and it will be ready soon."

The odor of frying seafood came wafting out through the doorway.

The guests jostled one another, each more eager than the next to get inside. Sostratos dipped his head in greeting to Philodemos. "Hail, Uncle," he said.

"Hail," Philodemos said again, his voice more sour than not. "I thought, when you went down to the *Aphrodite,* you would keep Menedemos out of mischief. Instead, I find you joining in. Three hundred twenty-five drakhmai. *Pheu!"*

"Three hundred twenty-four and three oboloi, actually," Sostratos replied. "And we'll bring back more from Italy. I truly think we will." He was also truly annoyed Philodemos should reckon him hardly better than a pedagogue, a slave who took a boy to and from his teacher's and kept an eye on him to make sure he stayed out of mischief on the way.

"I hope you do." By the way his uncle said it, he might hope, but he didn't expect.

Menedemos stood in the entranceway to the andron, silhouetted by the torches and lamps within. "Hail," he said as Sostratos came up.

Sostratos sniffed again. The ambrosial aromas from the kitchen weren't all he smelled. "Roses?" he asked.

"And why not?" Menedemos replied. He'd always been something of a dandy. "Rhodes is the city of the rose. There's a rose stamped onto the port side of the *Aphrodite*'s ram, along with far-shooting Apollo on the other. I thought I'd deck myself out with scented oil tonight." He lowered his voice: "I hoped it would help sweeten Father, too, but no luck there. What did he say to you on the way in?"

"Nothing too good," Sostratos said, and his cousin winced. He went on, "But the bargain stands. We still have the chance for the last laugh—as long as the birds don't take sick." Menedemos spat into the bosom of his chiton to avert the evil omen. Sostratos asked, "Where will you have us reclining?"

"Almost all the way over to the right, of course, on the couch next to Father and me," Menedemos said. "Why? Did you think we would slight you?"

"Not really," Sostratos said.

He must have sounded hesitant. His cousin said, "Father may be angry at you and me, but he'd never insult Uncle Lysistratos by moving him, and he can't very well move you alone and give your father a new couchmate. As far as the outside world knows, all's well—mm, well enough—among us."

"The outside world certainly knows about the peafowl," Sostratos said. "I hope Himilkon hasn't been going through the wineshops boasting of getting the better of us. That'd be all we need."

Menedemos made as if to spit into his bosom again, but refrained. "Go on in," he said. "We'll eat, then we'll drink, and we'll have fun with the flutegirls and the acrobat. And tomorrow is another day, and we'll drink our morning wine fast and eat raw cabbage to ease our sore heads."

To Sostratos' way of thinking, the best way to ease back into things after a night of excess was to drink well-watered wine the next day. That didn't seem to cross Menedemos' mind. Sostratos' cousin had never been one to do things by halves.

"Go on in, boys, go on in," Telephos said. "If you stand in the doorway, a hefty fellow like me can't squeeze by." He patted his paunch and wheezed laughter.

If you spent more time at the gymnasion and less with a bowl of sweetmeats beside you, you'd have no trouble fitting through a doorway, Sostratos thought. But he and Menedemos went into the andron, and Telephos followed. Menedemos' father, bustling about like a goose trying to keep track of all her goslings at once, escorted the plump merchant to the couch he'd chosen for him.

Cushions rested on all the couches. Sostratos took his place beside his father on the couch next to that of their hosts. Lysistratos, being the elder, leaned on his elbow at the head of the couch. Sostratos reclined farther down, so that his feet hung off the edge.

He prodded his cushion, trying to get comfortable. It wasn't easy. In a low voice, he told his father, "I'm not what you'd call fond of fancy dinners. My arm goes to sleep, and I always spill food on my clothes."

Lysistratos shrugged. "It's the custom, and custom—"

"Is king of all," Sostratos finished, quoting Herodotos quoting Pindaros. His father dipped his head in agreement.

"All right, where's Kleagoras?" Menedemos said when only one space on one of the seven couches remained unfilled. "Late again, I see."

"Kleagoras would be late to his own funeral," Philodemos said sourly.

"Well, there are worse things," Sostratos' father remarked. "I wouldn't mind being late to mine, to tell you the truth." That drew chuckles from the three sides of the open-fronted rectangle in which the couches were arranged.

"Yes, Uncle, but at your funeral you wouldn't be waiting to eat Sikon's good fish and hoping it didn't burn," Menedemos said.

Kleagoras came bustling in just then. He always moved as if in a hurry, but somehow never got anywhere on time. "A thousand pardons, best ones," he said, wiping sweat from his forehead. "Very good to be here, very good indeed." He was panting as he slid down onto his couch. He might have run all the way from his house to this one, but running hadn't done him much good.

"You made it at last, Kleagoras, and I'm glad you did." Philodemos sounded welcoming and annoyed at the same time. Kleagoras' answering smile was sheepish. Philodemos turned to a slave who hovered by his couch. "Go to the kitchen and tell Sikon we can begin." The young man trotted away.

A moment later, more slaves came into the andron, setting a low, small table in front of each couch. They brought out bowls of pickled olives and onions to start the meal. Sostratos took an olive with his right hand and popped it into his mouth. When he'd worked off all the tart flesh, he spat the pit on the floor. After the feast was over and before the symposion began, the house slaves would clear away the debris.

Bread came next, with olive oil for dipping. Like everyone else, Sostratos ate the bread with his left hand. From his couch over on the far side of the andron, the long-winded merchant named Xanthos said, "Did you know—I have it for a fact, certain sure—that Kassandros murdered Alexandros and Roxane? Killed them both, I tell you, sent their souls down to the house of Hades. They're dead. Both of them are dead, dead as salt-fish, no doubt about it."

That got exclamations from everyone who hadn't already heard it. The exclamations got Xanthos to tell the news over again. He took longer the second time through, but, as far as Sostratos could see, he added no new details. The other feasters seemed to notice the same thing, for they quickly stopped asking him questions. That, of course, didn't stop him from starting to give the news a third time.

Lysistratos leaned over toward Philodemos and asked, "Did you have to invite him?" He yawned behind his hand.

But Menedemos' father dipped his head. "Unfortunately, I did. I heard from someone who ought to know that he's got some new perfumes we ought to have aboard the *Aphrodite*. I think he'll let me have them, because his ships stick to the Aegean and don't risk the longer trips west."

"All right." Sostratos' father sighed. "The things we do in search of profit."

A moment later, though, Xanthos fell silent: the slaves brought in baskets of rolls dusted with poppy seeds and plates of shrimp fried in their shells. "The opson!" someone said reverently.

Sostratos and his father, like Menedemos and his, had no trouble sharing from the plate set before their couch. Sostratos took each shrimp with his right thumb and index finger; had he been eating salt-fish, he would have used his middle finger, too. He couldn't remember when he'd learned the rules—sitos with the left hand, opson with the right; one finger for fresh fish, two for salt. But, like anyone with manners, he had. He wondered if some of the feasters did have manners. Where the two men on a couch were just acquaintances, they seemed to race to see who could eat the shrimp faster.

Sostratos savored the garlic and pungent silphium from Kyrene that flavored the shrimp. "Sikon's done it again," he told Menedemos, tossing an empty shell to the plastered floor after getting the last of the meat from the tail.

Out came more rolls, with squid to accompany them. Then the slaves brought in flat sheets of barley bread, and chunks of eel cooked in cheese with leeks to serve as their relish.

"Truly our host is a prince of generosity!" said portly Telephos. He plainly thought the eel the last course of opson. So did Sostratos, who joined in the applause when the dogfish came in afterwards. "A *king* of generosity!" Telephos cried, and no one contradicted him.

Some of the feasters left their bread all but untouched to concentrate on the opson. Not Sostratos; to him, the relish *was* relish, and the sitos the staple. *Sokrates would have approved,* he thought, even if he got rather less fish than some others.

Honey cakes and dried fruit finished the meal. Slaves brought in little bowls of water so the guests could wash their fingers, then carried the tables out of the andron. They returned to sweep away the shells and fish bones and scraps of bread that littered the floor.

When they came back, they brought garlands and ribbons for the feasters to put on their heads. And they brought shallow, long-handled, two-eared drinking cups, along with jars of wine, jars of water, a great mixing bowl, a pouring jug, and a ladle. Sostratos eyed the preparations for the symposion with an odd mixture of anticipation and dread. Dionysos' ocean of wine could be as stormy as Poseidon's watery sea.

THE FIRST CUP of wine at a symposion was always drunk neat, and the last bit of it poured out as a libation for Dionysos. Menedemos savored the sweet, rich, potent goodness of the golden Khian vintage. Letting the god have any seemed a shame and a waste, but he poured his libation onto the floor along with everyone else and sang Dionysos' hymn.

"Now," his father said, "we'll need a symposiarch, to guide us through our night together. Who will lead us over the wine-dark sea?"

Everybody smiled at the allusion to the *Iliad*. Xanthos promptly put up his hand. Everyone pretended not to see him; he was even less interesting drunk than sober. Sostratos also raised his hand. That was what made Menedemos decide to put up his. He liked his cousin, but he felt like getting properly drunk tonight, and he knew Sostratos would order the wine well-watered and drunk from shallow cups all night long.

"Let it be Menedemos," Telephos said. "We've all seen he knows how to have a good time." Amid laughter and clapping, he was elected.

Sostratos leaned toward him and said, "My father and I are close enough to get home clinging to the wall like that gecko we saw this morning, but the gods help our friends who live farther away."

Before Menedemos could answer that, his father tapped him on the shoulder. "There are better reputations to have than that of a roisterer," Philodemos said.

"Everything in its place," Menedemos replied, as philosophically as if he were Sostratos. "When it's time for business, business. When it's time for a symposion, wine." He waved to a slave. "Are the flute-girls and the acrobat here?"

"Yes, sir," the man answered. "They got here a little while ago."

"All right, good. We can bring them on after we've had a couple of rounds." Menedemos felt like a general arraying his army as he reckoned best. He clapped his hands together. All the feasters—the symposiasts, now—and the slaves looked his way. "Let the wine be mixed." Everybody leaned forward. As symposiarch, he set the strength. "Let it be . . . three parts water and two of wine."

"I thought you were going to say even measures, and have us as drunk as Macedonians in nothing flat," his father said. "Even three to two is a strong mix."

Menedemos grinned. "The symposiarch has spoken." No one but Philodemos was complaining. Even Sostratos just leaned on his elbow, watching a slave mix wine and water in the big krater in the center of the andron. Maybe he'd expected Menedemos to order equal measures, too.

I should have called for neat wine, Menedemos thought. But he tossed his head, rejecting the idea. That would make everyone fall asleep too soon. He wanted to feel the wine, yes, but he wanted to enjoy himself other ways while he was doing it, too.

When the wine was mixed, the slave filled the oinokhoe from the krater and used it to fill the symposiasts' cups. He started at the couch farthest from Menedemos and his father and worked his way toward them.

When Menedemos' cup was full, he lifted it by the handles. Even watered, the wine was sweet and strong. Everyone drank along with him. Where he led, they would follow. When he'd emptied the cup, he pointed to the slave, who filled the oinokhoe from the krater and then refilled the cups.

Before drinking this time, Menedemos said, "Let's have a bit of a song or a speech from everyone." The speeches ran in the same direction the wine had. As soon as Xanthos began to declaim, Menedemos knew he'd made a mistake: the merchant delivered, word for word—and there were a great many words—the speech he'd presented to the Assembly not long before.

"I've heard it today twice now," Lysistratos said, draining his own cup faster than was required of him.

"I'm sorry, Uncle," Menedemos said. "I didn't expect—that."

Sostratos gave Brasidas' speech at Amphipolis, explaining, "Great things happened there before Kassandros' day."

Lykon said, "That's an Athenian writer putting words in a Spartan's mouth, or I'm an Egyptian. Spartans aren't used to speaking in the Assembly, and they grunt and stammer instead of coming out with everything just so."

"It could be." Sostratos courteously dipped his head to the older man. "No one but Thoukydides ever knew how much of what was really said went into his speeches, and how much of what he thought men should have said."

"And what will *you* say, Uncle?" Menedemos asked Lysistratos.

Sostratos' father took a lyre down from the wall and accompanied himself as he sang a poem of Arkilokhos', in which he promised the girl he was seducing that he would spend himself on her belly and pubic patch, not inside her. The symposiasts loudly clapped their hands. "Sure, you always tell 'em that beforehand," somebody called, and everyone laughed.

Lysistratos waved to Menedemos. "Your turn now."

"So it is." Menedemos got to his feet. "I'll give you the *Iliad,* the section where Patroklos kills Sarpedon." The Greek he recited was even older, and more old-fashioned, than that which Arkilokhos used:

"Then Sarpedon missed with his shining spear.
    The spearpoint passed over Patroklos' left shoulder,
    But did not strike him. Patroklos made his
    Second attack with the bronze. No vain cast left his hand,
    But it struck just where the heart throbbed in his chest.
    He fell, as an oak or a white poplar
    Or a stately pine falls when men—carpenters—fell it
    In the mountains with newly sharpened axes to make ship
        timber.
    So he fell in front of his horses and chariot and lay
        outstretched,

Shrieking, clutching at the bloody dust,
As when a lion attacks a herd and kills
A great-hearted brown bull among the shambling oxen.
The bull bellows as it is slain by the lion's jaws.
So the warlike Lykians' commander raged after taking his
    death wound
From Patroklos, and addressed his friend and companion—"

Menedemos didn't get the chance to say what Sarpedon had told Glaukos, for Xanthos burst out, "By Zeus of the aegis, the Argives didn't kill enough Lykians during the Trojan War. We've still got too many of the stinking pirates no more than a stone's throw from Rhodes."

"Not even Herakles could throw a stone from here to Lykia," the literal-minded Sostratos said, but heads all around the andron dipped in agreement with Xanthos. Lykia lay less than eight hundred stadia to the east, and every Lykian headland was liable to have a pirate crew's swift pentekonter or even swifter hemiolia lurking behind it, waiting to swoop down on an honest merchantman.

Instead of going on, Menedemos dipped his head to his father, who also chose Homer: the passage in the *Odyssey* where Odysseus, with his comrades, blinded Polyphemos the Cyclops after first cleverly giving his name as Nobody. When the other Cyclopes asked him what was wrong, he blamed Nobody—Outis, not Odysseus. The symposiasts smiled at the wordplay.

"Another round," Menedemos told the slave tending the krater. "Deeper cups this time, and then bring on the flutegirls and the acrobat." He raised his voice: "Drink, my friends! We've plenty of wine still ahead of us."

The deeper cups were businesslike mugs. They weren't nearly so pretty as the shallow, high-footed cups with which the symposion had begun, but they held more than twice as much. Menedemos poured the wine down his throat. Since he was the symposiarch, the rest of the men had to follow his lead.

In danced Eunoa and Artemeis, both playing a drinking song from Athens on their double flutes. The flutegirls wore silk chitons filmy enough to show they'd singed away the hair from between their legs with a lampflame. The symposiasts whooped and cheered. A moment later, those cheers redoubled, for Phylainis the acrobat followed the flutegirls into the andron walking on her hands. She was naked; her oiled skin gleamed in the lamplight.

Philodemos nudged Menedemos as the symposiasts' cheers got louder yet. "The girls are pretty enough," the older man said. "I can't very well deny that."

"I'm glad you're pleased," Menedemos answered. His father was a hard man, but fair. "I hope the racket won't bother your wife, up in the women's quarters." Menedemos' mother was dead; his father had married a young bride a couple of years before, and was hoping for more children.

"We've had symposia here before," Philodemos said with a shrug. "She can put wax in her ears if the noise gets too bad, as Odysseus' men did sailing past the Sirens." He cocked his head to one side, listening to the music. "They don't play the flute badly, either."

"One of them can play my flute in a while," Menedemos said. "They're good at that, too." His father chuckled. Then they both laughed out loud. After a series of cartwheels across the andron, Phylainis had ended up in Sostratos' lap. Instead of feeling her up or starting the lovemaking then and there, Menedemos' cousin dumped her off as if she were on fire.

"She doesn't bite, Sostratos," Menedemos said. "Not unless you want her to." He threw back his head and laughed; he could feel the wine, all right.

Sostratos shrugged. "She picked me because I'm young, and she hoped I'd fall head over heels for her." He shrugged again. "I'm afraid not."

"All right—someone else will put his mortise in her tenon before long," Menedemos answered, as if talking of the shipwright's business rather than Aphrodite's. Sostratos seemed to stay sober even when drunk. *Poor fellow,* Menedemos thought.

Sure enough, Phylainis soon pressed herself against Xanthos, who started talking a great deal. *Are you going to bore her or bore her?* Menedemos wondered. With wine in him, that seemed very funny. He ordered the slave to go round and fill the symposiasts' cups again. Telephos let Artemeis drink from his mug. As she gulped wine, the merchant ran his hand up under her tunic. "What a smooth little piggy you've got," he said, fondling her.

"It's even smoother inside," she said, and took hold of the side of the couch and stuck her backside in the air. Telephos got behind her and put her words to the test.

Menedemos waved to Eunoa. He was the host's son. He'd hired her and the other girls. She hurried to him. "What would you like?" she asked. He sat up on the couch. She squatted in front of him on the floor, her head bobbing up and down, then, at his gesture, got up onto the couch and squatted on him. Her breath was sweet with wine fumes. And she was smooth inside, too.

2

WAVING A CLOTH, ERINNA RAN AT A PEAHEN. "GET OUT of my herbs, you nasty thing!" Sostratos' sister shouted. "Shoo!"

"What's it got in its beak?" Sostratos asked from the edge of the courtyard as the peahen beat a reluctant retreat.

"A wall lizard," Erinna answered. Sure enough, the tail disappeared down the peahen's gullet. Erinna went on, "I don't mind when the peafowl eat lizards and mice. But they eat the cumin and the fennel, too. I don't think you feed them enough."

"I do so." Sostratos indignantly pointed to the barley set out in a broad bowl, from which two other peahens were eating. "They get almost as much as a slave does. I just think they like some opson with their sitos, the same as we do."

Erinna rolled her eyes. "Well, they can get it somewhere besides my herb garden."

"It could be worse," Sostratos said. A horrible, vaguely hornlike noise from next door showed how it could be worse. "Menedemos has the peacock at his house. It does everything the peahens do, and squawks four times as much besides."

"I can't wait till you've bred all the peahens to it," his sister said. "I can't wait till you take them to the *Aphrodite* and sail far, far away with them."

"It won't be long," Sostratos said. "Now that ships are starting to put in to our harbor, Menedemos grudges every day the galley stays here."

"I'll miss you," Erinna told him. "But I won't miss these miserable, obnoxious birds at all." The peafowl she'd chased from the herb garden sidled back toward the plants, undoubtedly hoping she'd forgotten about it. Forgetting about a bird that big wasn't easy, though. Erinna flapped the cloth again, and the peafowl drew back.

Sostratos would have taken oath he saw anger in the bird's beady black eyes. He said, "You don't have to watch the garden yourself, you know. You could set a slave woman to doing it."

"I tried that yesterday," Erinna said darkly. "She paid more attention to her mug of wine than to the peahens, and we'll go short of garlic for a while—either that or get some from people whose gardens just have snails or caterpillars, not these, these—goats with feathers, that's what they are."

Before Sostratos could answer, the peacock next door let out its blatting cry again. Dogs in the neighborhood started barking. They'd been yapping their heads off every since the peafowl came to Sostratos and Menedemos' houses. The birds probably smelled like a banquet to them, and the peacock especially made enough noise to remind them he was around even when the wind blew from the wrong quarter.

Another horrible noise came from next door, followed by some equally horrible curses. "Hades stuff you with olives and boil you in a saucepan!" Menedemos shouted. "Roast you over a low fire! May your peahens give you the bird clap, so you can't pee through your peacock cock!"

Erinna giggled. Sostratos felt more inclined to applaud. That wasn't Aristophanes, but it almost could have been. Then Menedemos shouted again, this time in pain. Sostratos didn't need to be able to see through the walls between them to be sure the peacock had had its revenge. He wondered whether it had kicked or pecked. Peafowl were formidable at both ends—and with their buffeting wings— as the luckless sailor who'd chased the peacock had discovered to his sorrow.

Erinna said, "You really should have kept Menedemos from buying these pestilential birds."

Sostratos tossed his head. "Once Menedemos sets his heart on doing something, the twelve Olympians couldn't stop him. He'll go far—you mark my words. Of course, he may have to go pretty fast, too, to stay in front of all the husbands he's outraged."

"Oh." Erinna had to flap her cloth at the peahen yet again. Sostratos hoped that would distract her, but it didn't. After forcing the bird to retreat, she said, "Is that really true? About Menedemos, I mean."

"Some of it is, anyhow," Sostratos answered.

His sister clicked her tongue between her teeth. "Respectable women have to make do with a leather sausage if their husbands don't please them. Men can have all the women they want. It hardly seems fair for them to go after wives when they could dip their wicks with slaves and whores."

"I suppose so." Sostratos thought of the redheaded Thracian slave girl. But Erinna hadn't been talking about him; she'd been talking about Menedemos. He said, "You know how our cousin is. For him, sometimes, half the reason for doing something is knowing he shouldn't."

"It could be." Erinna considered. "It probably is, in fact. But what would he say of you if he had the chance?"

"Of me?" Sostratos echoed in surprise. "Probably that I'm too boring to say anything much about." He yawned to emphasize the point.

"Xanthos is boring—or at least that's what everybody says," Erinna answered. "You just don't care to talk about fighting and drinking and women all the time, that's all."

Sostratos went over and gave her a brotherly hug. The peahen, seeing the protector of the herb garden distracted, darted forward. Sostratos and Erinna shooed it off again together. *The trouble is, most people like to hear about fighting and drinking and women,* Sostratos thought. He did himself, sometimes. And Menedemos could indeed go on most entertainingly about any or all of them.

I'd better give it up, Sostratos thought, *or I'll convince myself that I am boring after all.* He took a warning step toward the peahen. It backed away, looking as if it hated him.

GETTING A SHIP ready to sail was always a tricky business. Menedemos was convinced he had a harder time with the *Aphrodite* than he would have had with a round ship, a sailing ship. The reason was simple: with forty oars to man, he needed far more sailors than the master of a sailing ship did.

"We're still a couple of men short," he said to Diokles, his keleustes.

The oarmaster dipped his head in agreement, but didn't seem particularly upset. "We'll hire harbor rats, that's all," he answered, "and if they drink up their wages the first good-sized port we come to, well, to the crows with 'em. Plenty more of that kind to be picked up in any harbor of the Inner Sea."

"I want as good a crew as I can get." Menedemos pointed toward the *Aphrodite*'s bow. "That ram isn't there just for show. Crete breeds pirates the way a dog breeds fleas, and Italy's the same way. And the war between Syracuse and Carthage goes on and on, so the Punic navy's liable to be prowling around, too."

Diokles shrugged. He was about halfway between Menedemos and his father in age, burnt brown by the sun, with the massive shoulders and heavy arms of a man who'd spent a lot of years working an oar himself. "The way I look at it is like this," he said "if a Carthaginian galley with four or five men to a bank of oars comes after us, it won't matter whether a couple of our rowers aren't everything they might be, because we'll get sunk any which way."

Since he was probably—no, almost certainly—right, Menedemos didn't argue with him. Instead, he turned to Sostratos and asked, "How's the cargo shaping?"

His cousin held out a three-leafed wooden tablet faced with wax, on which he'd written the manifest with the sharp end of his bronze stylus. As items came aboard, he'd either erased them with the blunt end or drawn a line through them, depending on how harried he was at any given moment. "We've still got some papyrus to take on board," he answered, showing Menedemos the tablet, "and the peafowl, and their feed, and wine and water and oil and bread for the men."

"We don't need that much," Menedemos said, "for we'll be putting in to real ports most nights."

"I know, but we do need some, and we haven't got it yet," Sostratos replied. "There *will* be nights when we just haul the ship up onto the beach wherever we happen to end up, and there may be storms."

Menedemos spat into the bosom of his tunic. Diokles had on only a loincloth, so he couldn't turn aside the omen that way. But he wore a ring with the image of Herakles Alexikakos, the Averter of Evil. He rubbed it and muttered a charm under his breath.

"On land, I'm not particularly superstitious," Menedemos remarked. "When I'm about to go to sea . . . That's a different business."

"You'd best believe it," Diokles agreed. "You never can tell with the sea. You can't trust it." He stopped—and started. "What's that dreadful noise?"

"Oh, good." Menedemos spoke with considerable relief. "Here come the peafowl."

Slaves from his father and uncle's houses carried the caged birds down to the *Aphrodite*. They'd managed to attract a fair-sized crowd of curious onlookers; men didn't carry half a dozen big, raucous birds through the streets of Rhodes every day. *And a good thing, too,* Menedemos thought. The peacock wasn't the only one screaming its head off. The peahens were squawking, too, though less often and not quite so loud.

"Where are you going to want these miserable things stowed, sir?" one of the slaves asked Menedemos.

He looked to Sostratos. Menedemos was captain; his cousin didn't tell him how to command the akatos. As toikharkhos, Sostratos had charge of the cargo. Since Sostratos was good at what he did, Menedemos didn't want to joggle his elbow.

"We have to keep them as safe as we can," Sostratos said. "They're the most delicate cargo we've got, and the most valuable, too. I want them as far away from the water in the bilges as I can get them. We'd better put them up on the little stretch of foredeck we've got."

That made Menedemos frown, regardless of whether he wanted to joggle his cousin's elbow or not. "Can we stow them there and still have room for the lookout to get up to the bow and do his job?" he asked. "If he can't see rocks ahead or a pirate pentekonter, a whole shipload of peafowl won't do us any good. If you could stack the cages . . ."

"I don't want to do that," Sostratos said unhappily. "The birds above would befoul the ones below, and they could peck at one another, too."

"Will you make up your mind?" asked the slave at the head of the procession. "This stinking cage is heavy."

"Take them up and put them on the foredeck," Sostratos said, speaking with more decision than he usually showed. "We'll just have to find out whether there's room up there for them and the lookout, too."

Down the gangplank and into the *Aphrodite* trudged the slaves. The peafowl screamed bloody murder; they liked descending at an angle even less than they liked being carried on level ground. By the way the slaves let the cages thud to the pine timbers of the foredeck, they'd got very sick of the birds.

Menedemos came up behind them. "Put those cages in two rows, with a lane in the middle," he said. When the slaves were done, he surveyed the result and reluctantly dipped his head. "I suppose it will do," he called to Sostratos. "But we'll have to warn the lookouts to steer the middle path. If they come too close to the birds on either side, they'll get their legs pecked." He laughed. "We've got Skylle and Kharybdis right here aboard the *Aphrodite*."

"Homer never saw a peacock—I'm sure of that." Sostratos pointed. "Here comes the last of the papyrus . . . and here comes something else, too. What's in those jars, Menedemos? They aren't on my list here."

"Oh, I know about those," Menedemos answered. "They're crimson dye from Byblos. Father just got them yesterday, from a ship that just came in from Phoenicia."

"Crimson dye . . . from Byblos." Menedemos' cousin spoke with exaggerated patience: "How many jars did Uncle Philodemos get? Why didn't anyone bother to tell me about them till now?" He looked daggers at Menedemos.

"Sorry," Menedemos said, more contritely than he'd thought he would. "It's two hundred jars, by the way."

"Two hundred jars." Sostratos still sounded furious. "This had better not happen again. How am I supposed to do my job if nobody tells me what I'm supposed to be doing?" He pointed to the men who were loading oiled-leather sacks of papyrus beneath the rowers' benches. "Shift those farther astern. We've got to make room for the crimson dye."

Menedemos gave his attention back to Diokles. "Go get us those rowers. I want to be at sea before noon. We probably won't make Knidos even so. No help for it; we'll just have to beach ourselves on Syme."

"Right, skipper." The keleustes dipped his head. "I'll take care of it." He went up the gangplank to the quay at which the *Aphrodite* was tied up, and shouted for rowers in a great voice.

"Have we got all our cargo aboard?" Menedemos asked Sostratos.

"Unless there's more you haven't told me about, yes," his cousin

answered tartly. Menedemos tossed his head, denying even the pos-
sibility. Sostratos didn't look appeased, but said, "In that case, everything's loaded." He peered down the quay, though he, unlike
Menedemos, wasn't following Diokles with his eyes. "I was wondering if we'd get any passengers."

"I was hoping we would—they're pure profit," Menedemos said.
"But it's still early in the sailing season, so some lubbers won't care
to put to sea so soon. We'll probably get some in Hellas. There are
always people who want to go across to Italy." He clapped his hands
together. "Here comes Diokles. That was fast."

"I wonder what'll be wrong with the rowers," Sostratos said.

"We'll find out. At least they aren't falling-down drunk in the
morning: a little something, anyhow," Menedemos said. "Get their
names, tell 'em it's a drakhma a day, and it'll go up to a drakhma
and a half when they show they're worth it. And then..." He
clapped again, hard this time. "Then we're off."

He hurried past the mast and back to the raised poop deck at the
stern of the *Aphrodite,* slapping rowers on the back as he went and
also making sure the jars and sacks that held the cargo were securely
stowed under their benches. He'd watched Sostratos attend to that,
but he checked it anyhow. The *Aphrodite* was his ship; if anything
went wrong, it was his fault.

He took the tiller bars to the new steering oars in his hands and
tugged experimentally. He'd done the same thing every time he came
aboard after the *Aphrodite* went into the sea: the steering oars pleased
him that much. Khremes the carpenter had been right—a little old
man could handle them all day and never get tired. He'd never felt
a pair that pivoted so smoothly.

Diokles came up onto the poop beside Menedemos. Sostratos
joined them a moment later, tying his tablet closed with a thin strip
of leather. "Let's have a lookout forward," Menedemos called. He
pointed to a sailor naked but for a knifebelt round his middle. "Aristeidas, take the first turn there. You've sailed with me before—I
know you've got sharp eyes. Mind the peafowl, now."

"Right, captain." Aristeidas hurried up onto the foredeck. The peacock tried to peck him, but he darted past and took hold of the
forepost. He waved back to Menedemos.

"Bring in the gangplank," Menedemos commanded. At his shouted order, a couple of longshoremen undid the lines that held the *Aphrodite* to the quay and tossed the coarse flax ropes into the akatos. With what was almost a bow to Diokles, Menedemos asked, "You have your mallet and your bronze square?"

"I'm not likely to be without 'em," the keleustes answered. "My voice'd give out if I had to call the stroke all day." He stooped and picked up the little mallet and the bronze square, which dangled from a chain so as to give the best tone when he struck it. The stern-facing rowers poised themselves at their oars. Diokles dipped his head to Menedemos. "When you're ready."

"*I've* been ready for months," Menedemos said. "Now the ship is, too. Let's go."

The keleustes smote the bronze with the mallet. The rowers took their first stroke. To leave the harbor, Menedemos had every oar manned—as much for show as for any other reason. The quay shifted. No: the *Aphrodite* began to move. Diokles used the mallet again. Another stroke. Again. "Rhyppa*pai*!" the oarmaster called, using his voice to help give the men their rhythm.

"Rhyppa*pai*!" the rowers echoed: the old chant of the Athenian navy, used these days by Hellenes in galleys all over the Inner Sea. "Rhyppa*pai*!! Rhyppa*pai*!"

"You can tell they haven't had oars in their hands for a while," Sostratos remarked.

"They're pretty ragged, aren't they?" Menedemos agreed. Even as he spoke, two rowers on the port side almost fouled each other, and one on the starboard dug the blade of his oar into the water as he brought it back for a new stroke. Menedemos shouted at him. "Nikasion, if you're going to catch a crab, make it the kind you can cook next time!"

"Sorry, skipper," the rower called back, dropping the chant for a moment.

Clang! Clang! After a while, Menedemos knew, he would hardly hear the keleustes' mallet striking the bronze square. At the beginning of every voyage, though, he had to get used to it all over again. A tern plunged into the water of Rhodes' Great Harbor less than a bowshot from the *Aphrodite* and came out with a fish in its beak. A screeching gull chased it, but the smaller bird got away with the prize.

A sailing ship was coming into the harbor as the akatos neared the narrow outlet between the two moles that protected it from bad weather. Menedemos tugged on the tillers to steer the *Aphrodite* a little to starboard and give the clumsy, beamy round ship a wider berth. Under the forward-pointing, goose-headed sternpost, the fellow at the sailing ship's steering oars lifted a hand to wave and thank him for the courtesy.

"Where are you from?" Menedemos called across a plethron of blue water.

"Paphos, in Cyprus," the other ship's officer answered. "I've got copper and olive oil and some shaped cedar boards. Where are you away to?"

"I'm bound for Italy, with papyrus and ink and perfume and crimson dye—and peafowl," Menedemos added with no small pride.

"Peafowl?" the fellow on the sailing ship said. "Good luck to you, friend. The peacocks are pretty, sure enough, but I've seen 'em—they're mean. I wouldn't have 'em on my ship, and that's the truth."

"Well, to the crows with *you,*" Menedemos said, but not loud enough for the fellow on the beamy merchantman to hear. He turned to Sostratos. "Fat lot he knows about it."

Only about three plethra separated the tips of the two moles from each other. Inside, the waters of the Great Harbor were glassy smooth. As soon as the *Aphrodite* passed out into the Aegean proper, the light chop made the motion of the ship change. Diokles smiled. "Your rowing may get a little rusty over the winter," he said, never missing a beat with the mallet, "but you never forget how to stand when she rolls and pitches a little."

"No," said Menedemos, who'd made the adjustment so automatically, he hadn't even noticed he'd done it. He scratched his chin, then shot Sostratos an amused glance: his cousin's beard was a handy thing to be thoughtful with. "I'll keep them all at the oars till we round the nose of the island. Then, if the wind holds, we'll lower the sail and let it do the work."

The keleustes dipped his head. "That seems good to me." Diokles paused, then asked, "You'll want to drill them, though, on the way out, won't you? If we have to fight, the practice'll come in handy. It always does."

"Of course." Menedemos dipped his head. "Yes, of course. But let's give ourselves a couple of days to shake off the cobwebs and rub oil on our blisters. There'll be time for sprints and time for ramming practice, believe me there will."

"Good enough," the oarmaster said. "I just wanted to make sure it was in your mind, skipper, that's all. I think we'll have a pretty fair crew once we do shake down. A lot of the men at the oars have rowed in triremes or in fours or fives. Nothing like serving in the polis' fleet to turn out a solid rower."

As if on cue in a comic play, Aristeidas sang out from his post at the bow: "Trireme off to starboard, captain!"

Menedemos shaded his eyes from the sun with the palm of his hand. So did Diokles and Sostratos. Menedemos saw the ship first. "There she is," he said, pointing. The trireme, twice the length of the *Aphrodite* but hardly beamier, glided along southeast under sail, the rowers resting easy at the oars. As the lean, deadly shape drew nearer, he made out Rhodes' rose in red on the white linen of the sail.

"Pirate patrol," Sostratos remarked.

"Nothing else but," Menedemos agreed. "Unless a pentekonter or a hemiolia can run away, it's got even less chance against a trireme than we do in the *Aphrodite* against a pirate ship. But the other side of the coin is, you wouldn't want to take a trireme up against a bigger war galley these days."

"By Poseidon the earthshaker, I should hope not," Diokles said. "Anything from a four on up will have extra timbers at the waterline to make ramming tougher, and it'll have a deck swarming with marines. I wouldn't want to fight a big old mean spur-thighed tortoise like that in a trireme, and I don't know anybody who would, either."

"When we Hellenes fought Persia—even when Athens fought Sparta less than a hundred years ago—all the warships were triremes," Sostratos said. "No one knew how to build anything bigger."

"When the Argives sailed to Troy, they all went in pentekonters," Menedemos said. "Nobody back then even knew how to build triremes." He laughed at how surprised Sostratos looked to find himself topped. Menedemos grinned. "You can keep your fancy historians. Give me Homer any day."

"That's right," Diokles said, though Menedemos didn't think the keleustes could read or write. But everyone, literate or not, had heard the *Iliad* and *Odyssey* countless times.

Stubborn as usual, Sostratos tossed his head. "Homer is where you start. No one would argue with that. But Homer shouldn't be where you stop."

There were times—at supper, say, or in a symposion with his cousin leading the drinking and keeping things moderate—when Menedemos would have been glad to argue that. Now he had the *Aphrodite* to run, and the ship came first. She'd traveled past the northernmost spit of land on the island of Rhodes. Looking south, Menedemos could see into the city of Rhodes' small western harbor.

"Lower the sail!" he called, and sailors leaped to obey. Down it came from the main yard, canvas flapping till the wind took it and filled it. Like any sail, it was made from oblong blocks of cloth sewn together; the light horizontal lines and the vertical brails gave it the appearance of a gameboard.

Even before Menedemos could give the orders, the men swung the great square sail to take best advantage of the wind coming down from the north. They brailed up the leeward half so as to get the precise portion and amount of sail needed.

"They're good," Sostratos said.

"Diokles said it," Menedemos answered. "They know what they're supposed to do, because they've done it before. The *Aphrodite*'s not so big as a trireme, let alone a four or a five or those new ships the generals are making with six or seven men to a bank of oars, but we do things the same way the bigger ships do. And a sail's a sail, no matter what kind of ship you're in. Only difference between us and a proper warship there is that we're not big enough to need a fore-sail."

His cousin grinned a sly grin. "You make me feel as if I were back at the Lykeion in Athens. Here, though, it's not Theophrastos lecturing on botany; it's Menedemos on seamanship."

Menedemos shrugged. "If your fancy philosophers would want to listen, I'd fill their ears for them. This is what I know, and I'm good at it." Like any Hellene, he was justly proud of the things he was good at, and wanted everyone else to know about them, too.

"And because you know these things so well, do you think you know others every bit as well?" Sostratos asked.

"What's that supposed to mean?" Menedemos gave him a suspicious stare. "When you start asking that kind of question, you're trying to lure me into philosophy myself, and I don't care to play."

"All right, I'll stop," Sostratos said agreeably. "But when Sokrates was defending himself in Athens, he talked about artisans who knew their own trade and thought they knew everything on account of that."

"And the Athenians fed him hemlock, too—even I know that much," Menedemos said. "So maybe he should have found something else to talk about."

For some reason—Menedemos couldn't fathom why—that seemed to wound his cousin, who subsided into sulky silence. Menedemos gave his full attention back to the *Aphrodite*. Getting the most from both sails and oars was a subtle art, one most merchant captains with their tubby roundships didn't have to worry about. He let the wind on the quarter drive the akatos westward, while using half the rowers—the others rested at their oars—to head the ram at her bow north as well, toward the little island of Syme.

As the island seemed to rise up out of the sea. Diokles pointed toward it and said, "Miserable little place. Not enough water, not enough decent land for it to amount to anything."

"Well, you're not wrong," Menedemos said. "If it weren't for sponges, nobody would remember the place was here."

That brought Sostratos out of his funk. He tossed his head, saying, "Thoukydides talks about the sea-fight between the Athenians and the Spartans off Syme and the trophy the Spartans set up there in the last book of his history. That makes the island, like the history itself, a possession for all time." He slid from Doric to old-fashioned Attic for the last few words; Menedemos presumed he was quoting his pet historian.

Hearing Sostratos quote Thoukydides, though, jogged his own memory, and he quoted, too, from Homer:

" 'Nireus led three ships from Syme—
    Nireus son of King Kharopoios by Aglaie,
    Nireus, who was the handsomest man who came under Ilion
    Of the other Danaans except the illustrious son of Peleus,
    But he was not a powerful man, and only a small host
    followed him.'

So even in those days, Syme was nothing much."

"You know the *Iliad* even better than I thought you did, if you can recite from the Catalogue of Ships in Book Two," Sostratos said.

"Homer to sink my teeth into, Aristophanes to laugh at," Menedemos replied. "To the crows with everybody else."

Before Sostratos could come back with something indignant, Diokles asked, "Whereabouts on the island will you want to beach her tonight?"

"You know the gnarled finger of land that sticks out to the south, the one that points to the islet called Tetlousa?" Menedemos said. "There's a small inlet there, on the western side of it, with the best and softest beach on Syme. That's where I want to put us."

"I do know that inlet, captain, and I do know that beach." The oarmaster dipped his head. "I asked because I was going to speak of them if you didn't."

"And the town on the island is at the north end, isn't it?" Sostratos said. "We'll be as far away from a lot of people as we can—though on Syme, that's not very far."

If Sostratos was talking about practical matters again, and not about literature, that suited Menedemos fine. He said, "You're right. We haven't got that many choices on Syme, anyhow, not when most of the coast is rocky cliffs."

Before long, he ordered the sail brailed up again, for the *Aphrodite* swung almost due north once it got past Tetlousa—straight into the teeth of the breeze. He put more men back on the oars. The sun was sinking in the west, and he didn't want to have to feel his way into that inlet in the dark. He was all too liable to misjudge things and run the *Aphrodite* up against the rocks. Sooner than risking that, he would have spent a night anchored at sea, with the rowers sleeping on their benches. They wouldn't be happy about that. They'd have to do it a few times, especially on the journey across the Ionian Sea from Hellas to Italy, but it would be a bad omen the first night out.

But he had plenty of daylight left when Aristeidas sang out from the bow. "There's the inlet, captain!" The lookout pointed to starboard. A moment later, he let out a yelp. "*Papai!* That stinking peacock got me on the leg!"

"Now you've got to watch yourself," Menedemos said. He leaned on the tillers to the steering oars and swung the akatos into the tiny bay.

At the bow, Aristeidas cast a lead-weighted line into the sea to gauge its depth. "Ten cubits," he called. Menedemos waved to show he'd heard. That was enough water and to spare.

At Diokles' shouted orders, the portside rowers backed water while those to starboard pulled with the usual stroke, so that the *Aphrodite* spun through half a circle in very little more than her own length. When her stern faced the beach, the keleustes cried, *"Oöp!"* and the rowers rested at their oars. "Now," Diokles said, "back water all—at the beat, mind—and bring her up onto the sand." He smote the bronze square with his mallet.

After a few strokes, the *Aphrodite*'s false keel—of sturdy beech, to protect the true keel beneath it—scraped sand as the rowers grounded her. *"Oöp!"* the oarmaster cried again. Sailors sprang out onto the beach to drag the galley farther from the sea.

Menedemos dipped his head, more than a little pleased with the way things had gone. "This was a good first day," he said to anyone who would listen.

FIRES CRACKLED on the beach. Sailors sat around them, eating bread and olives and oil and drinking rough wine. Some of them rubbed their bodies, and especially their sore hands, with more olive oil. A few small fish from the bay and a couple of rabbits sailors had knocked over with rocks sizzled above the flames, adding savory smells to the air and a little opson to the sitos and wine.

Sostratos spotted his cousin over by the biggest, brightest fire. Menedemos spat out an olive pit and drank wine from the same sort of mug he'd called for at the symposion. Sitting there on the sand among the rowers, Menedemos seemed as much in his element as in the fanciest andron. Sostratos sighed. Save perhaps for the Lykeion, he'd never found anywhere he truly felt he belonged.

But he had to do what he had to do. "Hail, cousin," Menedemos called as he came over. "What have you been up to?"

"Checking on the peafowl," Sostratos answered. "I have to tell you, I don't like what I'm seeing."

"What's wrong?" Menedemos asked sharply. Then he checked

himself and asked the question a different way. "What do you think is wrong?"

The change angered Sostratos. If his cousin didn't like what he heard, he'd just given himself an excuse to do nothing about it. Trying to keep the ire out of his voice, Sostratos said, "They're looking peaked. I don't think they like staying cooped up in those cages. I don't think it's healthy for them."

Sure enough, Menedemos tossed his head. "Tell it to Aristeidas," he answered. "The peacock drew blood when it pecked him there a little before we landed."

"I don't care," Sostratos said. "Remember how unhappy the birds were when we brought them from Himilkon's warehouse to our houses? Remember how they perked up when they got to run around the courtyards? They *like* to run around. My sister ran herself ragged trying to keep them out of her herb garden. Now they're caged up again, and they're starting to droop again, too."

"They'll be fine." But Menedemos spoke without so much conviction.

"Three minai, twenty-four drakhmai, three oboloi," Sostratos said. "We want to keep them healthy, you know."

Talking about the birds hadn't got through to his cousin. Reminding Menedemos how much the peafowl had cost did. Wincing, Sostratos' cousin said, "What do you think we ought to do?"

Serious as usual, Sostratos began, "Well, my prescription would be—"

Menedemos burst out laughing. "What have we got here, Hippokrates for peafowl? You've already come halfway toward talking Attic. Will you start spouting Ionian dialect when you go on about doctoring them? ' 'E 'opped on 'is 'orse and 'ammered the 'ide off it with 'is whip.' " He dropped the rough breathings at the beginnings of words, as Ionian Hellenes were wont to do.

The sailors sitting around the fire laughed and poked one another in the ribs; Menedemos had laid on the dialect with a shovel. Sostratos fought to hold on to his patience. "My prescription would be," he repeated in tones threatening enough to make his cousin keep quiet and hear him out, "to let the birds run free whenever we possibly can."

"What? Now?" Menedemos' eyebrows flew upwards. "They'd run off and get away, and a fox would never know what an expensive supper it had."

"You ask me, any fox that tried to catch a peafowl would be sorry a heartbeat later." Sostratos kicked at the golden sand. Now he was annoyed at himself. Theophrastos would have had something sharp to say about irrelevance. Of course, Theophrastos had something sharp to say about almost everything. Sostratos went on, "I don't mean here, especially not at night. But they ought to have the chance to get some exercise while we're at sea, where they couldn't possibly escape."

"No, they can't escape at sea, that's true—not unless they jump into the drink," Menedemos allowed. "But they're pretty stupid, so they might do just that. And I'll tell you something else they'd do: they'd drive the rowers mad. Or do you think I'm wrong; O best one?"

His withering sarcasm failed to wither Sostratos, who answered, "Most of the time, we haven't got a full crew on the oars, nor anything close to one. The men who aren't at the benches could fend them off the ones who are."

"Maybe." But Menedemos sounded anything but convinced.

Sostratos shrugged. "You're the captain. It's up to you. But if the birds do come down sick, that's in your lap, too."

"No. That's in the lap of the gods." Menedemos gulped his wine and glowered at Sostratos. "Are you sure about all this?"

"No, of course I'm not sure," Sostratos answered, more than a little exasperated. "Unless you break your leg or something, a proper physician isn't sure what's wrong with you nine times out of ten. But I'm telling you what I've noticed."

If Menedemos was drunk enough or cruel enough to tell him where to head in, he could walk across Syme to the little town at the north end of the island and hire a fishing boat to take him back to Rhodes. He could . . . but he couldn't. The *Aphrodite* carried his family's wealth no less than Menedemos'. If he abandoned that investment while fearing Menedemos would make a hash of things with it, neither his own father nor Uncle Philodemos would ever forgive him. And how could he blame them for that? He couldn't.

But how could he stand Menedemos' berating him for doing what he was supposed to be doing and doing it as well as he could? He was every bit as much a free Hellene as his cousin. Slaves had to take abuse; that was one of the reasons no man wanted to be a slave. He waited, grinding his teeth from nerves.

By the look on Menedemos' face, he was about to let fly. But then, eyeing Sostratos, he choked back whatever he'd been on the point of saying. He took another swig of wine from his mug instead. When he did speak, he had himself under control again: "All right. I suppose we can try it, at least when the weather's good and we're in waters where we don't have to worry about pirates. But the birds go back in their cages the instant anything even starts to smell like trouble."

"A bargain," Sostratos said—a great gust of relief. "Thank you."

His cousin shrugged. "Every now and then, I'm tempted to forget why you come along when I take a ship out." His grin was on the nasty side. He'd given Sostratos what he wanted; now he would try to make Sostratos pay for it. And Sostratos, having won the point he had to win, was willing to put up with more than he would have otherwise. Then Menedemos surprised him by adding, "Even if I am tempted, I'd make a mistake if I did it."

Sostratos stared, Menedemos usually amused himself by giving him a hard time, not by paying him compliments. He did that so seldom, in fact, that Sostratos concluded he had to mean this one. He bowed. "Thank you, cousin."

"You're welcome." Menedemos' eyes glinted. Maybe it was just the firelight, but Sostratos didn't think so. And, sure enough, his cousin went on, "See how much you thank me when you're trying to round up the peafowl in a hurry because it's starting to blow a gale."

That didn't sound like anything Sostratos much wanted to do. Still . . . "I'd sooner chase them than throw them over the side with rocks tied to their feet so they'll sink."

"Oh, you're right, no doubt about it." But that glint remained in Menedemos' eyes. "Remember what you just said. It's the sort of thing the gods like to listen for."

Several sailors dipped their heads in agreement. Sostratos thought of himself as a modern, well-educated man. Unlike the sailors—even unlike his own cousin—he didn't get most of his ideas about the gods from the *Iliad* and the *Odyssey*. But what Menedemos said had a horrid feeling of probability to him, too. He spat in the bosom of his tunic to turn aside the omen.

"You don't do that very often," Menedemos remarked.

Sostratos answered with a shrug: "We're on the sea now. Diokles said it—things are different here."

"I know that," Menedemos said. "I'm surprised *you're* willing to admit it."

"We're on the sea," Sostratos repeated. "And we're on the sea with peafowl. If that doesn't make things different, I don't know what would." He plucked at his beard. Since he'd got what he wanted from his cousin, changing the subject looked like a good idea. And so he did, asking, "Do you plan on putting in at Knidos tomorrow?"

"I planned to, yes," Menedemos answered. "It's a good harbor, and a good day's journey from here, too. A couple of hundred stadia—we'll be able to use the sail some, I expect, as long as the breeze holds, but the boys will do some rowing, too. We can put some fresh water aboard, buy some food. . . . Why? Did you have some different scheme in mind?"

"No." Sostratos tossed his head. "I was just wondering if you intended to lay over for a day and do some business there."

"Not unless you find something that drives you wild," Menedemos said. "My thinking is, it's too close to home. What's the point to taking all our expensive goods for a short haul when we're bound to get a lot more for them farther west?"

"Good. We're sailing in the same direction," Sostratos said.

One of the sailors by the fire, a skinny bald man named Alexion, nudged Menedemos and said, "Once we're in the harbor at Knidos, skipper, you ought to charge folks a khalkos apiece, say, to watch master Sostratos here go chasing after all those peafowl." He laughed. So did the other sailors in earshot. So did Menedemos.

And so did Sostratos: if he found the joke funny, they weren't laughing at him . . . were they? But then he grew thoughtful. "Himilkon got half a drakhma from you for just a tail feather, cousin. If we charged people a khalkos or two to come to the edge of the quay and look down into the *Aphrodite* while the peacock was out of his cage—well, we wouldn't get rich doing it, but I bet we'd make a drakhma, maybe a couple of drakhmai, whenever we did it."

Menedemos looked thoughtful, too. "You're right. We probably would." He turned and slapped Alexion on the back. "Whatever we bring in the first day we try it, it's yours, for having the idea."

The rower's grin showed a broken front tooth. "Thanks, skipper. You treat a fellow right, no two ways about it."

"Fair's fair," Menedemos said. Sostratos dipped his head, wondering if he would have thought of the same thing himself. He hoped so, but he wasn't altogether sure.

The fires died down to embers. Sostratos wrapped himself in his mantle and lay down on the beach with his cloak under his head for a pillow. A nightjar's froglike call came from not far away. The sky was clear, a blue almost black. Only a faint gleam from the Milky Way lightened it near the southern horizon. Zeus' wandering star blazed brilliant, high in the southern sky; that of Ares, duller and redder, hung farther west. Sostratos stared up at them for a little while, then yawned, rolled over on his side, and fell asleep.

"ROSY-FINGERED DAWN!" Menedemos shouted to wake the *Aphrodite*'s crew. The tag from Homer had never seemed more apt. He wondered how the blind poet had been able to describe things so exactly. Beams of pinkish light in the east foretold the arrival of the sun, which couldn't be more than a quarter of an hour away. Even as he watched, the pink began to turn gold.

Sailors groaned and grunted and sat up, rubbing their eyes. Some of them kept right on snoring. Sostratos often did that. To Menedemos' disappointment, his cousin's eyes were open. Sostratos got to his feet and went off behind a bush to piss.

"Get some bread. Get some oil. Get some wine," Menedemos called as the men woke their sleepy comrades. "No slaves here— we've all got to work once we eat."

"What other cheery news have you got for us?" Sostratos asked around a yawn as he came back from behind that bush.

"Once we get the *Aphrodite* in the water, you can let the peafowl out—one or two at a time, mind, and the peacock by himself—to get whatever exercise they can," Menedemos answered. "Tell off as many sailors as you need to keep them from fouling the men who stay at the oars and mind the sail."

His cousin dipped his head. "Thanks again," he said. "I really do think the birds will be better for it."

"I hope so," Menedemos said, which was true; he didn't want to have to explain to his father that he hadn't been able to sell the peafowl because they'd all died before he got to Italy. "But there's one thing even more important," he added, and watched Sostratos raise a dubious eyebrow. But that was also true: "I hope the ship will be better for it."

"It will be all right," Sostratos said confidently. Menedemos clicked his tongue between his teeth and didn't answer. His cousin was a clever fellow—*cleverer than I am,* Menedemos thought, without rancor or envy—and a first-rate toikharkhos. But Sostratos had never had to give orders to a crew; he'd never been responsible for a whole ship and everybody in it. He could say things would turn out all right, but Menedemos was the one who had to make them turn out all right.

Just getting that akatos back into the sea was harder work than it would have been with a trireme or even a piratical pentekonter. The *Aphrodite* had fewer men and, because of the cargo she carried, was heavier in proportion to her size than a vessel meant solely for fighting. Menedemos put half a dozen oarsmen into the ship's boat, and ran a line from its stern to the *Aphrodite*'s stempost. While they rowed with all their might to help pull the beached ship forward, he and the rest of the crew pushed against her stern and sides.

She didn't want to move. Wiping sweat from his forehead with his hand, Diokles said, "We may have to lighten her before she'll get back where she belongs."

"To the crows with that," Menedemos said, though he'd been thinking the same thing. "Taking jars and sacks off, putting them back aboard—we'd never make Knidos by nightfall. The hours aren't so long as they will be come summertime." In the winter, a day's twelve hours were cramped, while a night's twelve stretched. In summer, the reverse held true. At this season of the year, daylight hours and those of the nighttime roughly matched.

"Shall we give it another try, then?" the keleustes asked.

"Unless you feel like swimming home," Menedemos answered. Diokles tossed his head. Menedemos raised his voice to a shout:

"Come on! Put your backs into it this time! One more good heave and we'll be off!"

He was anything but sure he was telling the truth, but it was what the sailors needed to hear. He heaved with them, his bare feet digging into the golden sand. At first, he thought this try would prove as fruitless as the last. But then the false keel grated as the ship lurched forward: not much, only a digit's worth or not even that, but some.

Everyone felt the tiny motion. "We *can* do it!" Menedemos cried. "At my count . . . one, two, *three*!"

Another scrape of timber on sand. The men grunted and cursed as they shoved. Out in the little bay, the rowers in the boat pulled as if they had a five full of Carthaginians on their tail. The *Aphrodite* moved a little more, and then a little more—and then, more than a little to Menedemos surprise, slid into the Aegean. The sailors raised a cheer.

"We'll spend the night tied up to a pier in Knidos," Sostratos said, "but the next time we have to go aground on a sandy shore, let's not beach ourselves so hard."

"Well, that isn't the worst idea I've ever heard," Menedemos answered. "Still and all, though, we do want to let the timbers dry whenever we get the chance. Rowing's harder work when you have to shove along the extra weight that goes into a waterlogged ship."

He waded out into the cool water of the bay and, agile as a monkey, swarmed up a rope and over the side of the *Aphrodite*. Rather less gracefully, Sostratos followed. Before long, all the men were in the *Aphrodite* and the akatos' boat tied to the sternpost once more for towing.

"Out of the inlet," Menedemos said, "then around the southern coast of Syme, and then west and a little north to Knidos." Still dripping, his hair wet and slick, he took his place at the steering oars and dipped his head to Diokles. "If you'd be so kind, keleustes."

"Right you are, skipper." The oarmaster clanged his mallet against the bronze square. "Rhyppa*pai*! Rhyppa*pai*!"

"Rhyppa*pai*!" the rowers echoed, taking their beat from him. Menedemos had only ten men a side at the oars. He would work the men in shifts, the way any captain not in a desperate hurry did.

Sostratos asked, "May I let a couple of peahens out now?"

"Wait till we're well away from Syme and in more open water," Menedemos answered. "We don't want the miserable birds trying to fly to land and going into the sea instead."

"You're right. I hadn't thought of that," Sostratos said. Menedemos couldn't imagine himself making an admission like that, even if it was true. If he hadn't thought of something, he didn't want anybody but himself knowing it. His cousin went on, "Tell me when the time is right, then."

"I will," Menedemos said, somewhat abstractedly: the bulk of the island was shielding him from some of the wind he wanted to use. He ordered the big square mainsail lowered from the yard, but it flapped and fluttered and didn't want to fill. Even after the sailors used the brails to haul up most of the canvas on the leeward side, he wondered if he should have bothered using it at all; it hardly seemed to add anything to the *Aphrodite*'s turn of speed. Then he shrugged. The men would think it helped, even if it didn't really do much. Keeping them happy counted for something, too.

After an hour or so, the *Aphrodite* glided between the narrow spit of land at Syme's southwestern corner and the closest of the three tiny islets that straggled out from the spit. Once the ship got free of Syme's wind shadow, the sail bellied out and went taut. "That's more like it," Menedemos exclaimed, and ordered more of the sail lowered to take advantage of the breeze.

"Now?" Sostratos asked: so much for waiting for Menedemos to give him the word.

Menedemos considered. Now that Syme no longer blocked his view, he could see the long, narrow Karian peninsula at whose end Knidos sat. But the peninsula lay perhaps forty stadia to the north: far enough away for it to seem a little misty, a little indistinct. He didn't suppose the peafowl would try to fly to it. "Go ahead," he said. "Let's see what happens. Pick your sailors first, though, and tell them what they're going to have to do."

His cousin dipped his head. Menedemos gave him no more specific instructions; he wanted to see how Sostratos would handle the business. Most of the sailors Sostratos chose were men Menedemos would have picked, too, men he reckoned sensible and reliable. But his cousin also pointed to the two rowers Diokles had plucked off the wharf as the *Aphrodite* was about to sail. Maybe he wanted to work them in with the rest of the crew. Maybe he just reckoned them expendable. Either way, Menedemos didn't think he would have wanted them for this work.

"Just keep the birds away from people who are doing things that need doing," Sostratos said. "Except for that, let them run around and eat whatever they can catch. We'll have fewer lizards and mice and cockroaches aboard the *Aphrodite* after a while."

He was probably right. Menedemos hadn't looked at that side of things. No man born of woman could keep down the vermin that inevitably traveled with men and cargo. Vermin were part of life; Menedemos suspected mice and roaches ate scraps of ambrosia on Olympos. Some ship captains took along Egyptian cats to try to keep down the mice, though he'd never been convinced the nasty little yowlers caught enough to be worthwhile.

His cousin stooped on the little foredeck to unlatch a peahen's cage. A moment later, Sostratos hopped back with a yelp of *"Oimoi!"* He wrung his hand.

"Still have all your fingers?" Menedemos called from the steering oars at the poop.

By the way Sostratos looked down, Menedemos guessed he was checking to make sure of that himself. His cousin dipped his head. "I do," he said, "though no thanks to this monstrous fowl." He shook one of the fingers he still had at the peahen. "You hateful bird, don't you know I'm doing you a favor?"

Maybe the peahen heeded him. At any rate, it didn't try to peck him again. He swung the cage door open. The bird emerged. A heartbeat later, so did another one. Menedemos and Sostratos called that second peahen Helen, because the peacock mated with her more enthusiastically than with the other peahens. When she walked past his cage now, he started screeching loud enough to make Menedemos wince even though he stood at the *Aphrodite*'s stern.

With a flutter of wings, the two peahens went down the wooden stairway and into the undecked bottom of the akatos. One of them pecked at something. "That was a centipede!" a sailor said. "Good riddance to the horrible thing."

The bird called Helen pecked at something else. A rower let out a howl: "That was my leg! You lefthanded idiot, you're supposed to keep the miserable creature away from me."

"I'm sorry, I'm sure," said the fellow called an idiot: one of Diokles' new men, a chap named Teleutas. He flapped the little net he was holding at the peahen, which didn't peck the rower twice. All the same, Menedemos didn't judge this the best way to blend the newcomers with the rest of the crew.

Another rower yelped. The sailor who hadn't kept the peahen from nipping at him had been rowing for Menedemos and Sostratos' families since they were both little boys. Maybe nobody could stop the peafowl from making nuisances of themselves. In that case, maybe Sostratos hadn't made such a bad choice with Teleutas and the other new sailor—whose name Menedemos kept forgetting—after all.

Helen the peahen hopped up onto an empty rower's bench and stretched her neck so she could peer over the gunwale at the Karian coastline in the distance. Would she know it lay in the distance? Or would she forget she had clipped wings and try to strike out for the land she saw?

Before anyone could find out, Sostratos threw a net over her. He didn't want fifty drakhmai of silver splashing into the Aegean. It was a fit home for dolphins—Menedemos saw three or four leaping out of the water off to port—but not for expensive birds.

Helen gave a screech the peacock might have envied and lashed out with feet and beak through the mesh of the net. Sostratos cursed, but didn't let her escape till he got her down where she couldn't do herself mischief.

"This is supposed to keep the birds healthy?" Menedemos called. "Looks like you'll just run them ragged."

Sostratos shot him a harried look. "I'm doing my best," he answered. "If you've got any better ideas—if you've got any ideas at all, Menedemos—suppose you tell me about them."

Menedemos went back to steering the akatos. His cheeks felt on fire; he hoped the flush didn't show. His cousin looked down his nose at him for preferring Homer and bawdy Aristophanes to Herodotos and Thoukydides, and for preferring wine and flutegirls to philosophical discussion at a symposion. But Sostratos didn't usually come right out and call him a fool, especially not when the whole crew of the *Aphrodite* could hear him. Of course, Sostratos wasn't usually so harassed as he was while trying to shepherd bad-tempered birds that didn't feel like being herded.

Occupied with the peafowl, Sostratos didn't even seem to notice what he'd done. He let Helen out of the net and gave her and the other peahen some more time to run around loose. If either one of them presumed to climb up to the poop deck, Menedemos told himself he'd kick it off no matter how expensive it was. But his cousin and the sailors kept the peafowl away. That left Menedemos disappointed. He was so angry, he wanted to kick something.

After Sostratos got the peahens back in their cages, he let out the peacock. All the sailors exclaimed: they hadn't seen the male bird uncaged. "Be careful of those tail feathers," Sostratos warned. "They're what makes the bird worth what he's worth. If anything happens to them—if anything happens to him—it'll come out of your hides."

Menedemos wouldn't have put it that way. Putting it that way, he thought, meant the sailors wouldn't dare do anything much to or with the peacock. And he proved a good prophet. The peacock ran around staring and pecking and kicking and screeching, and Sostratos had to take care of it and recapture it almost completely by himself. Irked at his cousin, Menedemos gave no orders to make life easier for him, as he might have otherwise. Had Sostratos complained, Menedemos would have told him where to head in. But Sostratos didn't complain. He netted the peacock as neatly as a fisherman might have netted some anchovies, and returned him to his cage without taking any wounds. Even Menedemos had to admit to himself it was a job well done.

As the *Aphrodite* made her way toward Knidos, Sostratos gave the other three peafowl some exercise time in turn. One of them drew blood from a rower. His friends had to grab him to keep him from bringing the bird to an untimely end.

Once the last peahen was back in its cage, Sostratos mounted the steps to the poop deck. He looked haggard. "I *hope* that's done the peafowl some good," he said. "It's certainly kept *me* on my toes."

"This is what you asked for," Menedemos reminded him. "If the birds *do* look perkier, you'll be doing it every day."

"Gods," Sostratos muttered. Menedemos, still feeling heartless, affected not to notice. His cousin spoke a bit louder: "They're liable to be more trouble than they're worth."

"Not when they're worth at least three and a quarter minai," Menedemos said. Sostratos groaned, not loudly but unmistakably. Again, Menedemos pretended not to hear.

KNIDOS HAD A FINE harbor. A little island sat just off the Karian coast. Part of the town was on the mainland, the rest on the island. Stone moles connected the two, dividing the harbor in twain. Sostratos breathed a sigh of relief as longshoremen tied the *Aphrodite* up to a pier. He looked forward to sleeping in a bed at an inn. It wouldn't match the bed he had at home, but it would have to be an improvement on wrapping himself in his himation and lying down on the sand.

A bald man with a gray-streaked beard pointed to the cages on the foredeck and asked, "What have you got in there?"

"Peafowl," Sostratos answered.

"Peafowl," Menedemos echoed, in an altogether brighter tone: he remembered Alexion's moneymaking scheme, which had slipped Sostratos' mind. He went on, "Peafowl from the steaming jungles of India. You can see them up close for only two khalkoi—the sixth part of an obolos." The man with the gray beard paid out the two little bronze coins without hesitation. He came aboard the *Aphrodite* and stared at the birds through the slats of the cages.

They gave him a good show. Two of them tried to peck him, and the peacock screeched loud enough to make him jam his fingers in his ears. "Nasty things, aren't they?" he said to Sostratos, who'd stayed by the birds. By worrying about the way they looked after staying in their cages all the time, he'd apparently appointed himself chief peafowl-keeper along with all his other duties.

Those screeches drew more people to the pier. With his usual eye for the main chance, Menedemos went up the gangplank and talked rapidly, fluently, and perhaps even truthfully about peafowl. His patter was plenty to send more curious Knidians down to the *Aphrodite* to take a look for themselves. He collected the khalkoi on the pier; nobody set foot on the galley without having paid. Sostratos remained by the peafowl to make sure nobody tried to poke them with a stick or yank out one of the peacock's tail feathers or do anything else he shouldn't have. He told what he knew about the birds and listened to the locals' news, not all of which he'd heard before.

Men and boys and even a few women kept coming aboard till the sun sank in the Aegean. By then, most of the sailors—everyone, in fact, except for six or eight guards Diokles chose—had gone into Knidos to sample the harborside taverns and brothels. Sostratos reluctantly resigned himself to spending the night on the *Aphrodite*: only a fool would wander through a strange town at night by himself with nothing but a torch to light his way.

Some of the akatos' crew brought back bread and oil and olives and wine for the men who stayed behind. It wasn't much of a supper, but better than nothing. Alexion happily counted the pile of small change Menedemos gave him. "Better than a drakhma here, sure enough," he said. "Thank you kindly, skipper."

"Thank *you*," Menedemos told him. "You earned it. The birds will make us money the rest of the trip."

"I heard a couple of interesting things," Sostratos said, dipping a chunk of bread into some oil as he sat on the timbers of the poop deck. "I think we can forget about the peace the four generals signed last summer."

"I don't suppose anyone expected it to last long." Menedemos spat an olive pit into the palm of his hand, then tossed it over the side. Sostratos heard the tiny splash as it went into the water. Colors faded out of the world as twilight deepened and more stars came out. Menedemos asked, "What happened?"

"They say here that Ptolemaios has sent an army up into Kilikia to attack Antigonos there," Sostratos answered. "The excuse he's using is that Antigonos broke the treaty by putting garrisons in free and independent Hellenic cities."

Menedemos snorted. Sostratos didn't blame him. Knidos, for instance, called itself a free and independent Hellenic city, but it did Antigonos' bidding, as did most Hellenic cities in Asia Minor—including those of Kilikia in the southeast. Rhodes, now, Rhodes truly was free and independent . . . since expelling Alexander's garrison. That didn't mean any of the squabbling Macedonian generals wouldn't be delighted to bring the city to heel again.

After another snort, Menedemos asked, "What else did you hear?"

"You know Polemaios, Antigonos' nephew?" Sostratos said.

"Not personally, no," his cousin answered, which made *him* snort in turn. Menedemos went on, "What about him?"

"A fisherman told me that a ship came into Knidos from Eretria on the island of Euboia," Sostratos said.

Menedemos impatiently dipped his head. "He's been holding the island—and Boiotia, too: all that country north of Athens—for Antigonos for the past couple of years."

"Not any more," Sostratos said. "He's gone over to Kassandros with his whole army."

"*Has* he?" Menedemos whistled softly. "I'll bet old One-Eye is fit to be tied. Why on earth would he do a thing like that?"

"Who can say?" Sostratos answered with a shrug. "But Antigonos' sons are grown men—Demetrios especially, though Philippos can't be more than a few years younger than we are. With two sons in the family, how much inheritance can a nephew hope for?"

"Something to that, I shouldn't wonder," Menedemos said. "If Antigonos gets his hands on Polemaios now, though, he'll give him his inheritance, all right: one funeral pyre's worth."

"I wouldn't want Antigonos holding that kind of grudge against *me*." Sostratos agreed. "And, of course, he'll be at war with Kassandros over this, because it really weakens him in Hellas. I wonder why the generals bothered making their treaty at all."

"It must have seemed like a good idea at the time," Menedemos said. "More often than not, that's why people do things."

There in the twilight—almost the dark, now—Sostratos eyed his cousin. Menedemos might well have been describing himself and his own reasons for doing this or that . . . which didn't mean he was wrong about the generals. Sostratos tried to take a longer view of things. He knew he often failed, but he did try.

"It shouldn't have anything to do with us, not directly," he said. "We won't be heading to the northern parts of Hellas or up to Macedonia, either."

"Not directly, no," Menedemos said. "But if Kassandros sends out a fleet and Antigonos sends out a fleet—they aren't pirates, but they'd both think we made tasty pickings. They aren't pirates, but they're liable to be worse than pirates. The *Aphrodite*'s got some chance of beating a pentekonter, but we'd need a miracle against a trireme, let alone anything bigger."

"Maybe it's a good time to get out of the Aegean and head west,"

Sostratos said, and then, before Menedemos could answer. "Of course, it would be even better if Syracuse and Carthage weren't fighting over there."

"No such thing as good times for traders," Menedemos said. "No such thing as safe times, anyway. My father would say that, anyway, and I think yours would, too."

"Probably." Sostratos yawned, then sighed. "I was hoping for a real bed tonight, and what do I get? Wood." He wrapped his himation around himself.

His cousin laughed. "I was hoping for a real bed with somebody warm and friendly in it, and what do I get? Wood and you." He too stretched out on the poop deck and made himself as comfortable as he could. "Good night."

"Good night." The planks were hard, but Sostratos had had a long, wearing day. He fell asleep almost at once.

He woke a little before sunup. The peacock, punctual as a rooster, announced the coming day with a squawk that probably shook half of Knidos out of bed. Sostratos yawned and stretched and rolled over so that he faced Menedemos. His cousin's eyes were also open. "Do you think Diokles is awake?" Menedemos asked.

"Yes, unless that horrible screech frightened him to death," Sostratos answered.

"Ha! If only that were a joke." Menedemos got to his feet. With his himation a blanket and his chiton a pillow, he was as naked as the day he was born: nothing out of the ordinary on a ship, in port or on the sea. He raised his voice: "Diokles."

The keleustes had slept on a rower's bench, leaning up against the planking of the *Aphrodite.* He waved back toward the poop. "Good day, captain," he said. "Gods, that's a sweet-voiced fowl we're carrying, isn't it?"

"Sweet as vinegar," Menedemos answered. "Sweet as rancid oil. How many rowers went into town yesterday and still haven't come back?"

Diokles didn't even have to look around to answer: "Five. Not too bad, all things considered."

"No, not too," Menedemos said. "But tell off some men and start scouring the wineshops and the whorehouses. I want a full crew when we sail, and I want to leave inside an hour's time. The wind'll be in our teeth all the way to Kos, so I don't want to head up there with any empty benches—we'll row every cubit of the trip."

"I'll see to it," Diokles promised. "Most of the dives are close by the harbor, so we shouldn't need long to sift through 'em. And if we're still a man or two short, there's bound to be somebody who'll want to ship with us."

"Let's try to round up our own first," Menedemos said, and the oarmaster dipped his head. He chose large, well-made men to come with him. They all had knives on their belts, and some of them carried belaying pins, too. "He's smart," Menedemos remarked to Sostratos. "The best way not to run into trouble is to show that you're ready for it."

"You're bound to be right." Naked as Menedemos, Sostratos strode to the gunwale and pissed over the side into the harbor water. Then he went up to the little foredeck to see how the peafowl were doing. The peacock greeted him with another raucous screech.

"How do they look?" Menedemos called from the stern.

"All right, I suppose," Sostratos answered. "We're still finding out how they're supposed to look. Nothing wrong with their voices, that's certain. I'm going to give them something to eat while the ship's still tied up to the quay."

He waited for his cousin to wave agreement, then undid a leather sack of barley and piled grain onto half a dozen plates, one of which he set in front of each cage. The slats in the doors were wide enough to let the birds stick their heads out and eat. That made anyone who walked by step lively, but it meant he didn't have to open the cages to feed the peafowl.

"Are they eating all right?" Menedemos asked. On land, he did as he pleased, indulging his passions far more than Sostratos chose to do. Aboard ship, nothing escaped his notice. The peacock had Argos' eyes in its tail; Sostratos' cousin seemed to have them in his head.

Sostratos watched the birds pecking away like so many outsized chickens, then dipped his head. Menedemos waved again to show he'd seen the answer. No, nothing got past him.

A couple of the missing rowers returned by themselves, one hung over and the other so drunk he almost fell off the pier before he got to the *Aphrodite*. "Are you going to dock his pay?" Sostratos asked.

His cousin tossed his head. "No, he's here on time—and he's here all by himself, too." An evil smile spread over Menedemos' face. "I'll do something worse—I'll wait till he's really starting to hurt, and then I'll put him on the oars. If that doesn't cure him, gods only know what will."

"Not a bad notion," Sostratos said, admiring the rough justice of it. He paused thoughtfully. "The exercise may help ease the confusion in his humors and cure him quicker than sitting idle would."

"Maybe." Menedemos chuckled. "Even if it does, though, he won't be happy while it's going on." Sostratos could hardly disagree with that.

One of the rowers came running up the pier toward the *Aphrodite*. "Diokles says to tell you we've got three of them, captain," he called. "No sign of the other two."

"They came back on their own," Menedemos answered. "Diokles can bring in the rest of the lost sheep, and then we'll be off."

The sailors had to carry one of their comrades, who'd guzzled himself into a stupor. By the glint in Menedemos' eye, Sostratos knew what his cousin had in mind for that fellow once he revived. *Fair enough*, Sostratos thought. *Drinking yourself blind is excessive.* Diokles giving the beat, the *Aphrodite* left the harbor of Knidos and headed for Kos.

3

"RHYPPAPAI! RHYPPAPAI!" DIOKELES USED THE OAR-master's chant along with the rhythm of mallet on bronze. As Menedemos had thought it would, the wind blew straight out of the north, straight into his face, as the merchant galley he commanded made for Kos. A sailing ship bound for Kos from Knidos would have had to stay in port; it could have made no headway against the contrary breeze. He just left the sail brailed up tight, so that the akatos proceeded on oars alone.

Waves driven by the headwind splashed against the *Aphrodite*'s ram and pointed cutwater. Striking the ship head-on, they gave her an unpleasant pitching motion. Menedemos, who stood on the raised poop deck handling the steering oars, didn't mind it so much, but he'd spent the night aboard ship. Some of the rowers who were rather the worse for wear leaned out over the gunwales and fed the fish of the Aegean.

"Keep an eye peeled," Menedemos called to the lookout at the bow. "The mainland of Asia belongs to Antigonos." He took his right hand off the steering-oar tiller to wave toward the misty mainland. "Kos, though, Kos is under Ptolemaios' thumb. And if the treaty the generals signed last summer is just a broken pot, the way it seems, they're liable to go at each other any time."

He kept a wary eye out for warships and pirate galleys himself. All he saw, though, were a few little fishing boats bobbing in the chop. A couple of them spread their sails and scooted away from him as fast as they could go. He laughed at that: the akatos looked too much like a piratical pentekonter for them to want to let it get close.

"You're the one who's been hearing most of the news lately, cousin," he said to Sostratos. "Do you have any idea what sort of fleet Ptolemaios has at Kos?"

But Sostratos tossed his head. "Sorry—haven't heard that. It had better be a good-sized one, though, because Antigonos has a lot of ports on the mainland and the islands farther north." He grimaced. "The same holds for Rhodes, you know."

"We *have* got a good-sized fleet, and a good thing, too," Menedemos said. "Antigonos knows better than to quarrel with us, the same as a dog knows better than to bite a hedgehog. Now, where have you got those perfumes stowed?"

"To port, a little aft of amidships," Sostratos answered. "Are you thinking of trading them for silk?"

"That's just what I'm thinking," Menedemos told him. "The Hellenes in Italy can make their own perfume. You can't get silk anywhere but Kos."

"If we can make a good bargain with the silk merchants, that's fine," Sostratos said. "If not . . ." He shrugged. "If not, we'd do better spending silver on silk and saving the perfumes for a market where they'll bring us more."

"You'll be the judge of that," Menedemos said. "That's why you're along."

"Nice to know you think I have some use," Sostratos said dryly.

"Some," Menedemos agreed, to make his cousin squirm. He pointed. "And you'd better keep an eye on that peahen, too, before she goes into the drink."

As one had done on the first day it was let out of its cage, a peahen had hopped up onto a vacant rower's bench and was peering over the side. Menedemos didn't know if the bird would try to fly off and fall into the sea, but he didn't want to find out the hard way, either. Sostratos was of like mind. He netted the bird before it could do anything the young men who'd bought it would regret.

The peahen pecked Sostratos through the mesh of the net. "Down to the house of Hades with you, you accursed, abominable thing!" he shouted, rubbing at his ribs through his chiton. He turned to Menedemos. "If it weren't for what we paid for them, I'd *like* to watch them drown."

"So would I," Menedemos said. "I'd hold them under myself, in fact."

"I never imagined sailing with a valuable cargo I hated," Sostratos said, releasing the peafowl by the socket that fixed the mast to the keel. He pointed a warning finger at the bird. "Stay down here where you belong, Furies take you!" To Menedemos, he added, "I don't much care for cargo that won't stay where I stow it, either."

"The birds would, if you left them in their cages," Menedemos said.

His cousin tossed his head. "We've been over that. I think they'll be better for getting out, though they may drive *me* mad by the time we make Italy."

Menedemos laughed. Sostratos rolled his eyes. That made Menedemos laugh more. But before he could twit his cousin any further, the watchman on the foredeck sang out: "Sail ho, off the starboard bow!" A moment later he amended that: "Sails ho! She's got a foresail, captain!"

"A big one," Menedemos muttered, peering in the direction the lookout's pointing finger gave. He had sharp eyes; he needed only a moment to spot the ship. When he did, he cursed. He'd hoped to see a big merchantman, bound perhaps for Rhodes and then Alexandria. No such luck: that low, lean shape could belong only to a war galley.

"He's seen us, too," the lookout called. "He's turning this way."

His voice held alarm. Menedemos didn't blame him. He was alarmed, too. "What do we do, skipper?" Diokles asked.

"Hold course," Menedemos answered. "Best thing we can do is put up a bold front. If we were in a pentekonter or a hemiolia, we might have hoped to turn and outrun him downwind, but we haven't got a prayer of that in this akatos—she's too beamy. We have every right to be here, and a proper warship won't give us any trouble, because nobody wants any trouble with Rhodes."

I hope. He'd spoken brashly to hearten his men—and to hearten himself, too. But brashness didn't come easy, not as the galley approached, now under sails and oars. "Eagles on the sails," the lookout called.

"He's one of Ptolemaios', then," Sostratos said.

Menedemos dipped his head in agreement. "Patrolling out of Kos, I suppose."

"Too big and broad to be a trireme," his cousin observed. "A four or a five."

"A five," Menedemos answered. "Three banks of rowers, see? One man on each thalamite oar down low, two on each zygite, and two on each thranite oar on top. If it were a four, it'd be two-banked, with two men on each oar."

"You're right of course." Sostratos thumped his forehead with the heel of his hand, as he often did when he thought he'd been foolish. "Whatever it is, it's big enough to eat us for opson and still be hungry for sitos afterwards."

"And isn't that the truth?" Menedemos said unhappily. "Got to be a hundred cubits long, if it's even a digit." For a merchant galley, the forty-cubit *Aphrodite* was of respectable size. Compared to the war galley, it was a sprat set beside a shark. The five was fully decked, too; armored marines with spears and bows strode this way and that, their red cloaks blowing in the breeze. The outrigger through which the thranite oarsmen rowed was enclosed with timber, making the ship all but invulnerable to archery.

"Catapult at the bow," Sostratos remarked. "From what Father says, they were just starting to mount them on ships when we were little."

"Yes, I've heard my father say the same thing," Menedemos agreed. He hadn't been paying the dart-thrower any mind; he'd been looking at the eyes painted on either side of the five's prow. The *Aphrodite* had them, too, as did almost every ship in the Middle Sea, but these seemed particularly fierce and menacing—not least because, at the moment, they were glaring straight at his ship.

One of the men on the war galley's deck cupped his hands in front of his mouth and shouted: "Heave to!"

"What do we do, skipper?" Diokles asked again.

"What he says," Menedemos answered, watching seawater foam white over the topmost fin of the five's ram. The green bronze fins had to be a cubit wide; they could smash a hole in the *Aphrodite*'s side that would fill her with water faster than he cared to think about. Even if he were mad enough to try to use his much smaller ram against her timbers, she had extra planking at the waterline to ward against such attacks.

"*Oöp!*" the keleustes shouted, and the akatos' rowers rested at their oars.

Up came the five to lie alongside the *Aphrodite*. Men brailed up the sails to keep the great ship from gliding away to the south. The war galley's deck rose six or seven cubits out of the water; the archers there could shoot down into the akatos' waist, while Menedemos' men could do next to nothing to reply.

A fellow in a scarlet-dyed tunic looked the *Aphrodite* over. By the way he put his hands on his hips, what he saw didn't much impress him. "What ship is this?" he demanded.

"The *Aphrodite*, out of Rhodes," Menedemos said. And then, deliberately mocking, he gave the galley the same sort of once-over her officer had given the akatos. It wasn't so easy for him, because he had to crane his neck upwards to do a proper job of it, but he managed. And, looking up his nose because he couldn't look down it, he asked, "And what ship are *you*?"

Perhaps taken by surprise, the war galley's officer replied, "The *Eutykhes*. General Ptolemaios' ship, out of Kos." Then he glared at Menedemos, who smiled back. He snapped, "I don't have to answer your questions, and you do have to answer mine. If you're lucky"—he played on the meaning of his ship's name—"you'll be able to."

"Ask away," Menedemos said cheerfully. Out of the corner of his eye, he saw Sostratos looking worried. Sostratos would never have baited the *Eutykhes'* officer. Because he was rational and sensible, he thought everybody else was, too. Menedemos had a different opinion. Insulting an arrogant ass was often the only way to get him to acknowledge you.

Of course, it also had its risks. With a scowl, the officer said, "You look like a gods-detested pirate to me, is what you look like. Rhodes? Tell me another one. Give me the name of the man you serve and give me your cargo and do it fast, or you'll never get the chance to do anything else."

"I serve two men: my father Philodemos and Lysistratos, his younger brother," Menedemos answered, all business now. "If you don't know of them, ask your crew; someone will."

And, to his relief, one of the marines aboard the *Eutykhes* came up to the officer. Menedemos couldn't make out what the fellow said, but the sour look on the officer's face argued that the other man did know of Philodemos and Lysistratos. A snap in his voice, the officer said, "Any rogue may hear a name or two, and put them in his own mouth when he finds them handy. I am not convinced you are what you claim to be. Your cargo, and be quick about it."

"Quick as you please," Menedemos answered. "We carry ink and papyrus and crimson dye and fine perfumes and . . ." He grinned slyly. "Five peahens and a peacock."

As he'd hoped, that rocked the *Eutykhes'* officer back on his heels. "A peacock?" he growled. "I don't believe you. If you had a peacock on board, I'd see it. And if you're lying to me, you'll be sorry."

"Sostratos!" Menedemos called. His cousin waved. "Show the gentleman the peacock, if you please."

"Right." Sostratos hurried up to the foredeck. He undid the latches on the peacock's cage and opened the door. The bird, which would have bolted out screeching at any other time, stayed where it was and kept quiet. Menedemos flicked a glance to the officer aboard Ptolemaios' five. The man stood on the deck with his arms folded across his chest. He wasn't about to believe anything Menedemos said, not till he saw it with his own eyes.

There had been times when Menedemos faulted Sostratos for dithering when he should have been doing. This wasn't one of those times. When the peacock refused to come out of its cage, Sostratos picked up the cage and dumped the bird out onto the foredeck. It squawked then, squawked and ran down into the waist of the *Aphrodite.*

"A peacock," Menedemos said smugly. "Tied up at anchor, we'd charge you a khalkos or two to see it, but here on the sea I give you the sight for nothing."

He was, perhaps, lucky: the *Eutykhes'* officer paid no attention to his patter. The fellow stared down at the bird and its magnificent tail. Marines and other officers hurried over to have a look, too. So many men rushing to starboard might have capsized the *Aphrodite,* but they gave the far bigger war galley only a slight list.

"A peacock," Menedemos repeated softly.

"A peacock," the officer agreed. Because the *Aphrodite's* sailors weren't watching the bird so closely as they might have been, it pecked a rower in the leg. He sprang up from his bench, howling curses. The men on the *Eutykhes* howled laughter.

"May we cage it up again now?" Menedemos asked. "It's pretty, no doubt about it, but it's a cursed nuisance."

"Go ahead." The *Eutykhes'* officer absently dipped his head in assent. His eyes remained fixed on the bird. He had to gather himself before finding a question of his own: "You'll be putting in at Kos today?"

"That's right," Menedemos answered. "We're bound for Italy, and we'll want to take some silk with us if we can get a decent price."

"Good trading, then," the officer said. He turned away from Menedemos and shouted orders to his own crew. The five's mainsail and foresail descended from their yards. The keleustes clanged on something louder and less melodious than the bronze Diokles used. The oars began to work. Eyeing the *Eutykhes*, Menedemos judged the crew had been together for a while. Their rowing was very smooth. The war galley resumed its southbound course, picking up speed quickly despite its massive bulk.

Once it had got out of arrow range, Menedemos allowed himself the luxury of a long sigh of relief. Diokles dipped his head to show he understood why. "That could have been sticky," the oarmaster said.

"That *was* sticky," Menedemos said. "But you're right. It could have been even stickier. He might not have stopped to ask questions. He might have just lowered his masts and charged right at us." He paused, imagining the *Eutykhes'* ram bearing down on the *Aphrodite*, driven toward her by three hundred rowers pulling like madmen. The mental picture was vivid enough to make him shudder. He tried to drive it from his mind: "Maybe we could have dodged."

"Maybe," Diokles said. "Once, maybe." He didn't sound as if he believed even that. And Menedemos didn't argue with him, because he didn't believe it, either.

Having wrestled the peacock into its cage once more, Sostratos made his way back to the stern. "Ptolemaios' men must be jumpy now that they're fighting Antigonos again," he said, and waved toward the mainland of Asia off to starboard. "Plenty of towns where old One-Eye could put a fleet together for the invasion of Kos. And the channel between the island and the mainland can't be more than twenty-five stadia wide. You can almost spit across it."

"You're right, and I'm an idiot," Menedemos said. Sostratos gaped at him, not used to hearing such things: Menedemos was more likely to call *him* an idiot. Not now, though. Menedemos went on, "I didn't see the connection between Kilikia and here till you rubbed my nose in it. I probably wouldn't have, either."

"All the pieces fit together," his cousin answered seriously. "That's what history is all about—showing how the pieces fit together, I mean."

"Well, maybe it's good for something after all, then," Menedemos said. "Maybe." He didn't quite know it, but he sounded as dubious as Diokles had when talking about the *Aphrodite*'s chances of escaping the *Eutykhes* had the five chosen to attack. He didn't worry about that, though. He had more important things to worry about: "On to Kos, and let's see if we can get some silk."

KOS, THE MAIN CITY on the island of Kos, was a new town, even newer than Rhodes. The Spartans, Sostratos knew, had sacked Meropis, the former center, during the Peloponnesian War after an earthquake left it half wrecked. Meropis had stood in southwestern Kos, looking back toward Hellas. The new city of Kos was at the northeastern end of the island, and looked across the narrow strait to Halikarnassos on the Asian mainland.

Like Rhodes', the new city's harbor boasted all the modern improvements: moles to moderate the force of the waves, and stone quays at which merchantmen and war galleys could tie up (though the galleys usually stayed out of the water in shipsheds to keep their timbers from getting heavy and waterlogged). "It's a pretty sight, isn't it?" Sostratos said as the *Aphrodite* eased up to a quay. "The red tile roofs of the city against the green of the hills farther inland, I mean."

"When I get a chance to look, I'll tell you," Menedemos answered, making a minute turn with the port steering oar. All his attention was on the quay, none on the scenery. He turned to Diokles. "I think that will do it. Bring us to a stop just as we come alongside here."

"Right you are, skipper." The keleustes raised his voice: "Back oars!" A couple of strokes killed the akatos' forward motion. *"Oöp!"* Diokles shouted, and the men rested at the oars with the *Aphrodite* motionless in the water only a short jump from the quay.

Sailors tossed lines to men on the quay, who made the akatos fast. "Who are you?" one of the Koans asked. "Where are you from?" another asked. "What's your news?" a third said.

Sostratos wasn't surprised that they already knew about the murders of Alexandros and Roxane, and of course they knew Ptolemaios had gone back to war with Antigonos. They hadn't heard that Antigonos' nephew had gone over to Kassandros, and one of them clapped his hands when Menedemos mentioned it. "Anything that keeps the Cyclops busy somewhere else is good for us here," the fellow said, and his friends chimed in with loud agreement.

"Remind me how I get to the shop of Xenophanes the silk merchant," Sostratos said.

"It's simple, sir," one of the harbor workers answered, and then paused expectantly. With a mental sigh, Sostratos tossed him an obolos. He popped it into his mouth, saying, "Many thanks, best one. Go up three streets"—he pointed—"then turn right and go over two. You can't miss it: there's a bawdy house full of pretty boys across the street."

"That's right." Sostratos dipped his head and turned to Menedemos. "Remember the fellows who were brawling in the street over that one boy when we were here last spring?"

"I certainly do," his cousin said. "That little chap with the gray hair was going for his knife when a couple of people sat on him."

"Foolishness," Sostratos said. "A brothel boy's not worth quarreling over. He wouldn't have cared a fig for either one of them, except for what he could squeeze out of them. Hetairai are the same way, most of the time: more trouble than they're worth, and more expensive, too."

"You sound like my father." By the way Menedemos said that, he didn't mean it as a compliment. He raised an eyebrow. "Besides, what do you know about hetairai?"

Ears burning, Sostratos hurried up the gangplank to the quay. Menedemos stayed aboard the *Aphrodite* for a little while, setting up a watch schedule that would keep enough men on the ship at all times to deter robbers. The delay let Sostratos recover his composure. Unlike Menedemos—unlike most young men of his wealth—he wasn't in the habit of keeping a mistress. His cousin made it sound as if there were something wrong with him. *But I've never met a hetaira who made me believe she cared about me more than she cared about my silver.* He didn't bother saying it aloud. Letting it drop seemed better than enduring whatever snide comeback his cousin would surely find.

Menedemos pranced up the gangplank, almost as if he were about to start dancing the kordax. He had one of the little pots of perfume in his left hand. "Let's go," he said cheerfully, and slapped Sostratos on the shoulder. He'd already forgotten he'd been teasing his cousin. Sostratos hadn't. Menedemos continued, "With any luck at all, we'll be able to make a deal before sundown and get back to the ship without having to hire torchbearers."

"Now who's fretting about every khalkos?" Sostratos said, and savored the dirty look Menedemos gave him.

Being a new city, Kos was laid out in a grid, as Rhodes was. Once they got directions, Sostratos and Menedemos had no trouble finding Xenophanes' establishment. A man came out of the establishment across the street with his tunic rumpled and a lazy smile on his face. Other than that, the bawdy house seemed as peaceful as if the proprietor sold wool.

A plump Karian slave bowed when Sostratos and Menedemos walked into Xenophanes' shop. "The gentlemen from Rhodes!" he said in excellent Greek.

"Hail, Pixodaros," Sostratos said.

"My master will be as pleased to see you as I am, best ones," Pixodaros said. "Let me go get him." He bowed again, beamed at Sostratos, and hurried into a back room.

"How did you remember his name?" Menedemos whispered. "You could set a vulture tearing at my liver, the way Zeus did with Prometheus, and I couldn't have come up with it."

"Isn't that why you bring me along?" Sostratos answered. "To keep track of details, I mean?"

"He's just a slave," Menedemos said, as if Pixodaros weren't important enough to be even a detail.

But Sostratos tossed his head. "He's more than just a slave. He's Xenophanes' right-hand man. If he's happy with us, his master will be, too. That can't hurt, and it might help."

Pixodaros returned, Xenophanes following him and leaning on a stick like the last part of the answer to the riddle of the Sphinx. The silk merchant's white beard spilled down over half his chest. A cataract clouded his right eye, but the left remained clear. He shifted the stick to his left hand and held out his right. "Good day, gents," he said, his Doric drawl more pronounced than that of the Rhodians.

Menedemos and Sostratos clasped his hand in turn. His grip was still warm and firm. "Hail," Menedemos said.

"What's that?" Xenophanes cupped a hand behind his ear. "Speak up, young fellow. My hearing isn't quite what it used to be."

It hadn't been good the year before, Sostratos remembered. Now, evidently, it was worse. "Hail," Menedemos repeated, louder this time.

Xenophanes dipped his head. "Of course I'm hale. If a man my age ain't hale, he's dead." He laughed at his own wit. So did his slave. And so, dutifully, did Sostratos and Menedemos. Xenophanes turned to Pixodaros. "Fetch us some stools from the back, why don't you? And a jar of wine, too. I reckon we'll chat for a spell before we commence to dickering."

Pixodaros made two trips, one for the stools, the other for the wine, some cool water to mix with it, and cups. He served Xenophanes and the two Rhodians.

"Thanks," the silk merchant said. He waved toward the stools. "Set a spell," he told Sostratos and Menedemos as he perched on the one Pixodaros had brought for him. The Karian had also brought one for himself, and sat down beside his master.

They sipped wine and swapped news. Like the rest of the Koans, Xenophanes hadn't heard about Polemaios' defection from Antigonos. "The nephew will have seen that the sons are rising men," Pixodaros remarked.

"My thought exactly," Sostratos agreed.

Xenophanes ran a hand through his beard. "I'd be just about of an age with One-Eye," he said. "Still a few old mulberry trees the wind hasn't blown down."

"Mulberry trees?" Sostratos said; he hadn't heard that figure of speech before.

"Mulberry trees," Xenophanes repeated, and dipped his head for emphasis. "Call it a silk-seller's joke if you care to, sir." He took another pull from his cup and declined to explain further.

After a while—a little sooner than Sostratos would have—Menedemos said, "I've got some fine perfumes with me, made from the best Rhodian roses."

Xenophanes' smile showed teeth worn down nearly to the gums. "My friend, no matter how fine your perfumes are—and I'm sure they're very fine; your father and I have been doing business longer than you've lived, and I know he handles the best—I doubt the maidens would beat a path to my door if I wore them."

"But they might beat a path to your door if you sold them," Menedemos said. "For that matter, the pretty boys across the street might, too."

That made the silk merchant laugh, but he tossed his head even so. "Making silk, selling silk—those I know. Selling perfumes? I reckon I'm too old to start picking up things I didn't learn when I was younger."

Pixodaros leaned forward on his stool. "Master, perhaps I could—"

"No," Xenophanes broke in. "I said it once, and I'll say it twice. You don't know a single thing more about perfume than I do. As long as I'm breathing, we'll do it my way."

Being a slave, the Karian had no choice but to accept that. Sostratos thought of the character types Theophrastos had discussed at the Lykeion in Athens. One of them was the later learner: the old man who was always trying something new and making a botch of it. Xenophanes was not an old man of that sort; he clung like a limpet to what he understood.

Then Sostratos had another thought. He snapped his fingers and said, "We've also got crimson dye from Byblos. If you like, we can trade you that for silk. Dye, sir, I'm sure you do know."

He and Menedemos would have got more for the dye in Italy, far from Phoenicia, than they could hope to here. But they would get still more for silk. He was sure of that. Menedemos murmured, "See? It comes in handy even if you didn't know about it till the last moment."

Sostratos only half heard him; his attention was aimed at Xenophanes. The old man's good eye lit up. "Dye? I should hope I know dye," he said. "Tyre, now, Tyre made the best crimson, back in the days before Alexander sacked it. It hasn't been the same since; the men who knew the most got killed or sold for slaves. Arados, I reckon, turns out the best nowadays, with Byblos down a notch."

"I wouldn't say that." Sostratos knew a negotiating ploy when he heard one. "Arados makes more dye than Byblos, true. But better? I don't think so, and I don't think you'll find many who do."

"Which of us dyes silk?" Xenophanes returned.

"Which of us sells dye all around the Inner Sea?" Sostratos asked. They smiled at each other. Their moves were as formal, as stylized, as those of a dance.

Pixodaros said, "My master is right." That was an inevitable response, too. He went on, "The crimson of Byblos may be brighter, but that of Arados holds its color better." Sostratos tossed his head to show he disagreed.

Again, Menedemos moved faster than Sostratos would have, saying, "Each jar of dye holds about a kotyle. That may not be very much wine, but it's a whole great whacking lot of boiled-down murex juice. How much silk might you trade for a jar?"

"And of what quality?" Sostratos added. "There's dye and then there's dye, and there's silk and then there's silk."

They haggled till the light in Xenophanes' shop faded. Pixodaros lit lamps that nibbled at the edges of oncoming night without really pushing it back. The familiar smell of burning olive oil filled the air. Xenophanes began to yawn. "I'm an old man," he said. "I need my sleep. Shall we go on come morning? We're pretty close, I reckon."

"Is there an inn close by?" Sostratos asked. "My cousin and I slept on the poop deck last night. We'd sooner have something a little softer tonight."

"That there is, just a couple of blocks over," Xenophanes answered. "I'll have a couple of slaves get torches and light your way there. And I'll give you some bread to eat for your suppers—Skylax will sell you wine till you're too drunk to walk, but you have to bring in your own food. He will cook meat or fish if you pay him."

The slaves were a couple of fair-haired Thracians. They chattered in their incomprehensible language while guiding Sostratos and Menedemos to the inn. Their torches didn't shed much light; Sostratos stepped in something nasty, and kept trying to scrape it off his foot till he got to Skylax's place. He and Menedemos each gave Xenophanes' slaves a couple of khalkoi. The torchbearers hurried toward the silk merchant's house.

More torches blazed inside the inn. Not all the smoke escaped through the hole in the roof; a lot of it hung in the main room in a choking cloud. The odor of hot oil fought with it: Skylax kept a vat bubbling over a fire. By the smell, Xenophanes lit his home with better oil than the innkeeper used for cooking.

His wine wasn't bad, though, and he didn't seem put out to see Sostratos and Menedemos eating bread and not giving him anything to throw into that bubbling vat. When Sostratos asked about his rooms, he said, "Two oboloi for the pair of you." He wouldn't haggle. When Sostratos tried, he just tossed his head. "If you don't like it, strangers, go somewhere else."

The two Rhodians couldn't very well do that, not in a strange city after dark. Sostratos thought he could have found his way back to the *Aphrodite,* but he didn't want to sleep on planking again. After a glance at his cousin, he paid Skylax the little silver coins. A slave carrying a lamp guided Sostratos and Menedemos to the room. It held only one bed. The slave set down the lamp and dragged in another one from across the hall. Then he departed, taking the lamp with him and plunging the room into stygian darkness.

With a sigh, Sostratos said, "We might as well go to sleep. Nothing else we could possibly do in here."

"Oh, there's one other thing," Menedemos said. "If you were a cute little flutegirl . . ."

"Me?" Sostratos said. "What about you?" They both laughed. Sostratos groped his way to a bed, took off his tunic, and draped it over himself. He wished he'd thought to bring his mantle, too; that would have made a better blanket. But the little room was too cramped and stuffy to get very cold. He twisted, trying to make himself comfortable. Creaks from the other bed said Menedemos was doing the same. Just as he heard the first snore from Menedemos, he fell asleep, too.

His cousin shook him awake. A little gray light was sneaking through the closed shutters over the narrow window. "You sound like a saw working through hard wood," Menedemos said.

"I'm not the only one," Sostratos answered. "Did they bother giving us a chamber pot? If they didn't, I'm going to piss in the corner." He looked under the bed. To his relief, both metaphorical and literal, he found one.

After buying more wine from Skylax to open their eyes, the Rhodians went back to Xenophanes'. "Good day, my masters," Pixodaros told them. "My master still sleeps. He told me to bring you food if you came before he rose." With a bow, the Karian slave went into the back of the house. He returned with bread and cheese.

"Thank you," Sostratos said, and then, "This business will be yours one of these days, won't it?"

"It could be." Pixodaros' voice was carefully neutral. "The gods gave my master no children who lived, so it could be."

Even if Xenophanes liberated Pixodaros on his deathbed, the Karian would never be a full citizen of Kos. His children might, though, depending on whom he married. *Life is a changeable business,* Sostratos thought—not original, but true.

He and Menedemos and Pixodaros made small talk till Xenophanes came out about half an hour later. "I still say you're asking too much for a jar of dye," the silk merchant began without preamble.

Menedemos put on his most winning smile. "But, my dear fellow . . ." he said. He could charm birds out of trees and wives into bed when he worked at it.

But he couldn't charm Xenophanes, who said, "No. It's too much, I tell you. I spent a deal of time thinking on it last night in bed, and my mind's made up."

"All right, then," Sostratos said before Menedemos could speak. Sostratos was the one who used bluntness, not charm, as his main weapon. He got to his feet. "I guess we'll go see Theagenes"—Xenophanes' chief rival—"if you won't see reason. And if Theagenes is stubborn, too, I guarantee we can get a better price for the dye in Taras or one of the other Italian cities than we can here."

That was likely true, though silk would bring more profit still. Mentioning Theagenes' name had the desired effect. Xenophanes looked as if he'd taken a big bite of bad fish. "He'll cheat you," he spluttered. "His silk is full of slubs. It's not nearly so thin and transparent as mine."

"No doubt you're right, O best one." Sostratos didn't sit down. "But he usually knows better than to price himself out of a bargain, and at least we'll have something to show the Italiotes. Come on, cousin." Menedemos rose, too. They both started for the door, though Sostratos was anything but eager to throw away most of a day's haggling.

"Wait." That wasn't Xenophanes—it was Pixodaros. He put his head together with his master. Sostratos stayed where he was. Menedemos started to get closer to try to hear what they were saying, but checked himself at Sostratos' small gesture.

"It's robbery, that's what it is!" Xenophanes spoke loud enough for the whole neighborhood to hear. Pixodaros didn't. The slave—the slave who might be a master himself one day—kept his voice low, but he kept talking, too. At last, Xenophanes threw his hands in the air and dipped his head to Sostratos and Menedemos. "All right," he said grudgingly. "A bargain. The Karian is right—we do need the dye. A hundred jars, for the bolts of silk you proposed last night."

Slaves carried the silk to the *Aphrodite* and took the dye back to Xenophanes' shop. Watching them go with the last of the jars, Menedemos said, "Gods be praised, our fathers don't have to worry about passing on what they've spent a lifetime building up to a barbarian slave."

"And here's hoping we never have to worry about it ourselves," Sostratos said, at which his cousin gave him a very peculiar look.

MENEDEMOS DECIDED NOT TO stop in Halikarnassos, even though it lay close by Kos. For one thing, he wanted to press north to Khios, to get some of the island's famous wine to take west. And, for another, he'd left an outraged husband behind on his last visit to the former capital of Karia, and he didn't care to appear there before things had more of a chance to settle down.

Instead, traveling under oars into the breeze, the *Aphrodite* went up the channel between the mainland and the island of Kalymnos, and beached itself for the night on Leros, the next island farther north. Sostratos quoted a fragment of verse:

    " 'The Lerians are wicked—not just one, but every one
      Except Proklees—and Proklees is a Lerian, too.' "

"Who said that?" Menedemos asked.

"Phokylides," his cousin answered. "Is it true?"

"I hope not," Menedemos told him. "Leros and Kalymnos are supposed to be the Kalydian isles Homer speaks of in the *Iliad*."

"If they are, they've changed hands since," Sostratos said, "for the Lerians nowadays are Ionians, colonists from Miletos on the Asian mainland."

The peacock started screeching. Menedemos winced. "You don't know how sick I am of that polluted bird," he said.

"Oh, I think I may," Sostratos replied. "I may even be sicker of it than you are, because you get to stay back at the steering oars most of the day, while I have to play peacockherd."

Before Menedemos could point out that his staying at the steering oars did have a certain importance to the journey, someone hailed them from the brush beyond the beach. " 'Ere, what's making that 'orrible noise?"

"Ionians, you see," Sostratos said smugly. "No rough breathings."

He didn't say it very loud. In similarly soft tones, Menedemos answered, "Oh, shut up." He raised his voice and called, "Come and see for yourself," to the stranger.

"You'll not seize me for a slave and 'aul me off to foreign parts?" the Lerian asked anxiously.

"No, by the gods," Menedemos promised. "We're traders from Rhodes, not pirates." In another soft aside to Sostratos, he added, "Some withered old herdsman wouldn't be worth our while grabbing, anyhow."

"True enough," Sostratos said. "And it wouldn't be sporting, not after you've promised to leave him alone."

Menedemos cared little for what was sporting and what wasn't. But the rustic who emerged from the scrubby brush was middle-aged and scrawny. He wore only a goatskin tunic, hairy side out. That by itself made Menedemos' lip curl; country bumpkins were the only ones who preferred leather to cloth. And, when the Lerian got closer, Menedemos' nostrils curled, too: the fellow hadn't bathed in a long time, if ever.

"All right," he said. " 'Ere I am. What was that screeching like it was being turned into a eunuch?"

"A peacock," Menedemos answered. "For a khalkos, you can go aboard and see it for yourself." He didn't think he would be able to get two bronze coins out of the local; even one might be pushing it.

As things were, the fellow in goatskins made no move to produce a khalkos. He just stared at Menedemos. "A what?" he said. "You're 'aving me on. You think because I live on a little no-account island you can tell me anything and I'll swallow it. Can't fool me, though. I know there's no such beasts, not for true. Next thing is, you'll be telling me you've got 'Ades' three-'eaded dog Kerberos on your ship, or else a tree nymph out of 'er tree. Well, you must think I'm out of mine, and I'm 'ere to tell you I ain't." He stomped off, his nose in the air.

"No, you can't fool him," Sostratos said gravely. As if to prove the Lerian couldn't be fooled, the peacock let out another screech.

"Sure can't," Menedemos agreed. "He knows what's what, and he's not about to let anybody tell him anything different."

"He would have voted to make Sokrates drink the hemlock," Sostratos said.

"How does that follow?" Menedemos asked.

"You said it yourself," his cousin answered. "He already knows everything he wants to know. That means anyone who tries to tell him anything else must be wrong—and must be dangerous, too, for wanting to tell him wrong things."

"I suppose so," Menedemos said with a shrug. "Sounds like philosophy to me, though."

"Maybe you don't want to know anything more, either," Sostratos said, which left Menedemos feeling obscurely punctured.

When the sun rose the next morning, he shouted his men awake. "Let's get the *Aphrodite* back into the sea," he called. "If we push hard, we make Samos tonight. Wouldn't you sooner do that than sleep on the sand again?"

"After that Koan inn, I think I'd just as soon stay on the beach," Sostratos said. "Fewer bugs."

"Don't think about bugs," Menedemos said. "Think about wine-shops. Think about pretty girls." He lowered his voice. "Think about making the men want to work hard, not about giving them reasons to take it easy."

"Oh." Sostratos had the grace to sound abashed. "I'm sorry." He made a splendid toikharkhos. He always knew where everything was and what everything was worth. He'd done well in the dicker with Xenophanes. When the old coot got mulish, he'd picked the right time to get mulish in return. But ask him to be a man among men, to understand how an ordinary fellow thought . . . Menedemos tossed his head. His cousin didn't have it in him, any more than a team of donkeys had it in them to win the chariot race at Olympos.

With men in the boat pulling and men on land pushing, the *Aph-*

rodite went back into the Aegean more readily than she had after beaching on Syme. Menedemos steered the akatos north and a little east, toward Samos. He wished the wind would swing round and come out of the south so he could lower the sail, but it didn't. Through most of the sailing season, winds in the Aegean would stay boreal.

"Rhyppa*pai*! Rhyppa*pai*!" Diokles called, amplifying the stroke he gave with mallet and bronze. Menedemos had ten men on the oars on each side of the galley. He planned on shifting rowers when the sun swung past noon, and on putting the whole crew on the oars if he was close to making Samos in the late afternoon. If not . . .

Sostratos asked, "What will you do if we come up short?"

"We have choices," Menedemos replied. "We could head for Priene, on the mainland. Or we could beach ourselves again. Or I might spend a night at sea, just to remind the men there will be times when they need to work hard."

"You didn't want to do that before," Sostratos remarked.

Patiently, Menedemos explained, "Before, it would have just annoyed them. If I can turn it into a lesson, though, that would be worthwhile."

"Ah," his cousin said, and stepped over to the rail: not to ease himself but to think about what Menedemos had told him. Sostratos was anything but stupid; Menedemos knew that. But he had a lot less feel for what made people work than Menedemos did. Once things were set out before him, though, as if at the highfalutin Lykeion at Athens, he could grasp them and figure out how to use them.

After a bit, Menedemos interrupted his musing, saying, "Why don't you give the peafowl some exercise?"

"Oh." Sostratos blinked his way out of contemplation and back to the real world. "I'll do that. I'm sorry. I forgot."

"The ship won't sink," Menedemos said as his cousin headed for the bow. *And you'll be too busy to do any philosophizing for a while.*

Except when Sostratos' antics were funny or his curses got frantic, Menedemos put him out of his mind for a while. He took in the *Aphrodite*'s motion through the soles of his feet and through the steering-oar tillers in the palms of his hands. It was almost as if he were peering out through the eyes painted at the merchant galley's bow, so much did he feel himself a part of the ship.

More ships were on the sea than had been true even when the *Aphrodite* set out from Rhodes a few days before. Fishing boats bobbed in the light chop. Some were hardly bigger than the akatos' boat. Others, with many more men dangling lines over the side or trailing nets behind them, were almost half the size of the *Aphrodite* herself. Menedemos saw most of them at a rapidly increasing distance, as he had the day before. The merchant galley really was beamier and slower than any proper pirate ship, but few skippers conning fishing boats cared to wait around till such details grew obvious.

Larger merchantmen—merchantmen big enough to dwarf the akatos—also spread their sails and scudded away, sometimes fast enough to kick up a creamy white wake at the bow. Their captains commanded bigger ships than Menedemos did, but he had more men aboard his. Like the men in charge of the more numerous fishing boats, they weren't inclined to take chances.

And then, not long before midday, Menedemos felt like scurrying aside himself when he spotted a five majestically making its way south under sails and oars. Instead of Ptolemaios' eagle, this war galley bore the Macedonian royal sunburst on foresail and mainsail both. "Ptolemaios and Antigonos are liable to start going nose to nose here along with their squabbles in Kilikia," Menedemos said.

"I wouldn't be surprised," Diokles answered. "And what can a free polis like Rhodes do if they start?"

"Duck," Menedemos said, which startled a laugh out of the keleustes.

Unlike the *Eutykhes,* Antigonos' five didn't change course to look over the *Aphrodite.* Menedemos watched the big ship glide over the waves in the direction of Kos with nothing but relief. Ptolemaios' crew hadn't turned robber. Maybe Antigonos' wouldn't have, either. Maybe. Menedemos was just as well pleased not to have to find out.

Little by little, the mountains of Samos and of Ikaria slightly to the southwest rose up out of the sea. Those of Samos, especially Mount Kerkis in the western part of the island, were taller than their Ikarian neighbors. Menedemos had noticed that every time he approached Samos—Ikaria, inhabited mostly by herdsmen, was hardly worth visiting—but hadn't wondered about it till now.

Diokles just gave him a blank look when he mentioned it. "Why, skipper?" the oarmaster said. "Because that's how the gods made 'em, that's why."

He might well have been right. Right or not, though, the answer wasn't interesting. Menedemos waited till Sostratos came up onto the poop deck and asked the question again. He might joke about philosophy, but it did sometimes lead to lively conversation.

"They are, aren't they?" Sostratos said, looking from the peaks of Samos over to those of Ikaria and back again. Then he did something Menedemos hadn't done: he looked to the Asian mainland east of Samos. "There's Mount Latmos, back of Miletos, and I'd say it's taller than anything on Samos."

"I . . . think you're right," Menedemos said; Mount Latmos was also farther away, which made its height hard to judge. "Even if you are, though, so what?"

"I don't know for certain, but it looks to me as if the islands carry the mountains of the mainland out into the sea," his cousin answered. "If that's so, it would stand to reason that the peaks would get lower the farther out into the sea the islands went. After a while, no more peaks—and no more islands, either."

Menedemos considered, dipped his head, and sent Sostratos an admiring glance. "That would make sense, wouldn't it?"

"It seems to me that it would," Sostratos answered. "I don't know whether it's true, mind you—that isn't the same as being logical."

"Close enough for me," Menedemos said. His cousin raised an eyebrow, but didn't rise to the bait.

Samos rose ever higher out of the sea, while the sun sank ever closer to the water. "Looks to me like we'll make it, skipper," Diokles said.

"We will if the boys put their backs into it," Menedemos replied. Actually, he was pretty sure the keleustes was right, but he wanted to get the rowers working as a team. "Call everyone to the oars and give them a sprint, why don't you? Let's pretend we've got a hemiolia full of Tyrrhenians on our trail."

Diokles stroked the ring with the image of Herakles Alexikakos on it to turn aside the evil omen. "That could happen, you know, even here in the Aegean. Those polluted whoresons don't stay in the Adriatic any more. They're like cockroaches or mice—they're all over the stinking place."

Like any merchant sailor, Menedemos knew that entirely too well. He dipped his head, but said, "They've got more teeth than mice, worse luck. Come on—get the men to the oars and up the stroke. We'll see what kind of crew we've got."

"Right you are." The oarmaster shouted the whole crew to their benches and kept right on shouting once they were in their places: "We're going to push it to get to port before sundown—and so we know what we can do if pirates come after us. Give it everything you've got, boys. Rhyppa*pai*! Rhyppa*pai*!"

Mallet met bronze in an ever-quicker rhythm. Diokles hit the bronze harder, too, so each clang seemed more urgent. The rowers didn't spare themselves. Panting, their bodies glistening with oil and sweat, their muscular arms working as if belonging to Hephaistos' automata from the *Iliad,* they worked like men possessed.

And the *Aphrodite* fairly seemed to leap ahead. She arrowed through the deep-blue water; a creamy wake streamed from her bow. After a very short time, Menedemos grew sure they would make Samos.

Diokles held the oarsmen to the sprint as long as he could, and eased off as slowly as he could. "Not too bad, captain," he said. "No, not too bad at all. And the rowing's smooth as that silk you bought. We knew we had some good men here, and this proves it."

"You're right," Menedemos answered. "I wouldn't quarrel with a single word you said. But tell me, would we have got away from a pirate ship?"

"Well . . ." The keleustes looked unhappy. "We'd've needed some luck, wouldn't we? They did get her up as fast as she'll go."

"I know they did," Menedemos said. "The trouble is, she won't quite go fast enough." The *Aphrodite* carried cargo, not just rowers who doubled as fighting men. She was beamier than a hemiolia or a pentekonter, too, which meant there was more of her to resist the sea than held true for their lean, deadly shapes. And she rode deeper in the water, because of her cargo and because her timbers were more waterlogged and heavier than those of pampered pirate ships, which dried out on the beach every night. Because of all that, odds were a ship full of pirates could overhaul them from behind.

"We're all right if we've got a friendly port we can run for," Diokles said.

"Of course we are. But if we don't, we're going to have to fight."

Menedemos drummed his fingers on the steering-oar tiller. "I'd sooner do it ship against ship, not man against man. They'll have bigger crews than we do."

"Pirate crews mostly aren't disciplined," the keleustes observed. "They don't want to fight unless they have to. They're out to rob and kidnap, either for ransom or for slaves."

"We've got a lot of men who've put in time aboard war galleys," Menedemos said. "Once we sail west from Khios—maybe even sooner—we will work hard."

"Good," Diokles replied.

Though the sun was not far from setting when the *Aphrodite* glided into Samos' harbor, Menedemos had enough light to reach the quays and tie up without any trouble. A temple dedicated to Hera lay to the left, where the Imbrasos River ran down into the sea from the mountains in the island's interior. To the right was a shrine for Poseidon that looked across a seven-stadia strait to the mainland.

As longshoremen made the akatos fast to the wharf, the rowers rested at their oars, still worn with the effort they'd put forth in the sprint. One of them said the worst thing he could think of: "I'm liable to be too tired to want to go into town and screw."

"Well, if you are, I hear there are girls up in Khios, too," Menedemos said.

"Likely there are," the sailor agreed, "but I hate to waste a chance." Since Menedemos hated to waste a chance, too, he just laughed and dipped his head.

As Kos lay under Ptolemaios' thumb, so Samos belonged to Antigonos. Sostratos wasn't surprised when a couple of officers in gleaming armor tramped up to the quay to inquire about the *Aphrodite* and where she'd been before coming to Samos. He *was* surprised when they started asking their questions: he could hardly follow a word they said.

"What *is* that gibberish?" Menedemos asked out of the side of his mouth.

"Macedonian dialect, thick enough to slice," Sostratos replied, also in a whisper. He raised his voice: "Please speak slowly, O best ones. I will gladly answer all I can understand." That might have been a lie, but the Macedonians didn't have to know it.

"Who . . . art tha?" one of them asked, his brow furrowed in concentration, his accent both rustic and archaic. *Homer might have spoken like that, had he been an ignorant peasant and not a poet,* Sostratos
thought. The Macedonian went on, "Whence . . . art tha from?"

"This is the *Aphrodite,* owned by Philodemos and Lysistratos of
Rhodes," Sostratos said. The officer dipped his head; he could follow
good Greek even if he couldn't speak it himself. Sostratos continued,
"We're for Khios, and we've stopped at Syme, at Knidos, and at Kos."

"Did you have to tell him that?" Menedemos murmured.

"I think so," Sostratos said. "Someone else may come in who saw
us in port or rowing up from the island."

Mentioning Kos got the Macedonians' attention. "What be there?"
demanded the one who could make a stab at real Greek. "Ships?
Ptolemaios' ships? How many of Ptolemaios' ships?"

"How gross?" the other one added, and then corrected himself:
"How big?"

"I wasn't watching all that closely," Sostratos answered, and proceeded to exaggerate what he had seen. No one gave him the lie;
though Rhodes' shipwrights had built war galleys for Antigonos, the
island inclined more toward Ptolemaios. Rhodes shipped a lot of
Egyptian grain all over the Hellenic world.

Sostratos didn't exaggerate enough to make the Macedonians serving Antigonos suspect him—only enough to give them long faces.
They spoke back and forth between themselves; he understood not
a word. Then, to his relief, they left.

Beside him, Menedemos let out a glad sigh to match his own. "I
thought they were going to jump out of their corselets when you
started talking about Ptolemaios' sixes and sevens at Kos," Sostratos'
cousin said.

"So did I," Sostratos said. "I wanted to give them something to
think about—something that wasn't quite true, but sounded as if it
could be."

"Well, you hit the nail on the head," Menedemos told him. "If
that doesn't set Antigonos' carpenters building like maniacs, to the
crows with me if I know what would."

"I wouldn't mind—but where will it stop?" Sostratos wondered.
"If you can build sevens, are nine better? What about thirteens, or
maybe seventeens?"

Menedemos shrugged. "Not my worry. Not Rhodes' worry, either, I shouldn't think. How many rowers would you need in a seventeen?" He held up a warning hand. "No, don't go trying to figure it out, by the gods. I don't want to know, not exactly. However many it is, Rhodes might be able to man one or two of them. No more, I'm sure."

He was stretching things; but not by that much. He did persuade Sostratos not to finish the calculation he had indeed started. Instead, Sostratos asked, "You don't intend to do much in the way of trading here, do you?"

His cousin tossed his head. "Not much point to it: ordinary wine and plain pottery. I mostly wanted the anchorage." Menedemos hesitated. "If we could get our hands on those statues in Hera's temple, though, they'd bring a pretty price in Italy, don't you think?"

"Myron's Zeus and Athena and Herakles?" Sostratos laughed. "I'm sure they would. But remember, Ikaria's close by, and it got its name because Ikaros fell to earth there after flying too close to the sun. You'd fall and fail if you tried to get those statues, too."

Menedemos laughed. "I know. Had you worried there, didn't I?" Before Sostratos could answer, the peacock screeched. Menedemos snapped his fingers. "That reminds me—time to make ourselves a little money. Do you want to show people the peafowl?"

"I'm dying to," Sostratos replied.

He might as well have saved his breath; Menedemos paid no attention to him. Menedemos paid attention to him only when that suited his purposes. Sostratos' cousin hurried up the gangplank to the wharf and started singing the praises of peafowl. In short order, he started collecting khalkoi. Nobody got to look at the birds without handing over a couple of the little bronze coins. Sostratos showed off the peafowl till it got too dark for spectators to see them.

"What's the take today?" he asked when Menedemos gave up on luring any more spectators aboard the *Aphrodite*.

Khalkoi clinked as Menedemos built them into shaky piles. "Half an obolos, an obolos, an obolos and a half . . ." When he was through reckoning piles, he said, "A drakhma, four oboloi, six khalkoi. Nothing that'll make us rich, but not bad, either."

"Sixty-three people," Sostratos said after a moment's thought.

"No, that isn't bad at all. Peafowl are interesting birds—it'll be interesting to see if we can get them to Italy without tossing them overboard, for instance."

For once, his cousin didn't rise to the bait of the joke. Instead, Menedemos gave him an odd look. "Without a counting board, I couldn't have figured out how many people saw the birds to save my life."

"It wasn't hard." Sostratos changed the subject: "Will you look for an inn?"

Menedemos tossed his head. "Too late now. I'll just sleep on the deck. I've done it before. I can do it again." He waved a hand. "If you want to go into town, though, don't let me stop you. Plenty of sailors heading in for a good time."

"No, thanks," Sostratos said. His cousin was the one who was fond of luxury. If Menedemos could stand another night wrapped in his himation on the poop deck, Sostratos could, too. A man of philosophical bent was supposed to be indifferent to bodily pleasures . . . wasn't he?

Sostratos wondered about that as he lay with his chiton bundled up under his head for a pillow. Even though he was wrapped in his mantle, he couldn't get comfortable on the planks. He'd had an easier time drifting off on the beach on Leros.

As Menedemos had said, some of the rowers went into Samos to roister. The rest dozed on their benches. Some of them snored. Others, probably even more uncomfortable than Sostratos, talked in low voices so as not to disturb their shipmates. Sostratos tried to eavesdrop on them till he finally fell asleep.

He woke once in the middle of the night, pissed into the water of the harbor, and fell asleep again almost at once. The next time he woke, it was daybreak. Menedemos was already sitting up, an almost wolfishly intent look on his face. He dipped his head to Sostratos. "A lot to do today," he said. "We won't make Khios in one day from here, not rowing all the way. A good two-day pull. Since we didn't pass the night at sea coming to Samos, I intend to do that, to give the men a taste of what it's like."

"Whatever seems good to you," Sostratos agreed. "Our fathers trust you to command the ship. I haven't seen anything that makes me think they're wrong." Saying that didn't come easy to him; Menedemos often wore on his nerves. But his cousin did know what to do with the *Aphrodite* and how to lead her crew. However much Sostratos might have wanted to deny that, he couldn't.

Menedemos jumped to his feet. He paused just long enough to ease himself over the akatos' side. Then, still naked, he shouted the sailors awake. They yawned and grunted and rubbed their eyes, much less enthusiastic about facing the new day than he was.

He laughed at them. "We're heading toward the finest wine in the world, and you whipworthy catamites complain? I thought I'd signed up a crew of real men." His scorn lashed them to their feet and into action. Sostratos wondered how they would have acted had *he* exhorted them like that. Actually, he didn't wonder. He knew. They would have flung him into the Aegean. Had they been feeling kindly, they might have fished him out again afterwards.

He had his own morning duties to attend to. He gave the peafowl barley and water for their breakfast. The birds ate with good appetite. He'd seen they ate better in harbor than while the *Aphrodite* moved across the open sea. That was nothing remarkable. A lot of people went off their feed on the open sea, too.

"How many men are we missing, Diokles?" Menedemos asked.

"Not a one, captain, if you can believe it." The keleustes shook his head in amazement. "I wonder about these fellows, I truly do. You're hardly a man at all if you can't go out and make a night of it."

"They want the Khian, too," Menedemos said. "Even a sailor can afford it when he buys it where they make it."

Sostratos said, "The dealers won't be so generous as the tavernkeepers will. They'll be selling their best, not the cheap stuff you get in taverns, and they'll squeeze us till our eyes pop."

Menedemos grinned at him. "That's why you're along. You're not supposed to let them squeeze us."

"Ha," Sostratos said. "Ha, ha." He brought out the syllables just like that, as if they were dialogue in a comedy. "I can't keep them from squeezing us, and you'd better know it. With a little luck, I can keep them from squeezing us quite so much."

"All right." Menedemos dipped his head. He seemed in a good mood this morning, likely because the *Aphrodite* wouldn't have to sit in the harbor while Diokles hunted down men who gave more thought to roistering than to how they earned the money to roister. He pointed to Sostratos. "Grab yourself some bread and oil and wine. I want to get out into the open sea as soon as I can."

"All right." Sostratos drummed his fingers on the gunwale. "We'll have to lay in some more supplies when we get to Khios. We're using them faster than I thought we would."

"Take care of it." Menedemos was already eating and spoke with his mouth full. Sostratos tried to resent his cousin's peremptory tone, but couldn't quite. He was the toikharkhos; taking care of such things was his job. As he came back to the poop, Menedemos added, "The sooner I can get out of this port, the better I'll like it."

"Those Macedonians?" Sostratos asked.

"Sure enough," Menedemos agreed. "I didn't like the way they asked questions—like they were demigods looking down their noses at ordinary mortals." He dipped a piece of bread into olive oil and took a big bite. As he swallowed, his lip curled. "Demigods would speak better Greek, though."

"Khios won't be any better when it comes to that," Sostratos predicted. "It bends the knee to Antigonos, too."

"Well, yes, but it's not sitting over Kos, the way Samos is," his cousin answered. "The officers up there won't be so . . . eager to squeeze everything we know out of us. I can hope they won't, anyhow."

"It makes sense," Sostratos said. "You have a pretty good idea of the way the politics work."

"For which I thank you." Menedemos sounded as if he meant it. Then he added, "I may not know everything that's happened everywhere since before the Trojan War, but I do all right."

"I don't pretend to know everything that's happened everywhere since before the Trojan War," Sostratos spluttered. Only after he was done spluttering did he realize Menedemos had been hoping he would. He shut up with a snap. That also amused his cousin, which only annoyed him more.

"Come on!" Menedemos called to his men. "Let's cast off and get going. Like I told you, we're two days away from the best wine in the world." That got the men working. It got the *Aphrodite* away from the harbor ahead of many of the little fishing boats that sailed out of Kos. And it got the akatos through the narrow channel between the island and the mainland of Asia in fine fashion.

Sostratos hadn't really thought about just how narrow the channel was. "If you had stone-throwers on both sides of it," he remarked to Menedemos, "you could make this passage very hard and dangerous."

"I daresay you're right," Menedemos answered. "It may happen one of these days, too, though I hope none of Antigonos' generals is as sneaky as you are."

Half her oars manned, the *Aphrodite* fought her way north. The broad stretch of sea between Samos and Ikaria on the one hand and Khios on the other was one of the roughest parts of the Aegean: neither the mainland nor any islands shielded the water from the wind blowing out of the north. The merchant galley pitched choppily as wave after wave slammed into her bow.

The motion gave Sostratos a headache. A couple of sailors reacted more strongly than that, leaning out over the gunwale to puke into the Aegean. Maybe they'd taken on too much wine the night before. Maybe they just had weak stomachs, as some men did.

As some men did, Menedemos had a quotation from Homer for everything:

" 'The assembly was stirred like great waves of the sea,
    The open sea by Ikaria, which the east wind and the south
    wind
    Stir up from Father Zeus' clouds.' "

"What about the north wind?" Sostratos asked. "That's the one troubling us now."

His cousin shrugged. "You can't expect the poet to be perfect all the time. Isn't it marvel enough that he's so good so much of the time?"

"I suppose so," Sostratos said. "But it's not good to lean on him the way an old man like Xenophanes leans on a stick. That keeps you from thinking for yourself."

"If Homer's already said it as well as it can be said, what's the point to trying to say it better?" Menedemos asked.

"If you're quoting him for the sake of poetry, that's one thing,"

Sostratos said. "If you're quoting him to settle what's right and wrong, the way too many people do, that's something else."

"Well, maybe," Menedemos said, with the air of a man making a great concession. *At least he's not sneering at using philosophers' ideas to judge what's right and wrong, the way he sometimes does,* Sostratos thought. *That* is *something.*

He soon discovered why Menedemos showed no interest in twitting him: his cousin's thought turned in a different direction. Setting a hand on Diokles' shoulder, Menedemos said, "It's two days to Khios no matter what we do. Shall we start putting them through their paces?"

"Not a bad notion," the keleustes replied. "The more work we get in, the better the odds it'll pay off when we really need it."

"With luck, we won't need it at all," Sostratos said. Both Diokles and Menedemos looked at him. He felt he had to add, "Of course, we'd better not take the chance."

His cousin and the oarmaster relaxed. "Enough trouble comes all by itself, even when you don't borrow any," Menedemos said. He raised his voice. "All rowers to the oars. We're going to practice fighting pirates—or whatever else we happen to run into on the western seas."

Sostratos had wondered if the men would grumble at having to work harder than they would have done if they'd rowed straight for Khios. A few of them did, but it was grumbling for the sake of grumbling, not real anger. And so, on the rough sea north of Samos and Ikaria, the akatos practiced darting to the right and to the left, spinning in her own length, and suddenly bringing inboard all the oars now on one side of the ship, now on the other. They worked on that last maneuver over and over again.

"This is our best chance against a trireme, isn't it?" Sostratos said.

"It's our best chance against any galley bigger than we are—best besides running away, I mean," Menedemos answered. "It's our *only* chance against a trireme: if we can use our hull to break most of the oars on one side of his ship, that lets us get away. Otherwise, we haven't got a chance."

"I suppose not." Sostratos sighed. "I wish someone would keep pirates down all over the Inner Sea, the way Rhodes tries to do in the Aegean."

"While you're at it, wish navies didn't hunt merchantmen when they saw the chance, too," Menedemos said. "Here close to home, we're fairly safe, because Ptolemaios and Antigonos both care about keeping Rhodes happy. Farther west . . ." He tossed his head. Sostratos sighed again. *One more thing to worry about,* he thought. *As if I didn't have enough already.*

4

MENEDEMOS WOKE IN DARKNESS, THE *APHRODITE* TOSSING NOT too gently under him. A couple of cubits away, Sostratos lay on his back on the poop deck, snoring like a saw grinding through stone. Menedemos tried to slide straight back into sleep, but his cousin's racket and his own full bladder wouldn't let him.

Short of kicking Sostratos and waking him up, Menedemos couldn't do anything about his snoring. And Sostratos wasn't the only offender, only the nearest one; a good many rowers buzzed away, making the night anything but serene. *I can ease myself, though,* Menedemos thought, and got to his feet to do just that.

As he stood at the rail, the *Aphrodite* might have been alone on the sea, alone in all the world. Zeus' wandering star was about to set in the west, which put the hour somewhere close to midnight. The moon, a waxing crescent, had already vanished. All he could see was the star-flecked dome of the sky, and the blacker black of the night-time sea. Khios to the north, the Asian mainland to the east . . . He knew they were there, but he couldn't prove it, not by what his eyes told him.

One after another in endless succession, waves lifted the merchant galley's hull. The swell was bigger than it had been during the day. Menedemos hoped that didn't mean a storm would be blowing down out of the north. This early in the sailing season, it might.

"Bring me safe to Khios, Father Poseidon, and I'll give you something," he murmured; the sea god had a temple on the island, not far from the city. Praying for good weather was as much as he could do. Having done it, he lay down again, wrapped himself in his himation, and tried to go back to sleep. He wondered if he would succeed with Sostratos making horrible noises almost in his ear. He yawned and pulled the thick wool of the himation up over his head and aimed several unkind thoughts at his cousin.

The next thing he knew, the sun was rising over the distant mainland to the east. He rolled over to wake Sostratos, only to discover that Sostratos was already among those present—was, in fact, fixing him with a reproachful stare. "I hardly slept a wink last night, you were snoring so loud," Sostratos said.

"*I* was?" The injustice of that all but paralyzed Menedemos. "*You're* the one who kept making the horrible racket."

"Nonsense," Sostratos said. "I never snore."

"Oh, no, of course not." Menedemos savored sarcasm. "And a dog never howls at the moon, either."

"I don't," Sostratos insisted. Menedemos laughed in his face. Sostratos turned red. He waved toward Diokles, who was stretching on the rower's bench where he'd passed the night. "He'll tell us the truth. Which of us was snoring last night, O Diokles?"

"I don't know," the keleustes answered around a yawn. "Once I closed my eyes, I didn't hear a thing till I woke up at dawn."

"I did." That was Aristeidas, the sharp-eyed sailor who often served as lookout. "You get right down to it, both of you gents were pretty noisy."

Sostratos looked offended. Menedemos felt offended. Then they happened to glance toward each other. They both started to laugh. "Well, so much for that," Sostratos said.

"I'm going to sleep on the foredeck from now on," Menedemos said. "Then I can blame it on the peafowl." He peered north. No clouds gathered on the horizon, though the breeze had freshened. "I hope the weather holds till we make Khios. What do you think, Diokles?"

If anyone aboard the akatos was weatherwise, the oarmaster was the man. Menedemos watched him not just turn to the north but scan the whole horizon. He smacked his lips, tasting the air as he might have tasted fine Khian wine. At last, after due deliberation, he said, "I expect we'll be all right, skipper."

"Good." Menedemos had made the same guess, but felt better to have someone else confirm it. He grinned at the keleustes. "If you're wrong, you know I'll blame you."

Diokles shrugged. "As long as the ship comes through all right, I won't worry about it." He shrugged again. "And if she doesn't come through, if I drown, I won't worry about it then, either, will I?"

Several sailors caressed amulets or muttered charms to avert the evil omen. Sostratos, thought, looked intrigued. "So you think a man's spirit dies with him, do you?" he asked Diokles.

Menedemos recognized a question like that as an invitation to philosophical discussion. Diokles responded as matter-of-factly as he had to the query about the weather: "Well, sir, folks say a lot of things: this one says this, and that one says that. All I know is, nobody who went down with his ship ever came back to tell me what it was like."

That touched off a lively argument among the sailors as they hauled in the anchors and slung them from the catheads at the bow: one more bit of ship's business that the peafowl cages on the foredeck made more awkward. By Sostratos' expression, though, it wasn't the sort of discussion he would have heard at his precious Lykeion. A lot of the men were loudly certain they'd seen, or sometimes talked with, ghosts.

After a while, Menedemos' cousin turned to him, frustration on his face. In a low voice, Sostratos said, "I don't want to offend anyone or make anyone angry, but I don't think I've ever heard so much nonsense all at once in my whole life."

"On land, I'm sure I would agree with you," Menedemos replied. "Out here . . ." As Diokles had done, he shrugged. "Out here, half the things I'd laugh at on land feel true." His chuckle held less mirth than he would have liked. "Out here, especially after we spend the night at sea, I don't even know exactly where I am. If I can't be sure of that, how can I be sure of anything else?"

If nothing else, he'd succeeded in distracting Sostratos. His cousin pointed toward the Asian mainland in the distance. "The shape of the coastline will tell you where you are."

"Well, so it will," Menedemos admitted, "though it wouldn't mean anything to a landlubber. But we'll spend some time out of sight of land when we sail west toward Hellas, and then again when we cross the Ionian Sea to Italy. No way to tell for certain where you are then. I wish there were."

Sostratos frowned. "There ought to be."

"There ought to be all sorts of things," Menedemos said. "That doesn't mean there are." Diokles struck his bronze square with the mallet. The rowers began to pull. The *Aphrodite* glided north, toward Khios. With the steering oars to tend to, Menedemos didn't have to worry about splitting hairs with his cousin.

Like Samos, Khios lay close to the mainland. The channel between the island and Asia was wider than that separating Samos from the shore, but also longer. Waves built in it, built and rolled toward the galley one after another. Even without a real storm, the going was heavier than it had been since the *Aphrodite* set out from Rhodes. Menedemos thought it wise to repeat his promise to Poseidon, this time so the whole crew could hear.

Coming up toward the city of Khios—which lay on the eastern coast of the island, looking at the mainland across about forty stadia of water—the *Aphrodite* fought her way past a temple to Apollo hard by a grove of palm trees, then past the small harbor of Phanai, and at last by a colonnaded building close to the shore. Pointing toward it, Diokles said, "There's the sea god's shrine, skipper."

"I knew where it was. I've been here before," Menedemos answered. The keleustes dipped his head, unashamed at having nagged him. Like any sailor, he wanted to make sure a vow to Poseidon got fulfilled.

Khios the city boasted a very respectable harbor. "How many war galleys do you suppose could shelter here?" Menedemos asked.

"If we're talking about triremes, I'd say eighty, easy," Diokles answered. "Fewer of the bigger ships they're turning out nowadays, though."

Sostratos came up onto the poop deck and pointed toward the sun, which still hung high in the west. "We made good time," he remarked. "We'll have the chance to do some business today."

"We'd have done better still without waves smacking us in the teeth all the way up from Samos," Menedemos answered, "but that's the kind of weather you're likely to run into this time of year. As for the business, you'll have to start without me. First thing I'm going to do is go down to Poseidon's temple and make that offering to thank him for getting us here safe."

"What did you have in mind?" his cousin asked warily.

"I was thinking of a lamb," Menedemos said, and Sostratos relaxed. Along with being the sea god and the earthshaker, Poseidon was also the god of horses, which were sometimes sacrificed to him. Horses, though, were beyond the means of any but the very rich. Menedemos might have thought about giving Poseidon one after coming through a true storm, but the god hadn't earned so great a reward for helping the merchant galley through seas that were rough but weren't really dangerous.

Sostratos said, "Go make your sacrifice, then, and meet me at Aristagoras the wine merchant's. I'll see him first. We can decide later whether to go to an inn or spend another night listening to each other snoring on deck."

"That seems good to me," Menedemos said.

No Macedonian officers came down the wharf to interrogate the men of the *Aphrodite,* as they had back at Samos. With the more southerly island shielding Khios from Ptolemaios' base on Kos, the local garrison didn't worry about raiders descending on them. Menedemos walked up the pier and into the city without drawing more than a couple of nods from longshoremen and fishermen.

He walked out through the southern gate just as casually. The countryside between the city of Khios and Poseidon's shrine was given over to olive groves and ripening grain; the grapes that yielded the famous Khian wine grew on the higher ground in the northwestern part of the island. Channels brought water from Khios' many springs to the fields and groves, for the island had no rivers worthy of the name.

Poseidon's temple was flanked by neatly trimmed laurel trees. A priest in a spotless white himation came up to Menedemos as he entered the sacred precinct. "Good day. 'Ow may I 'elp you?" he asked: like Samos, Khios was an island settled by Ionians.

"I just got into port. I want to give the god a lamb for letting me come in safe." Menedemos was much more conscious of his own Doric accent here than he would have been back on Rhodes, where everyone spoke as he did.

"I'd be 'appy to oblige you, sir," the priest replied. "Come with me, and you can pick out a beast for yourself."

"I thank you," Menedemos said. He chose a newborn lamb nursing at its mother's udder; the ewe let out a bleat of anger and dismay when the priest took the little white animal from her.

"Let me examine it to make sure it 'as no blemish." The priest looked at its eyes and ears and hooves. He dipped his head when he was through. "It is acceptable." His tone went from pious to businesslike in the blink of an eye. "That will be two drakhmai, sir."

Menedemos gave him two Rhodian coins. He accepted them without a murmur; Khios and Rhodes coined to the same standard, somewhat lighter than that of Athens and a good deal lighter than that of Aigina. Briskly, the priest tied a length of rope around the lamb's neck and led it to the altar.

An attendant brought up a bowl of water. Menedemos and the priest both washed their hands. Once the priest was ritually clean, he also sprinkled water on the lamb. Then the priest, Menedemos, and the attendant all lowered their heads and spent a moment in silent prayer. The lamb let out a bleat, not liking the fire that crackled on the altar or the odor of blood that clung to it.

The attendant sprinkled unground barley over the lamb, the altar, and the priest and Menedemos. The priest took a knife from his belt, cut a tight curl of soft wool from the lamb's head, and threw it into the flames on the altar.

A man with a flute and another with a lyre began to play, to help drown out the victim's death cry. The attendant handed the priest an axe. He killed the lamb with one swift blow, then used the knife to cut its throat. The attendant caught its blood in a silver bowl and splashed it on the altar.

Together, the priest and Menedemos chanted the Homeric hymn to Poseidon:

" 'I begin to sing about Poseidon, great god,
Mover of earth and of the unfruitful sea.
Deep-sea lord who also holds Helikon and broad Aigai.
The gods divided your rule in two, Earthshaker:
To be both tamer of horses and savior of ships.
Hail, dark-haired Poseidon, Earth-holder.
And, blessed one, have a kind heart and help those who go sailing.' "

"He's done that for me," Menedemos added. "I thank him for it."

While they were reciting the Homeric hymn, the attendant began butchering the lamb's little carcass. He gave the god his portion: the thighbones wrapped in fat. As he set them on the fire, the scent of the burning fat sent spit rushing into Menedemos' mouth. Like most Hellenes, he seldom ate meat except after a sacrifice.

With ease born of long practice, the attendant cut up the carcass into chunks of meat of roughly the same size. Butchery after a sacrifice got no fancier than that. The attendant skewered one piece of meat for Menedemos, one for the priest, and one for himself. The two musicians came forward to get their share.

They all roasted the tender bits of lamb over the fire on the altar. After he'd wolfed down his share, Menedemos asked, "Is it permitted to take the rest of the carcass out of the sacred precinct?" Some temples allowed that, some didn't.

The priest tossed his head. "I am sorry, but no—it is not permitted."

"All right, then," Menedemos said. "The god has his fair share of my thanks-offering; the people here are welcome to the rest."

"Many men would argue more," the priest said. When he smiled, he looked years younger. "Many men 'ave argued more. Good fortune go with you, Rhodian, and may the Earthshaker always smile on you."

"My thanks," Menedemos said, and started back toward the city of Khios.

ARISTAGORAS THE WINE seller dipped his head to his slave. As the Lydian scraped away the pitch around the stopper so he could open a new jar of wine, Aristagoras told Sostratos, "Truly, O best one, you must sample the vintages so you know what you are getting."

"I thank you for your generosity," replied Sostratos, "but if you keep feeding me even little cups of neat wine, pretty soon I'll be too drunk to tell one from another. My head's already starting to spin."

Aristagoras laughed heartily, just as if Sostratos were joking. "Oh, you are the funniest fellow," he said. The broken veins in his nose said he'd had a lot of practice pouring down wine, and it certainly didn't seem to affect him. He turned to the slave. " 'Aven't you got that yet, Alyattes?"

"Just now, master," the Lydian replied in his singsong accent. He pried the stopper out with the knifeblade, then lifted the jar and poured some of its golden contents into what were indeed small cups.

" 'Ere you are," Aristagoras said to Sostratos, and handed him one of the cups. "Now, this jar was laid down in the year Alexander died, which makes it"—he counted on his fingers—"thirteen years old now." He smiled the easy, friendly smile of a man who bought and sold things for a living. "It's getting close to a man's years on it. Go ahead and taste—don't be shy."

Sostratos sipped the sweet, fragrant wine. He smacked his lips and made polite appreciative noises. Had he not been trying to buy the stuff at something close to a reasonable price, he would have burst into cheers. "Very nice indeed," he murmured.

"Nice?" Aristagoras said. "Nice?" He donned indignation as readily as he'd put on friendship. "My dear fellow, that is the authentic Ariousian, the best wine on Khios—which is to say, the best wine in the world."

"I said it was good." Sostratos sipped again, determined to be as moderate as he could. It wasn't easy. The wine was so splendid, he wanted to guzzle like a Skythian. "But whether I can afford it is apt to be a different question. How much for a jar would you ask?"

"For one of the usual size, of a little more than half a metretes?" Aristagoras asked. Sostratos dipped his head. The wine merchant plucked at his beard, which had a couple of reddish streaks that were going gray. At last, voice elaborately casual, he answered, "Oh, twenty drakhmai sounds about right."

Sostratos jerked as if stung by a wasp. "I know I'm young," he said, "but I hope you won't take me for a fool. When I was in Athens, I could get a khous of Khian for two drakhmai, and one of those jars won't hold above seven khoes. So you're asking more—half again as much—wholesale as an Athenian tavernkeeper charged at retail. If that's not robbery, what is?"

"There's Khian, and then there's fine Khian, and then there's Ariousian," Aristagoras said. "Any Khian is worth three times as much as the cheap slop they make most places. I say nothing about Thasos or Lesbos, mind: they turn out pretty good wine, too. But most places?" He wrinkled his nose and tossed his head before continuing, "And Ariousian is to regular Khian what Khian is to regular wine."

"At twenty drakhmai the jar, the gods on Olympos couldn't afford to drink it, let alone mere mortals," Sostratos said.

"You're bound for Italy, you said." Aristagoras looked sly. " 'Ow much can you charge for it there?"

"That's not the point," Sostratos answered. "The point is, how much would you charge for it if I weren't going to Italy?"

"Not an obolos less," Aristagoras insisted. He looked so very sincere, Sostratos didn't believe him for even a moment.

"Are you going to tell me that a tavernkeeper here in Khios city pays you twenty drakhmai for a jar of Ariousian?" Sostratos rolled his eyes to show how likely he thought that was.

"No, I can't tell you that," Aristagoras said, but he held up a hand before Sostratos could pounce on him. "The reason I can't tell you that is, not many tavernkeepers will 'ave anything so fancy around, because there isn't much call for it from the sort of men who drink in taverns. But I've got twenty drakhmai the jar a good many times from people who wanted to put on a proper symposion and make their friends 'appy."

People who wanted to put on an expensive symposion and make their friends jealous, Sostratos thought. But Aristagoras didn't sound as if he were lying this time. A few rich Khians—and, very likely, some of Antigonos' officers here, too—wouldn't count the cost when they bought wine. Still . . . "If you've got twenty drakhmai a good many times," Sostratos said slowly, "that must mean there are times when you've got less, too."

Aristagoras bared his teeth in what only looked like a smile. "Aren't you a clever young chap?" he murmured, making it sound more like accusation than praise.

"And," Sostratos pressed, "they would be buying only a few amphorai at a time. You're bound to have a discount for quantity. Even twelve drakhmai a jar is outrageous, but I'm willing to talk about it for the sake of argument, provided we're talking about enough jars."

"Such generosity," Aristagoras said, and his expression didn't even resemble a smile any more. "Kindly remember who owns the wine you're generous enough to talk of buying."

Oh, a pestilence, Sostratos thought. *Now I've gone and put his back up.* He couldn't so much as look as if he knew he'd made a mistake: that would only give Aristagoras a greater edge. He wondered how to go about repairing the error.

Before he could say anything, Alyattes the slave came in and announced, "Master, the other trader, the one called Menedemos, is here."

"Bring 'im in. Maybe 'e'll be more reasonable," Aristagoras said.

"And if not . . ." The wine seller shrugged. "Many good-byes to them both. They can do business somewhere else."

"Hail," Menedemos said when the Lydian slave led him back to the room where Sostratos and Aristagoras were dickering.

"Hail," Sostratos answered in a distinctly hollow voice.

If Menedemos noticed that, he didn't let it show. He clasped hands with Aristagoras, then slapped Sostratos on the back almost hard enough to knock him off the stool Alyattes had given him. "By the dog of Egypt, cousin, you're the lucky one. I went down to Poseidon's temple and made my offering, and here you've been guzzling away at the nectar of the gods."

Remembering his own comment about the gods' being unable to afford Aristagoras' wine, Sostratos kept his mouth shut. Aristagoras said, "If you'd care to taste this for yourself . . . ?" When Menedemos dipped his head, Alyattes poured him a cup. Aristagoras went on, "Your—cousin, is it?—your cousin, yes, 'as been doing 'is best to persuade me the wine isn't worth what I say it is."

Menedemos shot Sostratos a hooded glance, but one so swift, it was gone almost before Sostratos was sure he saw it. With a laugh, Menedemos said, "Well, that's a merchant's job, after all, O best one." He sipped the Ariousian. His eyes widened. "We won't get this cheap, will we?"

"Your cousin was trying 'is best," the wine seller said dryly. "But no, my friend, you won't. I know what I've got, and I know what it's worth."

"I'm sure you do." Menedemos dipped his head. He sipped again. His eyes closed, as if a flutegirl at a symposion had started doing something extraordinarily pleasurable. "Oh, my. That is the real stuff. No one could mistake it, not even for a heartbeat. And what they'll pay in Italy!" His eyes closed again, this time contemplating a different sort of ecstasy.

"I should say it is, and I should say they will." Aristagoras dipped his head, too, and then looked daggers at Sostratos.

Sostratos, for his part, felt like looking daggers at Menedemos. The only reason he didn't was to keep Aristagoras from getting even more of the upper hand in the dicker. But, from everything Sostratos could see, the wine merchant already had a sizable edge, and Menedemos seemed intent on giving him more.

Menedemos drained the little cup Alyattes had given him and sighed. At Aristagoras' gesture, the Lydian slave filled it again. "I thank you," Menedemos told him. He gave Aristagoras a seated bow. "And I thank *you.*" He took another sip. "Exquisite, just exquisite. I wouldn't be surprised if you were getting twelve drakhmai for an amphora, maybe even thirteen."

"I'm getting twenty," Aristagoras said. But he didn't get angry, as he had with Sostratos. Menedemos' charm had softened him a little; he no longer glared like a blunt-nosed viper about to bite. Sostratos saw what he'd done wrong—saw it, as one usually does in such affairs, too late.

"I can well believe that you'd ask twenty." Menedemos' smile remained easy, ingratiating. "But it's a long haul from Khios to Italy, and I have expenses, too—and the Italiotes, in spite of what people say, aren't quite made of money. What do you say to fourteen drakhmai a jar?"

He'd come up twice now, and without even being asked. Would Aristagoras move at all? If he didn't, would Menedemos give him every obolos he demanded? Sostratos had the dreadful feeling his cousin would. If they bought wine, even Ariousian, at twenty drakhmai the amphora, could they sell enough of it in Italy at a high enough price to make it worthwhile? He doubted it.

"Your expenses aren't my worry," Aristagoras said, and Sostratos' heart sank.

"I know that, sir," Menedemos said. Suddenly, Sostratos' hopes began to rise. Whenever his cousin sounded that earnest, good things followed—good things for Menedemos, that is. This was the tone he used to sweet-talk other men's wives into bed with him. He went on, "I do so want to do business with you, but twenty seems the tiniest bit high. You'll have met my father, I expect. You know what he's like. Old-fashioned? I should say so!" He rolled his eyes. "I just don't think he could stay reasonable if he heard a number like that."

Sostratos waited. Had *he* haggled like that, Aristagoras would have thrown him out onto the street on his backside. He was sure of it. With Menedemos . . . With Menedemos, the wine seller said, "Well, you've gone up a couple of drakhmai. I don't suppose the Persian Empire will come back to life if I drop one."

They settled at sixteen drakhmai the amphora. Sostratos would have been happier at fifteen, but he hadn't been able to make Aristagoras move at all. Menedemos, now, Menedemos had Aristagoras eating out of the palm of his hand. "Have the slaves bring the jars to my ship tomorrow morning," he said.

"I'll do that," Aristagoras said. "Meanwhile, you and your cousin are welcome to take supper with me and to spend the night here if you care to."

"We'll do that, and thank you kindly for it," Menedemos said.

Sostratos added, "Would you send one of your slaves by the *Aphrodite* now, to let our men know where we'll be in case of trouble?"

"I suppose so, though you seem to worry about every little thing," the wine merchant said. The comment made Sostratos feel like breaking an amphora over Aristagoras' head, but he refrained.

As Aristagoras was instructing the slave, Sostratos managed to murmur a few words to Menedemos. "I'm glad you came along when you did. I managed to get him angry at me, and we wouldn't have had a bargain."

"Don't let it trouble you," Menedemos replied. "I almost queered the deal with Xenophanes, down on Kos. As long as things work out one way or another, who cares how?"

More often than not, Menedemos wouldn't say any such thing. More often than not, he would grab all the credit and leave all the blame for Sostratos. He might do that yet, on this very journey. For now, maybe the thanks-offering to Poseidon had left him feeling more charitable than usual. Sostratos could think of nothing else to account for it. Whatever the reason, he was glad his cousin answered lightly.

Supper included some splendid tuna steaks, enough to warm the heart of the most jaded opsophagos. Supper also included a very pretty serving-girl, with whom Menedemos wasted no time in coming to an arrangement. Aristagoras chuckled. "I'll make sure the two of you have separate rooms. Do you want a girl for yourself tonight, Master Sostratos?"

"No, thank you," Sostratos said. Menedemos looked at him as if he were daft. Aristagoras shrugged. Sostratos didn't regret his choice. The wine seller probably wouldn't have another girl as good-looking as this one, and a slave ordered to go to bed with him wouldn't show much enthusiasm, while the serving-girl seemed about ready to climb up onto the couch with Menedemos and ravish him on the spot.

That all made good sense to Sostratos till he and Menedemos went to bed. Whether from efficiency or cruelty, Aristagoras put them in adjoining rooms. The wall wasn't very thick. Sostratos got to listen to the fun Menedemos was having next door. By the noises he and the girl made, they were having lots of fun. Sostratos wrapped his chiton around his head. That did next to nothing to block the amorous racket. Eventually, he fell asleep in spite of it.

THE CLEAR *POO-POO-POO* call of a hoopoe woke Menedemos somewhere around sunrise. He started to sit up, and discovered he couldn't: the serving-girl's warm, bare body was draped over his. He smiled to himself as he patted her backside. It had been quite a night.

Her eyes came open. "Good day, Leuke," Menedemos said.

For a moment, she looked confused. He wondered how many of Aristagoras' guests she'd slept with. *Better not to wonder something like that,* he thought. Leuke didn't stay confused long. "Good day," she purred, and stretched languorously.

"One more before I have to go?" Menedemos asked. She hesitated. Menedemos gave her a silver coin, a half-drakhma. "For you either which way," he said, "whether you decide to or not."

"Not just a sweet lover but a generous lover, too," Leuke exclaimed, and rode him as if she were a jockey. He would have had to pay a lot more than three oboloi for that at a brothel; courtesans charged more for it than any other way. After the sweaty exertions of the night before, being ridden suited him fine.

He was whistling when he ate barley porridge and drank wine for breakfast. Sostratos wasn't whistling; he looked glum. "It's your own fault," Menedemos told him. "You could have had a good time, too."

"Maybe another time," Sostratos said, as he usually did when Menedemos asked him why he wasn't enjoying himself now. He ate porridge and drank wine with a concentration that said he didn't want to be disturbed.

But Menedemos said, "Don't spend all day over breakfast. I want us back at the *Aphrodite* before Aristagoras' slaves fetch the wine. I don't think he'd try to palm off anything but what we agreed to on us, but I don't want to find out I'm wrong the hard way, either."

"You won't really be able to tell unless you open an amphora or two and taste what's in them," Sostratos said.

"Don't remind me." Menedemos got down to the bottom of his bowl of porridge in a hurry. He sat there drumming his fingers till his cousin finished, too. They said their good-byes to Alyattes—Aristagoras was sleeping late, since the sun was well up—and hurried down toward the harbor.

"Where shall we head next?" Sostratos asked as they threaded their way along Khios' narrow, winding, grimy streets.

"West," Menedemos answered.

His cousin paused to give him a mocking bow. "Many thanks, O best one. I never should have guessed. I expected we'd go on to Italy by sailing north."

"I was afraid you might have," Menedemos said with a chuckle.

"Let me ask you some different questions, then." Sostratos was at his most formal, which meant at his most irritating. "Do you plan to put in at Athens? If you do, it's a good market for our papyrus and ink; they probably do more writing there than anywhere else in the world, except maybe Alexandria."

"I hadn't intended to, no," Menedemos said. "The more we sell in the far west, the better the prices we'll get for it. Or do you think I'm wrong?"

"No, probably not—if we can sell the stuff," Sostratos said. "If we can't, we might think about stopping at Athens on the way back to Rhodes." That made good sense. In such matters, Sostratos usually did. But before Menedemos could do more than begin to dip his head, his cousin went on, "How do you plan on getting to the west? Will you go over the Isthmus of Corinth on the diolkos, or do you intend to sail around the Peloponnesos?"

"That's a good question. I wish I had a good answer for it," Menedemos said unhappily. "Most times, I'd sooner have my ship dragged across the tramway from the Saronic Gulf to the Gulf of Corinth, but with Polyperkhon kicking up his heels in the Peloponnesos, who knows if some Macedonian army isn't going to come rampaging through Corinth?"

"Of course, rounding the Peloponnesos is no bargain, either, especially not with that mercenary hiring camp that's sprung up at the end of Cape Tainaron," Sostratos said. "Crete's not very far away, either, and pirates swarm out of Crete the way bugs swarm out from under flat rocks."

"I wish I could say you were wrong," Menedemos answered.

"What will you do, then?" his cousin demanded.

"Sail west," he said with a grin. Sostratos' scowl grew fiercer than ever, which only made Menedemos grin more widely.

Menedemos had wondered if Aristagoras would let Alyattes take charge of delivering the wine and collecting the money for it, but the merchant showed up in person. Menedemos decided he couldn't blame him. Aristagoras was getting more than a quarter of a talent of silver; that much money could easily tempt a slave into striking out on his own, especially with only a few stadia of water separating him from his native Lydia.

Sostratos gave the wine merchant his money, each mina in its own leather sack. "Thank you, young fellow," Aristagoras said, smugly dipping his head as he accepted the last pound of silver. "All I can say is, it's a good thing your cousin came along when he did, or you'd be sailing without my fine Ariousian."

"No doubt, sir," Sostratos replied, as ostentatiously polite as a Phoenician. "And, in that case, you'd be sitting in your house without our fine Rhodian drakhmai."

"Is that a joke?" Aristagoras demanded. "Are you trying to be funny with me?"

"Not at all," Sostratos said. If Menedemos was any judge, his cousin was trying not to kill the wine seller. "All I'm trying to do is tell the truth."

"You'll never make a trader that way," Aristagoras said. "Hail." He turned his back and walked down the wharf and into Khios. Menedemos could hear the silver clinking in the sacks almost until the wine merchant reached solid ground.

"May Athana turn him into a spider, as she did with Arakhne," Sostratos ground out. "She'd have an easier time of it with Aristagoras, because he's already halfway there." He was quivering with fury; Menedemos didn't think he'd ever seen his cousin so angry. He'd even let his dialect slip, calling the goddess *Athana* in broad Doric rather than speaking in the half-Attic style he usually used.

"Easy, there," Menedemos said, and reached up to put a hand on Sostratos' shoulder. Sostratos shook him off. Menedemos' cousin was bigger than he, but Menedemos could usually count on his strength and grace to give him an edge. Not this time. In Sostratos' fury, he might lash out wildly at the least little thing, and might not care about consequences till much too late. "Easy there," Menedemos repeated, as if gentling a spooked horse. "If you let him get under your skin, he's won."

In a deadly voice, Sostratos said, "I shall bind Aristagoras and his possessions and his thoughts. May he become hateful to his friends. I bind him under empty Tartaros in cruel bonds, and with the aide of Hekate under the earth and the Furies who drive men mad. So may it be."

Menedemos stared at his cousin as if he'd never seen him before. Calm, rational, mild-mannered Sostratos, ripping loose with a curse that would have chilled a Thessalian witch? All the sailors were staring at him, too. Several of the men closest to him edged away. They'd thought Sostratos mild-mannered, too, mild-mannered and ineffectual. But if he could call a curse like that down on a merchant's head, who was to say he couldn't also call its like down on one of them?

Rather nervously, Diokles said, "That was quite . . . something." He fingered his ring.

Sostratos blinked. The flush of fury faded from his cheeks. He looked like a man whose fierce fever had just broken. And when he laughed, he sounded like himself, not the savage stranger who seemed to have seized him for a moment. "It was, wasn't it?" he said.

"Are you . . . all right now?" Menedemos asked, and heard the caution in his own voice.

Sostratos considered that with his usual gravity. At last, he tossed his head. "All right? No. I won't be all right till Khios goes down under the horizon—and if it went down under the waves, I wouldn't shed a tear. But I'm . . . not mad any more, I don't think." He plucked at his beard, the picture of bemusement. "That was very strange. If he'd stayed here even another moment, I would have killed him."

"I noticed," Menedemos said dryly.

"I have to think about that," Sostratos said.

Diokles nudged Menedemos. Lost in thought, Sostratos didn't notice. The oarmaster said, "What *we* have to do is get out of here, skipper. I don't *think* anybody but us heard him, but I could be wrong."

"That's . . . probably not the worst idea I ever heard," Menedemos agreed. He raised his voice: "Bring in the lines. Bring in the gangplank. Man the oars. We've got what we came for, and we don't need to hang around any more."

None of the sailors argued with him. By the way they leaped to obey, they might have been thinking along with Diokles and wanted to get out of Khios while they still had the chance. The *Aphrodite* left the harbor in a hurry, almost as if several of Antigonos' war galleys were in hot pursuit. But the war galleys stayed snug and dry in their sheds, as they usually did when not on patrol.

Once out in the channel between Khios and the mainland, Menedemos swung the akatos south. "Lower the sail," he said. Again, the sailors hurried to follow his order. This time, escape wasn't on their minds. They'd rowed every digit of the way from Knidos up to Khios. Now the wind would do the work for them. The northerly breeze filled the sail. Running before it, the *Aphrodite* scudded over the waves. Her motion was different, smoother, now that she no longer fought them.

But that motion wasn't quite what it might have been. "Sostratos!" Menedemos called.

His cousin was making sure one of the peahens didn't do anything more than usually birdbrained. Not taking his eyes off the peafowl for a moment, he answered, "Yes? What is it?"

"Get the bird back in its cage," Menedemos said. "Then I'm going to ask you to shift those amphorai we got from Aristagoras farther toward the stern. I don't like her trim—she's down by the bow just a bit." He held his thumb and forefinger together to show he didn't mean much.

"Seems all right to me," Sostratos said, but then, before Menedemos could get angry, he went on, "You're the skipper, so it will be however it suits you." He chivvied the peahen forward and actually succeeded in chasing it into its cage without having to net it first.

That done, he told off several sailors to move the heavy jars of wine back toward the poop deck. He had plenty from whom to choose; with the sail sweeping the *Aphrodite* along, the oars went unmanned. Even so, the sailors grumbled. "Aristagoras had slaves lugging these miserable jars," one of them said, "and now *we've* got to do it."

"If you want to bring your slave along, Leontiskos, he can fetch and carry for you," Menedemos said sweetly.

"If I had one, I *would* bring him," Leontiskos said. But, seeing that his comrades were laughing at him, he settled down and helped do what needed doing.

"That's much better," Menedemos said when the work was finished. "My thanks to you all." It wasn't *much* better, but he could feel the difference; the *Aphrodite* responded to the sail and to the steering oars more readily than she had before.

Sostratos ascended to the poop deck and asked, "Now will you tell me what you plan to do?"

Menedemos considered. "I'll make you a bargain," he said at last. "I *will* tell you—if you answer a question of mine first."

"Go ahead," Sostratos said. Menedemos noticed that he hadn't promised to answer—he wanted to hear the question first.

Well, if he won't give, he won't get, Menedemos thought. Picking his words with care, he said, "Why did you let Aristagoras make you so angry?"

His cousin's face closed like a slamming door. "Why?" Sostratos echoed. "Isn't that obvious?" His voice showed nothing, either.

"If it were, I wouldn't ask," Menedemos told him.

"No?" Sostratos rolled his eyes, as if to call Menedemos an idiot without saying a word. Remembering how frayed his cousin's temper was, Menedemos fought to hold on to his own. When he didn't rise to the bait, Sostratos clicked his tongue between his teeth and said, "All right, I'll go through it like a mother teaching her little boy to count on his fingers."

There was another slap, another one Menedemos pretended not to notice. All he said was, "Thank you."

Sostratos stared out into the Aegean, as if that were easier than looking at Menedemos. In a voice Menedemos could barely hear, his cousin said, "That polluted whoremonger told me I'd never make a trader. He told me you were the only reason we made the bargain. He told me I told the *truth* too much, if you can believe the hubris in that."

"And he was trying to make you angry, and you let him," Menedemos said. "You still haven't told me why."

"Are you deaf? Are you blind?" Sostratos blazed. "Why? *Because I was afraid he was right,* that's why."

"Oh," Menedemos said. "Listen to me, O cousin of mine: if you let somebody like that get your goat, you're the fool." But Sostratos still stood there looking out to sea, his back as stiff as if he'd been cast from bronze. Menedemos knew he'd spoken the truth, but it wasn't the kind of truth his cousin needed to hear. He tried again: "It's like I told you after we finished the dicker: yes, I was the one who jollied Aristagoras into a deal, but you got Xenophanes moving when he turned stubborn on me. Sometimes one man's way works, sometimes another's."

That was better. Menedemos saw as much at once. Sostratos eased into a more nearly human posture. He actually looked back toward Menedemos as he said, "I suppose so."

"Of course!" Menedemos said heartily—but not too heartily, lest Sostratos see that he was jollying *him* and get angry again. Someone like Aristagoras was easy to manipulate, because he took flattery as no less than his due. Sostratos didn't. He examined everything to see how it worked, to see where the truth lay. And so, still choosing his words one by one, Menedemos went on, "You'd better believe it— and you'd better come out of your shell—because I'm going to need you every stop we make between here and Italy."

"Out of my shell, eh?" Sostratos hunched up his shoulders and forced his mouth into a tight, narrow line and otherwise did such an excellent imitation of a pond turtle that Menedemos' laughter came altogether unforced. His cousin said, "Now you have to keep your side of the bargain, too."

"Who, me?" Menedemos said. "What bargain?" He saw he'd almost been a better actor than he'd intended; his cousin looked ready to fling him over the rail. He pointed to Sostratos. "Before I answer, tell me what you would do if you were me."

"If I were commanding the *Aphrodite,* we'd go by way of Corinth," Sostratos said slowly. He scratched his chin. "But that's not what you asked, is it? If I were you, I expect we'd go by way of Cape Tainaron."

Doing his best not to show whether Sostratos was right or not, Menedemos asked, "And why is that?"

"Because you think we'll pick up mercenaries bound for Italy: either to Syracuse to fight against Carthage or to the mainland poleis to hold back the local barbarians," Sostratos answered. "Passengers are pure profit, after all."

"So they are." Menedemos dipped his head in agreement. "And that is just what I intend to do, and for your reasons. Take note— you're not useless after all, no matter what anybody says."

"You needn't sound so disappointed," Sostratos said. In a different tone of voice, that would have meant he still felt gloomy. As things were, he sounded more like his usual self. Because he sounded like his usual self, Menedemos could forget about him for a while, as he could forget about a parted line after it was spliced. He could—and he did.

As he passed the southern tip of Khios, he swung the *Aphrodite* west for the passage across the Aegean. The akatos sailed well enough with the wind on the quarter; at his orders, the sailors swung the yard to take best advantage of it, and also brailed up some of the canvas on the leeward side. "A little more," he called, and they hauled again on the lines that raised the fabric section by section. He waved to show he was satisfied.

First the Asian mainland and then Khios itself slid down below the horizon and out of sight astern. Nothing new appeared ahead, nor would anything till the next day. For the first time on the journey, the *Aphrodite* sailed out of sight of land. Besides his own ship, Menedemos saw a couple of fishing boats, a leaping dolphin, and a few birds. Other than that, nothing but sun and sky and sea.

Diokles said, "Always seems a little odd, doesn't it, being out here all by our lonesome?"

"It makes me wish there were a better way to guide a ship over the open ocean than steering by the sun and by guess," Menedemos answered.

"I've sailed with some skippers who'd rather cross the open sea

by night. They say they steer better by the stars than by the sun,"
Diokles said.

"I've heard others say the same thing," Menedemos replied. "One
of these times, I may try it myself. Not today, though. After a while,
I want to raise the sail to the yard, put everyone on the oars, and get
in more practice at fighting the ship."

The keleustes rumbled approval, deep down in his throat. "That's
a good notion, captain, no two ways about it. It's like most things:
the more work we do, the better off we'll be."

"With a sunny day, we can twist and turn however we like and
have no trouble picking up our course again later," Menedemos
added. "When it's all foggy and overcast, you have a hang of a time
figuring out which way's which—have to go by wind and wave, and
they can change on you before you know it."

"That's true, by the gods. And in a storm . . ." Diokles rubbed his
ring, as if speaking of a storm might make one blow up.

"In a storm, you worry about staying afloat first and everything
else later." Remembering his cousin for the first time in a while,
Menedemos raised his voice: "In a storm, we'll chuck the peafowl
over the side to lighten ship."

"Suits me fine," Sostratos said, "as long as you're the one who
explains to our fathers why we did it."

Menedemos spat into the bosom of his tunic, as if that were a
more frightening prospect than a storm. After a little thought, he
decided it was. A storm would either blow over or sink him, but
Sostratos' father, and especially his own, could keep him miserable
for years to come.

"LAND HO!" Aristeidas called from the foredeck. Pointing, he went
on, "Land off the port bow!"

Sostratos was on the foredeck, too, wrestling a peahen back into
her cage. He closed the door behind the squawking bird, slipped the
bronze hooks into their eyes, and got to his feet. Shading his eyes
with his hand, he peered in the direction the lookout's finger showed.
"Your sight is sharper than mine," he said. Not very much later,
though, he pointed, too. "No, wait—now I see it there." He turned
and called back to the stern: "What island is that?"

At the steering oars, Menedemos only shrugged. "We'll find out when we get a little closer. One of the Kyklades, anyway. I was aiming for Mykonos, but you don't always hit what you aim for when you get out of sight of land."

"If that is Mykonos, we'll see a couple of little islands off to the south and east," Aristeidas told Sostratos. "I mean *little* islands, not much more than rocks."

"Does anyone live on them?" Sostratos asked.

The lookout shrugged. "Probably—but they aren't places where you'd want to stop and find out, if you know what I mean."

In due course, the little islands did appear. Menedemos seemed as proud of them as if he'd invented them himself. "Is that navigating, or is that navigating?" he crowed when Sostratos came back to the poop deck.

"That's navigating, or else good fortune." Sostratos had been annoyed enough lately that he wanted to annoy his cousin in return.

But, to his own further annoyance, he couldn't. Menedemos just grinned at him and said, "You're right, of course. If you think I'll complain when the gods throw me a little good fortune, you're daft."

That didn't even leave Sostratos any room to quarrel. He said, "We ought to put in at the island and take on water. We're getting low."

"All right." Now Menedemos didn't look quite so happy. After a moment, though, he brightened. "I'll anchor offshore and let them bring it out in boats. That'll be easier and faster than beaching."

"More expensive, too," Sostratos pointed out.

"While we're going out to Italy, we spend money," Menedemos said airily. "When we get there, we make money." That was indeed how things were supposed to work. Menedemos took it for granted that they would work that way. Sostratos was the one who had to make them work that way.

He started to get annoyed all over again, but checked himself. *I take it for granted that we'll get to Italy so I can work on seeing that the voyage turns a profit. Menedemos is that one who has to make things work* that *way.*

The *Aphrodite* anchored off Panormos, on the northern coast of Mykonos. Her arrival at first produced more alarm in the little town than anything else. Only after a good deal of shouting could Menedemos convince the locals he wasn't commanding a pirate ship. "They think everything with oars is full of corsairs," he grumbled.

"Maybe they have reason to think so," Sostratos answered. "If they do, we need to be wary in these waters."

Menedemos clicked his tongue between his teeth. "I suppose so. Well, it's not as if it's something we didn't already know." With obvious relief at changing the subject, he pointed to the town. "Here comes the first boat."

After that first boatman—a fellow who, though only a few years older than Sostratos and Menedemos, had lost most of his hair—delivered water to the *Aphrodite* and came back unscathed, more islanders came out to the akatos. After a while, Sostratos turned to Diokles. "You must have come here before," he said, and the oarmaster dipped his head. Sostratos went on, "Is it my imagination, or are there a lot of bald men on this island?"

"No, sir, it's not your imagination," Diokles answered. "Haven't you ever heard somebody say, 'bald as a Mykonian'?"

"I don't think so," Sostratos said. "Of course, now I'll probably hear it three times in the next two days. That's how those things seem to work."

"So it is," Diokles said with a chuckle. Sostratos started to say something more, but the keleustes held up a hand. "Hold on a bit, would you? I want to hear what that fellow in the boat is telling the skipper."

Sostratos outranked the oarmaster. Not only that, he was the son of one of the *Aphrodite*'s owners. A lot of men, in such circumstances, would have gone right on talking. *Menedemos probably would,* Sostratos thought. But he fell silent, not least because he was also curious about what the local had to say.

"That's right," the fellow said to Menedemos. "A ship just about the size of yours. That's one of the reasons we all had the hair stand up on the backs of our necks when you sailed toward town." He had little hair save on the back of his neck—he was bald, too.

"Do you know where she's based?" Menedemos asked.

"Sure don't," the Mykonian answered, tossing his head. "Lots of beaches that'll hold a pirate ship. Plenty of little tiny islands here in the Kyklades, places where nobody lives, or else maybe a goatherd or two. A pirate crew could sail out of one of those and you'd never find it, except maybe by accident."

"You're probably right." Menedemos didn't sound happy about agreeing.

" 'Course I'm right," the bald man said with the sort of certainty only people who haven't traveled very far or done very much can have. He went on, "Plenty for the polluted son of a whore to feast on, too, what with all the ships bringing people to pray or to make offerings to Apollo on holy Delos."

"Ah, Delos. That's right," Menedemos said. Sostratos found himself dipping his head, too. Along with its larger but less important neighbor, Rheneia, Delos—famous for being the birthplace of Apollo and his twin sister, Artemis—lay just west of Mykonos. Pirates could easily make a comfortable living preying on the ships that brought pious Hellenes there.

"Since you ain't pirates, you'd be smart to watch out for 'em," the Mykonian said. "Otherwise, you might end up on Delos your own selves—in the slave markets, I mean."

"We'll be careful," Menedemos assured him. The local didn't seem convinced. But he also didn't seem much interested in what happened to a ship full of strangers. With a shrug, he rowed back toward Panormos.

"Well, well," Diokles said. "Isn't that interesting?"

"Interesting, yes." Sostratos did his best to sound as detached as the oarmaster. "It's not as if we didn't know there would be pirates along the way. And we haven't run into this ship yet, whoever it may be."

"If the gods be kind, we won't, either." Diokles rubbed the ring with the image of Herakles Alexikakos. But then a scowl darkened his weathered face. "Of course, if these pirates plunder ships bound for Delos, they don't fear gods or men. Too much of that these days, if anyone cares what I think. Back before so many men called themselves philosophers, most folks respected the gods. They didn't go around stealing from them."

Sostratos bristled at that. He was about to launch into a spirited defense of philosophy and philosophers when Menedemos called, "Raise the anchors! Lower the sail! Let's be away—and everybody keep a sharp eye out for pirates, because there's supposed to be one in the neighborhood."

"I wonder how many of your rowers brought swords aboard," Sostratos said to Diokles.

"There'll be some—don't know how many myself, not offhand," the keleustes said. "Everyone'll have a knife. Belaying pins . . . Did your cousin bring his bow?"

"I don't know," Sostratos answered. "I'm sorry."

Diokles made unhappy clucking noises. "We ought to have at least one aboard. That way, nobody can start shooting at us without us shooting back." He rubbed the ring again. "Maybe I'm worrying about the reflection of a bone, like the dog in the fable. The sea is a big place. Maybe we won't have to worry about these pirates at all. I hope we don't."

As the *Aphrodite* pulled away from Panormos, Sostratos asked Menedemos, "Do you have your bow? The keleustes is worried about it." He was worried about it, too, but didn't care to admit that to his cousin. Menedemos too often made him pay when he showed anything that looked like weakness.

"I've got it," Menedemos answered. "I hope it's not the only one aboard. What I wish we had is a dart-thrower at the bow, like the ones Ptolemaios and Antigonos' fives carry. That would make a pirate ship sit up and take notice." He sighed. "Of course, we've got nowhere to put it, especially not with the peafowl all over the foredeck, and it'd be heavy enough to ruin the ship's trim. But I still wouldn't mind carrying one, not at times like this."

The *Aphrodite* sailed through the channel between Mykonos and Tenos, the larger island to the northwest. Delos, which seemed hardly more than a speck of land, lay to port after the akatos cleared Mykonos. The polis of Delos stood on the island's west side. The white stone of the temples gleamed dazzlingly under a warm spring sun.

Several boats went back and forth between Delos and Rheneia; the channel separating the two islands couldn't have been more than four stadia wide. "I wonder who's dying," Sostratos murmured.

"What's that?" Menedemos said.

"I wonder who's dying," Sostratos repeated. "Delos is sacred ground, you know—too sacred to be polluted by death. If somebody's in a bad way there, they take him across the channel to Rheneia to finish the job. They do the same for women in childbirth, too."

"Childbirth's just about as bad as dying when it comes to pollution," Diokles said.

Menedemos dipped his head. "Women's things are a strange business. I thank the gods every day for making me a man." Neither Sostratos nor the oarmaster disagreed with him.

A tubby sailing ship approaching Delos from the northwest sheered off sharply when her crew spied the long, lean shape of the *Aphrodite*. Diokles grunted laughter. "If we were pirates, we'd have them for supper," he said.

Sostratos' cousin steered the merchant galley south past Rheneia's western coast, which held a town even smaller and less prepossessing than Mykonos' Panormos. Menedemos clicked his tongue between his teeth. "Poor Rheneia," he said, "always running second behind its little neighbor. That must be hard."

You wouldn't know, would you? Sostratos thought. He almost said it out loud, but ended up keeping quiet. What was the use? Menedemos might not even realize what he was talking about.

Far to the south, beyond Rheneia, clouds swirled above Paros, twisting into all sorts of improbable patterns. Sostratos merely admired their beauty. To Diokles, the view of the island helped define the *Aphrodite*'s route. "One nice thing about the Kyklades," the keleustes said. "There's always an island or two on the horizon somewhere, so you can figure out where you are."

"It's a lot easier than navigating out of sight of land," Menedemos agreed.

He had lynx-eyed Aristeidas at the bow as a lookout, but it was one of the sailors one the starboard side who sang out, "Sail ho!" and pointed west.

As Sostratos had when Aristeidas sighted Mykonos, he peered in the direction in which the sailor pointed. This time, he scratched his head and said, "I don't see anything."

"It's there," the man insisted. After a moment, a couple of other sailors added loud—and alarmed—agreement. Sostratos kept peering. He knuckled his eyes, for he kept on seeing nothing.

From the poop, Menedemos shouted, "All men to the oars! Diokles, give us a lively beat. We'll see if we can't show the polluted robbers our heels."

Sailors rushed to their benches. A couple of them trod on Sostratos' toes as they hurried past. He cursed, not from pain but from

frustration: he still couldn't see the sail that had everyone else jumping like chickpeas on a hot griddle. He rubbed his eyes again. People
said reading could make you shortsighted. Sostratos had never believed that. His vision, if not of the very best like Aristeidas', had
always been good enough. Now he began to wonder.

And then, just as the *Aphrodite,* propelled now by sail and oars,
seemed to gather herself and leap forward over the wine-dark water
of the Aegean, he did spy the sail and understood at once why he
hadn't seen it earlier. He'd been looking for a white square of linen
against the blue sky. This sail, though, was blue itself, making it
harder to see at any distance.

Now he pointed. "There's the pirate," he called back to Menedemos.

"There's *a* pirate, anyhow," his cousin agreed. "Whether that's *the*
pirate or not, the one the fellow on Mykonos talked about, I don't
know and I don't care. But no honest skipper makes his sail into a
chameleon."

"Not just his sail." Now that Sostratos knew where to look, he
had much less trouble spying the other ship. "His hull's painted the
color of the sea, too."

"If you're going to do those things, you don't usually do them by
halves," Menedemos said. He turned to Diokles. "Up the stroke,
keleustes. They're gaining on us."

"Skipper, we can't row any harder than what we're doing," the
oarmaster answered. "In fact, we won't be able to hold this sprint
very long."

Menedemos cursed. So did Sostratos, all over again. Sure enough,
the pirate ship was visibly bigger than when he'd first spotted it. As
did those of the *Aphrodite,* its oars rose and fell, rose and fell, in
smooth rhythm, digging into the water and then breaking free once
more. The pirates were stroking no more rapidly than the *Aphrodite*'s
crew, but they had a faster ship: they didn't have to worry about
hauling cargo, only fighting men.

It hardly seemed fair, Sostratos thought as he counted the oars on
the pirate's port side, which he could see better than the starboard
as her captain steered on a course that converged with the *Aphrodite*'s. He counted the oars, muttered to himself, and then counted

them again. "Menedemos!" he called, his voice rising nearly to a shout. "Menedemos!"

"What is it?" His cousin, understandably, sounded harried. "By the gods, it had better be something good, if you're bothering me at a time like this."

"I think so," Sostratos answered. "If you take a long look at that pirate ship, you'll see she's just a triakonter—she's got fifteen oars on a side, and that makes thirty altogether."

"What?" Menedemos sounded astonished. When he saw the pirate ship, all he'd tried to do was get away, as any skipper would have done. He hadn't bothered taking its measure. Now he did, and started cursing all over again. "We've got more men than he does." He pulled back on the tiller to one steering oar and forward on the other, so that the *Aphrodite* swung sharply toward the pirate ship. The shout he let out was in much harsher, broader Doric than he usually spoke: "Now let's *git* him!"

Even as the akatos turned toward the triakonter, Menedemos called more orders. Up went the sail, brailed tight against the yard. Aboard a war galley, the sail and the mast would have been stowed away so as not to interfere with the attack run, which always went in under oar power alone. Menedemos couldn't do that in the *Aphrodite,* but he did the next best thing.

Sostratos kept his eye on the pirate ship. How many times had potential prey turned on the robbers and killers and slavers that green-blue hull carried? Were they ready to fight? If they were, and if they wanted to do it ship against ship and not man against man, they had a chance, and probably a good one: that triakonter was both faster and more maneuverable than the *Aphrodite*.

Closer and closer the two galleys drew. Faint across the water, Sostratos heard shouts aboard the pirate ship. Several men stood on its little raised poop deck. By the way they waved their hands and shook their fists, they were arguing about what to do next.

When the ships were only a couple of stadia apart, the pirate suddenly broke off his own attack run, swinging away toward the southwest. Staying aggressive, Menedemos went right after him. But the smaller, leaner ship was now running straight before the wind, and she had a better turn of speed than the merchant galley. Little by little, she pulled away.

"Can I ease the men back, skipper?" Diokles asked. "We're not going to catch those bastards no matter how hard we pull."

"Go ahead," Menedemos answered, and the oarmaster slowed the rhythm of his mallet on bronze. The men sensed the relaxation at once. They let out a great cheer. Some of them took one hand off their oars to wave to Menedemos, and he took his right hand off the steering-oar tiller for a moment to wave back. "Thanks, boys," he called. "I guess those villains didn't know who they were messing with when they tried to mess with us, did they?"

The sailors cheered louder than ever. Menedemos grinned, basking in the praise. Sostratos wondered how he would respond if people cheered him like that. Then he wondered what he could do to make people cheer him like that. He was the one who'd noticed the pirate ship was only a triakonter. Nobody else had even thought to look.

But he'd just been accurate. Menedemos was the one who'd made the bold, unexpected move, the move anybody could see had saved the ship. He got the credit. He knew how to get the credit, and he knew what to do with it once he had it.

Me? Sostratos thought. *I'm a good toikharkhos, is what I am.* He might wish he were bold, but he wasn't. *Well, the world needs reliable men, too.* He'd told himself that a good many times. It was, without the tiniest fragment of doubt, true. It was also, without the tiniest fragment of doubt, small consolation.

"Did you see those polluted bastards run? *Do* you see those polluted bastards run?" Excitement still crackled in Menedemos' voice. He pointed ahead. Sure enough, the pirate ship seemed to shrink every moment.

"Many good-byes to them," Sostratos said as he mounted to the poop deck. "May they try to outrun a trireme next, or one of Ptolemaios' fives."

His cousin dipped his head. "That would be sweet. I wouldn't mind seeing every pirate in the Inner Sea sold to the mines, or else given over to the executioner." He reached up and slapped Sostratos on the shoulder. "That was clever of you, seeing he wasn't so big as he wanted us to think."

"Thanks," Sostratos said, and then, "Do we really have to visit Cape Tainaron? More pirates there than you'll find here in the middle of the Aegean. The only real difference between a pirate and a mercenary is that a mercenary's got someone to pay him his drakhma a day and feed him, while a pirate has to make his own living."

"There's one other difference," Menedemos said. "A mercenary who's looking for someone to pay him his drakhma a day and feed him will pay us to take him over to Italy. I like that difference. It makes us money."

"So it does," Sostratos said. "But it also makes us trouble, or it can. Those who run too hard after money often end up regretting it."

"And those who don't run hard enough after it often end up hungry," Menedemos replied. "We've been through this before. I'm not going to change my mind. I say the profit is worth the risk, and we're going on to Tainaron."

He *was* the captain. He had the right to make such choices. Sostratos asked a rather different question: "Suppose that pirate ship had been a pentekonter or a hemiolia, the way so many of them are. Would you still have turned toward it?"

"I don't know. I might have," Menedemos said. "Most pirates don't want a sea fight. What they want is an easy victim. Sometimes, if you show you're ready to give them a battle, you don't have to."

"Sometimes," Sostratos said. But his cousin had a point. Pirates were no more enamored of hard, dangerous work than anybody else. After a moment, another thought struck Sostratos. "Maybe we ought to paint our hull and dye our sail, too. If we look like a pirate ourselves, the other pirates won't bother us."

He'd meant it as a joke, and his cousin did laugh. A moment later, though, Menedemos said. "That's a long way from the worst idea I ever heard. The only thing wrong with it is, we'd never get an honest cargo again if we sailed into a harbor looking as if we didn't want anybody more than a plethron off to be able to see us."

"I suppose not," Sostratos said. "And then, instead of worrying about pirates all the time, we'd have to worry about real navies chasing us."

"True." Menedemos laughed again, but with little real mirth this time. "That might be a good bargain. By all the signs, there are more pirates running around loose than real warships chasing them."

Sostratos sighed. "We live in troubled times."

"Do you think they'll get better any time soon?" Menedemos asked. With another sigh, Sostratos tossed his head.

5

ON THE FOURTH AFTERNOON AFTER THE BRUSH WITH the pirates, the lookout at the bow called, "Land! Land dead ahead!" and Menedemos knew it had to be Cape Tainaron, the most southerly point on the mainland of Hellas. The *Aphrodite* had sailed through the narrow channel with Cape Maleai and Cape Onougnathos on the right hand and the little island of Kythera on the left not long before, so he'd been expecting the call, but it still sent a jolt of mixed excitement and alarm through him.

We'll pick up some mercenaries here, he thought. *We'll take them to Taras—maybe even to Syracuse, depending on what kind of news we hear when we get to Italy—and we'll rake in the silver doing it.* He did his best to keep that thought uppermost, but another one kept intruding. *We'll rake in the silver, provided we get away from Tainaron in one piece.*

Diokles said, "Even if the lookout hadn't seen land, all these other ships bound for the tip of Tainaron would tell us we were heading towards a fair-sized town."

"A fair-sized town at the tip of the cape has to be supplied by sea," Menedemos answered. "You can't get much in the way of grain down there by road. You can't get much of anything down there by road—which is why the mercenaries have their camp there."

"True enough." Diokles pointed to the rocky peninsula leading down to the sea. "A handful of men could hold off an army coming south just about forever."

"That's why this place is where it is," Menedemos agreed. "And, since Kassandros and Polyperkhon haven't got much in the way of ships, the mercenaries can do what they want—and hire out to whomever they want." He started to say more, but Sostratos came running back toward him, excitement on his face. Menedemos wasn't sure what sort of excitement it was. He tried to forestall his cousin, asking, "All right, who spilled the perfume into the soup?"

"No, no." Sostratos tossed his head so emphatically, a couple of locks of his hair flew loose. As he brushed them back from his eyes, he explained, "I was going to let the peahen called Helen out for a run when I found she'd laid an egg!"

"Ahh." Visions of drakhmai danced in front of Menedemos' face. "That is good news. And if Helen has started laying eggs, the others won't be far behind her. We can sell eggs for a nice price once we get across the Ionian Sea." He scratched his chin. Bristles rasped under his fingernails. "Have we got any straw, so the birds can make nests?"

Sostratos tossed his head again. "No, but I can get some light twigs from the dunnage without having amphorai knock together or anything like that. Those would probably be better than nothing."

"Good. Do it," Menedemos said. Sostratos turned to go. Menedemos pointed at him. "Wait. I didn't mean you personally go and do it right this instant. It's important, but it's not *that* important. Tell off a couple of sailors and have them take care of it."

"Oh. All right." Plainly, that hadn't occurred to Sostratos. He pointed ahead. "They've got themselves a real polis here, haven't they?—and not the smallest one in Hellas, either."

"No. Nor the worst-governed city in Hellas, probably," Menedemos said. As he'd thought it would, that made his cousin squirm. In musing tones, Menedemos went on, "This really *is* a polis, or something close to one. It's not just the mercenaries, not even close. They've got their wives here, and their concubines, and their brats, and their slaves—"

"And the people who sell things to them, like us," Sostratos put in.

"And the people who sell things to them," Menedemos agreed. "But you won't find too many merchants' shops right there in the mercenaries' encampment. Most of the traders come here by sea, too, and anchor out of bowshot from the shore."

Diokles said, "I hope you're going to do the same thing, skipper."

"I hope I am, too," Menedemos said, which made the keleustes laugh and Sostratos smile. Dipping his head, Menedemos went on, "I want to get away from Tainaron nice and safe myself, you know."

"That would be good," Sostratos said. "The generals and the Italiote cities aren't the only ones recruiting here." He pointed toward a couple of low, lean craft painted blue-green. "If those aren't pirates, I'd sooner eat the peahen's egg than sell it."

"Even without that paint job, they'd be pirates," Menedemos said. "Not much else hemioliai are good for." The galley had two banks of oars, but the upper, or thranite, bank stopped short just after the mast, to give the crew plenty of space to stow mast and yard and sail when they took them down for a ramming attack. No other variety of galley was so fast and so perfectly suited to predation.

"I hope they aren't watching us the way we're watching them," Sostratos said.

"They aren't," Menedemos assured him. "The fox doesn't look at the hare the way the hare looks at the fox."

"You so relieve my mind," Sostratos murmured. Menedemos grinned.

"We're not your ordinary hare, though," Diokles said. "We showed that triakonter we're an armored hare." He chuckled. "*Aphrodite*'s a good name, mind, but I wouldn't mind sailing in a ship called *Hoplolagos,* just for the sake of surprising people."

"No one gives ships names like that," Menedemos said. "You name them for gods, or after the sea or the waves or the foam or something like that, or you call them swift or fierce or bold—or lucky, like that five of Ptolemaios' we met. I've never heard of a ship with a silly name."

"Does that mean there should never be one?" Sostratos asked, a certain glint in his eye. "Is the new bad merely for being new?"

With most men, that glint would have been lust. With Sostratos, Menedemos judged it likelier to be philosophy. He tossed his head. "Save that one for the Lykeion, cousin. I'm not going to thrash my way through it now. We've got more important things to worry about, like coming away from Tainaron without getting our throats cut."

He wondered if Sostratos would argue about that. When his cousin was feeling abstract, the real world often had a hard time making an impression on him. But Sostratos said, "That's true enough. It's so true, maybe you should have thought about it sooner, thought about it more. I tried to get you to, if you'll recall."

"I did think about it. You know that," Menedemos said. "I decided the chance for profit picking up men to go to Italy outweighs the risk. That doesn't mean I think there's no risk."

Diokles pointed. "There's the temple to Poseidon. It looks like the one building hereabouts that's made to last, set alongside all these huts and shacks and tents and things."

"That's the temple with the bronze of the man on the dolphin, isn't it?" Sostratos said. "I'd like to see it if I get the chance: it's the one Arion the minstrel offered after the dolphin took him to shore when he jumped into the sea to save himself from the crew of the ship he was on."

The keleustes gave him a quizzical look. "How do you know about that bronze? You've never been here before, have you?"

"No, he hasn't." Menedemos spoke before his cousin could. He pointed a finger at Sostratos. "All right, own up. Whose writing talks about it?"

"Herodotos'," Sostratos said sheepishly.

"Ha!" Menedemos wagged that finger. "I thought as much." He turned back to Diokles. "Let them bring us a couple of plethra closer to land, but no more than that. Then we'll go ashore and see if we can hunt up some passengers. Pick some proper bruisers to man the boat, too—I don't want to come back to the beach and find it's been stolen from under our noses."

"Right you are," the oarmaster said. "Matter of fact, if you don't think you've got to have me here aboard, I wouldn't mind taking boat duty myself."

Menedemos looked Diokles up and down. He dipped his head. "As far as I can see, any mercenary who's stupid enough to get frisky with you deserves whatever happens to him."

"I'm a peaceable man, captain," Diokles said. A slow smile spread over his face. "But I might—I just might, mind you—remember what to do in case somebody else didn't happen to feel peaceable."

"Good," Menedemos said.

"*Oöp!*" Diokles called. The other rowers in the *Aphrodite*'s boat rested at their oars. The boat grated on the sand. Sostratos wore only a tunic and a knife belt. As he stepped onto the beach, he wished he had on a bronze corselet and crested helm, greaves and shield, and long spear and shortsword. Armor and weapons might have made him feel safe. On the other hand, they might not have been enough.

"This is a place with no law," he murmured to Menedemos. "If anyone takes it into his mind to try to kill us, what's to stop him?"

"We are," Menedemos replied. Sostratos found that unsatisfactory. But his cousin was grinning from ear to ear and strutting a jaunty strut. Just as some men were wild for women or wine or fancy opson, so Menedemos was wild for trouble. He sometimes seemed to get into it deliberately so he could have the fun of getting himself out.

A couple of mercenaries dressed like Sostratos and Menedemos except for wearing sandals and having swords on their belts instead of knives came up to them. " 'Ail," one of them said in Ionian dialect. "What are you selling, sailors?"

"Passage to Italy," Menedemos answered. "We're bound for Taras. Always something lively going on in Great Hellas." He used the common name for the colonies the Hellenes had planted in southern Italy and Sicily.

"That's so." The second mercenary dipped his head. "How much for the trip?" He sounded like an Athenian—his dialect wasn't far removed from Ionian, but preserved rough breathings.

Menedemos turned to Sostratos. As toikharkhos, he set fares. "Twelve drakhmai," he said.

Both mercenaries winced. "You won't find many who'll pay you that much," said the one who spoke Attic.

"We can't take many," Sostratos answered. "We've got a full crew and not a lot of room for passengers. But you'll get where you're going if you travel with us. We don't have to stay in the harbor for half a month if the winds are against us, and we won't get blown to Carthage if a storm comes up at sea."

"Even if all that's true, it's still robbery," the mercenary said.

He looked as if he knew plenty about robbery. *How many men have you murdered?* Sostratos wondered. *How many women and boys have you forced?* He didn't let any of what he was thinking show on his face. If he had, the mercenary probably would have yanked out that sword on his belt and gone after him with it. Instead, he just shrugged. "No one says you have to pay it if you don't want to."

Grumbling, both mercenaries walked on. Menedemos said, "Don't take such a hard line that you turn away business."

"I won't," Sostratos answered. "I think we can get five or six passengers at twelve drakhmai, and we don't want any more than that. If it turns out I'm wrong, I'll come down a little. But I don't want to do that too soon."

"No, I suppose not," Menedemos said. "You'd get a reputation like a girl who's easy with her virtue."

"That's right." The comparison was apt. Several others might have been, too, but Sostratos wasn't surprised that that one had occurred to his cousin.

Along with huts and tents, the mercenaries' encampment at Tainaron did boast taverns and cookshops and armorers' shops and swordsellers' establishments. Sostratos and Menedemos stopped at several of them, letting the proprietors know the *Aphrodite* lay offshore and where she was bound. Word would spread fast.

When one of the taverners heard they were coming from Khios, he surprised Sostratos by asking if they carried wine, and surprised him more by paying twenty-five drakhmai an amphora for some of the Ariousian without so much as a whimper. "I'll get it back," he said. "You bet I will. Some of these fellows won't take anything but the best, and they don't care what they have to pay to get it, either."

To celebrate the bargain, he poured cups of wine a long way from the best for Sostratos and Menedemos. Sostratos had taken one sip from his own when the ground jerked beneath his stool. The flimsy walls of the tavern rattled for a moment, then were still. "Earthquake!" he exclaimed, as a nearby dog barked. "Just a little one, though."

"Gods be praised," the tavernkeeper said, and everybody else in the place, Sostratos and Menedemos included, dipped his head in agreement. Even though the quake had been small, Sostratos' heart still thudded in his chest. When the earth started to shudder, you couldn't tell ahead of time whether it would stop again right away— as it had here, as it did most of the time—or go on and get worse, sometimes bad enough to level a city. Everyone living around the Inner Sea knew that too well.

Menedemos said, "Let me have another cup of wine." When the taverner gave it to him, he poured a small libation onto the dirt floor. "That's for the Earthshaker, for not shaking too hard this time." Then he drained the cup. "And *that*'s for me."

"It's the Spartans' curse, that's what it is," the tavernkeeper said.

"The what?" Menedemos asked.

Sostratos spoke before the taverner could: "A long time ago, back before the Peloponnesian War, some helots took refuge in Poseidon's temple here. The Spartans hauled them out and killed them. Not long afterwards, a big earthquake almost knocked Sparta flat. Plenty of people claimed it was Poseidon's vengeance."

"How did you know that?" The tavernkeeper stared at him. "You said you were a Rhodian."

"I am," Sostratos said.

"He must have read it in a book," Menedemos said. "He reads all sorts of things in books." Sostratos had trouble gauging his cousin's smile: was it proud or mocking? *Some of each,* he thought. Menedemos asked, "Is that your pal Herodotos again?"

"No, it's in Thoukydides' history," Sostratos replied.

"A book," the tavernkeeper said. "A *book*. Well, ain't that something? Don't have my letters myself, nor much want 'em, neither, but ain't that something?"

"Ain't that something?" Menedemos echoed wickedly as Sostratos and he headed for a cookshop not far away.

"Oh, shut up," Sostratos said, which made his cousin laugh out loud. Irked, he went on, "Natural philosophers say that earthquakes aren't Poseidon's fault at all, that they're as much a natural phenomenon as waves stirred up by wind."

"I don't know that I can believe that," Menedemos said. "What could cause them, if they're natural?"

"No one knows for sure," Sostratos replied, "but I've heard people suggest it's the motion of gas through subterranean caverns pushing the ground now this way, now that."

He'd always thought that seemed not only probable but sober and logical to boot. Menedemos, however, took it another way. His whoop of delight made several passing mercenaries whirl to gape at him. "Earthfarts!" he said. "Instead of Poseidon Earthshaker, we've got Kyamos Earthfarter. Bow down!" He stuck out his backside.

"No one ever made a bean into a god until you did just now," Sostratos said severely, resisting the urge to kick the proffered part. "You complain about the way I think sometimes, but you're more blasphemous than I'd ever be. If you ask me, all that Aristophanes has curdled your wits."

His cousin tossed his head. "No, and I'll tell you why not. Aristophanes has fun mocking the gods, and so do I. When you say you don't believe, you mean it."

Sostratos grunted. That held more truth than he cared to admit. Instead of admitting it, he said, "Come on, let's tell this fellow we're looking for passengers."

"All right." Menedemos made a very rude noise. "Earthfarts!" He giggled. Sostratos wished he'd never started talking about the natural causes of earthquakes.

To get a measure of revenge—and perhaps expiation as well—he all but dragged Menedemos to Poseidon's temple. Sure enough, there among the offerings stood the statue of Arion astride the dolphin. Sostratos clicked his tongue between his teeth. "It's not so fine a piece of work as I thought it would be. See how stiff and old-fashioned it looks?"

"Arion jumped into the sea a long time ago," Menedemos said reasonably. "You can't expect the statue to look as if the sculptor set it there yesterday."

"I suppose not," Sostratos said, "but even so—"

"No. But me no buts," Menedemos said. "If you laid Aphrodite, you'd complain she wasn't as good in bed as you expected."

If I laid Aphrodite, she'd complain I wasn't as good in bed as she expected, Sostratos thought, and then, *Or would she? She being a goddess, wouldn't she know ahead of time what I was like in bed?* He scratched his head. After pondering that for a little while, he said, "The problem of how much the gods can see of the future is a complicated one, don't you think?"

"What I think is, I haven't got the faintest idea of what you're talking about," Menedemos answered, and Sostratos realized he'd assumed his cousin could follow along in a conversation he'd had with himself. While he was still feeling foolish, Menedemos went on, "Let's get back to the boat and see if we've got any passengers looking to go west."

"All right," Sostratos said. When they left the temple precinct, he let out a sigh. "Except for this shrine, Tainaron's about as *un*holy a place as I've ever seen."

"It's not Delphi," Menedemos agreed, "but we wouldn't pick up mercenaries bound for Italy at Delphi, now would we?" Sostratos could hardly argue with that. What he could do—and what he did— was keep a wary eye out for thieves and cutpurses all the way down to the beach. He credited his eagle eye for their getting to the boat unmolested.

A couple of brawny, sun-browned men with scars on their arms and legs and cheeks were talking with Diokles when Sostratos and Menedemos came up. The oarmaster looked very much at home with them: but for the scars, he might have been one of their number himself. "Here's the skipper and the toikharkhos," he said. "They'll tell you everything you need to know."

"Twelve drakhmai to Syracuse, we heard," one of the mercenaries said. "That right?"

Sostratos tossed his head. "Twelve drakhmai to Taras," he answered. "I don't know if we'll be putting in at Syracuse at all. There's no way to tell, not till we hear how the war with Carthage is going."

"Twelve drakhmai to Italy is a lot of money," the other mercenary grumbled, "especially when I've got to pay for my own food, too."

"That's the way things work," Menedemos said. "That's the way they've always worked. You don't expect me to change them, do you?"

To Sostratos, expecting things to work a certain way because they always had was nothing but foolishness. He started to say so, then shut up with a snap; as far as a dicker with mercenaries went, his cousin had come up with an excellent argument. "All right, all right," the second hired soldier said. "When do you figure you'll sail?"

"We have room for five or six passengers," Menedemos replied. "We'll stay till we've got 'em all, or till we decide we're not going to."

"Well, you've got one, even if you are a thief," the second mercenary said. "I'm Philippos."

"Two," the other Hellene said. "My name's Kallikrates son of Eumakhos."

"I'm the son of Megakles myself," Philippos added. He pointed out to the *Aphrodite*. "You're not sailing today, though?"

"Not unless we get three or four more passengers in a tearing hurry," Sostratos assured him. "We have some cargo to unload, too. Come down to the beach every morning for the next few days, and we won't leave without you."

"Fair enough," Philippos said. Kallikrates dipped his head in agreement. They both ambled off the beach and back up toward the town that had sprung into being at Tainaron.

"Well, there's two," Menedemos said to Sostratos. "Not so bad, the first day we anchor offshore."

"No, not so bad, provided we get away with coming here in the first place," Sostratos replied. "If this were a proper harbor, a harbor where honest men came, we wouldn't have to anchor offshore."

"This *is* a harbor where honest men come," Menedemos said with a grin he no doubt intended as disarming. "We're here, aren't we?"

"Yes, and I still wish we weren't," Sostratos said. His cousin's grin turned sour. That didn't keep Menedemos from getting into the boat with him and returning to the *Aphrodite*. Sostratos raised an eyebrow as they climbed up into the akatos. "I don't see you spending the night ashore, honest man."

This time, Menedemos was the one who said, "Oh, shut up," from which Sostratos concluded he'd made his point.

They got another passenger the next day, a Cretan slinger named Rhoikos. "I'm right glad to get out of here," he said, his Doric drawl far thicker than that of the Rhodians. "Everything's dear as can be in these here parts, and I was eating up my silver waiting around for somebody to hire me. Don't reckon I'll have much trouble getting 'em to take me on over across the sea. Always a war somewheres in them parts."

He tried to haggle Sostratos down from his price. Sostratos declined to haggle; Rhoikos had made it clear he didn't want to stay in Tainaron. The slinger complained, but he said he'd come down to the beach every morning, too.

For the next three days, though, nobody showed any interest in going to Italy. Menedemos grumbled and fumed up on the foredeck. Sostratos tried to console him: "The peahens are laying more eggs."

"You were the one who wanted to get out of here," Menedemos snapped. "D'you think you're the only one?"

Sostratos stared at him. "I thought you were as happy as a pig in acorns."

"Do I look that stupid?" his cousin said in a low voice. "I put up a bold front for the men. So I took you in, too, eh? Good. We'll make money here, and that's why we came, but I'll thank all the gods when the cape slides under the horizon."

Plucking at his beard, Sostratos murmured, "There's more to you than meets the eye."

"You don't need to sound so accusing," Menedemos said with a laugh.

When the sailors rowed them to the beach the next morning, Philippos, Kallikrates, and Rhoikos were all waiting for them. As Sostratos had for the past several days, he said, "Not today, not unless we get lucky." The mercenaries growled things that didn't sound complimentary under their breaths.

And then Menedemos pointed in the direction of the huts and tents and said, "Hello! Somebody wants to see us."

Sure enough, a man was trotting down toward the beach. He wore a tunic and sandals, and carried a soldier's panoply in a canvas sack. "You there!" he called. "Do I hear rightly that you're sailing for Italy?"

"Yes, that's so," Sostratos answered.

"I'll give you a quarter of a mina to take me there," the fellow said, "as long as you sail today."

Sostratos and Menedemos looked at each other. Here was somebody who didn't just want to go to Italy; here was someone who *needed* to go there. "You'd be our fourth passenger," Sostratos said. "We were hoping for six."

"What are you charging for each?" the newcomer asked.

"Twelve drakhmai," Sostratos answered. He and Menedemos exchanged another look, this one not altogether happy. If the other three mercenaries hadn't been standing right there, he could have named a higher figure.

"All right, then. I'll give you"—the newcomer paused to count on his fingers—"thirty-six drakhmai to leave today." He rummaged through the sack and pulled out a smaller leather bag that clinked.

Philippos and Rhoikos muttered under their breath. Rhoikos stared at the fellow with the fat moneybag, or perhaps at the moneybag itself. Along with the silver, they saw the same thing Sostratos had: anybody willing to spend so freely was bound to have an urgent reason to be so willing. "Hold on," Sostratos said. "Tell me who you are and why you're in such a hurry to leave Tainaron."

Menedemos looked sour. Sostratos pretended not to see him. No matter how sour Menedemos looked, no matter how anxious he was to come off with a profit, Sostratos didn't want to carry a murderer, say, away from justice—assuming any justice was to be found at this southernmost tip of the mainland of Hellas.

"I'm Alexidamos son of Alexion," the mercenary answered. "I'm a Rhodian—like you, if what I heard is right." Sostratos dipped his head. Alexidamos' accent wasn't far removed from his own. The fellow continued, "I, ah, got into a disagreement with a captain named Diotimos, and all his men are looking for me, or will be soon."

Kallikrates pointed. "So you're the fellow who buggered Diotimos' boy! I'd get out of Tainaron, too, if I were you."

That told Sostratos what he needed to know. It told Menedemos the same thing. "Pay my toikharkhos now," he said dryly. "Something tells me you won't be so grateful once we've put Tainaron under the horizon."

Alexidamos glared, from which Sostratos concluded his cousin was right. But the mercenary started counting out Athenian drakhmai with their familiar staring owls. Sostratos accepted the coins without a word and with his face carefully blank. Attic drakhmai were heavier than those of Rhodes, so he was getting more silver from Alexidamos than he'd expected. If Alexidamos didn't worry about that, Sostratos didn't feel obligated to bring it to his notice.

Having paid, Alexidamos said, "Now can we leave?" He looked anxiously over his shoulder.

"What about us?" the other three mercenaries chorused. Still in unison, they went on, "We haven't got our gear here."

Menedemos took charge. "Go fetch it," he said briskly. He turned to Diokles. "Take this fellow to the *Aphrodite*. Come to think of it, take Sostratos and me, too. Things are liable to get lively here."

"Thank you," Alexidamos said as he stowed his sack in the bottom of the boat.

"Don't thank me yet," Menedemos said. "If there's a commotion and those other fellows can't come aboard, you'll pay their fares, too. I'm telling you now, so you can't say it's a surprise."

"That's robbery," Alexidamos yelped.

"Call it what you want," Menedemos said coolly. "The way I see things, you might be hurting my business. If you don't see them that way, you can always talk them over with Diotimos, or whatever his name was. Now—have we got a bargain, or haven't we?"

"A bargain," the mercenary choked out.

"I thought you'd be sensible," Menedemos said. He climbed into the boat. So did Sostratos. The sailors pushed the boat into the sea, scrambled in themselves, and rowed back to the *Aphrodite*.

Once they'd come aboard, Diokles pointed back toward the beach. "I think maybe we got out of there right in the nick of time, skipper," he said.

Along with the oarmaster and Menedemos, Sostratos looked over to the shore. Several men stood there, looking across the water toward the *Aphrodite*. The sun glittered from swords and spearheads. One of the men shouted something, but the akatos stood too far out to sea for his words to carry. Even if Sostratos couldn't hear them, he didn't think the shouter was paying Alexidamos any compliments.

"Pity about those other chaps," Sostratos said to Menedemos. "How are we going to get them off the beach if these soldiers keep hanging around?"

Menedemos shrugged. "We end up with the same fare either way."

"I think you ought to try to get them, too," Alexidamos said, which surprised Sostratos not at all: he wouldn't have wanted to pay an extra thirty-six drakhmai, either. In its cage on the foredeck, the peacock screeched. Alexidamos jumped. "By the dog of Egypt, what's that?"

"A peacock," Sostratos answered. "Leave it alone."

"A peacock?" Alexidamos echoed. "Really?"

"Really." Sostratos looked in the direction of the beach again. He couldn't be sure, but he thought he saw Philippos, Kallikrates, and Rhoikos returning: three newcomers, at least, were staring out toward the merchant galley. Plucking at his beard, he beckoned to Menedemos. They put their heads together and talked in low voices for a little while.

Not much later, four rowers and Alexidamos got into the ship's boat. The boat made for one of the blue-green-painted pirate ships anchored a few plethra away. Diotimos and his bully boys hurried along the beach after the boat. It pulled up behind the pirate ship. When it came back to the *Aphrodite,* only the rowers were to be seen. They climbed back up into the akatos.

The angry mercenaries on the beach shouted at the pirate ship through cupped hands. A pirate shouted back. Neither side seemed to have much luck understanding the other.

Sostratos had counted on that. Quietly, he told the rowers, "I think you can try picking up the others now. Tell them to move fast. If they don't, or if Diotimos' men make trouble, turn around and come back."

"That's right," Menedemos said. "That's just right."

As Diokles had before, he headed this expedition to the beach. He didn't let the boat go aground. Instead, the three mercenaries who wanted to go to Italy waded out into the sea; the rowers helped them into the boat. They were on the way back to the *Aphrodite* before Diotimos and his pals came trotting back along the sand toward them.

Up came the rowers, into the merchant galley. Up came Rhoikos and Kallikrates and Philippos. And up came Alexidamos, who'd lain in the bottom of the boat since it used the pirate ship to screen it from Diotimos' men for a moment. He clasped Sostratos' hand. "Very neat. Very clever. You should be an admiral."

Sostratos tossed his head. "I leave that sort of thing to my cousin." He glanced toward Menedemos, about to suggest that sailing on the instant would be a good idea. But Menedemos had already gone to the bow. He was urging the men at the anchor lines to haul the anchors up to the catheads. He was plenty savvy enough to see what wanted doing here without any suggestions from Sostratos. And that suited Sostratos fine.

*   *   *

THREE DAYS AFTER leaving Cape Tainaron, the *Aphrodite* sailed northwest out of Zakynthos. "I could be Odysseus, coming home at last," Menedemos said, pointing out over the akatos' bow. "There's Kephallenia ahead, with Ithake just to the northeast of it."

"But you're not going to stop either place, or go up to Korkyra, either," Sostratos said. "You're going to strike straight across the Ionian Sea for Italy." He sighed. "And you the man who loves Homer so well."

Menedemos laughed and pointed a finger at him. "You can't fool me. You don't care a fig for trade. You just want to see the islands. I had to drag you away from Zakynthos."

"It's an interesting place," his cousin answered. "It's still a woody island, as the poet says. And the people speak an interesting dialect of Greek."

"Interesting?" Menedemos tossed his head. "I couldn't understand what they were saying half the time. It's almost as bad as Macedonian."

"I didn't have too much trouble with it," Sostratos said. "It's just old-fashioned. But are you sure you don't want to go up the coast and cross the sea where it's narrowest? We'd only spend one night—two at the outside—on the water that way, and sailing straight across we'll be out of sight of land for five or six days."

"I know. I have my reasons." That should have been all Menedemos needed to say; he was captain of the *Aphrodite,* after all. And Sostratos didn't argue, at least not with words. But he did raise an eyebrow, and Menedemos found himself explaining: "For one thing, most merchantmen sail from Korkyra across to Italy just because it's the shortest way."

"Exactly," Sostratos said. "Why are you doing something different, then?"

"Because all the pirates around—Hellenes, Epeirotes, Illyrians, Tyrrhenians—know what the merchantmen do, and they hover around the passage where the Adriatic opens out into the Ionian Sea the way vultures hover over a dead ox. Even if this trip across the open sea is longer, it should be safer."

"Ah." Sostratos spread his hands. "That does make good sense. You said it was one reason. You have more?"

"You've got no business grilling me," Menedemos said.

"No doubt you're right, O best one." Sostratos could be most annoying when he was most ironically polite. And then he struck a shrewder blow yet: "If anything goes wrong, though, our fathers will grill you, and it will be their business. Wouldn't you sooner practice your answers on me?"

The thought of having to explain things to his father made Menedemos spit into the bosom of his tunic. He said, "I'm sure you want me to tell you for my own good, not for yours." Sostratos looked innocent. He looked so innocent, Menedemos burst out laughing. "The other reason I don't want to stop at Korkyra is, it's about the most dismal place in the world."

"Not surprising, after all the wars it's lost," Sostratos said. "And it was the place where the Peloponnesian War began, and that ruined all of Hellas. But Korkyra's free and independent nowadays." He raised that eyebrow again—more irony.

"Yes, Korkyra is free and independent, all right." Menedemos raised an eyebrow, too, and quoted a proverbial verse: " 'Korkyra is free—shit wherever you want.' "

His cousin snorted. "Well, all right. Maybe it's just as well you didn't go up the coast. You would have recited that in a tavern after you'd had some wine, and got yourself knifed."

Since he was probably right, Menedemos didn't argue with him. Instead, he said, "I just wish the wind weren't right in our teeth. We'll have to row all the way. But it always comes out of the northwest hereabouts during sailing season."

With the passengers aboard, and with the peafowl cages taking up much of the foredeck, the poop deck was more crowded than usual. Philippos said, "You'll put right into the harbor at Taras, won't you?"

Menedemos didn't laugh out loud. Neither did Sostratos. But Diokles did, and so did Alexidamos and Rhoikos. They knew what an inexact art navigation was. Turning to his fellow mercenary, Rhoikos spoke in his broad Doric drawl: "Don't sail a whole lot, you tell me?"

"What's that got to do with anything?" Philippos asked.

At that, Menedemos did laugh. He couldn't help himself. He wasn't the only one, either. He said, "Best one, I'm sailing northwest. I'm keeping my course as true as I know how. And if the weather holds, we'll make the Italian coast within a couple of hundred stadia of Taras either way, and then sail along it to the city. If the weather doesn't hold . . ." He shrugged. He didn't want to talk about that, or even to think about it.

Philippos looked as astonished as a young boy might on first learning where babies come from. In tones that said he had trouble believing what he'd just heard, he asked, "But why can't you get right where you're going?"

Patiently, biting down on new laughter, Menedemos answered, "We'll be out of sight of land pretty soon. Once we are, what have we got to go on? The sun—the stars at night—the wind and the waves. That's all. I haven't got a magic pointer to tell me which way north is. I wish I did, but Hephaistos has never shown anybody how to make such a thing."

"If I'd known that, I'd've stayed at Tainaron till I found a general who'd march me off to his army," the unhappy mercenary said.

"You're welcome to go back," Menedemos said. Philippos brightened, but only till he added, "Provided you can swim that far."

"Perhaps the dolphins would carry him, as they did Arion," Sostratos said helpfully.

"You're making fun of me," Philippos said, which was true. He pushed by Menedemos to the *Aphrodite*'s stern. There he stood, staring out past the sternpost toward Zakynthos, which steadily dwindled in the southeast and finally vanished below the horizon. Philippos kept staring anyhow.

Menedemos fancied himself Prometheus rather than Epimetheus: he looked ahead, not behind. Fluffy white clouds drifted across the sky from north to south. The sea was low; the *Aphrodite* pitched a little because she headed straight into the swells, but the motion wasn't enough to make even a lubber like Philippos lean out over the rail.

In a low voice, Menedemos asked Diokles, "Do you think the weather will hold for the crossing?"

The oarmaster shrugged. "You'd do better asking the gods than me. We've got a pretty fair chance, I think—couldn't hardly ask for anything better than we've got right now. But it's still early in the sailing season, too."

"Would you head up to Korkyra?" Menedemos asked. "We could still swing back in that direction."

Diokles shrugged again. "If a blow comes, odds are we'd be at sea either which way. And we're a lot less likely to run into pirates cutting across—you're dead right about that, skipper. Six oboloi one way, a drakhma the other. You don't go to sea unless you're ready to take a chance now and then."

"That's true enough." Menedemos was about to say more when a yelp from the foredeck distracted him. Alexidamos stood there with a finger in his mouth. Menedemos raised his voice so it would carry. "Leave the peafowl alone, or you'll be sorry."

"I'm sorry already." Alexidamos inspected his wounded digit. "I didn't realize the polluted things could peck like that. I'm bleeding."

"Bandage yourself up, or get a sailor to do it for you." Menedemos showed no sympathy. No matter how much Alexidamos had paid, each peafowl was worth more. "You're lucky you won't have to face your foes nine-fingered from here on out."

"I'd have gone to law with you in that case," Alexidamos said.

"Go right ahead," Menedemos said cheerfully. "You're meddling with my cargo, and I've got the whole crew as witnesses." Alexidamos sent him a sour stare. Menedemos stared back. If the mercenary thought he could intimidate him on his own ship, he was daft. *Maybe I should have let that Diotimos have him, in spite of getting three fares out of him,* Menedemos thought. *He's nothing but trouble.*

But then Menedemos shrugged. Any passenger who made too much trouble aboard ship might unfortunately fail to reach his destination.

Diokles was thinking along with him. "Be a real pity if that fellow fell overboard, wouldn't it?" he murmured. "My heart would just break."

"Can't do that unless he really earns it," Menedemos answered. "Otherwise, the rowers start blabbing in taverns, and after a while nobody wants to go to sea with you."

"I suppose so," the oarmaster said. "If I had to guess, though, I'd say nobody would miss that chap much."

"Don't tempt me, Diokles, because I wouldn't miss him at all," Menedemos said. The keleustes laughed and dipped his head.

Menedemos kept twenty men on the oars, changing shifts every

couple of hours to keep all the rowers fairly fresh. By the time the
sun set ahead of them, they might have been alone on the sea. The
bow anchors went into the water with twin splashes. The rowers ate
bread and olives and cheese and drank wine. So did the mercenaries.
"Are we really going to be several days at sea?" Alexidamos asked.
"I fear I didn't bring enough in the way of victuals. Shall I hang a
fishing line over the side?"

Yes, or else starve, Menedemos thought. But Sostratos said, "We'll
sell you rations from the crew's supplies, at four oboloi a day."

"Still charging me triple, are you?" Alexidamos said with a nasty
smile.

"Passengers are supposed to bring their own victuals—everyone
knows that. If you don't . . ." Sostratos shrugged. "Whose fault is it?"

"I had to leave Tainaron in rather a hurry," Alexidamos pointed out.

Sostratos shrugged again. "And whose fault is *that?*" he answered,
perfectly polite, perfectly deadpan. Alexidamos took a moment to
realize he'd been skewered. When he did, he snarled a curse and let
a hand fall to the hilt of his sword.

"Remember where you are, friend," Menedemos said. He wondered if he would have to say something more than that, if the mercenary from Rhodes was too dense to take a hint. But Alexidamos
looked around and saw not a single friendly face anywhere. He also
saw not a speck of land anywhere on the horizon. His hand jerked
away from the sword as if the hilt were hot.

Menedemos sent Kallikrates and Philippos up to sleep on the foredeck; they'd shown no signs of causing trouble. With the other two
mercenaries sharing the poop with him and Sostratos and Diokles, it
was crowded. Even so, they all had room to stretch out. The rowers
at their benches had to lean up against the ship's planking to steady
themselves as they slept.

When Menedemos woke the next morning, the swells were bigger
than they had been. The breeze had freshened, and brought more
clouds out of the north with it. The sunrise was redder than he would
have liked to see, too.

"We may be heading into a blow," he said to Diokles, hoping the
oarmaster would tell him he was wrong.

But Diokles dipped his head. "Looks that way to me, too, skipper.
One thing: no lee shore to be washed up on. We've got a good many

stadia between us and the nearest land. If we ride it out, we're fine."

"Let's batten things down," Menedemos said. "We'd better do it, and then hope we don't need to." Rather to his dismay, Diokles dipped his head again.

When he gave the order, the sailors who weren't rowing hurried to obey. He drew the obvious conclusion from that: they thought a storm was coming, too. "Make sure the peafowl cages are well lashed down," Sostratos called. "We can't afford to lose any of the birds over the side." By the time the men were done with them, a spider-web of lines secured them to the ship.

Philippos came up to Menedemos. "Is it . . . going to blow?" the mercenary asked nervously.

"Only cloud-gathering Zeus knows for certain," Menedemos answered, watching large, dark clouds gather in the north and spread across the sky. "We don't want to take any chances, though." Philippos dipped his head and went away. Menedemos didn't know how reassuring he'd been, but he didn't have a lot of reassurance to offer. The other mercenaries asked him no questions. They could see for themselves what was likely to happen.

"This is what's wrong with sailing in the Ionian Sea," Diokles said. "A storm will start building at the top of the Adriatic and just blow all the way down."

"How bad do you think it will be?" Menedemos asked: the oar-master had been going to sea about as long as he'd been alive, and he valued Diokles' experience. Only after the question passed the barrier of his teeth did he wonder if he wasn't looking for some reassurance himself.

Diokles shrugged. "We'll find out. I've seen skies I liked more, but you can't always tell ahead of time, either."

The wind kept freshening, and shifted till it came straight out of the north. It was a chilly wind, as if, wherever it had started from, winter hadn't yet decided to give way to spring. The waves built, and struck with greater force now that they weren't quite head-on. The akatos yawed a little at each impact. Kallikrates clapped a hand to his mouth and dashed for the rail. Menedemos' smile wasn't pleasant. It would get worse before it got better. He could see that.

Rain began falling about an hour later. By then, all the sky save a blue strip in the south was the dirty gray of a sheep's back. That last reminder of good weather vanished a moment later. The rain, blowing into Menedemos' face, was cold and nasty. He did his best to keep the *Aphrodite* headed northwest, but without the sun to steer by he had much less idea how good his best was.

Thinking along with him once more, Diokles said, "Navigation's gone to Tartaros, hasn't it?"

"You might say so." But Menedemos did his best to sound cheerful: "Italy's a big place. We probably won't miss it."

The keleustes rewarded him with a chuckle. "That's good, captain. I'll tell you what I wouldn't miss right now: I wouldn't miss being in port."

"If sailing were easy all the time, any fool could do it." Menedemos relished the tossing timbers under his feet, the resistance the sea gave the steering oars. He particularly relished those steering oars. Once again, he discovered what fine work Khremes and the other carpenters had done. He was able to keep the *Aphrodite* on the course he wanted—the course he thought he wanted, judged by shifting wind and wave—with far less effort than he would have needed before the repair.

Off in the distance, a purple spear of lightning stabbed from sky to sea. Diokles rubbed the ring with the image of Herakles Alexikakos as thunder rumbled through the hiss and splash of the rain. Menedemos wished he had a ring, too. Lightning could so easily wreck a ship, and ships seemed to draw it.

Another flash, this one brighter. Another peal of thunder, this one louder. Menedemos did his best to put them out of his mind. He couldn't do anything about them. The waves slapped the akatos' flank harder and harder. After a while, seawater started splashing over the gunwale.

"I wish we had more freeboard," Menedemos said. "That five of Ptolemaios' can ride out seas that'd swamp us."

"That five of Ptolemaios' is back in the Aegean," Diokles answered. "The sun's probably shining on him."

"To the crows with him," Menedemos said. Diokles raised an eyebrow. Menedemos said it again, louder this time. Diokles dipped his head to show he understood. The wind was starting to howl, and to make the rigging thrum. Menedemos cocked his head to one side, gauging the notes from the forestay and backstay. They didn't sound as if they were in danger of giving way . . . yet.

Sostratos made his way up onto the poop deck. Like everyone else aboard the *Aphrodite*—*including me, no doubt,* Menedemos realized— he looked like a drowned pup. Water dripped from his nose and the end of his beard. He said something, or at least his lips moved, but Menedemos couldn't make out a word of it. Seeing as much, Sostratos bawled in his ear: "How do we fare?"

"We're floating," Menedemos shouted back. It wasn't any enormous consolation, but, as with Philippos, it was what he had to give. He shouted again: "How are the peafowl?"

"Wet," his cousin answered. "Too much moisture can affect a man's humors and give him a flux of the lungs. We have to hope that doesn't happen to the birds."

Menedemos grimaced, not because Sostratos was wrong but because he was right. When it came to the peafowl, hope was all he could do. He hated that. He wanted to be able to make things happen. As the captain of a ship at sea, he was usually able to do just that. But how could he do anything about derangement of the humors, or whatever caused sickness? He couldn't, and he knew it. The best physicians could do precious little. And so . . . he would hope.

"Are the cages lashed down well enough?" he asked. He could do something about that if he had to.

But Sostratos dipped his head. "The ship will sink before they come loose."

"Don't say such things!" Menedemos exclaimed. He thanked the gods he was the only one who could have heard it. With any luck, the wind would blow it away so even the gods couldn't hear it.

"*Will* we sink?" Sostratos didn't sound afraid. As he usually did, he sounded interested, curious. It might have been a philosophical discussion, not one whose answer would decide whether he lived or died.

"I don't think so," Menedemos answered. "Not if the storm doesn't get any worse than this, anyhow." But it was getting worse, the wind blowing ever harder, the lines howling ever more shrilly. He had no idea how long the storm had been going on; he couldn't gauge time without the sun's motion across the sky, and the sun had long since vanished.

He turned the *Aphrodite* straight into the wind. That made the pitching worse; he felt as if the ship were climbing hills and sliding down into valleys every few heartbeats. But the yawing eased, and the ram and the cutwater meant that the akatos didn't ship quite so much water.

And so the merchant galley fought her way north. A couple of big waves did crash over the stempost, but only a couple. Sostratos made his way forward. His waving hand told Menedemos the peafowl still survived. Menedemos wanted to wave back, but didn't dare take a hand off the steering oar for even an instant.

The sky grew blacker yet. At first, Menedemos feared the storm was growing worse. Then he realized it was only night coming. "Do you want me to spell you, skipper?" Diokles asked. "You've been at it a goodish while."

Until the keleustes spoke, Menedemos didn't realize how worn he was. But he'd been standing on one spot for a long time. His legs ached. So did his arms and shoulders; the steering-oar tillers sent every shock from the sea straight through him. When he started to answer, he found himself yawning instead. "Will *you* be all right?" he asked.

"I think so," Diokles answered. "If I feel myself wearing down, I'll get one of the rowers to handle her for a bit. We've got a double handful of men, likely more, who've spent enough time aboard ship to have put their hands to a set of steering oars now and again. All you'll want to do is keep her straight into the wind, right?"

"I don't want those waves smacking us broadside-to," Menedemos said. "We're liable to end up on our beam-ends."

Diokles rubbed his ring again. "Right you are. Get some rest then, if you can."

Menedemos doubted he'd be able to, not with the *Aphrodite* pitching as much as she was and the rain pouring down in sheets. He lay down on the poop deck even so. He didn't bother with a wrapping. What point, in such weather? He closed his eyes. . . .

When he opened them, it was still dark. He didn't think he'd slept till he noticed how the galley's motion had eased. It was still raining, but not so hard. "What's the hour?" he asked the man at the steering oars.

"Middle of the night sometime, captain—about the sixth hour, I'd say," the man replied—not Diokles, but a burly sailor named Hagesippos.

"How long has the oarmaster been off?" Menedemos asked.

"I've had the steering oars about an hour," Hagesippos answered. "He gave 'em to me not long after the weather started easing off a bit."

"That sounds like him." Menedemos yawned and stretched. He still felt abused, but he could return to duty. The *Aphrodite* was his ship. "I'll take them now, Hagesippos. Get some sleep yourself. Stretch out where I was, if you care to."

The sailor tossed his head. "All the same to you, I'll go back to my bench. That's how I'm used to sleeping when we're at sea."

"Suit yourself." Menedemos slapped the sailor's bare shoulder as Hagesippos went down into the waist of the akatos. The slap rang louder than he'd expected: his hand was wet, and so was Hagesippos' flesh.

As the rain diminished, men's snores came through it. The rowers who weren't at their oars grabbed rest as they could. Menedemos wondered how the peafowl had come through the storm. He peered up toward the bow, hoping to spot Sostratos' long, angular form silhouetted against the sky. When he didn't see his cousin, he felt miffed. He knew that was foolish—Sostratos had the right to rest, too—but he couldn't help it.

Because he was miffed, he took longer than he should have to realize he could see stars, there in the north. The rain died to spatters, and then stopped. The clouds blew past the *Aphrodite*. By the time rosy-fingered dawn began streaking the eastern sky, the storm might never have happened.

Diokles opened his eyes, saw Menedemos at the steering oars, and said, "Well, I might have known you'd be there. When did you take 'em back from Hagesippos?"

"Middle of the night sometime," Menedemos answered with a shrug. "That's what he told me, and how can I guess any closer?"

"You can't," the keleustes agreed. He got up, stretched as Menedemos had, and looked around. "Good weather after the storm."

"I'd sooner it were *instead of,* not *after,*" Menedemos said. Diokles laughed. Easy to laugh under blue skies on a calm sea. Menedemos laughed, too.

A few at a time, the sailors woke up. So did Sostratos, who'd slept between the rows of peafowl cages. "They all seem sound," he called to Menedemos. Then he stripped off his chiton to let it dry and went around as naked as most of the sailors. That struck Menedemos as a good idea, so he did the same. Bare skin proved a lot more comfortable than soaked wool.

When the whole crew had awakened, Menedemos ordered the men not rowing to break out the several wooden buckets the *Aphrodite* carried and start bailing the water she'd taken on during the storm. Getting the water out a bucketful at a time was slow, hard work, but he knew no better way to do it, nor did anyone else.

Philippos the mercenary said, "Where are we at, captain? I'm all topsy-turvy on account of that horrible storm."

"We're somewhere in the Ionian Sea," Menedemos answered. Philippos looked as if he wanted a more precise answer. Menedemos wanted one, too; again, he didn't know where to get one. "I couldn't have told you any more than that if the weather'd stayed perfect. If we sail northwest, we'll raise the Italian mainland. Once we do that, I promise we'll find Taras. Fair enough?"

"I suppose so." The mercenary didn't seem convinced. With a shudder, he went on, "Wasn't that the worst blow you ever went through in all your born days?"

"Not even close." Menedemos tossed his head. "We didn't have to lower the yard"—he pointed up to the long spar at the head of the sail—"let alone start throwing cargo overboard to make sure we stayed afloat. This wasn't a little storm, but there are plenty worse."

"Zeus strike me dead if I ever set foot on another boat as long as I live," Philippos said, and descended from the poop deck into the akatos' waist before Menedemos could dress him down for calling the ship a boat.

SOSTRATOS HADN'T SPENT quite so much time asea as Menedemos. He was also a more thoughtful man, more in the habit of imagining things that could go wrong than was his cousin. Both those factors had made the storm seem worse to him than it had to Menedemos.

For once, he almost welcomed the attention he had to give the peafowl. As long as he was busy, he didn't have to think so much. He couldn't let the birds exercise while the sailors were bailing. They wouldn't have had much room to run around, and they would have made nuisances of themselves. He didn't need to give them water, not for a while; they'd had plenty during the storm. But he could pour barley into bowls for their breakfasts, and he did. His spirits lifted when the birds ate well. That was the surest sign the storm had done them no harm.

And he could check on the eggs in the peahens' cages. Being the meticulous man he was, he knew exactly how many each peahen had laid. One, to his annoyance, had broken the day it was laid, falling from the nest to the planks of the foredeck. He imagined drakhmai broken with it. How much would a rich man who couldn't get his hands on one of the peafowl pay for an egg? He didn't know, not to the last obolos, but he'd looked forward to finding out.

Checking the nests was easiest when the peahens came off them to feed. Helen had five eggs in her clutch. That made sense to Sostratos. The peacock had mated with her more than with any of the others, which was how she'd got her name.

"One, two, three, four . . ." Sostratos frowned. He leaned closer to the cage, risking a peck from Helen. He saw only four eggs. He didn't see any bits of shell that would have shown one had fallen out of the nest during the storm. The slats were too close together to have let an egg escape the cage altogether. His frown deepened as he went on to the next cage.

After finishing with the peafowl, he hurried back to the poop deck, pushing past anyone who got in his way. His face must have spoken before he did, for Menedemos asked, "What's wrong?"

"We're missing three eggs," Sostratos answered. "One from Helen's cage, one from the peahen with the scar on her leg, and one from the smallest bird."

"Are you sure?" Menedemos asked. Again, Sostratos' expression must have spoken for him, for his cousin said, "Never mind. You're sure. I can see it. They didn't fall out and break during the storm?"

"No. I thought of that." Sostratos explained why he didn't think it had happened. Menedemos dipped his head to show he agreed. Sostratos went on, "No, somebody's gone and stolen them. How much would a peacock egg be worth? Never mind—we don't know exactly, but more than a little. We can be sure of that. And it's money that belongs to us, not to some thief. We've earned it." As much as his sense of justice, his sense of order was outraged. That anyone else should try to take advantage of all the hard work Menedemos and he had done infuriated him.

"We'll get them back," Menedemos said, and then, less happily, "I hope we'll get them back. When was the last time you counted them?"

"Yesterday morning," Sostratos answered.

"Before the storm." Menedemos still didn't sound happy. "A lot of people have been up on the foredeck since, either securing the cages or just looking at the peafowl. The passengers have all been interested in them." He rubbed his chin. "I wonder if one of them got *too* interested."

In a low voice, Sostratos said, "I know which one I'd bet on."

"So do I," Menedemos said, also quietly. "Anybody who needed to come aboard in such a tearing hurry isn't to be trusted, not even a little. And Alexidamos is a Rhodian. He's liable to have a better notion of what those eggs are worth than the other fellows. Well, we'll find out." He turned to Diokles, who'd been listening. "Tell off the ten men you trust most. If they're on the oars, set others in their places. Belaying pins and knives should be plenty for this job, but nobody's going to raise a fuss when we search his gear."

"What do we do if we catch the thief?" Sostratos asked.

"If it's one of the rowers, we'll give him a set of lumps and he'll forfeit his pay and we'll put him ashore at Taras—and good riddance to bad rubbish," Menedemos answered. "If it's one of the passengers . . . well, we'll come up with something." Seeing the look on his cousin's face, Sostratos would not have wanted to be the thief.

Diokles gathered his sailors near the stern. He dipped his head to Sostratos and Menedemos to show they were ready. Sostratos raised his voice. He couldn't make it carry the way Menedemos did, but he managed: "Three peafowl eggs have been stolen. We are going to search for them. We *will* find them, and we *will* punish the thief. Each man will turn out his gear, starting with the passengers."

He eyed the four mercenaries. Philippos and Kallikrates looked astonished. Alexidamos and Rhoikos showed no expression. Rhoikos was Sostratos' second suspect. He hadn't done anything illicit Sostratos knew about, but to Rhodians Cretans were thieves and pirates till proved otherwise.

Rhoikos also stood closest to Diokles and his search party. "Let's see your duffel," the oarmaster told him.

"I'll watch to make sure you don't take anything," Rhoikos said, and handed Diokles the leather sack. The keleustes and a couple of sailors started going through it.

Sostratos, meanwhile, kept his eye on the other mercenaries. "Let that be," he called to Kallikrates when the latter made a move toward his sack. "Your turn will come." Alexidamos stood calmly, watching everything going on as if it had nothing to do with him. *Isn't that interesting?* Sostratos thought. *Maybe I was wrong. Maybe Menede-mos was, too.* Seeing his cousin wrong might almost be worth the blow to his own pride at making a mistake.

Diokles looked up from Rhoikos' weapons and tunic and mantle and kilt and his little sack of coins. "No eggs here."

"Kallikrates next," Sostratos said.

Reluctantly, the mercenary handed the keleustes the sack with his worldly goods: cuirass, greaves, helmet, wool headcover to fit inside the helm, sword, a wooden game board with ivory pieces and a pair of bone dice, and a leather sack. Diokles blinked when he picked it up. "Got to be three, four minai in there," he said.

"It's mine, every obolos of it," Kallikrates growled, warning in his voice.

"Nobody said it wasn't," the oarmaster replied, and set it down. "No eggs here, either." Kallikrates visibly relaxed.

"Now Alexidamos," Menedemos called from the steering oars.

The mercenary who'd paid a triple fare to come aboard the *Aph-rodite* pointed to his sack. One of the sailors brought it back to Diokles. He took out Alexidamos' sword and his greaves and his helmet, in which the protective headcloth was bundled. Sostratos stooped and pulled up a corner of the cloth. Under it lay three large, off-white eggs, one of them speckled. "Oh, you bastard," Alexidamos said mildly, as if Sostratos had thrown a double six with Kallikrates' dice. "I thought I'd get away with it."

"You must have, or you wouldn't have done it," Sostratos answered. "Of course, you must have thought you'd get away with it when you took up with that captain's boy, too."

"Of course I did," the mercenary said. "And I would have, too, if the wide-arsed little fool had kept his mouth shut."

Sostratos looked back toward Menedemos. "It's your ship, cousin. What do we do with him?"

"If I threw him over the side, nobody would miss him," Menedemos said. That was true and more than true. No one but the *Aphrodite*'s crew and the other three passengers would even know what had happened to Alexidamos, and none of them seemed likely to care. Menedemos scratched his head. "How much silver has he got there, Diokles?"

"Let's have a look." The keleustes went through the canvas sack till he found Alexidamos' money bag. He hefted it. "Not as much as Kallikrates, but a couple minai, easy."

"I wonder how much is his by right, and how much he's stolen," Sostratos said.

"By the gods, it's mine," Alexidamos said.

"You're not in the best position to be believed," Sostratos pointed out.

"No, you're not," his cousin agreed. "Here's what I'll do. For stealing from the cargo, I fine you a mina of silver. Diokles, count out a hundred drakhmai. Take Athenian owls like he paid us before or turtles from Aigina: we'll make it a nice, heavy mina. And we'll keep him in bonds except when he eats or eases himself till we sight land. Then we'll put him ashore by himself wherever it happens to be, and many good-byes to him, too."

"You might as well kill me now," Alexidamos muttered.

"If that's what you want, you'll have it." Menedemos' voice held no hesitation. If anything, it held eagerness. Alexidamos quickly tossed his head. "No?" Menedemos said. "Too bad." He took a hand off one steering oar to gesture to the sailors. "Tie him up."

They did, ignoring the mercenary's yelps of pain and protest. Diokles counted coins. They clinked musically as he stacked them in piles of ten. Sostratos took the eggs back to the peafowl cages on the foredeck. He got pecked twice replacing them. As far as he was concerned, Diokles was welcome to make a few drakhmai, or more than a few, disappear on his own behalf, too. Maybe the oarmaster would. Diokles was a practical man in every sense of the word.

Alexidamos kept whining and complaining till Menedemos said, "If you don't shut up, we'll put a gag on you. You did this to yourself, and you've got no cause to moan." The mercenary did quiet down after that, but the look on his face was eloquent.

Flying fish jumped from the water and glided through the air. One unlucky fish, instead of falling back into the sea, landed in a rower's lap. "Isn't that nice?" the fellow said, grabbing it. "First time I ever had my opson come to me."

Dolphins leaped from the water, too. Sostratos recalled that Arion had set out from Taras on the journey where the dolphins carried him to shore at Cape Tainaron. When he said as much to Menedemos, his cousin answered, "Well, of course. That's why the Tarentines put a man riding a dolphin on their coins."

Sostratos made an irritated noise. He'd forgotten that, and he shouldn't have. He said, "Now that we've bailed out the ship, may I start exercising the peafowl again? We'll want them at their best when we get in to Taras."

"Yes, go ahead," Menedemos said. "It does look to do them good."

Sure enough, the birds seemed eager to run up and down the length of the *Aphrodite*. After a while, Sostratos wasn't so eager to run after them. But he and the sailors he detailed to help him stayed with the peafowl. Each one got its exercise and went back into its cage. Sostratos hoped being away from the peahens hadn't hurt the eggs Alexidamos had purloined.

As he hurried past Alexidamos after the peacock, the mercenary growled, "Who would've thought anybody'd keep track of how many eggs each miserable bird laid?"

"I keep track of all sorts of things," Sostratos answered. Alexidamos suggested something rude he could keep track of. He contrived to step on the thief's foot. Alexidamos cursed. Sostratos said, "I told you I keep track of all sorts of things," and went on by to keep track of the peacock.

So things went until, on the afternoon of the sixth day out from Zakynthos, the lookout at the bow—it wasn't Aristeidas, but Teleutas, one of the men Sostratos had taken on at the last moment when they set out from Rhodes—sang out: "Land ho! Land ho dead ahead!"

From his station at the steering oars, Menedemos said, "That's not bad. That's not bad at all. The storm hardly slowed us at all." He raised his voice to call to Teleutas: "Can you make out what land it is? It's got to be Italy, but whereabouts along the coast are we?"

"I'm sorry, captain, but I'm not the one to tell you," the sailor answered. "This is my first time in these waters."

Sostratos peered northwest, too, along with everyone else aboard the *Aphrodite* except the men at the oars, who naturally faced the other way. He couldn't see land yet. He stood in the waist of the ship, beside a peahen that had hopped up onto a rower's bench. The peahen looked toward the bow, too, but only for a couple of heartbeats. Then, taking advantage of Sostratos' momentary distraction, it leaped into the air and, wings whirring, struck out as if for that distant shore.

The motion drew Sostratos' eye—just too late. "*Oimoi!*" he cried in horror, and grabbed for the bird. One tail feather—one drab, worthless tail feather—was all he had to show for the desperate lunge. "*Oimoi!*" he cried again, as the peafowl went into the sea perhaps ten cubits from the *Aphrodite*.

"Back oars!" Diokles shouted. "Bring her to a stop!" Sostratos yanked his tunic off over his head and jumped onto the rower's bench himself, ready to dive in after the peahen—unlike most of the sailors, he knew how to swim. But, before he could go into the water, the peahen, which had been swimming with surprising strength, let out a squawk and vanished. He never knew what took it—tunny? a shark? one of the playful dolphins?—but it was gone. A few bubbles rose. That was all.

"Go on," Menedemos told the rowers, his voice frozen with shock. "You might as well go on." As they resumed their usual stroke, Menedemos added one word more—"Sostratos"—and gestured for him to come back to the poop.

Alexidamos laughed when Sostratos hurried past him. Not even pausing, Sostratos backhanded the mercenary across the face. He mounted the stairs to the poop deck as if about to be put to the sword. Diokles silently stepped out of his way. When he came up to Menedemos, he said, "Say what you want to say. Do what you want to do. Whatever it is, I deserve it."

"It's over," Menedemos said. "It's done. I've thought all along that we'd be lucky to get to Italy with all the peafowl. We came close. Gods be praised, we didn't lose the peacock." He slapped Sostratos on the back. "We'll sell the birds we've still got for a little more, that's all. Forget it."

"Thank you," Sostratos whispered. Then, to his own astonished dismay, he burst into tears.

6

THE *APHRODITE'S* BOAT CAME THROUGH THE LIGHT SURF
and beached itself a couple of hundred stadia southeast of Taras—
that was Menedemos' best guess of the landfall. He dipped his head
to a couple of the rowers. "Take this bastard"—he pointed at Alexidamos—"off and untie his hands. Let him tend to his feet himself.
It should take him a while—we tied him tight."

"What if the barbarians find me before I get loose?" Alexidamos
said. He had a black eye where Sostratos had hit him.

I expect I'd have cut his throat just then, Menedemos thought. He
said, "Tough luck. You've got nobody to blame but yourself. I ought
to keep your gear, too. If you say one more word, I will."

Alexidamos shut up. The sailors hauled him out of the boat like
a sack of barley. They dumped his canvas duffel beside him; his
weapons and armor clattered together. A man freed his hands. Then
the sailors and Menedemos shoved the boat out into the water again,
scrambled into it, and rowed back to the *Aphrodite,* which lay two
or three stadia offshore.

"Who are the barbarians hereabouts?" a sailor asked.

"I think the Salentinoi live in these parts," Menedemos answered.
"They're a lot like the Illyrians, over on the other side of the Adriatic."

"Nasty bastards, then," the sailor said. "I hope they *do* come for
Alexidamos. What makes it even worse is, he's from Rhodes just
like us."

"I don't care where he comes from," Menedemos said. "I only
hope I never see him again."

When they came alongside the *Aphrodite,* Sostratos gave Menedemos his hand and helped him up into the akatos. "Thank you,"
Menedemos' cousin said again. "I thought you were going to—I
don't know what I thought you'd do when the bird went overboard."

Menedemos hadn't know what he would do when the peahen

sprang into the Ionian Sea, either. His first impulse had been to do something a great deal more drastic than what he did. He explained why he hadn't: "You're flogging yourself harder right now than I could if I tried for a year."

"That's true." Sostratos hesitated, then added, "I know that's true. I didn't know if you'd know it."

"Well, I do." Menedemos looked back toward the shore. "I don't see Alexidamos. He must have got loose. Too bad." Then he looked toward the westering sun. "And we won't make Taras by nightfall, either. That's too bad, too."

"I don't suppose you intend to beach us for the night?" Sostratos said.

"Not likely!" Menedemos exclaimed. "Do you think I'm mad, or just stupid? These Italian barbarians would land on us like a fox on a rabbit." Only when one corner of his cousin's mouth curled up ever so slightly did Menedemos realize he'd been had. He stabbed out an accusing finger. "You set me up for that."

"I don't know what you're talking about." Sostratos might have convinced a jury, but he didn't convince Menedemos.

Here close to the mainland, the wind didn't blow steadily out of the northwest any more. Menedemos ordered the sail lowered from the yard. The sailors sprang to obey. They'd spent a lot of time taking turn and turn again at the oars, and were glad to let the breeze push the akatos along for a while. The *Aphrodite* probably would have gone faster had Menedemos kept the men rowing, but he didn't worry about it. They wouldn't have made Taras before sundown if he'd tried a sprint with a man at every oar. That being so, he was content to loaf along with the fickle breeze.

"Sail ho!" Aristeidas called, and pointed out to sea.

"Maybe we'll see what all that rowing practice got us," Diokles said.

"Maybe," Menedemos said. The lookout's call had been plenty to bring the crew back to full alertness. He liked that.

But the sail, when they got closer, proved to belong to a little fishing boat. Menedemos relaxed. So did his crew. The fishermen tried to flee, as fishermen usually did on spotting the *Aphrodite*. The wind, though, chose that moment to fail. Menedemos put some men on the oars and easily overhauled the boat.

When the frightened fishermen found out he aimed to trade and not to rob, they were so relieved, they gave him enough squid to feed the whole crew to the point of gluttony in exchange for a couple of jars of wine—not golden Ariousian, but the rough red the men drank at sea. Fried in olive oil on little charcoal-burning braziers, the squid smelled wonderful. Menedemos' mouth watered. His belly rumbled.

"Sitos is all very well," he said, "but we can be opsophagoi to our hearts' content tonight."

"I'll eat bread with my squid," Sostratos protested.

But Menedemos pounced. "Ha! From your own mouth you stand convicted. If you weren't going to be an opsophagos, you'd eat squid with your bread."

Sostratos considered that, then dipped his head. "Guilty, sure enough." He grinned. "Why not? We've got plenty." He popped a little one into his mouth.

The sun was still low in the east the next morning when the *Aphrodite* came to Taras. Plenty of ships were on the water there: fishing boats like the one whose crew they'd frightened, beamy merchant-men, and a couple of patrolling fives. One of the war galleys came up to give the akatos a closer inspection.

"We're the *Aphrodite,* out of Rhodes," Menedemos said in some annoyance as an officer shouted questions. "We're not fornicating pirates, and I'm getting tired of being taken for one." He cupped a hand behind his hear. "What's that? Cargo? We've got fine Khian wine—the best—and papyrus and ink, and Rhodian perfume and Koan silk for your ladies. And we've got peafowl and peafowl eggs, the likes of which you've never seen here in Great Hellas."

"We hope they've never seen them," Sostratos said softly.

By the way the Tarentine officer exclaimed in astonishment, that hope looked like coming true. "Go ahead, *Aphrodite,*" the fellow called when he'd regained his composure. "Pass on into the Little Sea and tie up where it suits you. Good trading."

"Thanks." Menedemos let himself be mollified. And he had a question of his own: "What's the news in the war between Syracuse and Carthage?"

"Not good for the Hellenes," the Tarentine answered. "From what we hear, Carthage may be able to lay siege to Syracuse, maybe even by land and sea at once. I don't know what Agathokles can do to save his polis this time."

"That's not good," Menedemos said, to which the officer aboard the five dipped his head. Menedemos turned to the mercenaries he'd brought west from Cape Tainaron. "If you want to go on to Syracuse, you'll have to get there on your own. Doesn't look like we'll be sailing to Sicily this season."

"Not if you're smart, you won't," the Tarentine officer agreed. "If Syracuse falls, that will give Carthage rule over the whole island, and then she's liable to come after us next. I wish Alexander hadn't died before he could head west and smash up the Carthaginians the way he did the Persians."

Like any Rhodian, Menedemos worried more about Macedonian marshals left over from Alexander's day. But he politely said, "That is too bad," and added, "What are things like in the Hellenic cities along the west coast of Italy? The war between Syracuse and Carthage isn't troubling them, is it?"

"Not very much—they're too far away," the Tarentine answered. "The Samnites and the Romans are still brawling up in those parts, though. But that's a land war, and shouldn't trouble you—neither set of barbarians has much in the way of a fleet."

"Thanks," Menedemos said. The Tarentine didn't even think of pirates. In a five, he didn't need to unless he was hunting them. But any trader who sailed into Italian waters—any trader who ventured far from Rhodes, for that matter—had to keep them in mind.

Her three banks of oars working in smooth unison, the five glided away from the *Aphrodite*. Menedemos waved to Diokles. The oarmaster struck his bronze square with his mallet. The merchant galley's rowers, who'd rested while their captain talked with the Tarentine officer, began to stroke once more. Menedemos guided the ship through the narrow entranceway into the Little Sea, the enclosed lagoon that gave Taras perhaps the finest natural harbor in all of Great Hellas.

Taras itself lay on the eastern spit of land forming the mouth of the lagoon. Small boats, some of them close enough to let Menedemos see the nets they trailed in the water, dotted the calm surface of the Little Sea. "Do you suppose they actually catch anything?" Sostratos asked as he came up onto the poop deck. "Is there anything left *to* catch, after they've been fishing here so long and so hard?"

"There must be something, or they wouldn't try," Menedemos said.

His cousin pondered that, then slowly dipped his head. "I suppose you're right, but none of them will get rich."

"When did any fisherman anywhere ever get rich?" Menedemos returned. "Hang of a way to make a living." Sostratos agreed with that much more quickly than he had with Menedemos' earlier opinion.

Diokles pointed. "Look, skipper—there's a pier where we can tie up. See it? The one not far from the shipsheds where they keep their galleys dry, I mean."

"Yes, I see." Menedemos' eyes swept the harbor. "Looks good, and nobody else seems to be making for it, either." He pulled one steering-oar tiller forward, the other back, and guided the akatos toward the pier.

"Easy there—easy," Diokles told the rowers as the *Aphrodite* came alongside. "Back oars . . . a couple more strokes, stop her nice and smooth. One more . . . *Oöp!*" The rowers rested. Longshoremen trotted up the pier toward the *Aphrodite*. Sailors near the bow and stern tossed them lines. They made the akatos fast.

"What are you carrying?" one of them asked in the broad Doric spoken through most of Great Hellas.

"We have papyrus and ink," Menedemos answered in a loud voice: not only the longshoremen but also the usual gaggle of spectators were listening. "We have the finest perfume, made from Rhodian roses. We have fine Koan silks and fine Khian wine—not just Khian, mind you, but Ariousian." That sent a hum through the Tarentines, though Menedemos doubted whether any of the people standing on the wharf could afford the splendid wine. He struck a dramatic pose. "And, for the very first time ever in this part of the world, we have for sale a peacock, five—uh, four—peahens, and eggs to yield more peafowl."

That produced another buzz, but less than he'd hoped for and expected. A moment later, somebody's question explained why the buzz was subdued: "Just exactly what kind of a thing is a peacock, anyways?"

Before Menedemos could answer, the thing in question let out one of its horrible, raucous screeches. Smiling, he said, "*That's* a peacock."

"You're selling it for its pretty song, right?" a wag in the crowd asked, and got a laugh from the Tarentines.

Menedemos laughed, too. He said, "I'll show you why we're selling it. Sostratos . . ." He waved to his cousin, who'd already gone up onto the foredeck. This would be a free show, unlike the ones they'd put on at other stops. They hoped to do business here.

"Ladies and gentlemen," Sostratos said, fumbling with the hooks and eyes on the cage, "behold—the peacock!" He threw open the door. The bird, however, declined to come forth. That drew more laughter. Sostratos muttered something uncomplimentary to every bird ever hatched. Having cared for the peafowl all through the voyage, having finally failed to keep one of them from leaping into the sea, he loathed them with a pure, clean loathing that far outdid Menedemos' dislike for them. "Behold the peacock!" he repeated, and got ready to drag out the bird by main force.

But, perverse as usual, it chose that moment to emerge on its own. And then, instead of running around and making a nuisance of itself as it often did, it peered up at the people on the pier like an actor looking up at the crowd in a theater—and, like an actor taking his cue, spread its tail feathers as wide as they would go.

"Ahhhh!" That was the sound Menedemos had hoped to hear when he announced they had peafowl for sale. It was a little late, but it would do.

"That's a pretty bird, sure enough, but what good is it?" somebody asked.

"If you're pretty enough, you don't have to be anything else," Menedemos replied. "What *good* is a beautiful hetaira?"

The wag spoke up again: "I'm not doing *that* with a peacock!"

He got another laugh. Menedemos didn't have a comeback ready. But Sostratos said, "A polis with a peacock is surely more splendid than one without. You'll be the envy of all the other cities of Great Hellas, and of the local barbarians, too." Menedemos feared the response was too serious, but it seemed to go over well.

"How much do you want for that creature?" asked a fellow whose threadbare chiton made him a most unlikely candidate to buy.

"Ah, that would be telling," Menedemos said slyly. "Suppose you ask the man who buys him, and see if you get a straight answer."

"Fat chance," the Tarentine said mournfully. Menedemos smiled. *That's just what it is,* he thought: *a chance to get fat. And I intend to make the most of it.*

TARAS' CENTRAL DISTRICT had the streets laid out in a neat Hippodamian grid. Farther west, they ran every which way, as they had throughout the city in the old days. Sostratos rented a house right on the border between the grid and the alleyways. But for the peafowl, he would have sold from the ship or from a stall in the agora, but he didn't want to keep them caged up any more than he had to. They could also be displayed to better advantage strutting around the central courtyard than huddled behind wooden slats.

"And," Menedemos said, "this is a much more comfortable arrangement for us."

"That's not why I did it," Sostratos said.

"I know." Menedemos grinned at him. "That doesn't make it any less true."

Sostratos started to get huffy. Before he launched into a lecture, though, he checked himself—that was just what his cousin wanted him to do. "All right," he said mildly, and Menedemos looked disappointed.

"Maybe we should have got a stall, too," Menedemos said.

"If our goods don't move so well as we'd like, I'll get one," Sostratos said. "But for now, I think going through the agora and letting people know where we are and what we've got for sale will work well enough. We've already moved a lot of the Ariousian—and all that papyrus, too."

Menedemos laughed out loud. "Didn't that Smikrines say he was going to write a history? You should have made him promise to have a copy made for you when he finished."

"If I'd thought he'd do it, I would have," Sostratos answered.

"If you thought he'd do which?" Menedemos asked. "Finish the work, or have a copy made once he did?"

"Either one," Sostratos said. "Writers are an unreliable lot." He knew that was true. How much writing had he done himself, after all? What he wanted to do was leave behind a work to rival those of

Herodotos and Thoukydides, but what was he doing? Selling wine and silk and peafowl and papyrus and perfume.

You're traveling, he told himself. *Herodotos traveled all over the world so he could learn things at first hand, and Thoukydides went all over Hellas and got to know men on both sides of the Peloponnesian War. If you don't see things and come to know about people, your history can't possibly be any good.*

That was some consolation, but only some. To keep Menedemos from knowing what was in his mind—and perhaps to keep himself from dwelling on it, too—Sostratos said, "I'm going over to the market square myself."

"You just want to make me keep an eye on the peafowl for a while," Menedemos said, which also held some truth. But Sostratos' cousin slapped him on the back. "Go on, then. I don't blame you. You had charge of them all the way from Rhodes to here."

Taras' agora lay a few blocks south of the rented house, close by the Ionian Sea—the Tarentines called it the Big Sea, in contrast to the Little Sea that was their sheltered harbor lagoon. Fishermen sold their wares there. So did potters and weavers and cobblers and net-makers and all the other sorts of craftsmen who worked in the city. And so did merchants from other Hellenic poleis and Italians from the interior with wool and tanned hides and honey and other products of the countryside.

Some of the customers were Italians, too. A good many of them wore tunics and mantles like Hellenes, and couldn't be told from Tarentines till they opened their mouths and spoke Greek with an accent. Others, though . . . In the midst of calling out the wares the *Aphrodite* had brought from Rhodes, Sostratos broke off and asked one of them, "Excuse me, sir, but what do you call that garment you're wearing over your chiton?"

"It is called a toga," the Italian answered in good Greek. "I am a freeborn citizen, so I have the right to wear it."

"I see. Thank you," Sostratos said. "Do you mind my asking *how* you wear it?"

"You Hellenes are always curious, and about the strangest things, too." The Italian's eyes twinkled. "Well, why not? You ask politely enough, I must say." He pulled off the toga and displayed it for Sostratos in his outstretched arms.

"What an unusual shape for a piece of cloth," Sostratos exclaimed. "We Hellenes just use rectangles, which are simple. This is ... a broad octagon, except that two of the sides are curved instead of straight. Now I have another question: *why* do you wear such an oddly shaped mantle?"

"It's our custom," the stranger replied with a shrug. "Many people here in Italy wear the toga. We Samnites do, and so do the Lucanians, and even our enemies the Romans farther north. As for how we wear it ..."

He folded the toga in half at its broadest point, then draped it over his left shoulder so that one corner was level with his left foot. He wrapped the rest of the garment over his back under his right arm, and back over his left shoulder again, then slowly turned so Sostratos could see how the enormous mantle covered him.

"Thank you very much," Sostratos told him. "I hope you will not mind if I say a himation seems much less ... cumbersome."

"No, I don't mind," the Samnite answered. "I often wear a himation myself. But I am Herennius Egnatius, a man of some importance among my people, and so I sometimes wear the toga to show who and what I am."

To Sostratos' way of thinking, a barbarian coming into a Hellenic city should have wanted to make himself look as much like a Hellene as he could. He gave his own name, and clasped the Italian's hand. Then he stroked his beard in thought. If this Samnite with the cumbersome name was important, he might well be rich. And if he was rich ... "Sir, as I've been saying all through the agora, among the things my cousin and I have brought from the east are fine Khian wine—Ariousian, in fact; the best of the best— and several peafowl. I am sure no Samnite today is lucky enough to own a peacock. In fact, the birds we brought are the first of their kind in Great Hellas." He wasn't absolutely sure that was true, but he thought so—and no one in Taras seemed to have seen one before.

"I know something of good wine," Herennius Egnatius said. "But what sort of a bird is a peacock?" He pronounced the unfamiliar name with care. "If I have one of these birds, will it show I am a man not of the common sort?"

"That it will, O best one—it will indeed." Sostratos coughed delicately. "Because these birds are rare, you will understand that we do not sell them for a few oboloi."

"Of course," the Samnite said. "One of the marks of a man's distinction is what he can afford. Is your ship in the harbor on the Little Sea?"

"Yes, but Menedemos—my cousin—and I have taken a house here in Taras, the better to show off the peafowl to men who might want to buy them," Sostratos said.

Herennius Egnatius drew himself up very straight. He was at least a palm shorter than Sostratos, but, like Menedemos, acted as if he were taller. "Take me there," he said. "My toga made you curious. Your . . . peafowl do the same for me."

Sostratos thought about going through the agora for a while longer, but then wondered why. He'd been trying to drum up customers, and here he . . . might have one. *Worth finding out,* he decided and dipped his head to the Samnite. "Come with me."

Aristeidas looked surprised when he knocked on the door to the rented house. "I didn't expect you back so soon, sir," he said.

"This foreign gentleman"—Sostratos nodded to Herennius Egnatius—"is interested in peafowl."

Just then, the peacock started screaming. Herennius Egnatius' eyes widened. "What is that appalling racket?" he asked.

"Those are the noises peafowl make." Sostratos wished he hadn't had to admit it quite so soon. He also wished Menedemos hadn't chosen that precise moment to shout, "Oh, shut up, you miserable, polluted thing!"

Herennius Egnatius smiled a thin smile. As the funny man at the harbor had, he said, "I take it you do not sell them for the beauty of their song?"

"Well . . . no." Again, Sostratos admitted what he could hardly deny. He tried to rally: "Come with me to the courtyard, and you'll see why we do sell them."

He led the Italian through the entry hall and into the rather cramped courtyard at the center of the house. There stood Menedemos, hands on hips, glowering at the peacock. Maybe he'd dozed off and it had wakened him. And there stood the peacock himself, his ocellated tail fully spread as he displayed himself to a peahen that took no notice whatever of him. *Maybe that's why he's screaming,*

Sostratos thought—in some ways, the peacock wasn't so different from a man.

"Oh," Herennius Egnatius said softly, and then something in his own language—Oscan, Sostratos supposed it was. The sounds weren't so very different from those of Greek, though of course Sostratos couldn't understand the words. After a moment, the Samnite recovered and returned to Greek: "Now I do understand. What is your price?"

"Before we speak of such things, let me introduce you to my cousin, Menedemos son of Philodemos," Sostratos said. "Menedemos, here I have Herennius Egnatius, who is interested in peafowl."

Menedemos instantly went from grouchy to charming, clasping the Italian's hand and saying, "Very pleased to make your acquaintance, sir. May I get you a cup of wine? It's just a local vintage, I'm afraid, though if you should want our Ariousian I could get you a sample."

Herennius Egnatius shook his head; as it did to Himilkon the Phoenician and to many other barbarians, that meant no to him. "The local wine will do well enough for me. I am looking for a way to make myself stand out. Many traders bring fine wine to Italy; some even bring it up to Samnium. But I have never seen such a bird as that." His eyes kept going back to the gleaming polychrome splendor of the peacock's plumage.

"We have only the one peacock." Menedemos stuck his thumb in the air to emphasize the point. "We have four peahens, and we have—how many eggs now, Sostratos?"

"Twenty-nine," Sostratos answered: he was the fellow who kept track of things. "The first of them should start hatching in less than half a month."

"Thanks." Menedemos dipped his head and went on, "Twenty-nine eggs, then. Unless you make us an extraordinary offer for the peacock, we would rather sell you a peahen or some eggs, to let you start your own flock in . . . ?"

"I live in Caudium." The Samnite shook his head again, and pointed at the peacock. "This is the bird I want. I will also buy a peahen, so that I may breed peafowl for myself."

He didn't lack for arrogance. Gently, Sostratos said, "As my cousin told you, you would have to make an extraordinary offer, because we probably would not be able to get so much for the other peahens and the eggs without the peacock to show what the buyer is really getting."

"I understand," Herennius Egnatius said. "I also understood your cousin. For the pair of birds, I will pay five minai of silver in the money of Taras."

"Five minai." Sostratos did his best to sound thoughtful rather than delighted. That was a good deal more than Menedemos and he had paid for all six peafowl. Of course, the Samnite didn't know what they'd paid.

No sooner had that thought crossed his mind than Menedemos said, "I'm sorry, sir, but we do have to make a profit. Ten minai for the pair would, but five?" He tossed his head. If he had any trouble concealing his delight, he didn't show it.

"I am sure you would make a profit on ten minai," Herennius Egnatius said. The haggling began. It followed familiar lines—except that the Samnite didn't realize how high his opening offer was. Sostratos and Menedemos made sure he didn't figure it out, either: they bargained with him as hard as if that first offer were outrageously low. By fighting over every drakhma, they made him think it was.

"Is the Tarentine drakhma lighter or heavier than ours?" Menedemos asked as the dicker drew toward a close.

"A little heavier," answered Sostratos, who'd had to change money—and to pay the fee for doing it.

"Well, shall we take eight minai, fifty drakhmai, then?" Menedemos said.

But now Sostratos was the one to toss his head. "No. I think eight minai, seventy-five drakhmai is the least we can take. I hate going below nine minai at all." He folded his arms across his chest and gave Herennius Egnatius as stony a stare as he could. He didn't think the Samnite would walk away from the deal—the fellow had already talked himself into buying the birds, which meant he had to talk the men who owned them into selling.

And, sure enough, Herennius Egnatius nodded to show he agreed. "I shall pay you eight minai, seventy-five drakhmai of Taras for the peacock and a peahen," he said, and held out his hand. Sostratos and Menedemos clasped it in turn. The Samnite went on, "Let me go back to the house of my guest-friend. My slaves and I will bring you the money this afternoon."

"That will do," Sostratos said, and Menedemos dipped his head. Sostratos went on, "If you don't mind my asking, why did you bring so much money here to Taras in the first place? It can't have been for peacocks."

"No," Herennius Egnatius said. "I came here to buy a fancy woman and bring her back with me. But your birds will set me apart from my neighbors even better. Anyone can buy a fancy woman, but not just anyone can have a peacock."

"I see," Sostratos said, and he did, too. *A social climber, that's what he is.* Sostratos had to fight to hold his face straight. *Who would have thought a backwoods Italian town spawned social climbers?*

Anticipation in his voice, Herennius Egnatius added, "I should like to see Gellius Pontius match me now." He bowed to Sostratos, and then to Menedemos. "Thank you, gentlemen. I shall see you this afternoon."

As soon as he'd left, Menedemos said, "Aristeidas!"

"What is it?" asked the sailor serving as doorman.

"Hurry over to the *Aphrodite*," Menedemos answered. "Round up six or eight sailors and get 'em back here as fast as you can. Have 'em bring swords—not knives, swords—and wear helmets if they've got 'em. Don't waste time—get moving."

Aristeidas dipped his head and was gone. Sostratos said, "You don't think—?"

"That he'd try to steal the birds instead of paying for them?" Menedemos shrugged. "The Samnites are warriors, which means they're robbers if they see the chance. If he doesn't see the chance, I think he'll be mild as overwatered wine and sweet as honey."

Sostratos didn't have to ponder that for very long before he said, "You're probably right. Better safe than sorry."

"Just what I thought myself," Menedemos said. "I'm going to wear my sword, too. And you ought to dig yours out and belt it on."

"Me?" That hadn't occurred to Sostratos. "But I'm a hopeless dub when it comes to fighting."

"You know that, and I know that, but Herennius Egnatius doesn't know it," Menedemos said. "All he knows is that you're taller than anybody has any business being and that you'll have a sword on your belt. Nobody who hasn't seen you working in the gymnasion wants any trouble with you."

The obvious implication was that anyone who *had* seen Sostratos at his exercises wouldn't worry about him very much. Since the obvious implication was true, he said no more than, "Let me rummage through my gear. I hope I didn't leave the blade back on the *Aphrodite*."

"You'd better not have!" Menedemos exclaimed.

"Taras is a civilized city," Sostratos said with dignity. "Am I a barbarian, to go armed inside a polis?" But then, automatically looking at the other side of things, he went on, "Of course, Taras isn't an ordinary polis, like the ones back in Hellas, not with the Italian barbarians just over the border. And there are some towns farther north that used to be Hellenic, but that the Italians have overrun."

"Thanks for the history lesson, but save it for another time," Menedemos said dryly. "What you need to do now is find that sword."

Sostratos went through the two duffel bags he'd brought from the ship. Somewhat to his own surprise, he discovered the sword at the bottom of the second one. The bronze scabbard slapped against his left thigh after he put on the sword belt. He felt as if he should lean a little to the right to compensate for the weight of blade and sheath.

Menedemos, by contrast, looked quite impressively martial with a sword on his hip. "What I wish I had is a hoplite's spear," he said. "But there's not much point to bringing one aboard ship, is there?"

Someone knocked on the door to the rented house. "If that's the Samnite here so soon, I wish you had a spear, too," Sostratos said. But it wasn't—it was Aristeidas, back from the *Aphrodite* with half a dozen men, Diokles among them.

"So you've sold a couple of birds, have you?" the oarmaster said. "That'll make a nice pile of silver, I expect. Don't blame you a bit for wanting to make sure you get it." He carried a stout, iron-headed club in place of a sword. Sostratos wouldn't have wanted to stand against him.

A couple of the sailors looked a little the worse for wear from wine, but they all seemed ready to fight if it came to that. Sostratos hoped it wouldn't. But his cousin was right: being ready for trouble made it less likely.

Half an hour later, another knock sounded. Sostratos opened the door again. There stood Herennius Egnatius. He had a sword on his hip, too. The four stocky, broad-shouldered men at his back didn't look like slaves—they looked like soldiers. They all wore helmets, three of bronze, one of iron. One of them did carry a spear; the others wore swords. Seeing the blade on Sostratos' belt, the Samnite said, "I don't care to be robbed carrying money through the streets."

"Of course not," Sostratos answered smoothly. He stood aside. "Come in."

The Samnite's retainers and the sailors from the *Aphrodite* eyed one another. Herennius Egnatius took the armed Hellenes in stride. "I see you are men who let no one use you unjustly," he said. "That is very good."

"Not that you would have done such a thing," Sostratos said, not raising an eyebrow—much.

"Of course not," Herennius Egnatius said blandly. "Perhaps it is just as well that we have no misunderstandings."

"Indeed." Sostratos' eyebrow climbed a little higher. "I hope you did bring the money as well as your retainers, on the off chance you might need it."

"I did." If Herennius Egnatius noticed Sostratos' sarcasm, he didn't acknowledge it. He spoke to one of his own men in Oscan. Again, Sostratos was struck by how similar the sounds of the language were to those of Greek, though he could make out none of the words. The Samnite had to repeat himself, raising his voice the second time; his retainers were as captivated by their first sight of the peacock as he had been. The bird's display even kept them from sending quite so many mute challenges to the sailors from the *Aphrodite*.

The leather sack the Samnite retainer handed to Sostratos was nicely heavy with silver. "I thank you," Sostratos said. By the shrug the Samnite gave him, the fellow knew no Greek. Sostratos turned back to Herennius Egnatius. "As soon as I have counted the coins, the birds are yours."

Counting out 875 drakhmai took some little while. There were fewer than 875 coins in the sack, for it held didrakhms and tetradrakhms as well as the pieces of silver worth a single drakhma. Not all of them were Tarentine coins; a fair number came from Syracuse. Sostratos went into a back room and weighed a Syracusan drakhma against a Tarentine counterpart. When the coin from Syracuse proved heavier, he came back and went on counting without another word.

At last, he dipped his head. "This is payment in full for the peacock and for one peahen," he said formally, and held out his hand to Herennius Egnatius. As formally, the Samnite clasped it.

"How shall I take the birds back to my guest-friend's house?" Herennius Egnatius asked.

"If you'd like, I can sell you the cages in which we brought the birds from Hellas," Sostratos replied. "Or, if you would rather, you can put ropes round their necks so they don't run away. I wouldn't try just herding them through the streets of Taras—they can run about as fast as a man can."

Herennius Egnatius drew himself up straight again. Speaking as proudly as a Hellene might have, he said, "I think five men can control two birds." He switched languages. After a couple of sentences of Oscan, his followers nodded. They thought they could handle the peafowl, too.

Sostratos shrugged. "The birds are yours, O best one. Do with them as you please. You asked me a question, and I answered it as best I could."

Maybe a couple of the Samnites had experience herding geese, for they managed to chivvy the peacock and peahen out the door and onto the street without too much trouble. Sostratos closed the door after them. When he came back into the courtyard, Menedemos said, "There's two of the miserable birds gone, anyhow."

"Many good-byes to them, too," Sostratos said. "May we get rid of the rest soon." The two cousins both dipped their heads.

GYLIPPOS WAS A FAT FELLOW who'd made a fortune in dried fish. His andron was large and, by Tarentine standards, splendidly decorated, though to Menedemos the wall paintings, the couches, and even the wine cups in the men's chamber were gaudy and busy. Gylippos himself was gaudy, too, with heavy gold rings on several fingers.

He wagged one of those fingers at Menedemos, who reclined on the couch next to his. "You were a naughty fellow, selling that barbarian the one peacock you had," he said.

Menedemos answered, "He paid me well. His silver's as good as anyone else's." *Better than yours would have been,* he thought, *because you'd have been careful to give me the exact weight of metal we agreed on, and not an obolos more.* Had all cities coined to the same standard, life would have been simpler. As things were, the fellow who took pains in his dealings with money had the edge on the man who didn't.

Gylippos wagged that finger again. His slaves had already cleared away the supper plates—he'd served squid and octopus and oysters and eels with the sitos: no dried fish for his guests—but the symposion that would follow hadn't started yet. He said, "And the scene he made in the streets getting the peacock to the house where he's staying! My dear fellow, you couldn't have done more to build demand for the birds if you'd tried for a year. Everybody saw the peacock, and everybody wants it."

Sostratos shared the couch with Menedemos. As usual, Menedemos had taken the head, though his cousin was older. Sostratos hadn't complained; he never did. He did speak up now, though: "That parade was the Samnite's idea, not ours. I offered to sell him two peafowl cages. I even suggested that he use ropes to keep the birds from running every which way. He wouldn't listen."

"And so," Menedemos added with a grin, "he had half the people in Taras chasing his precious peacock—and the peahen, too. You're right, best one"—he inclined his head to Gylippos—"we couldn't have made more folk notice the birds with anything we did on purpose."

"You certain couldn't." The purveyor of dried fish looked past Menedemos to Sostratos. "As for trying to tell an Italian anything, well . . ." He tossed his head. "I don't think it can be done. Samnites are stubborn as mules, and the Romans to the north of them are just as bad. It's no wonder they're bumping heads again."

"Again?" Sostratos looked interested. Menedemos recognized the eagerness in his cousin's voice—he hoped he'd find out about some obscure bit of history he hadn't known before. Sure enough, Sostratos went on, "They've fought before?" It was, Menedemos supposed, a harmless vice.

"Yes, a generation ago," Gylippos answered. "The Romans won that fight, and the Samnites went to war with them again ten or twelve years ago. They won a big battle early on, but the Romans were too stubborn to quit, so they've just been hammering away at each other ever since."

Another guest of Gylippos', a Tarentine with a face like one of the host's dried fish, said, "The Samnites who overran some of our poleis in Campania are almost civilized these days."

"Well, so they are, Makrobios—some of them." But Gylippos didn't seem much impressed. "And some of the Hellenes who have to live under their rule are *almost* civilized, too, if you know what I mean. Greek with an Oscan accent is ugly whether it comes out of a Samnite's mouth or out of a Hellene's."

"It sounds better than Greek with a Latin accent," Makrobios said.

"What's Latin?" Menedemos and Sostratos asked the question at the same time.

"The language the Romans speak," the fish-faced Makrobios answered. He held up his hand with the fingers spread. "We say *pente*. When the Samnites mean *five,* they say *pumpe*—not much different, eh? So you can understand a Samnite when he talks Greek."

"That Herennius Egnatius didn't speak badly," Menedemos agreed.

"But when the Romans mean *five,* they say *quinque.*" Makrobios pronounced the barbarians' word with obvious distaste. "I ask you, how can anyone who makes noises like that learn good Greek?"

"Some of those Campanian cities are doing pretty well for themselves, though, even if they've got Samnites ruling them," Menedemos said. "I was thinking of taking the *Aphrodite* up that way after I've done all the business here I can."

Makrobios shrugged. "Whatever you like, of course. Perhaps I'll see you again afterwards. On the other hand, perhaps I won't, too." His clear implication was that perhaps nobody would see Menedemos again afterwards.

With some irritation, Menedemos asked, "Do you think I'd be wiser to go to Syracuse? I don't, by the gods."

"Well, neither do I," the Tarentine admitted. "Unless Agathokles does something extraordinary, I don't see how he can keep Carthage from taking his city. And he's been ruling Syracuse for seven years now, so I don't know what he can do that he hasn't already done."

"You see my problem, then," Menedemos said. "I'm not going to turn around and go straight back to Hellas when I leave Taras, so what else can I do?"

"Believe me, I'm glad it's not my worry." Makrobios leaned forward. "Tell me, what price are you asking for peafowl eggs?"

"Thirty drakhmai," Menedemos answered at once; he and Sostratos had been over that ground, and had sold a couple of eggs at that price. "From their size, I'd also say you'd do better to have a duck or a goose brood them than a hen."

"And suppose I spend thirty drakhmai and the egg doesn't hatch? What then?" Makrobios demanded.

It was Menedemos' turn to shrug. "I'm afraid that's the chance you take. I'm not a god, to look inside an egg and tell whether it's good or bad."

"We'll soon have chicks for sale—for a good deal more," Sostratos added. "You can save some money if you want to gamble a little."

"You'll ask something outrageous, I'm sure," Makrobios muttered.

Menedemos smiled his suavest smile. "You have some fellow citizens who don't think so. You even have a barbarian neighbor who didn't think so. If you want to be among the first, O best one, you have to pay the price. If we had the second shipload of peafowl into Taras, we couldn't charge nearly so much—because the first ship would have."

Makrobios looked so unhappy, he might have been a hooked fish. But he said, "The house you're renting is north of the market, isn't it? Maybe I'll see you tomorrow." Before Menedemos could answer, Makrobios pointed to the doorway. "Ah, here come Gylippos' slaves with the wine."

Menedemos pointed in surprise. "Those are jars of our Ariousian."

"I sold them to his majordomo this afternoon," Sostratos said, a little smugly. "You were dickering with somebody over a peahen."

"Krates the potter," Menedemos answered in a low voice: the man in question reclined a few couches away. "He wouldn't meet our price."

"Well, Gylippos' majordomo did. He talks so strangely, he may be one of these Romans." Sostratos leaned forward to whisper in Menedemos' ear: "And now we get to drink some of the wine we just sold. I quite like that."

"So do I." Menedemos chuckled.

Gylippos' slave poured some of the Ariousian into the metaniptron from which they drank the first, neat, toast of the symposion and poured the libation to Dionysos. The guests murmured appreciatively. Menedemos wondered if they would be appreciative enough to elect him symposiarch, but they chose Krates instead. Menedemos wasn't surprised or offended; the potter was one of their circle, while he was a guest.

Krates was a solid man in his late thirties or early forties, handsome enough that he'd probably been much pursued as a youth. "Ariousian, eh?" he said, and Gylippos dipped his head and waved to Menedemos and Sostratos to remind the men in the andron where it had come from. Krates stood up and declared, "Since the wine is so very fine, let it be mixed one to one with water."

Everyone clapped. Menedemos laughed out loud. Turning to Sostratos, he said, "It's not *his* wine, so why shouldn't he mix it lavishly?"

"We're all going to get very, very drunk." Sostratos sounded disapproving. "I don't remember the last symposion I went to where they mixed it one to one. That's too strong."

"No wonder you don't remember, then." Menedemos laughed again. His cousin looked annoyed at him for deliberately misunderstanding. Menedemos had been at a good many symposia where the wine went around evenly mixed with water. They weren't like the ones at his father's house, or his uncle's, but they were fun in their own right. He asked Gylippos, "Where's that house called 'the trireme'? I know it's somewhere in Great Hellas. Is it here?"

" 'The trireme'?" Sostratos echoed. "I don't know that one."

"I do," their host said. "No, it's not here—it's in Akragas, on the south coast of Sicily. The symposiasts got so drunk, they thought they were in a storm at sea, and started throwing furniture out the windows to lighten ship. When people heard the racket, they came by to see what was going on and started carrying off couches and tables and chairs, and the fellow whose house it was had a nasty time getting things back once he sobered up." He grinned. "That's what I call a symposion."

He didn't seem to mind Krates' ordering strong wine. Back in Hellas, the Italiotes had a reputation for debauchery. Sostratos still looked primly unhappy. Menedemos enjoyed his father's symposia, but he enjoyed the wilder kind, too. Looking back to his cousin as the slaves mixed the wine, he said, "I don't think you'll have to remember your Euripides tonight."

"Probably not," Sostratos agreed, "though his verses ransomed some of the Athenians the Syracusans captured in the Peloponnesian War."

Instead of the long-dead past, Menedemos thought about the cup of potent wine Gylippos' slave—a short, broad-shouldered Italian—handed to him. Before drinking, he paused to admire the kylix. Its pure shape argued for the Athens of a hundred years before, but the yellow and purple glaze accompanying the usual red, white, and black and its obvious newness said otherwise. He nodded to Krates. "A work from your establishment?"

"Why, yes, as a matter of fact," the potter answered with a pleased smile. "How good of you to guess."

"It's nicely done," Menedemos said. Krates hadn't bought a peahen today, but he might come back.

He smiled again. "Thank you." He tasted the wine. His eyebrows rose. "Oh, this is very fine. I'm fond of the local vintages—don't get me wrong—but this makes them seem like vinegar by comparison. If you don't mind my asking, what did Gylippos pay?"

"Sostratos?" Menedemos said; he didn't know himself.

"I don't mind at all," his cousin said. "He paid forty-eight drakhmai the amphora."

Menedemos waited for Krates to wince. And Krates did, but not too badly. "That's steep," he said, but then he sipped again. "I can see why he paid it, though." A couple of other symposiasts also made enthusiastic noises.

"You'll understand, O best one, it wasn't cheap for us at Khios," Menedemos said, "and the one drawback of a merchant galley, of course, is the high cost of the crew's wages. I really don't see how I can come down." He'd sold for less at Cape Tainaron, but Tainaron was a good deal closer to Khios. And the Tarentines didn't need to know what he'd sold it for there.

Two flutegirls came in, one with a single flute, one with a double. They both wore short tunics of thin, gauzy linen. Before they began to play, Menedemos called out to them: "Hail, girls! Who's your master? He might want to know I've got fine Koan silk for sale, so transparent the men'd be wondering if you were wearing anything at all. You'd probably get some extra tips for yourselves that way, too."

"We belong to a man named Lamakhos, sir," replied the girl with the double flute. "You can find him not far from Poseidon's temple." She sighed. "I'd like to wear silk."

"Thanks, sweetheart." Menedemos blew her a kiss. "You'd look good in it." She smiled at him in a marked manner. He smiled, too, even if he didn't think she was especially pretty. Pretty or not, a willing slave made a much better partner than one who was only doing what she had to do.

Sostratos said, "I don't know how you do it, but you always do. You've got her eating out of the palm of your hand."

"It's not that hard," Menedemos answered. "You could do it yourself, if you set your mind to it."

"I don't think that much of her looks," Sostratos said. Menedemos had expected him to say something like that. His cousin most often seemed to find reasons not to have a good time.

"Send the wine around again," Krates told Gylippos' slaves—sure enough, this symposion would center on drinking. The symposiarch waved to the flutegirls. "Let's hear some music, too." The girls raised the flutes to their lips and began to play a love song in the wailing Lydian mode. It wasn't a tune Menedemos knew, but a couple of guests started singing along to it.

He leaned over toward his host. "Is that a Tarentine song?"

Gylippos tossed his head. "I think it comes from Rhegion, the town right opposite Sicily on the Italian coast. It's been all the rage in Great Hellas for the past year or so, though."

"I wonder how I missed it when I was in these parts last summer." Menedemos shrugged. "These things happen."

As the two flutegirls played, a handsome young juggler came into the andron. He was naked; his oiled body gleamed in the torchlight. Gylippos' eyes and those of several other guests hungrily followed him as he kept a stream of balls and knives and cups in the air.

Menedemos turned to Sostratos. "He's not bad at all. How'd you like him to play with *your* balls?" His cousin had been taking a sip of wine. He snorted and spluttered and did a good impression of a man choking to death. Menedemos laughed. He held up his own cup to show the slaves it was empty. One of them hurried to refill it.

As the juggler went from table to table, Krates got up from his couch and came over to Gylippos. "What's next?" he asked. "Have you got dancers out there in the courtyard?"

"I certainly do," Gylippos answered, "a pair of Kelts from the Keltic country this side of the Alps. Are you ready for them to come on?"

"I think so," Krates said. "People are getting jolly, and there's nothing like a couple of naked girls to liven things up." He spoke to one of Gylippos' slaves, who went over to the doorway and called out into the darkness beyond.

The symposiasts clapped and whooped as the dancers, graceful as leopards, bounded into the andron and began turning cartwheels. Menedemos joined the applause, but more for politeness' sake than anything else. The girls were nicely shaped, but almost fishbelly pale, with hair the color of untarnished copper—not to his taste at all. Both of them also were several digits taller than he.

He took a pull at his cup of wine, then leaned toward Sostratos. "I don't know about you, but I wouldn't want to bed a woman who looks like she can beat me up."

Sostratos didn't answer. After taking a look at his cousin, Menedemos doubted whether he'd even heard him. Sostratos was staring at the two redheaded dancers as if they were the first naked women he'd ever seen in his life, the expression on his face somewhere between awe and raw lust. "Aren't they beautiful?" he murmured, more to himself than to anyone else.

"Funny-looking, if you ask me," Menedemos answered. That made Sostratos notice him, and look at him as if he'd never heard anything so idiotic in all his born days. Menedemos patted him on the shoulder. "Never mind. Some men would sooner chase boys. Some like their women thin, others like them round. If you want to try to tame a wild Kelt or two, go ahead. You're bigger than they are, anyhow."

"They're—unusual," Sostratos said. Menedemos just shrugged. What was unusual, as far as he was concerned, was Sostratos' showing interest in women at a symposion. He was much more likely to want nothing to do with them.

"Enjoy yourself," Menedemos told him. "That's what they're for." He finished the wine in his cup, then set the kylix down and got to his feet. The andron seemed to sway a little as he rose. The Ariousian was potent to begin with, and cutting it with only its own measure of water left it still very strong. He dipped his head to Gylippos and walked out into the courtyard to ease himself.

However bright the torchlight was inside the men's room, it didn't reach far past the door. Menedemos paused for a moment to let his eyes adapt to the darkness outside, then walked over to the far wall and hiked up his tunic. Behind him, the snatches of song accompanying the flutegirls' music grew more raucous. Then a chorus of men's voices let out a loud, bawdy cheer. He knew what that meant: at least one of the girls had started doing something for one of the men. He hoped she'd chosen his cousin. Sostratos deserved more fun than he usually got.

As Menedemos turned to go back to the andron, a woman only a few cubits away gasped in surprise. "Who are you?" she said. "What are you doing here?"

She must not have noticed him in the gloom till he moved. He hadn't seen her, either. "I'm Menedemos son of Philodemos, one of Gylippos' guests," he answered. "And who are you, dear?"

"My name is Phyllis," she told him. "I came down from the women's room for some fresh air because it's so hot and stuffy up there, and I couldn't sleep with all the noise from the symposion. I didn't expect anyone inside there to notice me."

"I had to get rid of some of the wine I'd drunk." Menedemos tried to make out what she looked like, but didn't have much luck in the dim light. She wasn't taller than he was, though—on the contrary— and she sounded young. "How about a quick one, sweetheart? Do you want to lean forward against the wall?"

She laughed quietly. "You work fast, don't you?" she said, and then, giggling again, "Why not? Come over here where it's darker— and hurry."

"I'd follow you anywhere," Menedemos said. She led him into a corner that was dark indeed, then bent forward and down. Menedemos stood behind her and tugged at her chiton, then yanked up his own. He went into her from behind, his hands clutching her backside. She gave a little mewling cry of pleasure that would have worried him more had the andron not been so noisy—and had he not spent himself a moment later.

Phyllis quickly set her clothes to rights. "I've got to go back upstairs," she said. "You were sweet."

"Let me give you half a drakhma," Menedemos said.

She looked back at him over her shoulder as she hurried toward the stairway. "Did you think I was one of the house slaves?" Her laugh was all breath and no voice, but full of mirth just the same. With a toss of her head, she told him, "I'm Gylippos' wife." She hurried up the steps and was gone.

Menedemos gaped after her as if she'd hit him in the head with a rock. "Oh, by the gods," he muttered, "how *do* I get myself into these things?" But the answer to that was only too obvious—and getting into her had been most enjoyable. He laughed, too, though it wouldn't be so funny if his host found out.

When he strolled back into the andron, Gylippos said, "What were you doing out there so long? Diddling one of the slave girls?"

"As a matter of fact, yes," Menedemos answered—he couldn't very well brag to the husband he'd just cuckolded. The answer produced whoops from most of the couches. He rocked his hips forward and back, which produced more whoops. "She said it was too hot in the women's quarters, but I made it pretty hot out there, too."

"Resourceful Odysseus," Gylippos said.

But your Phyllis is no Penelope, Menedemos thought. He wondered if he would have taken her had he know she was the dried-fish magnate's wife. He didn't wonder long. He was no philosopher, but he knew himself pretty well. He hadn't put in at Halikarnassos because a certain prominent merchant there would have done his level best to kill him on account of the good time he'd had with the fellow's wife.

A slave handed him a fresh cup of wine. "Thanks," he said. "Looks like I'll have to drink this standing up—no room for me on my couch right now." Sostratos and the redheaded Keltic dancing girl with him were both big people, and the way they were thrashing about left the couch barely big enough for the two of them, let alone anyone else. The flutegirls and the juggler were entertaining other guests, while the other dancing girl, sweaty and unhappy, stood leaning against a wall: aside from Sostratos, nobody seemed much interested in an outsized barbarian bed partner.

By the time Sostratos finished what he was doing, Menedemos had almost finished his wine. He admired his cousin's stamina. So, evidently, did the Keltic girl. "I hadna thought to find sic a man amongst the Hellenes, indeed and I hadn't," she said in musically accented Greek. Sostratos' face lit up till he seemed to glow brighter than the torches. That that might well have been purely professional praise never seemed to enter the mind of Menedemos' usually so rational cousin. Menedemos didn't intend to enlighten Sostratos, either. A happy man was easier to deal with than a gloomy one.

Sounds of revelry came from the street. Somebody pounded on the door to Gylippos' house. When one of the house slaves opened it, another band of symposiasts swarmed into the courtyard and then into the andron. Wreaths and ribbons garlanded their hair; more dancing girls came in with them. They seemed a younger, rowdier, drunker crowd than most of Gylippos' guests.

Gylippos, by then, was far enough into his cups not to care. "Welcome, welcome, three times welcome!" he cried, and called to his slaves for more wine.

SOSTRATOS WOKE the next morning with a head he would gladly have traded for anything small and worthless and quiet, not that anyone would have wanted his head in its present sorry condition. He dimly remembered reeling back to the rented house arm in arm with Menedemos behind a couple of torchbearers, each of them trying to sing louder than the other and both succeeding too well.

Then he remembered the Keltic girl. All at once, his head didn't hurt quite so much. Maybe he liked her looks because he'd bedded the red-haired Thracian slave his family owned. And maybe he'd bedded both of them because redheaded women appealed to him. He chuckled as he got out of bed and threw on his chiton. That sounded as if it might be the subject of one of the dialogues Platon had put in Sokrates' mouth, even if it was on the bawdy side.

When he walked out into the courtyard, Menedemos was scattering barley for the peafowl. Menedemos looked about the way Sostratos felt. He managed a smile nonetheless. "Hail," he said. "That was quite a night, wasn't it?"

"So it was," Sostratos agreed. "I could do with a little wine—well-watered wine—to take the edge off my headache."

"I've already done that," his cousin said. "It helps a little—not much."

"Nothing helps a hangover much." Sostratos went into the kitchen, dipped up some water from a hydria, and poured wine into the cup with it. After a few sips, he walked back out into the courtyard. "I was thinking I might go and find this Lamakhos' place today, to see if he wants to buy some of our silk to deck out his girls."

He kept his voice elaborately casual, but not casual enough. Menedemos laughed at him. "I know what else you're after. You want another look at that Kelt you had at Gylippos'—maybe another go at her, too."

"Well, what if I do?" Now Sostratos knew he sounded embarrassed. He wanted to rule his lusts, not let them rule him. But he did want to see the girl again, and he wouldn't have minded taking her to bed again, either—not at all.

"It's all right with me," his cousin said expansively. Menedemos rarely wondered about whether he or his lusts had the upper hand. He smiled an ever so knowing smile. "I did all right for myself last night, too, thank you very much."

"What? A quick poke with a slave girl out in the dark?" Sostratos said. "Since when is that anything to brag about?"

Menedemos looked around. Seeing none of the *Aphrodite*'s sailors who guarded the rented house close by, he leaned toward Sostratos and spoke in a whisper: "She wasn't a slave girl, though I thought she was when I asked her. She was Gylippos' wife."

"Gylippos' . . . wife?" Sostratos repeated the words as if he'd never heard them before and had trouble figuring out what they meant. Then he clapped a hand to his forehead. "You idiot! He could have killed you if he'd caught you. He could have shoved one of those big radishes up your arse. He could have done anything he bloody well pleased, especially since you're a foreigner here."

"Thank you. That's the lecture my father would have given me, too," Menedemos said. "I told you, I didn't know she wasn't a slave till after she'd stuck her bottom out and after I'd stuck my lance in. Do you know what I want to do now?"

"What?" Sostratos asked apprehensively.

"I want to sell Gylippos a peafowl's egg, to go along with the cuckoo's egg I may have put in his nest." Menedemos' grin was foxy and altogether shameless.

Nevertheless, Sostratos let out a sigh of relief. "I was afraid you'd say you wanted to go after her again."

"I wouldn't mind," Menedemos said, and Sostratos considered smashing the winecup over his head. But then his cousin sighed and went on, "I probably won't get another chance, though, worse luck. Wives have to keep to themselves. It's what makes them so tempting to go after, don't you think?"

"I certainly don't!" Sostratos exclaimed, and Menedemos laughed at him. He stood on his dignity: "I'm going out with some silk. Try not to get murdered before I come back, if you'd be so kind."

Menedemos chuckled, for all the world as if Sostratos were joking. Sostratos wished he were. His cousin had always been like that: if someone said he might not have something, he wanted it the more for its being forbidden. Taking Gylippos' wife once, not knowing who she was, might make him want to go back to the man's house and do it again, this time with premeditation. Sostratos spat into the bosom of his tunic to avert the evil omen. Menedemos laughed again, as if he could see the thoughts inside Sostratos' mind. Muttering under his breath, Sostratos took a bolt of Koan silk and hurried out of the rented house.

Poseidon's temple lay only a few plethra from the house; he had no trouble finding it. When he asked the way from there, the fellow to whom he put the question went into what was almost a parody of deep thought. "Lamakhos' place? I ought to know where that is, I really should. . . ." He fell silent, his brow furrowed.

Sostratos gave him a couple of khalkoi. His memory improved remarkably. He gave quick, precise directions. Sostratos turned right, turned left, and there it was.

"Hail, friend," said a man whose hard face and watchful eyes didn't match the warmth he tried to put in his voice. "Well, well, you're here early this morning. Some of the girls are still asleep— they had a busy night last night. I can boot 'em out of bed if you want something special, though." He looked Sostratos up and down. "You're a long-shanked fellow. You might fancy a couple of the prettiest Kelts you ever did see. They're big girls, but full of fire."

"You must be Lamakhos," Sostratos said, and the brothelkeeper dipped his head. Sostratos went on, "I met your Keltic girls last night."

"Did you?" Lamakhos' eyes lit up. Sostratos had little trouble thinking along with him. If he, Sostratos, had been at the symposion, he was prosperous. And if he was here so early, he was probably besotted with at least one of the Kelts—which could only profit the man who owned them. "If you want to meet 'em again, friend, I'll be glad to get 'em for you."

I'm sure you would, Sostratos thought. Lamakhos wasn't so far wrong, either, but Sostratos didn't want him realizing that. And so, as casually as he could, he said, "Later, maybe. The real reason I came here was that I noticed your flutegirls were decked in thin linen last night."

"Well, what about it?" Lamakhos' bonhomie dropped away like a himation in hot weather.

"They'd make more for themselves and more for you if they wore silk." Sostratos showed him the bolt of Koan cloth he'd brought along.

"Ah." Now Lamakhos looked thoughtful. This was business, too, if not quite the business he'd had in mind. He pointed. "Come on into the courtyard, so I can have a look at this stuff in the sunlight."

He led Sostratos through the main reception room, where the girls sat around waiting for customers. Some of them wore linen tunics, as the flutegirls had the night before. Others were altogether naked. As they sat, most of them spun wool into thread—if they weren't making money for Lamakhos one way, they'd do it another.

"Hail, little brother!" one of them called to Sostratos, and fluttered her eyelashes at him. Her bare breasts jiggled, too.

"Shut up, Aphrodisia," Lamakhos said. "He's not here for a piece. He's here to try and sell me some silk."

Telling that to the whores proved a mistake. By their excited squeals, they all wanted to wear the filmy, exotic fabric. Sostratos displayed the bolt. The women reached for it. Lamakhos looked sour, but took Sostratos into the courtyard, as he'd said he would. Sostratos displayed it again. "Oh, look!" one of the girls said. "You can see right through it. What the men wouldn't pay if we went to a symposion dressed like *that*!" The other whores loudly agreed.

Lamakhos looked harassed. Even though the women were slaves, they could make his life miserable. "Well, what do you want for it?" he growled at Sostratos.

"Fifteen drakhmai for each bolt," Sostratos answered. "Plenty of silk in each one for a chiton, and your girls will make the price back inside a few months."

The women put up a clamor that hamstrung Lamakhos' tries at dickering. They made such a racket, they woke up the flutegirls and dancers who'd been at Gylippos' symposion the night before. The fluteplayer who'd given Menedemos the name of her master and the redheaded dancer with whom Sostratos had enjoyed himself both waved to him. They and the other girls joined in the outcry for silk.

Despite that outcry, Lamakhos did his best, but he couldn't get Sostratos down below thirteen drakhmai a bolt for twenty bolts. "You've seduced my girls, that's what it is," he said unhappily.

"You'll make money in the long run," Sostratos said again. Since the brothelkeeper seemed prepared to pay and didn't argue, he concluded Lamakhos held the same opinion. And then inspiration struck. "If you'll do something for me, I'll knock five drakhmai off the total."

"What's that?" Lamakhos asked.

Sostratos pointed to the Keltic girl. "Let me come by and have Maibia"—the name she'd given him didn't fit well in a Hellene's mouth—"whenever I like for as long as I'm in Taras this year."

Lamakhos pursed his lips, considering. "I ought to say no. I'd get more than five drakhmai out of you that way."

"You might," Sostratos replied. "On the other hand, you might not. You should know that I am not one who spends wildly on women."

That made Lamakhos look unhappy again. "You haven't got the look, I have to say. You'd probably stay away just to spite me, too, wouldn't you?" Sostratos only smiled. Lamakhos drummed his fingers on the side of his thigh. "All right—a deal, as long as you don't hurt her or do anything that makes her worth less. If you do, I'll take you to law, by the gods."

"I wouldn't," Sostratos said. "I'm not somebody who hurts slaves for sport. In fact, I'll even ask her if it's all right." He turned to Maibia.

She shrugged. "Why not? You weren't cruel last night, even with wine in you, and your breath doesn't stink." Such tiny praise—if that was what it was—made Sostratos' ears burn. The Keltic girl went on, "And if you want me enough to bargain for me, I expect you'll be giving me summat every so often to keep me sweet."

"I . . . expect I will." Sostratos didn't know why such a mercenary attitude surprised him. What did Maibia have to bargain with, except the favors she doled out?

Lamakhos stuck out his hand. Sostratos clasped it. "A bargain," they said together. The brothelkeeper went on, "I'll pay for this bolt now, and come to the house you're renting for the rest this afternoon or tomorrow."

"Good enough," Sostratos said. "Ah . . . You ought to know we have some stout sailors keeping an eye on things."

"Everybody knows that, on account of the Samnite," Lamakhos said. "I wasn't going to try and rob you." But he smiled, as if Sostratos had complimented him by thinking he might. In the circles in which he traveled, maybe that *was* a compliment.

7

MENEDEMOS PROBABLY WOULD HAVE GONE TO GYLIPPOS' house even without a good excuse. He knew that much about himself, from experience: that was how he'd got in trouble with the merchant he'd cuckolded in Halikarnassos. But he had a perfectly good excuse here—two perfectly good excuses, in fact, which he carried in a canvas sack.

When he knocked on Gylippos' door, the dried-fish merchant's majordomo, a stonefaced Italian of some sort named Titus Manlius, said, "Hail, sir. My master is waiting for you." He did speak Greek with an an accent different from Herennius Egnatius', so maybe Sostratos was right in guessing him a Roman.

As Menedemos walked across the courtyard toward the andron, his eye naturally went to the dark corner near the stairs where Phyllis had bent herself forward for him. The corner wasn't dark now, of course, not with the warm sun of southern Italy shining down on it. Menedemos had hoped for a glimpse of Gylippos' wife, but he was disappointed in that. He shrugged as he walked into the andron. He wasn't sure he could have told her from a slave woman, anyhow. All he really knew was that she was short and young—and friendly, very friendly.

"Hail," Gylippos said. "Have some wine. Have some olives." He pointed to a bowl on the round three-legged table in front of him.

"Thank you." Menedemos popped one into his mouth, worked off the pulp with his teeth and tongue, and spat the pit onto the pebbles of the floor mosaic.

Gylippos pointed to the canvas sack. "So those are the chicks, eh?"

"Either that or I've caught a kakodaimon in there," Menedemos replied with a grin.

The purveyor of dried fish chuckled. "Let's see 'em."

"Right." Menedemos upended the sack on the floor. Out spilled the two peafowl chicks. "Here—I brought some barley for them."

Menedemos scattered the grain over the mosaic. The chicks started contentedly pecking away. They were a good deal bigger than newly hatched chickens, brownish above and buff below. The little noises they made were louder and sharper than ordinary chicks', too, though not nearly so raucous as those of adult peafowl.

"I see they can take care of themselves," Gylippos said, and Menedemos dipped his head. "Figures that they would—most birds of that sort can," the fish dealer went on; he was no fool. "Still, it's good to see with your own eyes. Now—d'you know how to tell the peacocks from the peahens when they're this little?"

"I'm sorry, but I don't," Menedemos replied. "These are the first chicks I've seen, too, you'll remember. Either way, though, you'll have something unique in Great Hellas."

"The fellow who got something unique in Great Hellas will be heading out of Great Hellas pretty soon: the gods-detested Samnite you sold the grown peacock to," Gylippos grumbled.

"He paid for it, too," Menedemos answered. "I'm not asking nearly so much for the little ones." He ate another olive and spat out the pit. One of the chicks gulped it down. Menedemos wondered whether it could get nourishment from the pit or would use it as a gizzard stone.

"Well, how much *are* you asking?" Gylippos asked.

"A mina and a half apiece," Menedemos said lightly.

"A hundred and fifty drakhmai?" Gylippos howled. "By the dog of Egypt, Rhodian, either you're mad or you think I am."

Dickers always began with such cries. Menedemos sold the two birds for two Tarentine minai, just about the price he'd wanted to get. "My cousin will curse me when I get back to the house where we're staying," he complained, not wanting Gylippos to know how pleased he was.

Gylippos laughed. "He's probably off spending the money you make, screwing that barbarian with the ugly whey-colored skin and the hair like copper. He's welcome to her, you ask me."

"I'm with you." Menedemos laughed, too. He was far more likely to be accused of squandering silver on women than was his cousin.

"Speaking of which," Gylippos went on, "which of the house slaves did you have at the symposion? None of them owns up to it, and they usually brag about such things."

Alarm shot through Menedemos, though he did his best not to show it. One of the chicks wandered over and pecked experimentally at his toe. He thought fast while shooing it away. "I didn't ask her name," he said when he straightened. "It was dark—I can't even tell you what she looks like. But I will tell you this: I gave her three oboloi."

"Ah. That could be it." The dried-fish merchant looked wise. "I suppose she thinks I'd take it away from her. She ought to know better—I'm no skinflint, not like some people I could name—but you never can tell with slaves."

"True." Menedemos let out a sigh of relief. Gylippos didn't suspect him. Gylippos didn't suspect his own wife, either. Maybe Phyllis was good at keeping her affairs secret, or maybe she hadn't strayed till she met Menedemos. He preferred the latter explanation.

"Do you know," Gylippos said, "I offered Herennius Egnatius ten minai for the peacock, and he wouldn't take it. I still say it's not right to let him go off with a prize like that instead of selling it to a Hellene."

"Well, O best one, if you'd offered me ten minai, you'd have a peacock in your courtyard right now. Since you didn't . . ." Menedemos shrugged.

Gylippos gave him a sour look. Before Herennius Egnatius bought the peacock, he hadn't thought it was worth ten minai, or even five. He wanted it more because somebody else had it. Menedemos thought he was entitled to look sour himself, too. He would have loved to get ten minai for the bird. Because of her many rowers, sailing in the *Aphrodite* cost a lot more than a regular merchantman would have. The two chicks he'd just sold Gylippos were worth about three days of wages for the crew. Sostratos was the one who did most of the mumbling over a counting board, but Menedemos worried about turning a profit, too.

Instead of scowling, though, he gave Gylippos a broad, friendly smile, one so charming that the Tarentine couldn't help smiling back. Gylippos wouldn't have smiled had he known what Menedemos was thinking: I will *lay your wife again, by the gods. Do I want her more because you've got her? What if I do?*

Gylippos called to Titus Manlius. His majordomo went off, soon to return with a leather sack pleasantly full of silver. Menedemos opened the sack and began to count the coins. "Don't you trust me?" Gylippos inquired in injured tones.

"Of course I trust you," Menedemos lied politely. "But accidents can happen to anyone. With the money out in the open between us, there's no room for doubt." Before long, he was saying, "A hundred ninety-three . . . ninety-five . . . This nice fat tetradrakhm makes a hundred ninety-nine . . . and a last drakhma for two hundred. Everything's just as it should be."

"I told you so." Gylippos still sounded huffy.

"So you did." Menedemos started scooping the coins back into the sack. "When you sell your fish, best one, do you always take your customers' payments on trust?"

"Those thieves? Not likely!" But Gylippos didn't, wouldn't, see that anyone could reckon him anything less than a paragon of virtue. Menedemos sighed and shrugged and said his farewells.

Titus Manlius closed the door behind him as if glad to see him go. The Italian slave didn't seem to approve of him. Menedemos chuckled. From what he'd seen, the majordomo didn't seem to approve of anyone, save possibly his master. Some slaves got to be that way: more partisan for the families they served than half the members of those families.

Menedemos didn't go straight back to the house he shared with Sostratos. Instead, he walked around the corner so he could look up to the second-story windows. The women's quarters would be up there. Phyllis and the house slaves were doing whatever women did when shut away from the prying eyes of men: spinning, weaving, drinking wine, gossiping, who could say what all else?

The shutters were thrown back to let some air into the women's rooms. Looking up from the dusty street, Menedemos could see only ceiling beams stained with smoke from the braziers that would fight the cold in wintertime. Experimentally, he whistled one of the tunes the flutegirls had played the night of the symposion.

A woman came to the closest window and looked out at him. She was small and dark and young—not any great beauty, not to Menedemos' eyes, but not ugly, either. Was she the one who'd leaned forward against the wall for him? He started to call her name, but checked himself. He silently mouthed it: *Phyllis?*

She dipped her head. Her own lips moved without a sound: *Me-*

nedemos? He bowed low, as he might have to Ptolemaios or Antigonos or another of Alexander's generals. She smiled. Her teeth were very white, as if she took special pains to keep them that way. She mouthed something else. Menedemos couldn't make out what it was. He did his best to look comically confused. It must have worked, for Phyllis raised a hand to her mouth to keep from laughing. Then she repeated herself, moving her lips more exaggeratedly.

Tomorrow night. This time, Menedemos understood what she was saying. He blew her a kiss, waved, and hurried off. When he looked back over his shoulder as he rounded the corner, she was gone.

You're mad. He could hear Sostratos' voice inside his head. *You're a stupid little cockproud billy goat, and you deserve whatever happens to you.* That wasn't Sostratos' voice; it was his father's, and it held more than a little gloating anticipation.

He didn't care. For years, he'd made a point of not listening to Sostratos, and his father was back in Rhodes. *If I can sneak over here and get it in, I'll do it, by Aphrodite's tits.* That was his own voice, and he heard it louder and stronger than either of the other two.

MAIBIA LOOKED OVER at Sostratos from a distance of perhaps a palm and a half; the bed they shared in Lamakhos' establishment was none too wide. "Sure and you're so rich and all," she said, "so why don't you buy me for your very own self?"

Sostratos had heard ideas he liked much, much less. He enjoyed himself with the Keltic girl even more than he'd expected. If she didn't enjoy herself with him, she was artful at concealing it.

Of course, she might well have been artful at concealing it. What girl in a brothel didn't hope to escape it by becoming a rich man's plaything? He ran a hand along her smooth, pale curves. She purred and snuggled against him. "I have something for you," he said.

"Do you, now?" Maibia didn't speak Greek according to any rules of grammar Sostratos recognized, but her odd turns of phrase only made the language more interesting. "And what might that be?"

"It might be anything," Sostratos replied, precise as usual. "It is . . ." He reached down and picked up a small bundle of woolen cloth closed with twine that lay on the rammed-earth floor with his tunic and sandals. "This, or rather, these." He handed Maibia the bundle.

She fumbled at it. With her long, pointed fingernails, she made short work of the knot he'd tied to keep it closed. "Ahh!" she said when she saw the earrings inside. "Are they gold, now, or nobbut brass?" Before Sostratos could answer, she bit one. She squeaked in delight. "Sure and they *are* gold! What a sweet man y'are! How can I be after thanking you?"

"Oh, you might think of something," Sostratos answered lightly, though his heart pounded in anticipation.

And she did. By the time they finished, he was ready to stagger back to the rented house and sleep for a long, long time. As he put on his chiton, Maibia said, "You could be doing this every day if you were to buy me, now."

"If I did this every day, I'd fall over dead before long," Sostratos said.

"Not a big, strong man like your honor," she said with a shake of the head that sent coppery locks flying.

"I meant it as praise for you," he said, which made her eye him from under lowered lids and tempted him not to leave no matter how sated he was. But, though his body might have been satisfied, his curiosity never was. He asked, "How did you come to be a slave? Why aren't you up in the north of Italy married to a Keltic solder?"

"Indeed and I might have been, were it not for three Roman traders, bad cess to 'em forevermore," she answered. "I was out in the fields minding the cows—'tis a young man's job, but my father had no sons left alive—when they came along the road. They saw me and decided I was worth more nor whatever they had to sell. They lured me close by asking where they might be after finding water, then laid hold of me and carried me off. It wasna far to take me out of the Keltic country, and they got me away without a man of my village the wiser. They raped me and they sold me and"—she shrugged—"here I am."

Sostratos dipped his head. Most slaves not born to servitude had some such tale of horror to tell.

Maibia went on, "I look at that Titus Manlius, the which is majordomo to Gylippos, and I laugh to know it can happen to a Roman, too—though likely them as caught him didna hike up his tunic, with him so ugly and all."

"So he *is* a Roman, then?" Sostratos said. "I have to tell you, I can't keep all these different Italian tribes straight. It's not likely that any of them will ever amount to much."

When he kissed Maibia good-bye, she clung to him and murmured, "Would you not like to be after taking me along thee now?"

One of his eyebrows rose. He said, "My dear, you are very sweet, and great fun in bed. I am going to tell you something that will help us get along better: don't nag me. The more you tell me to do something, the more likely you are to make me want not to do it. Have you got that?"

"Aye," she said softly. A spark of anger flashed in her green eyes, but she did her best to hide it, adding only, "You're a cool one, aren't you?"

"So people keep telling me," Sostratos said, and went on his way.

She wants me to fall in love with her, he thought as he walked back to the house. *Men who fall in love spend a lot of money and do all sorts of other foolish things.* Menedemos seemed to fall in love with at least one woman in every city he visited. The life of a trader, never staying very long in any one place, probably kept him from landing in even worse trouble with some of them than he found.

Menedemos was beaming when Sostratos returned to the house. He was also singing one of the songs from the symposion at Gylippos' house. Sostratos pointed an accusing finger at him. "You're after another go with the fish merchant's wife!"

"I haven't the faintest idea what you're talking about, my dear fellow." Menedemos could be most annoying when he tried to seem most innocent.

"Not much, you haven't," Sostratos said.

"Oh, keep quiet," his cousin said, and then, turning the tables on him, "While you've been out buying trinkets for your mistress and screwing yourself silly, *I've* been doing business. Krates finally paid our price for a peahen."

"That is good," Sostratos said. "We're down to two of the miserable things now, and all these chicks." The little birds ran all over the courtyard, peeping and squawking and pecking at grain and at bugs and lizards and, every now and then, at one another.

"I bought a goose to help the peahens sit on the eggs that haven't hatched yet," Menedemos said. "From all I've seen, they don't make the best of mothers."

"No, they don't," Sostratos agreed. "It's a good thing the chicks can take care of themselves almost as soon as they hatch, because they need to." He glanced over to the goose, which indeed showed more interest in sitting on a nest than did either of the two remaining peahens. With a sigh, he went on, "I *am* sorry that one stupid bird jumped into the sea."

"So am I," Menedemos replied, "but neither one of us can do anything about it now." He raised an eyebrow. "Are you going to buy that little Kelt—no, by the gods, she's not little: that big Kelt, I mean—and take her along with you?"

"She wants me to," Sostratos said.

"Of course she does," Menedemos said. "If you were stuck in a brothel, wouldn't you want to get out?"

"It'd be a pretty desperate brothelkeeper who put me in amongst his pretty boys," Sostratos observed, and startled a laugh out of his cousin. He went on in more serious tones. "She's very pretty—"

"If you say so," Menedemos broke in.

"I think she is, which makes it true for me," Sostratos said. "She's pretty, and she has plenty of reason to treat me well, and—"

Menedemos interrupted again: "What more do you want?"

"Someone who treats me that way even though she doesn't have any special reason to," Sostratos answered. "But we weren't talking about me. We were talking about you, at least till you changed the subject. You and this Phyllis . . ."

"Yes?" Menedemos said when he paused.

"Never mind," Sostratos mumbled. Menedemos again raised an eyebrow, this time in astonishment. But Sostratos realized he'd just undercut his own argument. Gylippos' wife had no special, self-interested reason to bestow her favors on Menedemos. She'd done it anyway. No wonder he was eager to get back to her. With another sigh, Sostratos said, "For the gods' sake, be careful. I'm not the sea-man you are; I don't want to have to take the *Aphrodite* back to Rhodes by myself."

"I'm so glad you care." Menedemos chuckled. "When have I not been careful?"

"Halikarnassos springs to mind," Sostratos said dryly.

"I got away," his cousin answered.

"So you did, but you can't go back there," Sostratos pointed out.

"And we're not ready to leave Taras in a hurry, the way we were in Halikarnassos. You could put the ship in trouble, not just yourself." He hoped that would get through to Menedemos if nothing else did.

But Menedemos just reached up to pat him on the back and said, "Everything will be fine. You'll see."

Sostratos threw his hands in the air. He wasn't going to change his cousin's mind. "Be careful," he repeated. He wished he hadn't thought about the difference between a woman who gave herself because she wanted to and one who did it for money. Now he didn't feel right about urging Menedemos to slake his lust in a brothel, no matter how expedient that advice would have been.

Menedemos grinned at him. "I'll tell you all about it in the morning."

"I don't think I'll want to hear," Sostratos said, which made Menedemos' grin wider. But then Sostratos thought, *I hope you'll have the chance to tell me in the morning.* He spat into the bosom of his tunic to avert that omen, even if he hadn't said the words aloud. Menedemos looked puzzled. Sostratos did not explain.

THE SUN SEEMED to be taking forever to set. Menedemos was sure it had gone down much earlier the day before. Once twilight had finally faded from the western sky, he walked to the door of the rented house and said, "I'm going out for a while."

Aristeidas was standing watch at the door. "See you later, then, skipper," he said. "You're not going to hire a torchbearer or two?"

"No. I know where I'm going," Menedemos answered. Aristeidas laughed, having a pretty good idea of what that was likely to mean. Menedemos, however, wasn't joking. He'd spent part of the day going along the streets and alleys that lay between this house and Gylippos'. If something went wrong—*Aphrodite, prevent it,* he thought—and he had to flee, he wouldn't flee blindly.

I hope I won't. That was the first thought through his mind when he stepped out into the street. Nothing looked the same as it had in daylight. He had to look around to find Zeus' wandering star—now considerably lower in the southwest than it had been in the early evening when the *Aphrodite* first set out from Rhodes—to get his bearings and remember which way to go.

He counted street corners as he made his way toward Gylippos'.

Can I do this if I'm running for my life? he wondered, and then angrily tossed his head. *I'm getting as jumpy as Sostratos.* He tried to imagine his cousin going off to make love to another man's wife. After a moment, he tossed his head again. The picture refused to take shape in his mind.

Nevertheless, he kept counting corners. He wasn't running for his life now. He was going quietly, cautiously, trying to attract no one's notice. Few men with good intentions walked about after dark in a polis. Fewer still went without a torchbearer or, sometimes, a party of torchbearers to light their way. When Menedemos heard footsteps coming up a street he was about to cross, he ducked into the deepest shadow he could find and waited. Two men went by, talking in low voices. He didn't think they were speaking Greek. He had no desire to make their acquaintance and find out for certain.

Was this Gylippos' house? He cocked his head to one side and studied it, stroking his chin the while. The skin felt smooth; he'd shaved that afternoon, using scented oil to soften his whiskers. After a bit, he decided it wasn't; the line of the roof didn't seem right. But he was getting close, unless he'd completely miscounted—in which case, Phyllis would be miffed and Sostratos relieved.

"There it is!" he hissed. And he'd even come to the street under the window to the women's quarters. Lamplight slipped through the slats of the shutter. *If I could navigate this well by sea, I'd count myself lucky.* He whistled the tune that had drawn Phyllis' notice before.

For some little while, nothing happened. Menedemos kept whistling. Then, around at the front of the house, the door came open with a scrape of the timbers against the rammed-earth floor of the front hall. Menedemos hurried inside. The door closed behind him. A woman—she had to be a house slave, for she spoke in accented Greek—said, "Go on upstairs. She will be waiting."

Menedemos was already hurrying across the courtyard toward the stairway: he knew well enough where it lay. He'd got more than halfway up before pausing in the darkness. What would surely have occurred to his cousin before entering Gylippos' house now struck him. What if this was a trap? What if, instead of Phyllis or along with Phyllis, Gylippos waited up there, and with him friends with knives or swords or spears? They'd have him where all his charm wouldn't do the least bit of good.

Of course, if they were waiting up there chuckling to themselves, they already had Menedemos where they wanted him. What was he to do now, turn around, dash down the stairs, and run for the door? He tossed his head. Would divine Akhilleus have done such a thing? Would resourceful Odysseus?

Resourceful Odysseus would have had too much sense to get himself into a spot like this in the first place, Menedemos thought. Resourceful Odysseus, unlike Gylippos, had also been lucky enough to marry a faithful wife.

The hesitation on the stairs lasted no more than a couple of heart-beats. Then, as if angry at himself for wasting time, Menedemos raced up to the women's quarter. One door stood slightly ajar. A lamp inside the room—if he had his bearings, the room from which Phyllis had looked out at him—spilled dim, flickering light into the hallway. He went to that doorway and whispered her name.

His own came back as softly: "Menedemos?"

He opened the door, slipped inside, and closed it after him. She lay waiting on the bed, a large himation covering her. His eyes flicked this way and that. No Gylippos. No armed friends. Everything was the way it was supposed to be. Even so, he couldn't help asking, "Where's your husband?"

"His brother is having a symposion," Phyllis answered. "Some lit-tle slave girl will be giving Gylippos what he wants tonight. And so—" She threw aside the mantle. She was naked beneath it, her body pale as milk in the lamplight. "You can give me what I want."

"I'll do my best." Menedemos pulled his chiton off over his head. As he lay down beside her, he asked, "The slaves won't blab?"

Phyllis tossed her head. "Not likely. I treat them better than Gy-lippos does. If he gets home early, they'll warn us." She reached for him. "But I don't want to think about Gylippos, not now."

Like any man among the Hellenes, Menedemos was in the habit of using women for his own pleasure. Here was a woman using him for hers. He smiled as his mouth came down on her breast. She might be using him for her pleasure, but he'd get some, too. She growled down deep in her throat and pressed his head to her.

Presently, she crouched on all fours at the edge of the bed. When Menedemos started to choose the way that would ensure she didn't need to worry about conceiving, she tossed her head. "That always hurts," she said. "And I'd sooner have your seed sprout in there than his."

"All right." Menedemos spread his legs a little wider and began anew. He went slowly, stretching out his own pleasure—and, incidentally, Phyllis'. Soon she was thrusting back against him as hard as he drove into her. She let out a little wailing cry like the one she'd made down in the courtyard the night of the symposion. A moment later, Menedemos spent himself, too.

Being a young man, he needed only a very little while to recover. When he began again, Phyllis looked over her shoulder at him in surprise. "Gylippos would already be snoring," she said.

"Who?" Menedemos answered. They both laughed.

Again, he took his time. For the first round, he'd chosen to; for the second, he had to. Even after Phyllis' cat-wail of pleasure burst from her, he went on and on, building toward his own peak.

He was almost there when the front door to Gylippos' home opened. "Master!" a house slave exclaimed, louder than she needed to. "What are you doing back so soon?"

Phyllis' gasp, this time, had nothing to do with delight. As her husband growled, "My idiot brother and I had a quarrel, that's what," she jerked away from Menedemos. He hissed in protest, but then Gylippos' voice came from the very foot of the stairs: "I blacked his eye, the decayed, impotent monkey."

"*Oimoi!*" the house slave exclaimed. She went on, "Master, I think the mistress is asleep. She didn't expect to see you till tomorrow morning."

"She'll have a surprise, then," Gylippos said, and started up the stairs.

Menedemos grabbed his chiton. Phyllis pointed to the window as she blew out the lamp. Down below in the courtyard, the slave woman asked Gylippos something else, trying to delay him. Menedemos didn't hear what it was. He flung the tunic out the window, then scrambled out himself. Instead of just leaping, he hung from the sill by his hands for a moment before letting go and dropping to the street: that made the fall as short as possible.

Even so, he turned an ankle when he hit. Biting down hard against an exclamation of pain, he grabbed the chiton as Gylippos spoke from Phyllis' bedroom: "What was that? Is there a burglar trying to break in?"

As Menedemos limped around a corner as fast as he could go, he heard Phyllis answer, "I think it was just a dog, O husband of mine."

"Pretty big for a dog. Pretty clumsy for a dog, too," Gylippos said dubiously. He must have looked out the window, for a moment later he continued, "I don't see any dog. But I don't see any burglar, either, so I suppose it's all right." Maybe he turned away from the window and back toward his wife—his voice was harder for Menedemos to hear when he went on, "Come here."

"I obey," Phyllis said, as demurely as if no other thought had ever entered her mind, no other man had ever entered her body.

Gylippos didn't get what he wanted from a flutegirl or a dancer tonight, so he'll take take what he can get from his wife, Menedemos thought as he wriggled back into his chiton. He hadn't quite got everything he wanted from Phyllis himself. *Inconsiderate of Gylippos,* went through his mind. *Why couldn't he have waited just a little longer to pick a fight with his brother?*

He took his bearings. Gylippos' house lay in the central part of Taras, the part where a neat grid of streets superseded the jumble of lanes and alleys going every which way marking the rest of the town. That made things easier. As soon as Menedemos figured out which way was west, he started counting corners. His ankle hurt when he put weight on it, but it bore him.

He had one bad moment: three or four burly men, plainly bent on no good, padded up a north-south street just before he crossed it. But he'd stayed in the shadows and done his best to move quietly. They kept on going without so much as turning their heads his way. He let out a silent sigh of relief, waited till he was sure they'd passed, and headed on toward the rented house.

When he knocked on the door, he expected Aristeidas to be the one who made sure he was himself and not a robber too clever for his own good. But instead, he heard his cousin's voice: "Is that you, Menedemos?"

"Almonds!" Menedemos quavered in a high, thin falsetto. "Who wants to buy my salted almonds?"

Sostratos opened the door. "If I wanted almonds, I'd buy them in the shell and crack them on your hard head," he said. "You're back sooner than I thought you would be. No all-night debauch?"

"Afraid not," Menedemos said as he came in. Sostratos closed the door behind him. He went on, "I had a good time. You don't need to worry about that." He still wished Gylippos had waited a bit longer before coming home from his brother's, but leaping out of the window, landing badly, and having to limp away made not quite finishing his second round seem much less urgent than it had a little while before.

Altogether too observant for his own good, Sostratos noticed the limp even by the weak light of the single torch burning in the court-yard. "What happened to you?" he demanded. "Does Gylippos know who you are?"

"No, he doesn't," Menedemos answered. "He's not even sure I'm anybody, if you know what I mean. He got into a fight at his sym-posion, and left in a huff. That's why I had to go out the window."

"You're lucky you didn't break your leg, or maybe your neck," Sostratos said. "Is a woman really worth running that kind of risk?"

"If I hadn't thought so, I wouldn't have gone there, would I?" Menedemos said, a little testily. Looking back on it, he supposed it *hadn't* been worth the risk, but he would sooner have gone up before a Persian torturer than admit that to his priggish cousin. If Phyllis wanted him to pay her another visit, he knew he just might do it.

"Foolishness," Sostratos said.

"Yes, O best one." Menedemos used the honorific with intent to wound. By Sostratos' scowl, he succeeded. He said, "And now, if you'll excuse me, I'm going to sleep. It's been a busy night." Trying to walk as straight as he could, he headed for the bedchamber. His ankle complained. So did Sostratos. He ignored both of them.

A HOUSE SLAVE at Lamakhos' brothel shook her head, as barbarians were wont to do. "Maibia does not want to see you today," she said.

"What?" Sostratos stared as blankly as if she'd spoken Oscan or Latin rather than pretty good Greek. "She can't do that!" With a shrug, the slave just repeated herself. Sostratos started to push past her. A couple of other slaves—men: toughs with the look of bounc-ers—appeared behind her. He checked himself. "Let me talk to La-makhos, then." The woman nodded and went away.

"Hail, friend," the brothelkeeper said, his smile still broad and, Sostratos judged, still false.

"Hail," Sostratos replied. "We had a bargain, you know."

"Yes, I do know." Lamakhos shrugged. "Women are funny, that's all I can tell you."

"We had a bargain," Sostratos repeated: for him, that was sacred. Lamakhos shrugged again. Sostratos nervously cracked his knuckles. "Is she angry at me? If I did something to offend her, I'll apologize."

Lamakhos turned to the slave woman. "Go find out." She nodded again and hurried off in the direction of Maibia's chamber.

When she came back, she spoke to Sostratos: "She says it is not that. She says you should come back tomorrow. Maybe then."

Realization smote. *She's playing at being a hetaira.* A girl in a brothel had to take her customers as they came, do what they wanted when they wanted it. A high-class courtesan, on the other hand, had the looks and the charm and the wit to take men on her terms, not theirs. That made them more alluring, of course—if you had to persuade them, that showed, or seemed to show, they really wanted you.

Do I let her get away with it? Sostratos plucked at his beard. Maybe Maibia thought he really had fallen head over heels in love, in which case he would put up with anything from her. If she thought that, she was mistaken. What Menedemos thought of as foreign homeliness attracted him—but love? He tossed his head. He couldn't imagine falling in love with someone with whom he couldn't talk seriously . . . and Maibia's mental horizons were no wider than was to be expected of a girl kidnapped from a Keltic village and sold to a brothelkeeper.

That still didn't answer his question. He'd given Lamakhos a break on the price of the silk for free access to the girl. He supposed—no, he was certain—Lamakhos could make Maibia give herself to him now. But that would only make her sullen, and Sostratos wasn't one of those who enjoyed his girls resentful. Had he been, he would have bedded the Thracian slave back home more often.

Or he could ask Lamakhos for the five-drakhma discount back. He could—but the brothelkeeper would laugh in his face and tell him to go to law. The fuss and feathers would prove more trouble than the money was worth, and what were his chances of getting a fair judgment, even against a brothelkeeper, in a polis not his own?

"Well?" Lamakhos said. "Shall I go shake this nonsense out of her?"

"No, never mind," Sostratos answered—the blunt question made up his mind for him. "I'll come back tomorrow."

As he turned to go, he saw contempt in Lamakhos' eyes. The brothelkeeper tried to hide it behind his friendly mask. His slaves didn't bother. "Pussy-whipped," one of them said to the other, not quite softly enough to keep Sostratos from hearing. His ears tingled, but he kept walking.

Back at the rented house, Menedemos said the same thing. "Complain all you want about me and Phyllis," he added, "but that's nothing beside letting a barbarian slave lead you around by the prick."

"No, no, no—you don't understand," Sostratos said. "She isn't. I'm not mad for her, the way men get when they're assotted of a woman. By the gods, I'm not."

"Then why didn't march right in there and screw her?" his cousin demanded. "You let yourself look like a fool in front of a whoremaster."

"Maybe a little," Sostratos admitted—though it was more than a little. "But I'm not going to buy the girl and take her with me. This way, her owner will start thinking of her as somebody who could be a hetaira: after all, didn't she have the merchant from Rhodes wrapped around her finger? She'll have an easier time of it after I'm gone. Maybe she'll even get the chance to buy herself free."

His cousin gave him a quizzical look. "You'd never catch me acting the fool for the sake of some slave girl."

"You probably wouldn't catch me doing it back in Rhodes," Sostratos said. "Here in Taras"—he shrugged—"who cares?"

Menedemos didn't seem altogether convinced. "I still think she's got you by the balls, and you're making up excuses."

"Think whatever you like," Sostratos answered. "You'll see."

But when he went to Lamakhos' the next day, he had all the earmarks of a worried lover. He sighed with relief when the house slave said Maibia would deign to see him. "I brought her a present," he said, and showed the slave a small vial of cloudy green glass.

"Maybe she will like that," the slave said, but her eyes showed her scorn.

Maibia waited inside the chamber where they'd joined before. Sostratos had expected her to be naked, but she wore a chiton of the Koan silk Lamakhos had bought from him. Her nipples pushed against the filmy fabric; he could see their rosy pinkness through it. Down below, the thin silk showed him the groove between her legs—like most women who lived among Hellenes, she singed away the hair that grew around it.

"You look—lovely." Sostratos' voice sounded hoarse even in his own ears. He might not be madly in love with the Keltic girl, but that didn't mean he didn't want her. Oh, no, it didn't mean that at all.

"Indeed and I'm glad you think so," she said, cocking her hip at a provocative angle. She pointed to the glass vial. "And what might you have for me there?"

Sostratos started to say, *I might have anything,* but he'd used that joke before. Some people repeated themselves endlessly, not even noticing they were doing it. He wasn't—he hoped he wasn't—that sort of fool. Other sorts? Possibly. He handed her the vial. "It's rose perfume from Rhodes," he answered.

Maibia opened, sniffed, and sighed. "Sweet it is—like you." She dabbed on a little, then closed the vial and cast her arms around his neck. He could feel her body through the silk chiton as if she were bare, too.

Before very long, she was. The next little while passed most enjoyably indeed, at least for Sostratos. Maibia kissed him on the end of the nose, then leaned down and bestowed another, similar, kiss. "There, you see?" she purred. "Was I not worth waiting for?"

That brought Sostratos around to what he'd come to the brothel for—to one of the reasons he'd come to the brothel—faster than he'd expected. He sat up in bed and stroked Maibia's hair, which was a distracting mistake. "There's something you need to understand," he said.

"And that is?" Maibia found a way of her own to be distracting. She glanced up at him, mischief in her eyes. "How soon your spear's ready to pierce my flesh, now?"

"No." Sostratos tossed his head. To prove he meant it, he sat up in bed and pulled away from her. "What you need to understand is, I'm not nearly so wild for you as Lamakhos and his slaves think, and you're not going to squeeze me dry no matter how hard you try. The harder you try, in fact, the more annoyed you'll make me."

His tone got through to her. She was mercenary—considering what life had given her, she had to be mercenary—but she wasn't stupid. Fear replaced mischief on her face. "Why didn't you just have 'em thump me, then?" she asked sullenly. "I know some who'd take their pleasure from it, sure and I do."

"I wouldn't," Sostratos said. "Here is the bargain: I will not buy you, no matter what. I've already told you that. But I will let you play the hetaira with me and have your little ways—so long as you don't do it often enough to make me angry. That will give you a better chance to go on playing the hetaira after I leave Taras, it is not so?"

Maibia studied him as if she'd never really seen him before. Maybe she hadn't. Maybe hope and greed had kept her from noticing the person inside the man who enjoyed her body. "Not just cool, but cold-blooded as a frog y'are!" she exclaimed.

Sostratos shrugged. Most of the time, he would have taken that for a compliment. "I can only be as I am," he said. "Meanwhile, you didn't answer my question: is it not so?"

"Sure and it is," the redheaded Kelt said seriously. "Having to take any horny spalpeen who walks in . . ." She shuddered. "If you were in a boy brothel, would you care for that?"

As he had to Menedemos, he replied, "If I were in a boy brothel, I don't think I'd get much trade."

She laughed. "How many would say that?"

He shrugged once more. "What could be more important than the truth?"

That made Maibia laugh again. "Here in a brothel, what could be less important than the truth? If we told the men what we thought of 'em, if we told Lamakhos what we thought of him, how long would we last?" No sooner had she spoken than she looked worried. If Sostratos took her words to the brothelkeeper, what would he do to her?

He didn't intend to do that, but she couldn't know what he intended. He wondered what the girls who made symposia lively really thought of the men who used them. The question hadn't crossed his mind before; unless he badly missed his guess, it seldom crossed the mind of any Hellene. *Probably better not to know,* he thought. He didn't take advantage of such women very often—Maibia had been an exception. Would this keep him from doing it again if some other girl struck his fancy? *The truth,* he reminded himself. *No, it probably won't.*

Telling that to the Keltic girl struck him as less than wise. He did say, "Do we have a bargain, on the terms I put to you?" He might have been selling silk or papyrus.

"We do that," Maibia said at once. She held out her hand. He clasped it. Her skin was much fairer than his, but her hand was as large as many a man's and her grip firm. Yes, this did feel like commerce. But it was commerce of a particular sort, for she went on, "If I'm to hold up my end of the bargain, you need to hold up yours," and went back to what she'd been doing. This time, Sostratos didn't interrupt her. He set a hand on the back of her head, not quite holding her to him but urging her on.

He didn't need to pretend to seem sated when he left Lamakhos'. The brothelkeeper chuckled under his breath as Sostratos went by. He thought Sostratos was well and truly hooked. Sostratos chuckled, too. He knew he wasn't.

When he got back to the rented house, he was surprised—and a little alarmed—to find Gylippos and his Roman majordomo there. "Menedemos tells me you've made a pet of that redheaded wench," the dried-fish merchant said. "I think she's strange-looking, myself."

"I like things that are out of the ordinary," Sostratos said, and then, "What brings you here, sir?"

"I've decided to buy a couple of more peafowl chicks," Gylippos replied. "I want to have a better chance of having at least one peacock."

The little birds ran peeping and cheeping across the courtyard, stopping every now and then to peck at a bug or a bit of grain or another chick. Sostratos wondered how Gylippos would like having four full-grown peafowl in his own courtyard, but that was the Tarentine's worry, not his.

Menedemos had caught a couple of chicks. He limped back toward Gylippos, saying, "The choice is yours, of course, O best one, but I think these two are the biggest, strongest ones we have right now." As if to prove the point, one of them pecked him on the arm. He cursed.

Gylippos laughed. "They do seem lively," he said. "What did you do to your ankle?"

Sostratos started at the question, then tried to pretend he hadn't. Menedemos laughed easily. "Tripped over my own two feet—them and a pebble," he answered. "I feel like a fool. We rode out a nasty storm on the Ionian Sea coming over from Hellas, and I was steady on my legs no matter how the deck pitched and no matter how wet it got. Put me on dry land, and I go and do this."

"Bad luck," Gylippos agreed. Sostratos studied him from the corner of his eye. Was he disingenuous? He was a trader, too; Sostratos couldn't tell. Gylippos said, "I'll buy the one that pecked you, but go run down that mottled one over there for me, too."

The mottled chick didn't want to be run down. Menedemos had to chase after it. Gylippos eyed him as he limped around. The dried-fish dealer's face didn't show much, but Sostratos didn't like what he could see. Gylippos was paying altogether too much attention to his cousin's bad ankle. How much noise had Menedemos made when he left by that second-story window? Enough to raise Gylippos' suspicions when he saw an acquaintance with a limp? Evidently.

At last, after much bad language, Menedemos caught the little peafowl. He brought it over to Gylippos, saying, "Here you are, sir. As far as I'm concerned, now that you've got it, you can roast it."

"Not at these prices." Gylippos turned to Titus Manlius, who'd been standing there quietly, watching Menedemos with him. Sostratos couldn't read the slave's face at all. Did he know? If he did, had he told his master? Gylippos said, "Pay him the money."

"Yes, sir." The Roman might have been a talking statue. He handed Menedemos a leather sack. "Same price as for the last two chicks."

"I ought to charge more. These are bigger birds," Menedemos said.

Gylippos brusquely tossed his head. "Not likely."

Menedemos glanced toward Sostratos. Sostratos tossed his head, too, ever so slightly, as if to say he didn't think Menedemos could get away with it. With a small sigh, Menedemos said, "Well, never mind. Let me count the coins, and you can take your birds away."

Sostratos sat down on the ground beside him to make the counting go faster. The Tarentines minted handsome drakhmai, with an armored horseman holding a javelin on one side and with a man riding a dolphin on the other. Some people said that was Arion, others that it was the hero for whom the polis of Taras was named.

"All here," Sostratos told Gylippos when the counting was through. "We do thank you very much."

"You have things I can't get anywhere else," Gylippos answered. He dipped his head to Titus Manlius. "Let's go." Off they went, carrying one chick each.

Once the door closed behind them, Sostratos said, "I think he knows, or at least suspects. Did you see how he was watching you?"

"I doubt it," Menedemos said. "What kind of a man would do business with someone who'd been screwing his wife?"

"There *are* people of that sort," Sostratos said. "Back in Athens, Theophrastos called them ironical men: the sort who chat with people they despise, who are friendly to men who slander them, and praise to their faces men they insult behind their backs. They're dangerous, because they never admit to anything they're doing."

"Men like that aren't proper Hellenes, if you want to know what I think," Menedemos said.

"Well, I agree with you," Sostratos answered, "but that doesn't mean they don't exist. And it doesn't mean they aren't dangerous."

Menedemos waved his words away. "You worry too much."

"I hope so," Sostratos said, "but I'm afraid you don't worry enough."

MENEDEMOS DID STOP going round to Gylippos' house, even though checking on the peafowl chicks would have given him a perfect excuse to visit. He thought Sostratos was mistaken—Gylippos didn't strike him as lacking self-respect to the point of staying polite to an adulterer—but he decided not to take any needless chances. *And if Phyllis wants to try again, she knows where to find me,* he thought.

He sold the last adult peahen, along with four chicks, to a rich farmer who lived just outside of Taras. "To the crows with me if I know what I'll do with 'em," the fellow said, "but I think it'd be kind of fun to have a peacock strutting around the barn. I seen the one that Samnite bought, and I decided I wanted one my own self.

I figure my chances for getting one peacock out of all the chicks are pretty fair."

"Of course." Menedemos wasn't about to argue with him, not when he was putting down good silver for the birds. "And you can breed them and sell birds yourself and make back what you're paying me and more besides."

"That's right. I sure can," the farmer said. Menedemos wasn't so sure he could. Once these chicks grew up, a lot of people in and around Taras would be breeding and selling peafowl. There would be a lot more birds for sale, too. Prices were bound to drop. But if the farmer couldn't see that for himself, Menedemos didn't feel obliged to point it out to him.

The Tarentine had brought an oxcart and a couple of cages with him. The one for the peahen was a little small, but he got her into it. Off he went, the creak of the cart's axle almost as raucous and annoying as the peahen's screeches.

Sostratos was flicking beads back and forth on a counting board. "How does it look?" Menedemos asked.

"Not too bad," his cousin answered. "We'll show a tidy profit when we get home." Sostratos looked up from the beads. "Now that you've sold the last of the grown peafowl, do you plan on sailing back toward Rhodes?"

"Not yet, by Zeus," Menedemos answered. "Doesn't look like we'll be able to get to Syracuse, not with the Carthaginians pressing it so hard, but I was thinking of taking the *Aphrodite* up the western coast of Italy toward Neapolis. How often do the cities there get the chance to buy Khian wine and papyrus and ink and Koan silk? They should pay through the nose."

"Plenty of pirates in those waters," Sostratos observed.

"Plenty of pirates everywhere these days," Menedemos said. "We've been over this before." But Sostratos wasn't really arguing, not as he'd argued against stopping at Cape Tainaron. His tone was more that of a man pointing out the risks of doing business. Menedemos added, "Since we'll be sailing north once we pass between Italy and Sicily, maybe we'll find more of these redheaded women you like."

As he'd thought it would, that made his cousin splutter. "Don't talk to me of women, considering what you've been up to," Sostratos said. "We'd better be ready to sail at a moment's notice, in case Gylippos finds out for certain."

"We are," Menedemos said complacently, always pleased to be one step ahead. "I've let Diokles know, so he always has men ready to pull the crew out of the dives. They can't do so much drinking and wenching on a drakhma and a half a day as they could when they had back pay coming to them, either."

"True," Sostratos said. "Probably just as well, too. Men who rois- ter like that often die young."

"And men who don't roister like that also often die young, don't they?" Menedemos said with his most innocent smile. Sostratos gave him a sour look in return. Menedemos clapped his cousin on the back. "I'm going out for a while."

"Not to Gylippos', I hope," Sostratos exclaimed.

"No, no. I need to see a ropemaker. Diokles found some frayed lines on the ship, and I want to take care of that," Menedemos an- swered.

"He's a solid man, Diokles," Sostratos said. "He'd make a good captain, and I'd tell my father the same thing."

"We could do worse if we didn't have an owner aboard," Mene- demos agreed. He headed for the door. "See you later. I shouldn't be too long."

"All right," Sostratos replied in absent tones. He was already flick- ing beads up and down again. He paid as much attention to the counting board as he did to his precious books. When they engrossed him, Zeus might hurl a thunderbolt a cubit away without his noticing.

Amused at his cousin's foibles, Menedemos hurried off toward the ropemaker's shop. It lay close to the lagoon whose splendid harbor gave Taras its reason for being, not far from the shipsheds of the Tarentine navy—and not far from the *Aphrodite* herself.

And the haggle with the ropemaker turned out to be easier than Menedemos had expected. Cordage here cost only a little more than half as much as it did at Rhodes. The Tarentines made most of their rope from hemp rather than linen, but that didn't bother Menede- mos; the two were of comparable strength and weight. He left the shop well pleased with himself.

He was so well pleased with himself, in fact, that he didn't notice the four men following him quite so soon as he should have. They weren't doing anything in particular to keep him from noticing them. They came down the street after him shoulder to shoulder, and people walking in the other direction got out of their way in a hurry.

It was, in fact, a squawk of protest from one of those people that made Menedemos look back and spot the four bruisers. When they saw he'd seen them, they walked faster, closing the gap between themselves and him and making it plain he was their target.

Two of them wore knives on their belts. One carried a stick that would make an excellent bludgeon. The fourth had no immediately visible weapon, but that did little to reassure Menedemos.

I'm only a stadion or so from the house, and I ran the sprint almost well enough to go to Olympos, he thought. *If I can outrun them . . .*

He was about to flee when three other ruffians of similar sort came round a corner in front of him. One of them pointed his way. He'd been worried before. Now he was afraid. They weren't just toughs who'd chosen him at random, and might as easily have picked someone else. They wanted him in particular, which meant they were bound to want to do something especially dreadful to him in particular. What ran through his mind was, *Sostratos was right.* That bothered him almost as much as the ruffians did.

He took a couple of quick steps toward the three in front of him. But even as they opened their arms to grab him, he whirled and dashed back at the four behind, shouting at the top of his lungs. They shouted, too, in surprise—whatever they'd looked for him to do, that wasn't it.

One of them sprang at him. He dodged and kicked at the same time. The fellow went down with a groan. The tough with a stick swung. It struck Menedemos a stinging blow across the back, but then he was through and running like a man possessed back toward the harbor.

"After him, you fools!" one of the bruisers said. "Don't let him get away!" another added. Their sandals flapped on their feet as they began to run. Then one of them proved he had wit as well as brawn, for he shouted, "Stop, thief!"

Menedemos didn't stop. He did wiggle past a bystander who tried to stop him. His bare feet kicked up dust at every stride. He was glad sailing men seldom wore shoes even ashore—he'd always run races without them, and was convinced he ran faster that way. Now he wasn't running for his own pride or the glory of his polis. He was running for his life. His ankle screamed at him. He took no notice of it.

"Stop, thief!" That shout rose again behind him. But people did more staring than grabbing. Menedemos ran on, breath sobbing in his throat. He couldn't look back to tell whether his pursuers were gaining. A heartbeat's inattention and he might run into somebody or stick his foot into a hole in the ground and sprawl headlong. If he did, it would be the end of him.

There was the Little Sea, and there were the piers sticking out into the green-blue water of Taras' lagoon. A forest of masts sprouted from the ships tied up along those quays. Now Menedemos had to slow. Where was the *Aphrodite?* Right or left? If he went in the wrong direction, he would never get another chance to make a mistake.

There! The shipsheds farther east gave him his bearings. And most of the craft in the harbor were either little fishing boats or tubby roundships. Not many had the merchant galley's size and sleek lines. It lay only a couple of quays over to the left. Menedemos started running again—and just in time, too, for the footsteps behind him were getting closer fast. Now he was limping, but he kept going as best he could.

How many men would be aboard the akatos? Enough to keep off robbers, no doubt; Diokles was meticulous about such things. And they would be—Menedemos hoped they'd be—enough to stand off the ruffians on his tail.

Roustabouts and the usual sprinkling of quayside loafers pointed and called out as Menedemos raced past them. They pointed and called out again a moment later when his pursuers pounded after him. Gulls screeched and flapped into the air. Starlings let out metallic cries of alarm and flew off straight as arrows, their wings beating rapidly, the sunlight glistening from their iridescent feathers.

Menedemos' feet thudded on the planks of the pier that led out to the *Aphrodite*. He dashed down the gangplank and onto the poop deck. "By the gods, captain!" Diokles said. The oarmaster had been splicing a couple of lines. He and the double handful of sailors on the ship all gaped at Menedemos.

Gasping to get air back into his lungs, Menedemos pointed toward the ruffians advancing on the merchant galley. "Those whipworthy rogues set on me in the street," he panted, not mentioning the most likely reason why they'd set on him. "I broke through 'em and made it here."

"Oh, they did, did they?" Diokles got to his feet. He wore a knife on his belt. So did most of the other sailors aboard the *Aphrodite*. The ones who didn't were quick to grab belaying pins and other implements of mayhem. Diokles gave the local toughs a scowl that would have melted any of the akatos' rowers like beeswax in a fire. "Whatever you boys want, you'd better go find it somewhere else."

The ruffians stopped eight or ten cubits from the *Aphrodite*'s bow. They started arguing among themselves. "Well, to the crows with *him*!" one of them said loudly. "I didn't take this job to get my head broken. I took it to give the other guy some lumps. If he don't like it, he can go to Tartaros for all of me." He strode off.

A couple of the others turned toward the akatos. One of the sailors smacked the length of wood he was holding into the palm of his other hand. The sound seemed to make the toughs thoughtful. They put their heads together again. Two more walked away. That left four. Four were not enough to go up against the men on the *Aphrodite*. They left, too, looking back over their shoulders as they went.

"Somebody in Taras doesn't like you," Diokles remarked. Menedemos dipped his head. The oarmaster asked, "Any idea who?"

"I've got some ideas, but nothing I could prove," Menedemos said. Diokles grunted. Did he know? Some of the sailors who'd been at the house might have gossiped. For all Menedemos knew, the gossip might have got back to Gylippos. Or Gylippos might have drawn his own conclusions from Menedemos' limp, as Sostratos feared. It didn't really matter.

Now that he wasn't running any more, he had time to notice his ankle again. He wished he didn't. When he looked down at it, he saw how swollen it was. It felt as bad as it looked, too. *How did I run on it?* he wondered. But the answer to that was simple. You could do anything, as long as the alternative was worse.

Diokles asked, "You want a few of the boys to come along back to the house with you?"

"Now that you mention it, yes," Menedemos answered, and the oarmaster chuckled. Menedemos tried to laugh, too. It wasn't easy, not with the fire in his ankle—and his back hurt, too, where the ruffian had hit him with the stick.

He wished he had a stick of his own. On board ship, the sailors quickly found a length of wood that would do for one, at least long enough to let him get back to the rented house. He put as much weight as he could on it and as little as he could on his bad leg.

As he made his slow way up the pier, he managed a grin and said, "Look at me. I'm the last part of the answer to the Sphinx's riddle."

"Heh!" one of the sailors said. "That riddle's not so much. We see any of those scoundrels who set on you, skipper, we'll leave 'em on all fours even if they aren't babies." The other men with Menedemos dipped their heads. They all wore knives. They all had their right hands on their hilts—no, all but Didymos, who was lefthanded. He had a righthanded twin who was also a sailor, though not on the *Aphrodite*.

Menedemos saw none of the ruffians on the way back to the house where he and Sostratos were staying. Someone he didn't recognize was standing not far from the door when he and his escort came round the corner, but that fellow turned and walked off before Menedemos could find out what, if anything, he had in mind.

He brought the sailors in for a cup of wine. Sostratos, who was still muttering over the counting board, looked up in surprise. "What's all this in aid of?" he asked.

Trying to keep his tone light, Menedemos answered, "I had a little trouble coming back from the ropemaker's."

"Did you?" Sostratos raised an eyebrow, a characteristic gesture. He pointed to the sailors. "Looks as though you had more than a little."

"Well, maybe," Menedemos allowed. He told the story in a few bald words, leaving out any mention of either Gylippos or Phyllis.

"I'm glad you're all right," his cousin said when he finished. What Sostratos' eyes said was, *I told you so.* So he had, and he'd been right, too. That didn't make Menedemos any happier to be on the receiving end of his glare.

Menedemos took a cup of wine for himself, too, and mixed very little water with it. It didn't make his ankle feel much better—only time would do that—but it made *him* feel better. He gave the sailors a drakhma apiece (which made Sostratos mutter afresh) and sent them back to the *Aphrodite*.

Later, when he and Sostratos were both sitting in the house's cramped little andron, his cousin said, "You're lucky you're still breathing, you know."

"That thought did cross my mind, yes," Menedemos admitted.

"Then why did you do it?" Sostratos asked.

"Why did I do what? Run? Because I wanted to keep on breathing, that's why," Menedemos answered.

Sostratos let out an irritated snort. "Do you take me for a fool? You know perfectly well what I meant. Why did you go to Phyllis the second time? The first one doesn't count; you didn't know she wasn't a slave till afterwards."

"Thank you so much," Menedemos said. Sostratos snorted again, and glowered so fiercely that Menedemos felt he had to answer him. He did his best: "Why? Because I felt like it, and it was fun, and I thought I could get away with it."

"I'm sure you thought the same thing in Halikarnassos, too," Sostratos said. "How many lessons will you need before you realize that's a mistake? What will have to happen to you to get it through your head?"

"I don't know," Menedemos said sullenly. His father would have done a better job of raking him over the coals, but not much. Philodemos had a sharper temper—one closer to Menedemos'—but Sostratos sounded more self-righteous.

"One of these days, some husband will catch you in the act, and then . . ." Sostratos sliced a thumb across his throat. "Some would say you had it coming."

"If I'd already had it, if I were coming, he wouldn't catch me in the act." Menedemos managed a grin no matter how much his ankle hurt.

"You're impossible," Sostratos said, and Menedemos dipped his head, as if at a compliment. His cousin asked, "*Are* we ready to sail on short notice?"

That was a business question, whatever had spawned it. Menedemos dipped his head again. "Yes."

"Gods be praised," Sostratos said.

*   *   *

LAMAKHOS SMIRKED as Sostratos walked into his establishment. "Shall I find out if Maibia wants to see you?" he asked.

"Yes, if you'd be so kind." Sostratos did his best to ignore the brothelkeeper's scorn. Lamakhos gestured to a slave. She started back toward the Keltic girl's chamber. Sostratos called after her: "Tell Maibia we're sailing soon." The slave, an Italian, nodded to show she'd heard.

Lamakhos set his hands on his hips. "I wondered if you might want to buy her to take with you," he said; by *wondered* he doubtless meant *hoped*. "Plainly, you're more than fond of her. I could give you a good price."

"No, thank you." Sostratos tossed his head. "Taking her on board a merchant galley—that's just more trouble than it's worth."

"A bargain—" Lamakhos began.

Before he could launch into his sales pitch, the slave girl came back and told Menedemos, "She will see you." Her voice held faint contempt, too. Maibia was a slave in a brothel, but dictating terms to a free man. If that wasn't shameful, what was?

"Think about it," Lamakhos said as Sostratos hurried off toward the Kelt's room. "Maybe you could get your sailors to chip in if you don't want her for yourself. They could share her out on the sea."

"Bad for discipline," Sostratos said over his shoulder. The brothelkeeper, he thought, would make an excellent eunuch. If the fellow who did the cutting were to take his tongue, too . . .

He opened the door to Maibia's chamber. Such bloodthirsty thoughts flew from his head. She wore the tunic of Koan silk, in which she looked even more alluring than she did naked. "Is it true what Fabia told me, that you'll be leaving before long?" she asked.

"Yes, it's true." Sostratos closed the door behind him. "I'll miss you," he went on. "I'll miss you more than I thought I would."

"But not enough to be after taking me with you." Maibia sighed. Through the thin silk, the sigh was worth watching. "In spite of what you said and all, I did hope you might. I'd be good to you, Sostratos; you know I would."

She'd be good to him for as long as he kept her in the style she wanted, or until she found someone who'd keep her in higher style. He didn't blame her for wanting to escape from Lamakhos. Who wouldn't? But he tossed his head even so. "I'm sorry. I told you how things are. I didn't lie to you."

"Truth that," she said, and Sostratos felt the snugness one feels for playing the game by the rules and winning anyhow. Maibia promptly punctured it: "Sure and it is a truth, but not one that does me any good at all, at all. I'm still stuck here, still here to be stuck by any spalpeen with the silver to pay for it. And why should you be caring? You've had your fun."

How much did playing the game by the rules matter when those rules were stacked in your favor? She was only a woman, only a barbarian, only a slave; she had no business making him feel so guilty. But somehow she'd done it. "Here," he said roughly, and gave her his farewell gift: five heavy Tarentine tetradrakhms. "I hope this is better than nothing." He'd intended that for sarcasm; it come out sounding more like an apology.

Maibia took the silver coins and made them disappear. With luck, they'd disappear from Lamakhos, too. "Better nor nothing?" she said. "Sure and it is. What I'd hoped for?" She sighed and shook her head, then looked at him out of the corner of her eye. "And I suppose you'll be wanting it once more, for good-bye's sake?"

"Well . . ." Sostratos hadn't been able to keep his eyes from traveling along her sweetly curved body. *I could deny myself,* he thought. *That would make me feel virtuous.* Then he laughed at the absurdity of virtue in a brothel. And he *did* want her, virtue or no. He compromised with himself: "However you please. The silver is yours either way."

"What a strange man y'are, Sostratos," Maibia remarked. He couldn't tell whether that was meant for praise or curse. A moment later, she pulled the thin chiton off over her head, and he stopped caring one way or the other. "Why not?" she said as she stepped into his arms. "Better you nor plenty of others I can think of." Again, he wondered whether that was praise or something else. Again, he didn't worry about it for long.

He thought he pleased her when they lay down together. Afterwards, though, she started to cry. Awkwardly, he stroked her. "I'm sorry," he said. "I do have to go."

"I know," she wailed. "And I have to stay." Her tears splashed down on his bare shoulder. They felt hot as melted lead.

"There's no help for it," Sostratos said. "Maybe it will be better from now on. We've tried to do things so it would be." *Yes, I'm trying to salve my own conscience, too,* he thought.

"Maybe." But Maibia didn't sound as if she believed it, and Sostratos' conscience remained unsalved.

8

WITH THE COAST OF ITALY ON HIS RIGHT HAND, WITH THE *Aphrodite*'s steering oars firm in his grip, with the poop deck rolling gently beneath his bare feet, Menedemos felt at home once more. "By the gods, it's good to get back to sea."

"I suppose so." Sostratos didn't sound convinced.

"You've been sour ever since we left Taras yesterday morning." Menedemos eyed his cousin. "You're pining for that redhead girl. Foolish to get yourself in such an uproar over a slave."

"You're a fine one to speak of foolishness," Sostratos snapped: that had got his notice. "How's your ankle feeling these days?"

"It's doing pretty well," Menedemos answered blithely. "It hardly bothers me unless I turn just the wrong way." That exaggerated his improvement, but not by a great deal. He got in a jab of his own: "At least I never imagined I was in love with Phyllis."

"I wasn't in love with Maibia," Sostratos said. "She hoped I would be, but I wasn't. I'm not so silly as that."

"Well, what *is* your trouble, then? Was she *that* good in bed?"

"Never a dull moment—I will say that," his cousin replied. "I do feel bad about leaving her back there to take on all comers again."

"All comers, indeed," Menedemos said, and Sostratos gave him a dirty look. Trying to get Sostratos to show a little common sense, Menedemos went on, "Do you think she thinks *you* were all that wonderful?"

His cousin turned red. Stammering a little, he answered, "I—I like to think so, anyhow."

"Of course you do. But are you thinking straight? To a girl in a brothel, a man's just another man, a prick's just another prick." Menedemos leered at Sostratos. "Or are you another Ariphrades? *He* found a way to make the girls in the brothels happy with him." Grinning, he quoted from Aristophanes' *Wasps*:

" 'And so Ariphrades is the very cleverest fellow.
His father swore he learned from no one else,
But taught himself by his own wise nature
To work his tongue in the whorehouse, going in time after
time.' "

Sostratos looked revolted. "I wouldn't do anything like that,"
he said.

"I did hope not, best one," Menedemos said. "But if this girl was
really mooning over you, I wondered if you'd given her some strange
sort of reason." He quoted Aristophanes again, this time from the
Knights:

" 'Whoever isn't altogether disgusted with such a man
Will never drink from the same wine cup with us.' "

"Nor with me." Sostratos raised an eyebrow. "I read the historians,
and try to remember things they say that will help us when we trade.
You read Aristophanes, and what do you remember? The filthiest
parts, that's what."

"If you're going to read Aristophanes, that's the stuff worth remembering," Menedemos said. "And I read Homer, too, and there's
nothing filthy about him." He glared a challenge at Sostratos. His
cousin was so infected with radical modern ideas, he might even try
to argue about that.

But, to Menedemos' relief, Sostratos dipped his head. "Nothing
wrong with Homer."

"And nothing wrong with Aristophanes, either," Menedemos said
stoutly. "He's just different from the poet." Wherever Hellenes
lived—a vast stretch of ground indeed these days, after Alexander
opened the whole of the east—Homer was *the* poet.

"You're looking for a quarrel," Sostratos said. Menedemos didn't
deny it. If a quarrel would shake Sostratos out of his funk, Menedemos was ready to give him one. But his cousin just laughed. "I
don't really care to squabble today, if it's all the same to you."

"All right," Menedemos said. Whether Sostratos felt like squabbling or not, he sounded a little more like himself. And if he sounded
more like himself, he could be used: "Go forward and see how

the peafowl chicks are doing. They're still your babies, you know."

"*My* babies?" Sostratos exclaimed in moderately high dudgeon. "The peacock was welcome to his ladies, as far as I'm concerned. All I ever wanted to do with them was roast them, not screw them." Clicking his tongue between his teeth at the absurdity of the notion, he headed up toward the foredeck.

Menedemos chuckled a little, under his breath. Sostratos did seem a bit happier. And every heartbeat put Taras farther behind the *Aphrodite*. The longer Sostratos was away from Maibia, the more likely he was to stop brooding about her. Maybe he'd get himself another girl he enjoyed. That would help.

Sostratos had plenty of hands to help him now: a brisk breeze from the north meant the *Aphrodite* went by sail, with the rowers off their benches and free to chase chicks. Diokles pointed southwest and asked, "Do you aim to put in at Kroton, skipper?"

"I hadn't planned to," Menedemos answered. "It's a good-sized town, I suppose, but it's not a place where much ever happens." The keleustes raised an eyebrow, but said nothing. He knew his place; he wouldn't come right out and tell his captain he thought him wrong. But his expression was eloquent enough to make Menedemos pause and reflect. "Oh," he said. "You want to find out how the war is going before we try rounding Italy and heading up through the Sicilian Strait, don't you?"

"Might be a good idea." Diokles' voice was dry.

"Well, so it might," Menedemos admitted. "All right, we will put in at Kroton. Who knows? Maybe we'll sell something."

Kroton boasted the only real harbor between Taras and Rhegion— and to reach Rhegion, the *Aphrodite* would have to round the southwesternmost tip of Italy and start up into the strait. If the Syracusans or Carthaginians had ships in the neighborhood, that wouldn't be a healthy thing to do.

Menedemos worked the steering oars to change course to the southwest. At his command, the sailors swung the yard to take best advantage of the breeze on the new course. Had he not given the command, they might have done it on their own. They knew what wanted doing, and went about it without any fuss.

The harbor mouth faced northeast, so the men didn't even have to go to the oars to bring the *Aphrodite* into port. But the water inside the harbor remained choppy, for Kroton wasn't a town with all the latest improvements, and had built no moles to break the force of the sea. A lot of boats and even ships had simply been dragged up onto the beach, too, but Menedemos managed to find space at one of the piers.

"What do you hear from Sicily?" he called to a skinny fellow standing on the quay.

"Who're you, and what news have you got?" the Krotonite returned, his Doric accent much like that of Taras.

"We're out of Rhodes," Menedemos said. He gave his own name, and told of the deaths of Roxane and Alexandros, and of Polemaios' defection from Antigonos, his uncle. The local soaked up the news from the east like a sponge soaking up water. When Menedemos finished giving it, he repeated his own question: "What's the word from Sicily?"

"Well, the Carthaginians still have Syracuse harbor shut up pretty tight," the Krotonite answered. Menedemos dipped his head. He'd expected that; were it not true, he'd have seen more Syracusan ships in Taras. The dock lounger went on, "The barbarians have an army moving to lay siege to the place, too."

"Does it look like falling?" Menedemos asked anxiously; that would be a disaster.

With a shrug, the Krotonite said, "Who knows? They do say Agathokles pulled a fast one on his enemies in town, though."

"Ah?" Menedemos pricked up his ears. "Tell me."

"Rich folks in Syracuse never have fancied Agathokles," the local said. Menedemos dipped his head; he knew that. The Krotonite continued, "He said everybody who wasn't ready to stand siege and suffer should get out of town while the getting was good. Well, a lot of the folk who couldn't stand him upped and left—and as soon as they were gone, he sent a bunch of mercenaries after 'em and killed 'em all. Once they were dead, he confiscated their property and freed all their slaves who he reckoned could fight in his army."

Down in the waist of the *Aphrodite,* Sostratos let out a soft whistle. "That's one way to get your polis behind you."

"So it is," Menedemos said. "Not the way I'd choose, maybe, but one way. I'll tell you this: nobody who thinks Agathokles is wrong will dare open his mouth to say so, not for quite a while he won't."

"No," Sostratos agreed. "But then, no one would be much inclined to argue with him as long as the Carthaginians are outside the walls. No polis can afford factional strife with an enemy at the gates." His expression went bleak. "Of course, not being able to afford strife doesn't mean one can't have it. I can think of—"

The Krotonite cut short what would have turned into a historical lecture by pointing down toward Sostratos' feet and asking, "What's that funny-looking little bird there? Some kind of partridge? How much you want for it? I bet it'd be tasty, stewed up nice with leeks and cheese."

"It's a peafowl chick," Sostratos answered. "You can have it for a mina and a half." As the birds grew bigger, so did the asking price.

"A drakhma and a half, you say? That's not so. . . ." The Krotonite's voice trailed off as he realized what Sostratos had really said. His jaw dropped. His eyes bugged out. "You people are madder than Dionysos made Pentheus," he declared, and stalked off up the pier toward dry land with his nose in the air.

"I frightened him off," Sostratos said.

"Maybe, maybe not," Menedemos answered. "Look how he's talking to that other fellow and pointing back towards us. Word will get around. If there are any Krotonites with more money than sense, we'll do all right."

"Always some of those people," Sostratos said. "They just have to decide we're what they want."

To Menedemos' disappointment, no rich merchants or farmers came out to the *Aphrodite* before sunset. Only a few sailors went into town to drink themselves under the table or find the closest brothel. Most of the men had spent all their silver in the long stay at Taras, and seemed happy enough to stay close to the akatos: Sostratos came up onto the poop deck to spread out his himation. Catching Menedemos' eye, he glanced toward the jumble of buildings that made up Kroton and opened his mouth to speak.

Menedemos cut him off: "Don't even start. I don't know anyone's wife here, and I'm not trying to meet anyone's wife here, either."

"I didn't say a thing." Sostratos sounded innocent, but not quite innocent enough. He lay down on the himation, rolled himself up in it to hold mosquitoes at bay, and kept right on not saying a thing. Menedemos approved of that. He listened to his cousin start to snore.

After a little while, he stopped hearing Sostratos, which presumably meant he was doing some snoring of his own.

He jerked awake before sunrise when someone with a loud, harsh voice demanded, "Are those really peacock chicks you're selling?"

"Uh . . . yes," Menedemos said around a yawn. He untangled himself from his mantle and stood up, careless of his nakedness— Hellenes fretted much less about bare skin than most people. "Who are you?"

"I'm Hipparinos," the Krotonite answered, as if Menedemos ought to know who Hipparinos was. "Let me see these birds. If I like 'em, I'll buy a couple. A mina apiece, I hear you want."

"A mina and a half," Menedemos said. Hipparinos bellowed in outrage either real or faked as artfully as a fancy courtesan counterfeited the peak of pleasure. Menedemos went forward and got out a couple of chicks.

Hipparinos glared at them. "Those ugly little things really turn into peacocks? Why haven't you got any grown birds?"

"Yes, they turn into peacocks—or peahens," Menedemos said. "I haven't got any grown birds because I sold them all in Taras—and I got a lot more than a mina and a half apiece for them, too."

Hipparinos scowled. Menedemos would have been disappointed had he done anything else. He said, "Has anybody else in Kroton tried to buy these birds?"

"Indeed not, O best one," Menedemos replied. "And no one else will have the chance, for we intend to sail as soon as it gets light."

"I'll have the only ones, will I?" Hipparinos all but rubbed his hands in glee. He sounded much like Herennius Egnatius, but Menedemos would never have told him so: comparing him to a barbarian might have queered the deal. The Krotonite dipped his head in sudden decision. "I'll take two."

"At a mina and a half apiece?" Menedemos asked, to make sure there was no misunderstanding.

"At a mina and a half apiece," Hipparinos said. He took a leather sack from his belt and hefted it in his left hand. Menedemos went up the gangplank and onto the pier, a chick under each arm. Hipparinos gestured. A man—probably a slave—came up with a wickerwork basket in which to take the birds away. Before Menedemos could call anyone from the *Aphrodite*, Sostratos came of his own accord. Having equal sides went a long way toward keeping anything unfortunate from happening.

When Menedemos took the sack, it felt as if it weighed about three minai. He chuckled under his breath; Hipparinos had heard what his price was, sure enough. Menedemos handed the sack to Sostratos. "Count this quickly—you're good with numbers."

"As you say." His cousin made piles of silver coins on the pitch-smeared planks of the wharf. He did count money faster than Menedemos could. After a very brief time, he looked up and said, "Six drakhmai short. You can see for yourself." Sure enough, the last pile held only two didrakhms.

Hipparinos laughed. "Are you going to quarrel over six little coins?"

Menedemos had met this sort of small-time chiseler more often than he could count. He dipped his head. "As a matter of fact, yes. We agreed on a price. If you want the birds, you have to pay it."

Muttering under his breath, the Krotonite came up with the missing drakhmai. Menedemos was altogether unsurprised to find him able to. Down the pier Hipparinos went, the slave following him with the basket. In a low voice, Sostratos said, "I hope they both turn out to be peahens."

"That would be nice," Menedemos agreed. "Have you got the money back in the sack? The sooner we leave, the happier I'll be."

As THE APHRODITE came round Cape Herakleion, the southernmost bit of land in Italy, Sostratos exclaimed in astonishment and pointed west. "Is that really Mount Aitne, across all this distance?" he asked.

"Nothing else but," Menedemos answered, as if he were responsible for putting the volcano there and making it visible long before the rest of Sicily came into sight.

"How far from the mountain are we?" Sostratos wondered.

"I don't know." Menedemos sounded impatient. Where Sostratos found such details fascinating, they meant little to him. He made what was obviously a guess: "Five hundred stadia, maybe more."

"Ah," Sostratos said, in lieu of exclaiming again. "If we were coming from the southeast, where no land would block the view till the last moment, we could see it from much farther away, couldn't we?"

"I suppose so," Menedemos answered indifferently. "That would stand to reason, wouldn't it?"

"Of course it would," Sostratos said. "If we knew just how tall the mountain was and from exactly how far away we could see it, we could reckon up the size of the world."

His cousin shrugged. "So what?"

"Don't you care about knowing things for the sake of knowing them?" Sostratos demanded. He and Menedemos had had this argument a good many times before. He knew about how it would go, just as he knew about what Menedemos would try when they wrestled in the gymnasion. In the gymnasion, Menedemos almost always threw him despite that. When they wrestled with ideas, he had a better chance.

Sure enough, Menedemos said, "If knowing something will get me money or get me laid, I care about that. Otherwise . . ." He shrugged again.

Before Sostratos could tear him limb from rhetorical limb, one of the sailors at the bow yelped and made as if to kick the peafowl chick that had just pecked his ankle. *"Oimoi!"* Sostratos shouted. "Don't do that, Teleutas! You hurt that bird, it'll cost you just about all the wages you make on this cruise."

"Fine the stinking bird for hurting me, then," Teleutas said sulkily. "I'm bleeding."

"You'll live," Sostratos said. "Bind some cloth around it if it's really hurt. I doubt it is. I've had the grown birds get me more times than I care to remember, and the chicks don't peck anywhere near so hard." More sulkily still, Teleutas went back to whatever he'd been doing before he was wounded.

My, I sounded heartless, Sostratos thought, listening in his mind to the brief conversation. As Menedemos had, he shrugged. Rowers were easy to come by and cost a drakhma and a half a day. The peafowl chick, on the other hand, would bring in a mina and a half of silver, maybe even two minai.

It had other uses, too. One of the sailors near Teleutas said, "Look— it just ate a scorpion. That would have hurt you worse than the bird did." Teleutas grunted. But he didn't try to kick the chick again.

Sostratos thought about returning to the argument with Menedemos. In the end, he decided not to bother. He made his way up to the foredeck instead, and peered out past the forepost at Mount Aitne. It was blue with distance and pale near the summit, where snow still clung despite the season. No smoke rose from it; no stones and molten rock belched from it, as had happened many times in the past. Sostratos would not have cared to live in the shadow of a mountain that might let loose catastrophe without so much as a warning.

He made his way back to the poop, where Menedemos was turning the *Aphrodite*'s course from southwest to due west to approach the Strait of Sicily. Instead of resuming the argument the peafowl chick had interrupted, Sostratos asked, "Do you really think Polyphemos the Cyclops lived on the slopes of Aitne?"

That question interested Menedemos, even if it didn't involve money or girls. Sostratos had thought it would; his cousin truly cherished Homer. Menedemos answered, "It could well be so, I suppose. People have always put Skylle and Kharybdis in the Sicilian strait, so the Cyclops would have been somewhere nearby."

"But do you think people *ought* to put the monsters from the *Odyssey* in the real world?" Sostratos persisted. "No one but Odysseus and his comrades ever saw them."

"Egypt is in the real world, and Odysseus went there, or says he did," Menedemos said stoutly. "Ithake is in the real world, and you know he went there."

"But he doesn't talk about monsters in Egypt or Ithake," Sostratos said. "I think you'll find out where he saw the monsters when you find the cobbler who sewed up his sack of winds."

"I'd like to," Menedemos answered. "If I could pull out a south wind when we sent up the Strait, things'd be easier. As is, we'll have to row."

"Tomorrow," Sostratos said, eyeing the sun as it slid down toward Mount Aitne.

"More likely the day after, or even a day or two after that," Menedemos said. "I intend to put in at Rhegion, too, on the Italian side of the Strait. We may get rid of a couple of baby peafowl there."

Getting rid of peafowl chicks appealed to Sostratos, so he dipped his head. Sunset found the *Aphrodite* off Cape Leukopetra, which marked the Italian side of the entrance to the Sicilian Strait: the white stones of the bluffs just above the sea had given the cape its name. Menedemos chose to spend the night at sea, and neither Sostratos nor anyone else chose to argue with him, for beaching the akatos

here would invite every bandit for tens of stadia around to swoop
down on her.

After the anchors splashed into the sea, the sailors had hard barley-
flour rolls as sitos, with salted olives and crumbly cheese for their
opson. They washed supper down with cheap wine Sostratos had
bought in Taras. On dry land, he would have turned up his nose at
the stuff. Salt air and a gently rolling ship somehow improved it.

Diokles spat an olive pit over the rail and into the sea. "I don't
think the wind will shift," he said.

"Neither do I," Menedemos answered. "If we were in an ordinary
merchantman, we'd do a lot of waiting and a lot of tacking. As things
are . . . well, this is why we pay the rowers."

The men at the oars grumbled a little the next morning; they'd
had an easy time of it since leaving Taras, for the wind had been
with them all the way. But Diokles' mallet and bronze square gave
them the rhythm they needed. Menedemos set only ten men on each
side to rowing: no point in wearing out the crew. The *Aphrodite*
glided into Rhegion's harbor well before noon.

Because Menedemos intended to spend the day in the city, Sostratos went into the agora to let people know the merchant galley
had come and to tell them what his cousin and he had for sale.
Several men headed for the piers to buy chicks or wine or silk or
perfume or some of the other goods the akatos had brought from
the east.

And, being who he was, Sostratos also indulged his own curiosity.
"Tell me," he said to a potter who looked reasonably bright, "why
does this city have the name it does?"

"Well, stranger, I've heard a couple of stories about that, and I
have to tell you I don't know which one's true myself."

"Go on," Sostratos said eagerly. "I'm always glad to meet someone
who'll admit he doesn't know everything."

"Heh," the potter said. "I bet you it doesn't happen any too often,
either." That made Sostratos laugh out loud. The local went on,
"Anyway, one tale is that the name comes from the word that means
to break, because we have a lot of earthquakes in these parts, and
because it looks like Sicily broke off from Italy."

"That makes sense," Sostratos said; *Rhegion* could easily be derived from *rhegnumi*. "Aiskhylos says something similar, doesn't he?" he remarked. Without waiting for an answer, he continued, "What's the other story?"

"Some people say the name comes from one Italian language or another, because *regium* or some such word means *royal* in those tongues," the potter replied.

"Which do you think is true?" Sostratos asked.

"I'd sooner believe we Hellenes named the place ourselves than that we borrowed a word from the barbarians," the potter said. "I'd sooner believe that, mind you, but I can't prove it."

"Fair enough," Sostratos said. "Better than fair enough, in fact." He went off, hoping he would remember that when the day finally came for him to write his history.

That day wouldn't come if he didn't get back to letting the people of Rhegion know the *Aphrodite* had peafowl chicks for sale. *Of course it won't,* Sostratos thought: *Menedemos will kill me if I don't do my job.*

He went back to the merchant galley late in the afternoon. If the folk of Rhegion didn't know about the peafowl by then, it wasn't because he hadn't told them. "Any luck?" he called to Menedemos as he walked up the pier.

"I sold two," Menedemos answered. "Sold 'em to two different men, too, and it was almost like they were bidding against each other to see who could show what a rich fellow he was by paying more. I got close to five minai: you might have thought they each had to have the very last bird."

"That's splendid." Sostratos clapped his hands. "We sold two birds for the price of three, more or less, or earned a couple of extra days' wages for the whole crew."

"Tempts me to lay over here for one more day," his cousin said. "Maybe Rhegion holds some more rich fools—I mean, customers."

"Well, why not?" Sostratos said. "We can afford it now. And even if we only sell at the regular price, we still come out ahead."

"That's true." Menedemos dipped his head. "All right, then. I'll do it."

Sostratos went into the market square at first light the next morning. Not only did he talk about the *Aphrodite*'s cargo, he called, "Men of Rhegion, two of your fellows have already bought peafowl chicks. Do you want them to be the only ones in this polis lucky enough to own these beautiful birds?"

Men rich enough to buy peafowl chicks might not come to the agora themselves, but their slaves surely would. And he'd found that making people jealous of their neighbors was one of the best ways to get them to part with their silver.

After plucking at his beard in thought, he added, "We also have fine perfume made from Rhodian roses. How many women in Rhegion want to make themselves smell sweet for their husbands?" *How many want to make themselves smell sweet for somebody else's husband?* went through his mind, too, as it surely wouldn't have done had his cousin had a different nature.

Again, women who might buy Rhodian perfume for themselves— whether respectable matrons or rich hetairai—didn't frequent the agora, but their slaves did. Sostratos pitched that call to the slave women there. He smiled to himself when a couple of them hurried out of the market square. For good measure, he put some extra emphasis on the Koan silk, too.

He returned to the merchant galley at sunset, as he had the day before. "How did we do?" he called to Menedemos as he walked down the gangplank into the ship.

"Didn't sell any more birds." But Menedemos seemed happy enough, and explained why a moment later: "We had a run on silk and perfume, though. One fancy hetaira came herself, veiled up like a rich man's wife. When she took off her veil to haggle . . ." His eyes went big and wide. "Aphrodite, she was gorgeous! If she'd given me some of what she had under her chiton, I'd've let her have the perfume for free."

"I believe *that*," Sostratos said tartly. "I also believe I'd have let you explain to your father how it came to be that we ended up not having this perfume and not getting any money for it."

His cousin's expression changed to one of horror. "You're a nasty fellow, do you know that?"

"Thank you," Sostratos said, which did nothing to improve Menedemos' temper.

They left Rhegion the next morning. Sostratos expected Menedemos to go up the Italian coast, but his cousin chose to cross the Strait of Sicily to Messene instead. "Why not?" Menedemos said when Sostratos shot him a curious look. "We did well in Rhegion. No reason we can't do it there as well."

"No, I suppose not," Sostratos said, but then he added, "so long as the war in Sicily hasn't come that far north."

"We would have heard in Rhegion," Menedemos replied, which was probably true. He couldn't resist a gibe: "You always fuss."

"If you'd listened to my fussing back in Taras, your ankle would be better off," Sostratos retorted, and Menedemos mimed taking a wound.

From his usual station in the bow, Aristeidas pointed to starboard and called, "Something funny there." A moment later, he found a word for it: "Whirlpool!"

A few sailors exclaimed in alarm. More who weren't rowing hurried to the rail to get a look for themselves. Diokles said, "You get 'em in these waters now and again. It's the current, I expect. Most of 'em don't amount to anything much."

"They can pull a ship down to the bottom of the sea in less time than it takes to tell," a young rower quavered.

"Sure, a big one can," the oarmaster said. "But that one there? Don't be silly. It's not much more than you get when you mix water and wine in the jug called a dinos." That eased the sailors' worries and made several of them smile; the very name of the vessel meant *spinner*. Sostratos admired Diokles' quick wits.

After Menedemos saw that it wouldn't alarm the men, he began reciting from the twelfth book of the *Odyssey*:

" 'We sailed up the strait, lamenting.
    For there was Skylle, and on the other side divine Kharybdis,
    A wondrous thing, swallowed the water of the salt sea.
    I assure you, when she vomited it forth, she made it boil
    And stirred it up as if in a metal pot on a great fire.
    The foam fell on the high crags to either side.
    But when she gulped down the water of the salt sea
    Every place where she troubled came into view: echoing rock
    Appeared, a marvel, and the dark sandy earth—and green
    fear seized them.' "

The nervous young sailor pointed toward the whirlpool and asked, "Skipper, d'you think that's the real Kharybdis?"

Before Menedemos could speak, Sostratos did: "If it is, she's been washed in hot water once too often, because she's shrunk." That got a laugh from the men, and drew a grin and a wave from Menedemos. Sostratos mentally patted himself on the back for coming up with the right thing to say at the right time rather than two days too late. He prided himself on such moments, and wished they happened more often.

The *Aphrodite* passed within a couple of plethra of the whirlpool. Had it not been for Aristeidas' sharp eyes, nobody would have known it was there. An hour or so later, the merchant galley glided into the little sickle-shaped bay on whose south side the town of Messene sat.

Once the ship lay alongside a pier, Sostratos mentioned the whirlpool to one of the longshoremen who was making a rope fast. The fellow dipped his head. "You're lucky you came away with your lives," he said. "There's plenty of ships been sucked down to the bottom prow-first. They wash up, all broken to pieces, on the shore south of here."

Some of the sailors looked worried again. Sostratos said, "Sounds to me like a story to frighten strangers." The longshoreman gave him a sour stare. He concluded he was right.

As happened at any port around the Inner Sea, a small crowd of curious men gathered on the wharf by the *Aphrodite*. Menedemos began extolling the goods the akatos had brought to Messene. He also threw in tidbits of news from out of the east. In turn, the Messenians told him what they knew of the war raging farther south on the Sicilian coast. Unfortunately, they knew no more than the folk of Rhegion had.

Sostratos asked, "What will you do here if the Carthaginians do take Syracuse?"

That produced an unhappy silence in the crowd. At last, a skinny, gray-haired man said, "Hope they'll let us pay tribute and not put in a garrison."

"Not me!" a younger man said. "If it looks like the Carthaginians are going to take over all of Sicily, I'm getting out of here. I'm not taking any chances with those whoresons, not me. You know what happens when they sack a city?" He gave a melodramatic shudder.

Without a doubt, the Carthaginians did dreadful things when they took a city. So did Hellenes. Sostratos thought of what Alexander had done to Tyre not long after he was born. That story had been circulating for a generation now, and hadn't shrunk in the telling. Sostratos did a little discreet shuddering himself. Like every other Rhodian, he hoped none of Alexander's surviving generals would cast a covetous eye toward his polis.

As Hellenes had a way of doing, the Messenians standing on the pier divided into factions and started arguing with one another. Before long, they were paying hardly any attention to the *Aphrodite*: their own quarrel seemed more entertaining. Sostratos nudged Menedemos. "Why don't you run out the gangplank? I'll go into the agora and see if I can drum up some business."

"Good idea," his cousin said.

By the time Sostratos got up onto the pier, the locals were shouting insults at one another. A couple of them had hands on knife hilts, though nobody'd yet drawn a weapon. But with the shouts of "Traitor!" and "Liar!" flying back and forth, how long before someone did? Sostratos carefully picked his way around the edge of the crowd and headed up the pier toward dry land.

He hadn't been on that dry land more than a few heartbeats before he realized he'd have trouble finding the agora. Hippodamos and his ideas had never come to Messene. Streets and alleys and lanes didn't run in straight lines or intersect at right angles. They did exactly as they pleased, curving and twisting and doubling back on themselves. Had Sostratos gone out of sight of the harbor, he would have been lost in moments.

He was glad he figured that out before it happened. "How do I get to the agora?" he asked a man in a grimy chiton leading a donkey festooned with very plain clay pots.

The man didn't say anything. He just stopped in the middle of the street—incidentally blocking Sostratos' path—and waited. Sostratos wiggled his tongue to dislodge one of the oboloi he'd stashed between the inside of his cheek and his lower teeth. "Thanks, pal," the fellow with the donkey said as Sostratos handed him the wet, gleaming little coin. "What you do is, you . . ."

Sostratos made him go through it twice, then repeated the directions back to make sure he had them straight. "Is that right?" he asked when he was done.

"Sure is, pal," the Messenian said, and then added the words so often fatal to a stranger's hopes: "You can't miss it." Sostratos felt like spitting into his bosom to avert the omen. But that would have offended the local, who guided his donkey over by the mud-brick front of a house so Sostratos could squeeze past.

"Second right, third left, first right," Sostratos muttered, and, for a marvel, found the market square. He wondered if he could get back to the harbor again, and looked back into the alley from which he'd just emerged. "First left, third right, second left," he said, and then repeated it a couple of times so it would stick in his memory.

"Hail, stranger!" somebody called from behind a basket filled with dried chickpeas. "Where are you from, and what are you selling?"

Having sung his song in Rhegion the day before, Sostratos started singing it again. He traded news with the Messenians, though, as on the pier, they gave him none he hadn't already heard. Here, even more than in Rhegion and much more than in Taras, the people, while interested in what was going on in the east and in the struggles among Alexander's marshals, had other, more immediate, things on their minds. "D'you suppose there's a chance this Ptolemaios or Antigonos'd come west and put paid to the gods-detested Carthaginians once for all?" asked a fellow selling fried squid.

"I doubt it," Sostratos answered honestly. Everyone's face fell. He wished he'd been more diplomatic. Menedemos surely would have been.

A middle-aged man in a chiton of very fine, very soft wool came up to him and said, "Did I hear you say your ship had perfume on board?"

"You certainly did, perfume from the finest Rhodian roses." Sostratos studied the Messenian. The man had a sleek, prosperous look: just the sort of fellow to keep a mistress with expensive tastes. "If you like, you can tell your hetaira it came straight from Aphrodite. You don't have to say that's the name of my ship."

By the way the local started, Sostratos knew he'd made a good guess. "You're a clever chap, aren't you?" the Messenian said. "How much are you asking for this precious perfume?"

"For that, you need to go back to the harbor and talk to my

cousin," Sostratos replied. "Menedemos is much more clever than I am." He didn't really think so, not when it came to most things, but Menedemos was at least as good a bargainer. And Sostratos had an ulterior motive: "Maybe she'd like a peafowl chick, too, or maybe you'd like to buy one for your own house to keep your wife happy even if you do give your hetaira a nice present."

The Messenian rubbed his chin, which was shaved very smooth: another sign of wealth, and also of fastidiousness. "You *are* clever," he said. "You look young to be married, so how do you know such things?"

"No, I'm not married," Sostratos agreed, "but I'm not wrong, either, am I?"

"No, though I wish you were. A peafowl chick, eh? That *would* keep Nossis quiet for a while."

Of course it will, Sostratos thought. *Before long, the bird will make more noise, and worse, than even the most shrewish wife.* He kept that to himself; the Messenian would find out soon enough if he bought. All Sostratos did say was, "Well, there you are, then," as if it were settled. By the way the Messenian strode out of the agora and off in the direction of the harbor, maybe it was.

Sostratos went right on extolling the goods aboard the *Aphrodite* till the sun sank toward the hills in back of Messene. Then he headed back toward the merchant galley. Trying to find his way through a strange polis in the dark was the last thing he wanted to do. He remembered the turns the fellow in the ragged chiton had given him, and didn't get lost in a maze Minos might have envied.

There was the harbor, the wine-dark sea beyond dotted with fishing boats, almost all of them making for port now. There was the akatos, big and lean enough to frighten a fisherman out of his wits. And there, waving as Sostratos came down the pier toward the ship, was Menedemos. Sostratos waved back and asked, "How did it go?"

"Better than I expected," his cousin answered. "Sold a peafowl chick and some perfume and some Koan silk, all to a smooth fellow who wasn't too smooth to cough up more silver than he might have."

"If he's the man I think he is, he bought the perfume for a hetaira and the chick for his wife." Sostratos grinned. "I wonder who gets the silk."

"Not my worry—he can sort that out himself," Menedemos said.

"I also sold some papyrus and ink to a skinny little man who told me he aimed to write an epic poem on the war between Syracuse and Carthage."

"Good luck to him," Sostratos said. "If the barbarians win and head north toward Messene here, he won't have much leisure for his hexameters. And if Agathokles somehow manages to beat back the Carthaginians, well, Syracuse isn't shy about throwing its weight around, either."

"True." Menedemos dipped his head. "But I can't think of anything much Agathokles could do. Can you?"

"No," Sostratos admitted. "Still, when Xerxes invaded Hellas, I don't suppose he thought the Hellenes could do anything against him, either."

"That's also true enough," Menedemos replied. "Just the same, I'm not sorry we'll be sailing north, and away from that war. Trying to fight off a four or a five with our little akatos is a losing bet." He spat into his bosom to avert the omen. Since Sostratos agreed completely, he did the same.

CAPE PELORIAS, ABOVE Messene, marked the northeasternmost point of Sicily. With it falling astern and to port of the *Aphrodite,* Menedemos gave all his attention to the Tyrrhenian Sea ahead. Just because he'd escaped the war between Syracuse and Carthage didn't mean he or his ship was home free. He probably wouldn't fall foul of great war galleys here. But the Tyrrhenian Sea, not least because no great naval power lay anywhere near, swarmed with pirates.

"Keep your eye peeled," he called to the lynx-eyed Aristeidas at the bow. "Sing out if you spy any sail or mast." The sailor waved to show he understood. Menedemos turned to Sostratos, who was doing lookout duty at the stern. "The same goes for you."

"I know," his cousin said in injured tones.

"Well, see that you remember," Menedemos said. "Don't let your wits go wandering, the way you . . . do when you start thinking about history." He'd started to say, *The way you did when the peahen jumped into the sea,* but checked himself. If he hadn't thrown that in Sostratos' face when it happened, doing so now hardly seemed fair. By the sour look his cousin sent him, Sostratos had a pretty good notion of what he hadn't said.

To starboard, the Italian coast baked brown under the summer sun. Menedemos wore a broad-brimmed hat to help keep himself from baking likewise. Even so, sweat ran down his face. More sweat trickled down his torso, and down his arms to leave wet, dark patches where he gripped the steering-oar tillers.

He steered the *Aphrodite* farther out to sea, till the coastline receded to a brown blur low on the horizon. That would make him harder to spot. Some of the fishing boats bobbing in the chop between the merchant galley and the shore didn't notice him: his sail was brailed up tight against the yard as the galley traveled north under oars. *If I were a pirate and I wanted you, you'd be mine,* he thought. A few boats did spot the *Aphrodite* and got away from what they thought to be danger as fast as they could.

He was swinging northeast toward the harbor of Hipponion—not a splendid anchorage, but the best he could hope to find—when Aristeidas called out, "Sail ho! Sail ho to port!"

Shading his eyes against the late-afternoon sun, Menedemos peered out to sea. With more and more sailors pointing, he soon spotted the sail. It was of a good size, which warned him it might belong to a pirate. And it was of a color somewhere between sky blue and sea green, which argued that the captain of the ship to whom it belonged did not much want it seen.

"I'll show him, the son of a whore," Menedemos muttered to himself. He raised his voice to a shout: "All hands, grab your weapons and then to your oars!" As soon as the rowers had swords and knives and clubs ready to hand, he swung the *Aphrodite* toward the strange ship and told Diokles, "Up the stroke."

"Right you are, skipper," the keleustes replied. "You going to try and run him off, the way you did with that pirate back in the Aegean?"

"That's just what I'm going to do," Menedemos said. "And if he wants a fight, well, by the gods, we'll give him one."

Before long, he could see the pirate's hull as well as his sail. That the sail always came into sight before the hull made some people think the world was round. Menedemos had his doubts about that. If it were round, wouldn't all the water run off? He'd never found an answer to satisfy him there.

The question didn't worry him for long. Taking the measure of the enemy was much more urgent. "He's a pentekonter!" Sostratos called from the waist.

Menedemos dipped his head. "I see," he answered. The pirate had fifty rowers, then, to his own forty, and a hull shark-long and wolf-lean. The other ship sliced through the water like a knife. Menedemos saw at once that it had a better turn of speed than the *Aphrodite.*

But does he have the stones for a fight? Menedemos was betting his ship, his cargo, his freedom, his life, that the pirate didn't. Most sea raiders wanted nothing more than to rob victims who couldn't resist. What was better than profit without risk? If this pirate turned out to be an exception, though, he might end up naked and chained in a slave market in Carthage . . . or down at the bottom of the sea, with little crabs crawling in through the eyeholes of his skull to feast on whatever they could find inside.

Over in the pirate ship, men shouted and shook their fists at the oncoming *Aphrodite.* Some of the shouts were in Greek, others in one local language or another. The *Aphrodite*'s sailors shouted curses and obscenities in return. A naked pirate stood up on his bench and flapped his private parts at the *Aphrodite*'s crew, as if he were a man in the agora making himself disgusting to the slave women and poor farmers' wives who came there to shop and gossip.

"I've seen bigger pricks on a mouse!" Diokles yelled, not missing a stroke with mallet and bronze. The exhibitionist pirate sat down abruptly; he must have understood enough Greek for that shaft to strike home.

And then all the *Aphrodite*'s crew erupted in cheers: just out of bowshot, the pirate ship heeled hard to starboard as it turned away from the merchant galley. It headed north in a hurry, the sail coming up to lie against the yard. "Ease back on the men," Menedemos told Diokles. "Not a chance we'll be able to catch 'em. We saw that back in the Aegean, too."

"Right again," the oarmaster said. "The way he's running, you'd think he had a five on his tail."

"The way he's running, a five wouldn't catch him, either," Menedemos said. "A hemiolia might, or a trireme. But a five's too beamy and heavy and slow, just like us." He shook his fist at the receding pentekonter.

"I'd like to see everybody aboard there nailed to a cross," Diokles said. "Come to that, I'd like to see every pirate everywhere nailed to a cross."

"So would I, but I don't think it's going to happen," Menedemos answered. "For one thing, you'd run out of trees before you made enough crosses to put all the pirates on."

The oarmaster grunted and spat into the sea. "Heh. That'd be funny if only it was funny, you know what I mean?"

"Don't I just?" Menedemos raised his voice to call out to all the rowers: "Well done, men! We scared off another vulture. Now—portside back oars, starboard side forward." Almost in her own length, the *Aphrodite* spun to port. When her bow pointed back toward Hipponion, Menedemos took half the rowers from each side off the oars and headed toward the harbor, now a few stadia more distant than it had been when Aristeidas first spotted the pentekonter.

"Never a dull moment," Sostratos said, mounting the steps that led up from the waist to the poop deck.

"Did you expect there would be?" Menedemos asked. "If you wanted things dull, you should have stayed back in Rhodes."

"They're liable not to be dull even there," Sostratos said. "Who knows what the Macedonians are up to while we're out here in the west?"

"You're right," Menedemos said after a moment. "I could wish you were wrong, but you're right."

"I hope the generals aren't doing anything," his cousin said. "If they are doing something, I hope they're doing it to one another, not to Rhodes. But when you live in a polis in an age full of marshals, you can't help worrying."

"No, you can't." Menedemos thought about coming back to a Rhodes garrisoned by Antigonos' soldiers, or Ptolemaios'. He imagined mercenaries swaggering through the streets, with rich families hostages for the good behavior of the city as a whole. His own family was far from poor. Not for the first time, he wished Sostratos hadn't made him think so much.

Looking ahead to the Italian coastline bathed in the rays of the setting sun helped him not think about what might be happening far away to the east. Maybe Sostratos was doing his best not to think about that, too, for he pointed toward the shore and said, "It's greener by the town than it is most other places."

"Some people say Persephone used to come over there from Sicily to gather flowers," Menedemos answered. "I don't know whether that's true or not, but the girls from Hipponion go out to those meadows and make themselves flower garlands for festivals and such."

"How do you know that?" Sostratos asked. "You've never been here before."

"Tavern talk," Menedemos told him. "You miss a lot of things like that, because you don't like sitting around and chatting with sailors."

"I don't like going through a talent's weight of talk for half an obolos' worth of something interesting," Sostratos said tartly.

"But you never know ahead of time what will turn out to be interesting," Menedemos said.

Sostratos tossed his head. "No. You never know if anything will turn out to be interesting. Usually, nothing is. Most tavern talk is people lying about fish they say they caught and men they say they killed and women they say they had. I don't know how Persephone's name ever came up in a tavern, unless you were drinking with Hades."

That jerked a laugh from Menedemos. "I wasn't talking about Persephone, exactly. I was talking about Hipponion, and what the anchorage is like." He pointed ahead. "It's nothing much, is it?"

"No." Sostratos tossed his head again. "You almost wonder why anyone ever decided to build a polis here."

"You do. You really do," Menedemos agreed. "No proper bay to shelter a ship—just a long, straight stretch of coastline. The Hipponians haven't done anything to improve what they found here, either, have they? No mole to protect ships from waves and weather, hardly any quays. If Odysseus *did* sail up this way, he'd still feel right at home nowadays."

"If Odysseus *did* sail up this way, he did it in a pentekonter," Sostratos said. "Most of the Danaans who sailed to Troy went in pentekonters, if the Catalogue of Ships is right. To the Trojans, they were probably nothing but the biggest pirate fleet in the world."

Menedemos stared at his cousin. "Do you know something?" he said at last. "I care for Homer more than you do, I think."

"I'm sure you're right," Sostratos said. "He's a great poet, but he's not the man I turn to first."

"I know that," Menedemos said. "Still and all, though, you just made me look at the *Iliad* in a way I never did before. Who would have thought of trying to see things from the Trojans' point of view?"

He kept right on marveling as Diokles brought the *Aphrodite* to a stop not far offshore and the anchors at the bow splashed into the deep-blue water of the Tyrrhenian Sea. When Priamos and Hektor peered out from the windswept walls of Troy, how did they look at Agamemnon and Menelaos and Akhilleus and Odysseus? As a pack of gods-detested bandits who all deserved to be crucified? Menedemos wouldn't have been a bit surprised.

Sostratos might have been thinking along with him. He said, "I wonder how the *Iliad* would sound if Troy hadn't fallen."

"Different," Menedemos said, and they both laughed. Menedemos went on, "I'm sure it's better the way it really is." The effort holding that other perspective too quickly became too much for him. Sostratos didn't disagree. *When morning comes,* Menedemos thought as he stretched himself out on the poop deck, *my mind will work the way a proper Hellene's ought to again.*

WHEN MORNING CAME, Sostratos' mind was still buzzing with the notion he and Menedemos had had the night before. "When Alexander invaded Persia," he said, "Dareios probably thought the Macedonians were a horde of barbarians, too. And from what I've seen of Macedonians since, he probably had a point."

To his disappointment, Menedemos didn't feel like exploring the idea any further. "The Persians had it coming to them," was all he said.

Sostratos dipped a barley roll into olive oil. "I suppose you'll say the Trojans had it coming to them, too," he said, and took a bite.

"Well, of course they did," Menedemos answered with his mouth full; his breakfast was the same as Sostratos'.

"Why is that, O best one?" Sostratos asked with honey-sweet venom. "Because Paris ran off with Menelaos' wife?"

"Why else?" Menedemos answered. Then he must have realized Sostratos hadn't been talking only about the Trojan War. Sostratos enjoyed the dirty look his cousin gave him. "Funny," Menedemos said. "Very funny. If I see Gylippos in a fast pentekonter, then I'll start to worry."

"When we're going back toward Rhodes, do you plan on putting in at Taras?" Sostratos asked.

Menedemos gave him another dirty look. Sostratos didn't enjoy this one nearly so much, because his cousin looked harried, too. "Don't ask me things like that right now," Menedemos said. "It depends on how much we've still got to get rid of by the time we're heading back from Neapolis. I suppose it also depends on just how angry with me Gylippos really is."

"How many toughs did he send after you?" Sostratos asked. "Nine?"

"Only seven," Menedemos told him.

"Excuse me," Sostratos said. "I do like to have the details straight. I would say that sending even seven toughs after you is a pretty good sign you won't be welcome in Taras again any time soon."

"I'd have to be careful in Taras, no doubt," Menedemos said . . . carefully. "No way to tell yet if things will be as bad there as they are in Halikarnassos. I hope they won't."

"They'd better not be," Sostratos said. "I'm not sure you could bring a ship into the harbor at Halikarnassos without getting it burned to the waterline—which is a shame, because the family's done a lot of business there over the years."

Menedemos walked over to the rail, hiked up his tunic, and pissed into the Tyrrhenian Sea. Looking back over his shoulder, he answered, "Believe me, I've had this conversation with my father a good many times."

Then why didn't you listen to him? Sostratos wondered. *Why didn't you try to look at things from the point of view of the man whose wife you were enjoying?* He knew the answer well enough. *Because when your lance stood, that was all you cared about.* Some men were naturally bestial, and needed no Kirke to turn them into swine. But Menedemos wasn't really like that. He *could* think, and think quite well. Sometimes, though, he didn't bother.

He did handle the *Aphrodite* with his usual competence, sending her north up the coast. "No good anchorage tonight," he told the crew. "No proper harbor, I mean. Plenty of beaches, but do you really want to risk putting her ashore?"

Almost as one man, the sailors tossed their heads. Italy was a populous land, swarming with Samnites and other barbarians. Nobody was eager to give robbers a chance to swoop down on the ship.

"Sensible fellows," Menedemos said. Sostratos wondered what he would have said had the sailors wanted to beach the *Aphrodite*. Something interesting and memorable: of that Sostratos had no doubt. As things were, his cousin continued, "Since we don't have to hurry to make a port tonight, we're going to spend some more time pretending we're a war galley."

That didn't produce unanimous agreement from the crew. Sostratos hadn't thought it would. Practicing naval maneuvers was hard work, much harder than just sailing the akatos north would have been. And, of course, there was no guarantee the sailors would need what they were practicing. If they didn't, they would have put in all that effort for nothing.

Of course, if they didn't practice and ended up needing to fight, that would carry its own penalty, too: a penalty worse than blistered hands and weary backs. Sostratos could see that as plainly as he could look down and see his feet on the deck. He wondered why it wasn't obvious to everyone.

But the grumbling wasn't too bad. Before long, the *Aphrodite* zigged first one way, then the other. She spun in her own length, moving much faster than she had when turning back toward Hipponion after the pentekonter sheered off. "Starboard oars—*in*!" Diokles shouted, and the rowers on that side of the ship pulled their oars inboard at the same time.

The oarmaster glanced at Menedemos, who grinned back at him. "I've seen triremes where they didn't do it so smoothly," Menedemos said. Sostratos dipped his head.

"Same here." Diokles turned back to the rowers. "Resume!" The starboard oars went back into the water in the same unison with which they'd left it. The keleustes let the men row for a few strokes, then shouted, "Portside oars—*in*!" This time, the maneuver proved less successful; a couple of oars came in slower than they might have.

"That's not so good." Sostratos and Menedemos spoke together.

"I know it isn't." The oarmaster sounded angry and chagrined. When he yelled, "Resume!" this time, he didn't try to hide that annoyance. He went right on at an irate bellow: "Now listen to me, you worthless lugs—if we ever need that command, we'll need it *bad*. If you're late, it's your arms that'll get wrenched out of their shoulder sockets. We're going to keep working on this till we get it right— *right*, do you hear me?"

All the portside rowers were, of course, looking straight back toward the keleustes on the poop deck. Like Epimetheus in the myth, rowers had a perfect view of where they'd been and none of where they were going. Sostratos eyed their sweaty faces more openly than he could have most of the time, because they were paying him no attention at all, but were listening to Diokles' tirade. Most of them, especially the ones who'd been slow, looked embarrassed and angry— not at the oarmaster, but at themselves for failing him.

To Menedemos, Sostratos murmured, "If I talked to them like that, they'd throw me over the side."

"They'd do the same to me," his cousin answered. "They'll obey me; sure enough, but a skipper shouldn't scream at his sailors. That's what makes mutinies happen: they think you're a gods-detested whoreson. But they respect a tough keleustes—the fellow in that job's *supposed* to have a hide thick as leather."

Sostratos pondered that. Menedemos had the knack for getting men to do what he wanted because they liked him. Diokles was ready to outroar anyone who presumed to stand against him. *And what about me?* Sostratos wondered. Neither of those ways seemed open to him. When people did what he wanted, it was because he'd persuaded them that that was the right thing to do under the circumstances. Such persuasion had its uses, but not, he feared, in emergencies.

Again and again, Diokles shouted, "Portside oars—*in!*" After a while, Sostratos thought the rowers had the maneuver down cold, but the keleustes kept drilling them. When at last he relented, it was with a growled warning: "We'll do it again tomorrow, too. We're talking about saving your necks, remember."

At sunset, the anchors splashed into the sea. The *Aphrodite* bobbed in light chop, well off the Italian coast. Even if a storm blew up, the ship had plenty of leeway—and galleys were far less vulnerable to being driven ashore by hostile wind and wave than were ships that relied on sails alone.

The evening meal was about as frugal as breakfast had been. Sostratos ate bread and oil and olives and cheese. Menedemos bit into an onion pungent enough to make Sostratos' eyes water from three cubits away. He washed it down with a sip of wine. Catching Sostratos' eye, he said, "It's not what we got at Gylippos' supper, but it fills the belly."

"What you got at Gylippos' supper was trouble," Sostratos replied. "How's your ankle today?"

He'd meant that as a gibe, but Menedemos answered seriously: "Standing at the steering oars all day long doesn't do it any good, but it's healing. It would be worse if I had to run around a lot."

"You did that back in Taras," Sostratos pointed out.

"Yes, O most beloved cousin of mine," Menedemos said, so poisonously that Sostratos decided he'd pushed things about as far as he could go.

On the second evening out from Hipponion, the *Aphrodite* reached the town of Laos, which lay at the mouth of a river of the same name. Laos' harbor was rather better than that of Hipponion, and the merchant galley tied up at one of the piers. Hardly any of the longshoremen and loafers spoke more than a few words of Greek: they talked among themselves in one Italic language or another.

Across the pier was a sailing ship from Rhegion. Her skipper, a tubby, gray-haired fellow who gave his name as Leptines, ambled by to look over the *Aphrodite*. "I envy you your oars," he said. "I've been crawling up the coast—crawling, I tell you—tacking all the way. I'll be a month getting to Neapolis, maybe more. How am I supposed to make ends meet if I can't get from here to there?"

Sostratos poured him some of the same wine he was drinking himself and asked, "Why didn't you sail south, to take advantage of the winds?"

"I usually do." Leptines gulped the wine. "Ahh, that's good. I usually do, like I said, but not this year. Too big a chance of somebody's navy snapping me up if I went along the Sicilian coast."

Sostratos dipped his head. The *Aphrodite* hadn't tried sailing down to Syracuse, either. Menedemos gave Leptines an engaging smile. "Any special ports we should know about on the way up the coast?"

Leptines didn't directly answer that. Instead, he returned a question for a question: "What are you carrying?"

"Peafowl chicks and perfume, papyrus and ink, fine Khian wine, Koan silk, perfumes—things like that," Menedemos replied. "How about you?"

"Wool and timber and wheat and leather," Leptines said. "I should've known a merchant galley from out of the east would only come here for the luxury trade. If we were competing, I wouldn't give you the hour of the day, but you won't do my business any harm even if you will get up north ahead of me."

"Well, then?" Menedemos asked in his most ingratiating voice. Sostratos hoped his winecup hid his own snicker. His cousin sounded as if he were trying to talk a girl into bed. Had he sounded that way with Phyllis? Sostratos wouldn't have been surprised.

His tone certainly worked on Leptines. "There's one place by the coast south of Neapolis where there's more to it than you'd think," the trader from Rhegion said, "provided you don't mind doing business with Samnites, that is."

Menedemos glanced at Sostratos. Sostratos shrugged. Menedemos said, "When we were in Taras, we sold our peacock to a Samnite. He paid what he said he would. I'd do it again."

"What is this town?" Sostratos asked.

"It's on the Sarnos River," Leptines answered. "You can go a ways farther up the river, too, if you're really feeling bold. But this place I have in mind does duty as the port town for Nole and Noukeria and Akherrhai, too. Those places are all fat, fat, fat—some of the richest farming country in the world in those parts."

"Sounds promising," Sostratos agreed. "But you still haven't told us the name of this place."

Leptines snapped his fingers in annoyance at himself. "You're right, I haven't. It's called Pompaia."

"I never heard of it," Sostratos said. "What about you, Menedemos? You know more about Italy than I do."

"I think the name sounds familiar," Menedemos said. "I've never been there, though, and I don't know anyone who has."

Leptines tapped his own chest with a forefinger. "You do now. I'm telling you, the place is worth a visit. And the Pompaians are mad for anything from Hellas, too. They've got a Doric-style temple there that's kind of old-fashioned nowadays, but you wouldn't be surprised to see it in a real polis even so."

Sostratos eyed Menedemos. "What do you think?" Such decisions, in the end, were up to his cousin.

"I don't know." Menedemos rubbed his chin. Bristles rasped under his fingers; with the *Aphrodite* at sea the past two days, he'd had no chance to shave. "I hadn't planned to put in there; I was just thinking of heading on up to Neapolis."

"Don't listen to me, then—it'll be your loss," Leptines said. "I'm telling you, with the farms they've got up there, the rich men make a nice pile of silver. They'd be able to afford whatever you've got, and a lot of them speak Greek."

"That's good," Sostratos said. "We certainly don't speak Oscan, or whatever language they use there."

"Oscan, sure enough," Leptines said. "No, you wouldn't need to, not coming out from Rhodes the way you do. I've learned some over the years. It comes in handy now and again, if you do a deal of trading in Italian waters."

"Yes, I can see that it would," Sostratos agreed, and looked toward Menedemos again.

His cousin rubbed his chin once more. Then he reached out to Leptines. "Let me have your cup." He poured it full, and refilled his and Sostratos' as well. Then he raised his in salute. "To Pompaia!"

"To Pompaia!" Sostratos and Leptines echoed. Sostratos drank. Menedemos had watered the wine only a very little.

Leptines noticed that, too: the trader from Rhegion appreciatively smacked his lips. "Glad to help my fellow Hellenes," he said, "especially when I don't have to hurt myself to do it. If you boys were carrying wheat and wood, too, you couldn't pull the name out of me if you gave me to a Carthaginian torturer."

"Back in Rhodes, we'd speak of a Persian torturer," Sostratos said.

"All boils down to the same thing." Leptines tipped his head and his cup back. "Obliged to you boys for your hospitality. If you hang around in Pompaia for a bit, you'll eventually see me there. How much do you pay your rowers, anyway?"

"A drakhma and a half a day," Sostratos answered.

Leptines made a horrible face. "And you've got what, twenty-five rowers on a side?"

"Twenty."

"Even so. That's a lot of silver to have to lay out every day." Leptines chuckled. "I think about having to spend money like that and all of a sudden I stop caring so much that I don't get places in a hurry. Hail." He went back to his own ship.

"He's a piker," Menedemos said, but in a low voice so the other skipper wouldn't overhear. "He worries about money going out, but he doesn't think about how to bring lots of money in." He grinned. "All the better for us."

"I should say so," Sostratos answered. "And if this Pompaia place is even half as rich as he makes it out to be, we ought to do well for ourselves there."

"Worth a try," Menedemos said. "I don't expect it to reward us the way Aphrodite rewarded Paris, but worth a try."

"What would we do with Helen if we had her?" Sostratos pointed at Menedemos. "I know what *you'd* do, you satyr. But that's not profitable. Wouldn't you rather be rewarded as Kroisos the Lydian king rewarded Solon of Athens? He let Solon into his treasury to carry out as much gold as he could hold, and Solon went in wearing baggy boots and a tunic too big for him and even greased his hair with olive oil so gold dust would stick to it."

Menedemos laughed. "No, I wouldn't mind that. But I don't mind women, either. Why can't I want everything at once?"

"You can want everything at once," Sostratos said. "But you can't be too disappointed when you don't get it. How many men do?"

"Some must," Menedemos insisted.

"Some, maybe, but only a handful," Sostratos said. "When Kroisos asked Solon who the happiest man in the world was, he thought Solon would name him. But Solon picked Athenians who'd lived long and died well. Kroisos was offended, but Solon turned out to be right in the end, for the Lydian king first lost his son in a hunting accident and then lost his kingdom to the Persians. Was he happy at the last? Not likely."

"But he had plenty of good times before that last," his cousin said.

Sostratos sighed. "You're incorrigible." Menedemos gave him half a bow, as if at a compliment. Sostratos sighed again.

9

ON THE SECOND DAY AFTER LEAVING LAOS, THE *APHRODITE*
sailed between the island of Kapreai and the Cape of the Sirennousai.
As Menedemos swung the merchant galley east toward Pompaia, he
pointed to an old, tumbledown temple on the headland of the cape
and remarked, "They say Odysseus built that place. And they say
some of the rocky islands off Kapreai are the ones where the Sirens
lived."

"They say all sorts of strange things," Sostratos answered. "Do you
believe them?"

"I don't know," Menedemos said. "I truly don't. There was the
whirlpool off Messene, right where Skylle was supposed to be."

"Yes, there was the whirlpool," his cousin said, "but where was
the horrible monster sucking in the water to make it? Did you see
her? Has anyone since Odysseus heard the Sirens singing on those
rocks off Kapreai?"

"I don't know any of that, either," Menedemos said, a little testily.
"But if anyone did hear the Sirens singing, they'd lure him to his
doom, so how could he come back and say what he heard?" He
smiled a smug smile.

But Sostratos wouldn't let him get away with it. "Odysseus figured
out a way to do it. With Homer known wherever Hellenes live, don't
you suppose some other bold fellow would have put wax in his sailors' ears so he could listen to the song the hero heard?"

"Maybe." Menedemos gave Sostratos a sour look. "Sometimes
when you take things to pieces, you take all the fun out of them."

"No." Sostratos tossed his head in emphatic disagreement. "Taking things to pieces *is* the fun. If you leave them sitting there the way
they were when you found them, what have you learned? Nothing."

"Why do you have to learn something all the time?" Menedemos
asked. "Why can't something be interesting just because it is what it is?"

"If everyone thought that way, we'd still be sailing pentekonters and swinging bronze swords, the way the men of the *Iliad* and *Odyssey* did," Sostratos said.

"How do you know that's what they did?" Menedemos said. "You call the *Odyssey* nonsense when it suits you, so why do you choose to believe that?"

Sostratos opened his mouth, then closed it again. When at last he did speak, it was in thoughtful tones: "Do you know, I never once wondered about it. The strange pieces are those that seem the hardest to believe, not the homely little details of the heroes' world. We know pentekonters and bronze—we don't know Sirens and Skylle."

"Well, then, you believe what you want to believe and I'll believe what I want to believe, and we'll both be happy," Menedemos said. Sostratos did not look happy about that, but Menedemos didn't worry about it. He'd distracted his cousin, which served almost as well as convincing him, especially since he could cut the conversation short right after that by adding, "I believe we're just about to Pompaia, and I'm going to pay attention to that."

He had to pay more attention to it than he'd expected, for Pompaia lay not on the coast of the Tyrrhenian Sea, as Leptines had led him to believe, but a few stadia up the Sarnos River, on the northern side of the stream. Soldiers—presumably Samnites—peered down at him from the wall as his rowers guided the *Aphrodite* into place at one of the piers thrusting out into the stream.

As a couple of locals tied the akatos to it quay, Sostratos pointed north. "Look. That mountain there in back of the town has a good deal of the look of Aitne to it, doesn't it? It's not nearly so tall, of course, but it's got the same conical shape."

"So it does," said Menedemos, who, up to that moment, had had no chance to worry about the mountain.

"I wonder if it's a volcano, too," Sostratos said. "What did Leptines say its name was?"

"I don't think he did." Menedemos raised his voice to call out to one of the roustabouts: "Hey! Do you speak Greek?"

"Me?" The fellow pointed to himself. "Yes, I speak some. What do you want?"

"What's the name of that mountain north of your city here?"

"You must be from far away," the roustabout said, "not to know about Mount Ouesouion."

"Ouesouion?" Menedemos echoed, trying to imitate the local's pronunciation. "What an ugly name," he murmured in an aside to Sostratos, who dipped his head in agreement. Menedemos gave his attention back to the Pompaian: "We *are* from far away—we've sailed all the way from Rhodes."

"Rhodes?" The roustabout had almost as much trouble with the name as Menedemos had with *Ouesouion*. "Where's that at? Is it down by Taras, where so many of you Hellenes live?"

"It's farther away than that," Menedemos answered. "You have to cross the Ionian Sea to go from Taras to the mainland of Hellas, and then you have to cross the Aegean Sea to go from the mainland of Hellas to Rhodes."

"Do tell," the Pompaian said. "I went over to Neapolis once, I did. Had to walk two days to get there and two days back." Menedemos carefully held his face straight. Then he wondered how many people here had never gone two days' journey from their little town, if this fellow thought doing so was worth bragging about. The roustabout went on, "So what did you bring us from this Rhodes place, wherever it's at?"

Now Menedemos did smile, and launched into his sales pitch: "Fine wine from Khios, fine silk from Kos—"

"What's silk?" the local asked. "I don't know that word."

"It's a fabric, smoother and softer than linen," Menedemos answered. "And we have perfumes from Rhodian roses, and papyrus and ink"—*not that we're likely to sell any of those here,* he thought—"and . . . peafowl."

"What are peafowl?" the Pompaian said. "Don't know that word, neither."

"Sostratos . . ." Menedemos said, and Sostratos displayed one of the chicks. Menedemos gave a highly colored description of what an adult peacock looked like, ending, "It were not too much to call him the most magnificent bird in the world."

To his surprise, the roustabout burst into raucous laughter. "Tell me another one," he said. "You're going to sell us those ugly birds for half the money in the world, and they'll stay ugly, and you'll be gone. Do you think we're that stupid?"

Oh, a pestilence, Menedemos thought. *We've sailed so far, we've come to a place where the people have no idea what a peacock is like.*

How are we supposed to sell the chicks if no one believes they'll grow up to be beautiful? He hadn't thought of that when he decided to stop at Pompaia.

As Sostratos put the chick back into the cage, he said, "The rich folk here will know what peacocks are, I think. And even if they don't, the Hellenes up at Neapolis will."

"I hope so," Menedemos said. "We'll find out when we go into the market square, I expect."

"Silk and wine will sell," Sostratos said. "Silk and wine will sell anywhere."

"That's true." Remembering that it was true made Menedemos feel a little better. With a small sigh, he said, "I suppose we can sell leftover chicks back in Rhodes, too, but we'll get more for them here in the west—if we can get anything at all for them, that is."

"Shall we go find out?" his cousin asked.

Before answering, Menedemos gauged the sun. It was sliding down toward the western horizon, but would still be a while getting there. "Why not?" he said. "We'll do some business today, I expect, and we'll let word get around tonight."

When he and Sostratos entered Pompaia, they didn't go in alone. They made a procession of it. Menedemos led, his hands free. "Peafowl chicks!" he called in Greek. "Rare wines from Khios! Fine silk from Kos!" Sostratos carried a cage with several chicks in it. Behind them strode sailors with bolts of silk in their hands, and others hauling amphorai of Ariousian between them on carrying poles.

The procession would have been more impressive if Menedemos hadn't had to pause a couple of times to ask passersby how to get to the agora. Not everyone spoke Greek, either, which made things more complicated. Even though the blank housefronts and narrow, winding, smelly streets put him in mind of a polis that had never heard of Hippodamos and his grid, he was acutely aware of having come to a foreign part of the world.

Sostratos noticed something he hadn't: "Look! Some of the signs over the shops must be in Oscan, because that certainly isn't Greek."

"You're right," Menedemos said after a moment. "I hadn't paid much attention to them."

"I hadn't either, not at first," Sostratos said. "A lot of the poleis here in Great Hellas still use old-fashioned alphabets with characters you'd never see in Athens, for instance, but even when I can figure out what all the letters are supposed to sound like, the words they spell out don't make any sense."

"I suppose they do if you're a Pompaian," Menedemos said. "I didn't even know the Samnites could write Oscan. Looks like they can, though."

"So it does," Sostratos agreed. "I wonder if the Romans, up farther north still, have an alphabet of *their* own."

Menedemos looked back over his shoulder at his cousin. "There are times, O marvelous one, when you find the least important things in the world to worry about."

Sostratos chuckled. " 'O marvelous one,' is it? You sound like Sokrates when he's being sarcastically polite to some poor fool. And I wasn't worried. I was just—"

"Curious," Menedemos broke in. "You always are. But before you start learning to write history in Oscan, remember that we're here to sell things first."

"I know that." Sostratos sounded angry. "Have I ever disrupted anything because I'm interested in history?"

"Well, no." Menedemos admitted what he couldn't deny.

"Then kindly leave me alone about it." Sostratos still seemed hot enough to fire a pot.

Menedemos might have given him a hot answer, too, but they finally came out into Pompaia's agora, and he started crying his wares instead. Not far from the agora stood the temple Leptines had mentioned, its columns and walls cut from the rather dark local stone and the decorative elements brightly painted, just as they would have been in a Hellenic polis.

"Hardly seems like barbarian work," one of the sailors said.

"I was thinking the same thing," Menedemos answered. "The architect was probably a Hellene." Then he raised his voice again: "Perfume from Rhodes! Silk from Kos! Fine Ariousian, the best in the world, from Khios! Peafowl chicks!" He turned to Sostratos. "I wish you did know some Oscan. Then more of these people would be able to understand."

His cousin pointed. "I think we'll do all right." Sure enough, Pompaians were converging on the men from the *Aphrodite*.

One of them, a plump, prosperous-looking fellow in a toga—a

garment Menedemos found very strange and not very attractive—surprised him by going over to the cage with the peafowl chicks and addressing Sostratos in good Greek: "Are these the young of the big, shiny bird with the crest and the incredible tail?"

"Why, yes," Sostratos replied. "How do you know of peafowl? I didn't expect anyone here in Pompaia would."

"As it happens, Herennius Egnatius brought his through the town day before yesterday, on the way up to his home in Caudium," the man said. "Everyone who saw the male was amazed. He said he bought it from a couple of Hellenes in Taras. And so, when I saw you . . ."

"At your service, then," Sostratos said. "I would be lying, though, if I told you I knew which chicks would become peacocks and which peahens." Here in Pompaia, Menedemos might have told that lie. He didn't expect to be back any time soon to be called on it. But Sostratos had forestalled him, so now he had to make the best of it.

The Pompaian didn't seem displeased. "Life is full of gambles, is it not?" he said. "If I bought two of these little birds, I should have a reasonable chance of getting at least one peacock, eh? What is your price?"

Menedemos spoke before Sostratos could: "Two Tarentine minai apiece."

With a cough, the man in the toga said, "That is a lot of silver."

"It's a lot less than Herennius Egnatius paid for his birds," Sostratos put in.

"Which does not make what I said any less true," the Pompaian replied. "Half your price might strike me as reasonable."

"Half my price strikes me as unprofitable," Menedemos said. The Pompaian smiled. He might be a barbarian in a peculiar garment, but he knew the start of a dicker when he heard one.

And it turned out to be quite a quick dicker, too, for he wanted to buy as much as Menedemos wanted to sell. They didn't take long to settle on one mina, sixty drakhmai for each bird. The local spoke a couple of crackling sentences of Oscan to the retainers who stood near him, then returned to Greek: "I shall go to my house to get the money. And when I return, I may have a thing or two to say about your wine, as well."

Menedemos bowed, "Just as you say, O best one. Would you care to talk about the price now, so you'll know how much silver to bring back here to the market square?"

The Pompaian plucked at his graying beard. "Do you know, that is not a bad notion. You Hellenes have a knack for picking smooth ways to do things. How much will you try to steal from me?"

"Sixty drakhmai the amphora," Menedemos said calmly.

"What?" Now the local dug a finger in his ear, as if to make sure he'd heard right. He spoke in Oscan, presumably translating the price. His retainers all made horrified noises. *Not a bad ploy,* Menedemos thought. The Pompaian went back to Greek again: "You Hellenes say your gods drink something called nectar, is it not so? Have you got nectar inside those jars?"

With a smile, Menedemos said, "You are closer than you think. Any Khian wine is among the best that comes from Hellas, and Ariousian is to common Khian as common Khian is to ordinary wine. It's so sweet and thick and golden, you almost hate to mix it with water."

"As far as I am concerned, you Hellenes are daft for mixing wine with water in the first place." The Pompaian folded his arms across his chest. "I shall not pay even a khalkos, though, before I taste this wine for myself. Peafowl are hard to come by. Wine, now—wine is easy."

At Menedemos' dip of the head, one of the sailors unsealed an amphora. At the same time, one of the Pompaian's men borrowed a cup from a local wineseller. Menedemos poured some of the precious Ariousian into it and handed it to the local. "Here you are. See for yourself."

The Pompaian stuck his forefinger into the cup and flicked out a drop or two onto the dusty ground of the market square to do duty for a libation. He muttered something in Oscan, presumably a prayer to whatever god the Samnites worshiped in place of Dionysos. Then he sniffed the wine, and then, slowly and deliberately, he drank.

He made a good game try at not showing how impressed he was, but his eyebrows rose in spite of himself. After smacking his lips, he said, "Sixty drakhmai is too much, but I can see how you had the nerve to ask for it. I might give you sixty for two amphorai."

Now Menedemos tossed his head. "Again, there'd be no profit in it for me at that price, not when you reckon in the effort it took me to bring the wine from Khios all the way to Pompaia." Sincerity filled his voice, as sweetness filled the Ariousian. He wasn't even lying.

Maybe the local sensed as much. Or maybe he just had more silver than things he could readily buy in Pompaia, for, as with the peafowl chicks, he didn't seem to haggle so hard as he might have. Before long, he said, "All right, then, I'll give you a mina for the two jars."

"Fifty drakhmai the amphora?" Menedemos said, and the Pompaian nodded. Menedemos dipped his head. "A bargain." They clasped hands to seal it. Menedemos asked Sostratos, "How much does our friend owe us altogether?"

"Four minai, twenty drakhmai," Sostratos said at once, as if he had a counting board in front of him. Menedemos could have figured it out, too, but not nearly so fast.

"Four minai, twenty drakhmai," the Pompaian repeated. "I shall bring it. You wait here." Off he swept, retainers in his wake. When he returned, he brought back silver coined in most of the poleis of Great Hellas, as well as coins from Italian towns. Menedemos and Sostratos had to pay a jeweler three oboloi for the use of his scale.

Sostratos, as usual, did the weighing and calculating. When he dipped his head, Menedemos gave the Pompaian the birds and the wine. The local went off, seeming well pleased with himself. In a low voice, Menedemos asked, "How much extra did we make?"

"By weight, you mean?" his cousin answered. "A few drakhmai."

"It all adds up," Menedemos said happily, and Sostratos dipped his head once more.

THE NEXT MORNING found Sostratos spending one of those extra drakhmai on the hire of a mule in the market square and Menedemos loudly dismayed about it. "Why do you want to go riding around?" he demanded. "Somebody will knock you over the head, that's what'll happen."

"I doubt it," Sostratos said.

"I don't," his cousin snapped. "I ought to send a bodyguard out with you, is what I ought to do. You're a hopeless dub with a sword or a spear."

"You know that, and I know that, but these Italians don't know it," Sostratos answered. "All they'll see is a big man, one they'd think twice about bothering. And I want to look around a little. Who can guess when the *Aphrodite* will come back to Pompaia again, if she ever does?"

"All right. All right!" Menedemos threw his hands in the air. "You're more stubborn than that mule. Go on, then. Just remember, I'll be the one who has to explain to your father why I didn't bring you back to Rhodes in one piece."

"You worry too much," Sostratos said, and then started to laugh. "And do you know what else? You sound the way I usually do when I'm trying to keep you out of some madcap scrape. See how it feels to be on the other side?"

His cousin still looked unhappy, but stopped arguing. Menedemos even gave him a leg up so he could mount the mule. Once Sostratos swung aboard the beast—which gave him a resentful stare—his feet almost brushed the ground: he was indeed a large man on a smallish beast. And he did have a sword belted on his hip; he wasn't such a fool as to wander weaponless.

"Sell some more chicks," he told Menedemos. "I'll be back this afternoon."

"Why anyone would want to go wandering around a countryside full of half-wild Italians is beyond me," Menedemos said. "It's not like you've got a pretty girl waiting for you, or anything else worth doing. By the gods, you're just going around for the sake of going around, and where's the sense in that?"

"Herodotos did it." To Sostratos, that was answer enough—more than answer enough, in fact. His cousin just rolled his eyes.

Sostratos booted the mule into motion. It brayed resentfully, but then started to walk. Its motion put Sostratos a little in mind of that of the *Aphrodite,* though here he was feeling it through his backside rather than the soles of his feet. He picked his way toward the north gate through Pompaia's reeking alleys: he wanted a closer look at Mount Ouesouion. The *Aphrodite* probably wouldn't go back to Sicily and the environs of Mount Aitne, so this was his best—probably his only—chance to see a volcano.

He had to ask his way to the gate only once, and got lucky when he did: the first man to whom he put the question not only understood Greek but gave directions that proved detailed and accurate. The Pompaian didn't even ask for an obolos before answering. *Proves he's a barbarian—any Hellene would have,* Sostratos thought.

Once out of town, Sostratos guided the mule in the direction of the mountain. Farms and vineyards filled the rolling countryside. Leptines hadn't exaggerated: the land looked finer and broader than any Sostratos had seen in cramped, rocky Hellas, though the coastal lowlands of Asia Minor might have matched it.

The grainfields weren't planted, not in the heat of summer. When the fall rains came, the farmers would put in their wheat and barley, as they did in Hellas, to be harvested in the spring. But the vines were growing nicely. Sostratos had liked some of the Italian wines he'd drunk. He hadn't found any worth taking back to Hellas with him, but they weren't bad.

A fellow trimming vines not far from the road waved to him. Sostratos lifted a hand in return. The farmer no doubt took him for another Italian. His tunic and broad-brimmed hat were nothing out of the ordinary. He stroked his chin. Had he been clean-shaven like Menedemos, everyone would have known him for a Hellene at once: the fashion for scraping one's cheeks smooth hadn't yet reached the Samnites. He was less likely to find trouble if people didn't take him for a foreigner.

He rode past a couple of grave markers. One of the stelai had writing on it, in the odd-looking local alphabet. Sostratos wondered what the words meant. People were working in the fields a couple of plethra away, but he didn't call to them. Farmers were unlikely either to understand Greek or to be able to read their own tongue.

When he came to a roadside boulder convenient for remounting, he slid off the mule and tied it to a nearby sapling. Then he squatted, not to ease himself but to scoop up some dirt in the palm of his hand. The soil was grayish brown and crumbly; it had almost the look of ashes to it. His eyes went to the slopes of Ouesouion. What was more likely than that a burning mountain should scatter ashes far and wide?

Sostratos sniffed at the dirt, tasted of it. He was a trader, not a farmer, but, like most Hellenes, he knew something about judging soils. If this dirt wasn't rich with brimstone, he would have been astonished. No wonder the grapevines grew so exuberantly.

He led the mule over to the rock and climbed aboard it once more. It let out an amazingly human-sounding sigh, as if to say it had hoped its work was done for the day. But, being a reasonably good-natured beast, it consented to walk on with no more complaint than that.

After a while, Sostratos halted again, this time under the shade of a gray-branched, gray-green-leaved olive tree. The mule nibbled at grass that grew in little patchy clumps in the shade while Sostratos ate barley bread and sheep's-milk cheese and drank from a little jar of some local wine or another. He thought about sleeping for a while in the heat of the day, but tossed his head. Menedemos would say that was asking for trouble, and he'd very likely be right.

And so Sostratos mounted the mule once again—awkwardly this time, because he had no rock handy to give himself a boost, but he managed. The mule protested much more loudly and vehemently than it had before: it was convinced he was extorting an unfair amount of work from it. He had to whack its haunch with the flat of his hand to make it get going again.

He looked back toward the gray stone walls of Pompaia. He had no trouble spotting the town; he'd been riding mostly uphill, so it hadn't vanished behind higher ground. But he was surprised at how many stadia the mule, dismayed braying and all, had managed to cover. A glance at the sun showed noon already gone.

"Time to head back," he told the mule, and turned it toward the Sarnos River once more. It seemed no happier about going downhill than it had about going up-, and almost bucked him off over its head when an ocellated lizard as long as his arm dashed across the road in front of it.

"Hold still, you stupid, gods-detested thing!" Sostratos cried, hanging on to the mule's bristly mane for dear life till he got an arm around its neck. "It's not even a snake. It couldn't hurt you if it bit you." He didn't think the beast believed him.

Some time later, when he was a good deal nearer to Pompaia and the farms clustered more closely together, a large gray-and-white dog of a breed he'd never seen before advanced on the mule from a field. By the dog's fierce, stiff-legged gait and by the way it bared long, sharp teeth, Sostratos wouldn't have been the least surprised to learn it was half wolf.

As it came nearer and snarled again and again, he drew the sword that he hadn't needed against robbers. Fighting a dog from muleback was about as close as he cared to come to actual cavalry combat.

But the mule proved not to need his help. The harmless lizard had terrified it. It brayed at the dog—which really could have done it harm—and lashed out with its forefeet. The dog made one little barking rush, then decided it didn't feel like sampling either mule or Hellene after all. It loped off toward a round stone farmhouse with a thatched roof a couple of plethra from the road. The mule seemed inclined to pursue it.

Sostratos yanked back hard on the reins. The mule brayed and gave him a resentful stare. He stared back. "You really *are* a stupid creature," he told it. "You don't know the difference between what can hurt you and what can't." By the way it tried to pitch him off onto the dirt road again, it believed him no more than it had about the ocellated lizard.

He got into Pompaia a little before sunset, exactly as he'd planned, and succeeded in making his way back to the agora from the northern gate without having to ask directions of anyone. After returning the mule to the local from whom he'd hired it, he walked over to Menedemos: walked with a slow, rolling, bowlegged stride, for he'd done no riding for a long time before this.

His cousin laughed, recognizing the signs. "Don't you wish you'd stayed here with us?" Menedemos asked.

"I do not," Sostratos replied with dignity. "I've gone exploring, and I'm glad I did it."

"Have any trouble?"

"Oh yes—twice." Sostratos dipped his head. He made as if to draw the sword again. "Once I almost had to fight."

"Do you see? Do you see?" Menedemos said, his voice rising in excitement. "I told you it was dangerous out there. You're probably lucky to get back here alive. What happened, by the gods?"

"You're right—the Italian countryside is a rougher place than I ever thought it was," Sostratos said gravely. "The first time, a lizard tried to carry off my mule: that's what the mule thought, anyhow. And then we were assailed again, the second time by a . . . stray dog."

The sailors in the market square with Menedemos laughed. After a moment, so did Sostratos' cousin. He said, "All right, you got by with it. If you want to make me look the fool, I don't suppose I can blame you. But I still say you were the foolish one for going off by yourself."

Sostratos grunted. He'd hoped for more of a rise out of Menedemos. What was the fun of annoying him if he wouldn't get annoyed? Dissatisfied but doing his best not to show it, Sostratos asked, "How did you do here?"

Now Menedemos' face lit up. "I'll tell you, I'm tempted to stay here longer, to the crows with me if I'm not. I sold Ariousian, I sold silk, I sold perfume, I sold a peafowl chick. A lot of these Pompaians look to have more silver than fancy goods to buy with it, so they leap hard when they see something they want."

"Do you think the same won't hold true in Neapolis?" Sostratos asked. "That's a real polis, and the folk there won't have seen the kinds of things we've got any more than the Pompaians have."

"Some truth to that—but only some, I think," Menedemos said. "Ships from Hellas surely come to Neapolis more often than they put in here."

"You may be right," Sostratos said. "Even so, though, I've seen as much of Pompaia and the countryside as I care to."

"Well, yes, but have we seen as much of Pompaia's silver as we're going to? That's the real question, wouldn't you say?"

"You're the captain. I can't tell you when to sail," Sostratos answered. "I'm just thinking that in a small town like this, you do most of your business right at the start, and then it peters out after that." Menedemos looked mulish. Have had all too recent experience with a veritable mule, Sostratos had no trouble noting the resemblance. With a sigh, he said, "Very well, O best one. If you want to stay in Pompaia a while longer, stay a while longer we shall."

"That's right," Menedemos said smugly.

MENEDEMOS GLANCED OUT over the agora. He was beginning to hate Pompaians. Over the past two days, he'd sold one amphora of Ariousian, one bolt of Koan silk, and not a single peafowl chick. He wasn't even meeting the *Aphrodite*'s expenses, let alone turning a profit.

His glare reached over to Sostratos. His cousin only smiled back, which irked him further. Had Sostratos said something like, *I told you so,* they could have had a good, satisfying, air-clearing quarrel. Of course, had Sostratos said something like, *I told you so,* Menedemos' pride probably would have made him keep the *Aphrodite* tied up outside Pompaia for another couple of days. He knew that perfectly well. In fact, he was looking for the excuse.

But Sostratos kept his mouth shut. He just went on smiling that irritating, superior smile. As sunset of the second long, boring, empty day neared, Menedemos knew he was beaten. "All right," he snarled, as if Sostratos were arguing with him. "All right, curse it. Tomorrow morning we'll head up toward Neapolis."

"Fair enough," his cousin said. "All things considered, the stop was worthwhile—we did make money here."

"Well, so we did." Menedemos gruffly allowed Sostratos to let him down easy.

Later, he sometimes wondered what would have happened had Sostratos chosen that afternoon to squabble. His life, and his cousin's, would have been very different. He was sure of that, if of nothing else.

In Pompaia, the taverns and brothels lay close by the river. After returning to the *Aphrodite,* Menedemos sent Diokles and a double handful of sober sailors through them, making sure his crew would be in place and ready to go at dawn. "Tell 'em they can stay with the barbarians here if they don't want to come with you," he instructed the oarmaster.

"Don't you worry about a thing, skipper," Diokles said. "I'll take care of it."

And he did, too, with his usual unfussy competence. He had every sailor back aboard the merchant galley before the night could have been more than two hours old. That was a performance even Menedemos hadn't expected. "By the dog of Egypt, how did you manage?" he asked when Diokles returned with the last two sodden Hellenes.

"Not so hard," the keleustes answered. "All I had to do was listen for real Greek. It would've been a lot tougher job down in one of the towns of Great Hellas."

"All right. Good. You've done everything we've asked of you since we went out from Rhodes, Diokles, and you've done most things better than Sostratos or I would have hoped," Menedemos said. "When we get home, you'll find I haven't forgotten."

"That's mighty kind of you, captain," the oarmaster said. "Me, I'm just doing my job."

"And very well, too." Menedemos looked up to the flickering stars and yawned. "And now you'd better get some sleep. No matter how good a job you were doing, I'd bet you had maybe a cup of wine or two yourself while you were tracking down the boys who'd sooner drink or screw than row."

"Who, me?" Diokles was the picture of innocence. "I don't know what you're talking about." He and Menedemos both laughed. Then he went to perch on a rower's bench and leaned against the planking of the ship, while Menedemos spread his himation on the poop deck and, the night being fine and mild, slept on it rather than under it.

As he usually did, he woke with morning twilight in the air. When he went over to the rail to piss into the Sarnos River, he found Sostratos already standing there. "Good day," his cousin said.

"Good day," Menedemos answered. Having made up his mind to leave, he was already starting to look ahead: "We should squeeze more silver out of Neapolis than we got here—a lot more, with luck."

"Let's hope so," Sostratos said. "We should be there today, shouldn't we?"

"Oh, yes, by Zeus," Menedemos said. "We should be there by noon, or not much later. We'll probably have to row most of the way, though—the breeze feels like it'll be blowing right in our face."

"Maybe it'll swing round a bit once we get out onto the sea," Sostratos said.

"May it be so," Menedemos said. "Come on, let's get the men up. The more we can do before the sun gets hot, the happier we'll all be. One thing—" He chuckled. "We've got all the fresh water we'll need for the trip."

"There is that," his cousin agreed.

As they got ready to disembark, Menedemos instructed the crew: "When I give the order to back oars, I want you to row hard. Our boat has to be clear of the next wharf farther downstream before the

current pushes us into it. This business of moving is more complicated than it would be if we were moored in an ordinary seaside
harbor."

With Diokles calling the stroke, the *Aphrodite* did get out into the
middle of the Sarnos without any trouble. Menedemos swung the
ship's bow toward the mouth of the river. He took most of the men
off the oars, but kept half a dozen on either side busy to add speed
and precise direction to the current pushing the akatos out toward
the Tyrrhenian Sea.

A little naked herdboy watering his sheep at the riverbank waved
to the *Aphrodite* as she glided past. Menedemos lifted a hand from
the steering oars to wave back. Diokles said, "This is pretty settled
country. A lot of places, he'd run from a ship for fear we'd grab him
and sell him somewhere."

"That's true. He'd bring two, three minai, even scrawny as he is."
Menedemos shrugged. "More trouble than he's worth." He wondered if he would have said the same thing had the voyage not been
turning a profit.

At the bow, Aristeidas pointed ahead and called, *"Thalassa! Thalassa!"*

"The sea! The sea!" The rest of the sailors took up the cry.

Sostratos, on the other hand, started to laugh. "What's so funny?"
Menedemos asked.

"That's what Xenophon's Ten Thousand, or however many of
them were left alive by then, called out when they came to the sea
after they got away from the Persians," Sostratos answered.

"Xenophon was an Athenian, wasn't he?" Menedemos said. When
Sostratos dipped his head, Menedemos went on, "I'm surprised he
didn't write, *'Thalatta! Thalatta!'* instead." He pointed at his cousin.
"Some of that Attic dialect has rubbed off on you—I've heard you
say *glotta* for *glossa* and things like that."

Hearing his tongue mentioned, Sostratos stuck it out. Menedemos
returned the gesture. Sostratos said, "As a matter of fact, if I remember rightly, Xenophon did write, *'Thalattta!'* "

"Ha!" Menedemos felt vindicated. "I bet his soldiers, or most of
them, said it the way Aristeidas just did."

"You're probably right," Sostratos said. "But if you expect an Athenian to give up his dialect just because it doesn't match the way someone actually said something, you're asking too much."

"I never expect anything from Athenians," Menedemos said. "They'll come up with better excuses for cheating you than . . ." His voice trailed away. His cousin's face had gone hard and cold. A few words too late, Menedemos remembered just how much Sostratos had enjoyed his time at Athens, and just how gloomy he'd been when he first came back to Rhodes. Doing his best to sound casual, Menedemos continued, "Well, I'd better keep my mind on sailing the ship."

"Yes, that would be good." Sostratos sounded like a man holding in anger, too. Menedemos sighed. Sooner or later, he would have to make it up to his cousin.

The *Aphrodite* wouldn't give him a hard time, not on a fine bright day like today, with only a lazy breeze and the lightest of chop ruffling the blue, blue surface of the Tyrrhenian Sea. Even so, he steered away from land; he wanted a few stadia of leeway between the merchant galley and the shore. *You never can tell,* he thought. Ashore, with just his own neck to worry about, he took chances that horrified the cautious Sostratos. At sea, with everything at stake . . . He tossed his head. Not usually.

And so when, some time later that morning, Aristeidas called out, "Sail ho! Sail off the starboard bow!" Menedemos smiled and dipped his head. He wouldn't have to change course—that other ship, whatever it was, would pass well to leeward of him.

But then Aristeidas called out again: "*Sails* to starboard, skipper! That's not just a ship—that's a regular fleet."

Menedemos' eyes snapped toward the direction in which the lookout was pointing from the foredeck. He needed only a moment to spot the sails himself, and only another to recognize them for what they were. "All men to the oars!" he shouted. "That's a fleet of triremes, and they can have us for lunch if they want us!"

Sailors ran to their places on the benches. Oars bit into the sea. Without waiting for an order from Menedemos, Diokles picked up the stroke. Menedemos swung the *Aphrodite* away from those low, lean, menacing shapes.

They couldn't be anything but triremes: they sported foresails as

well as mainsails, which smaller galleys like pentekonters and hemioliai never did. Looking back over his shoulder, Menedemos did his
best to count them. He'd got to eighteen when Sostratos said, "There
are twenty."

"Twenty triremes!" Menedemos said. "That's not a pirate's outfit—
that's a war fleet. But whose?"

"Let's hope we don't find out," Sostratos said. "They're traveling
under sail, and they look as if they know just where they want to go.
May they keep right on going."

"May it be so," Menedemos said. "They look like they're heading
straight for the mouth of the Sarnos. Maybe they aim to raid Pompaia." He spoke before his cousin could: "If they do, it's a good
thing we got out of there this morning. If they'd caught us tied up
at the pier, they could have done whatever they pleased with us."

"That's true, and I'm glad we're away, too," Sostratos said—as close
as he came to *I told you so,* and not close enough to be annoying. Then
he grunted, as if someone had hit him in the belly. "The trireme closest
to us just brought out its oars. It's . . . swinging this way."

Menedemos looked back over his shoulder. "Oh, a pestilence," he
said softly. Sostratos was right, not that he'd really expected his
cousin to be wrong. And when a full crew rowed a trireme, she fairly
leaped through the water—she had a hundred seventy men at her
three banks of oars, compared to the *Aphrodite*'s forty on a single
level. "Pick up the stroke," Menedemos told Diokles.

"We're doing everything we can now, captain," the keleustes answered. "She's faster than we are, that's all." Menedemos cursed. He
knew that. He knew it much too well. And if he hadn't known it,
the way the trireme got bigger every time he looked at it would have
told him.

Sostratos was peering aft with a fascination somewhat less horrified
and more curious. "There's a wolf painted on the mainsail," he remarked. "Who uses the wolf for an emblem?"

"Who cares?" Menedemos snarled.

To his surprise, Diokles said, "The Romans do—those Italians
who're fighting the Samnites."

"How do you know that?" Sostratos asked, as if discussing philosophy at the Lykeion in Athens.

"Tavern talk," the oarmaster answered, as Menedemos had a few days before. "You hear all sorts of things sitting around soaking up wine."

"How interesting," Sostratos said.

"How interesting that we know who's going to sell us for slaves or knock us over the head and pitch us into the drink," Menedemos said. The trireme was gaining on the *Aphrodite* at a truly frightening rate. As he watched, the Romans—if they were Romans—brailed up the sails and stowed the mast and foremast. Like Hellenes, they would make their attack run under oar power alone.

They weren't the best crew in the world, nor anything close to it. Every so often, a couple of oars would bang together or a rower would catch a crab. Their keleustes was probably yelling himself hoarse, trying to get more out of them. But they had so many men at the oars, their little mistakes hardly mattered. Against another trireme, they might have, but against an akatos with fewer than a quarter as many rowers? Not likely.

Not likely if we keep running, anyhow—they'll just run us down, Menedemos thought. His men were rowing as if possessed, sweat streaming down their bare torsos. They couldn't hold such a pace much longer, and even this pace wasn't doing anything but putting off the inevitable.

If we keep running, they catch us. But what can we do except keep running? All of a sudden, Menedemos laughed out loud. It was a slightly crazed laugh, or perhaps more than slightly—both Sostratos and Diokles sent him sharp looks. He knew just what it was: the laugh of a man with nothing to lose.

"Port side!" he called, and the heads of the rowers on that side of the ship swung toward him. "Port side!" he sang out again, so they would be ready for whatever command he gave them. Then he shouted once more, and this time he gave the order: "Port side—back oars!"

He felt like cheering at the way the men on the oars obeyed him. He had a good, tight crew, one of which he could be proud. Most of the men had pulled an oar on a Rhodian warship at one time or another, and his work and Diokles' had, as the saying went, beaten them into a solid, steady unit. The Romans behind them, he was sure, would have made a hash of the maneuver.

He hauled back on one steering-oar tiller and forward on the other, aiding the *Aphrodite*'s turn back toward her pursuer. As she spun on the surface of the Tyrrhenian Sea, he called out to the handful of sailors not on the oars, "Get the sail brailed up to the yard!" They too leaped to do his bidding.

It was a godlike feeling, sure enough—and would have been even more so had he not known just how bad the odds against him still were. Sostratos said, "You're not going to *attack* them?" His voice broke like a youth's on the word he had trouble believing.

"They'll run us down and ram us if we flee," Menedemos answered. "That's certain sure. This way, we have a chance."

"A *small* chance," Sostratos said, which reflected Menedemos' thoughts altogether too well.

He bared his teeth in what only looked like a smile. "Have you got a better idea, O cousin of mine?" After a long moment, Sostratos tossed his head.

No sooner had he done so than Menedemos forgot about him. All his attention focused on the Roman trireme and on the rapidly narrowing stretch of water between them—down to a few stadia now. He raised his eyes from the trireme for an instant to look at the rest of the Roman fleet. The other ships were unconcernedly sailing on toward the mouth of the Sarnos. Their captains thought one trireme was plenty to chase down a merchant galley.

They're liable to be right, Menedemos thought. *No, by the gods— they're likely to be right.*

But then he tossed his head. He couldn't afford doubt now, not if he was to have even a small chance against that much larger ship. *If Sostratos were at the steering oars now, would doubt paralyze him?* Menedemos tossed his head again. He didn't have time to wonder, either.

He watched the Roman trireme. It was cataphract—fully decked— as a bigger ship, a four or a five, would have been. Marines in bronze helms and corselets and nearly naked sailors ran about on the deck. Some of them pointed toward the *Aphrodite*. Faint across the water, he heard their shouts.

They wonder what in Tartaros I'm up to. Maybe they think I've lost my mind. I wonder, too. Maybe I have.

On came the trireme, looking bigger and fiercer with every heartbeat. Its ram, aimed straight at Menedemos' ship, sliced through the sea as smoothly as a shark's snout. Its oars rose and fell, rose and fell, with almost hypnotic unity. Almost—sure enough, that crew either hadn't been together long or wasn't well trained. Menedemos' rowers were much more professional—but, again, he measured forty men against the Roman captain's one hundred seventy. That gave the barbarian a lot of room for error . . . and Menedemos none whatever.

More Roman marines came up on deck. The two ships were close enough now for Menedemos to see they carried bows. They were as jumpy as anyone else on either galley—they started shooting well before the ships were in range. One after another, their arrows splashed into the sea in front of the *Aphrodite.*

But that wouldn't last, and Menedemos knew it. "Anyone who's wounded," he called, "get up from your oar if you're too badly hurt to keep rowing. You men who aren't at the oars, jump in as fast as you can. And everyone, by the gods! Listen for my commands and obey them the instant you hear them. If you do, we can beat that big, ugly, clumsy trireme. We *can!*"

The rowers raised a cheer. Before Sostratos said anything, he came up close to Menedemos, which showed better sense than he sometimes used. In a low voice, he asked, "*How* can we beat that big, ugly, clumsy trireme?"

"You'll see." Menedemos did his best to show the confidence he was also doing his best to feel. He patted his cousin on the arm. "Now do get out of the way, best one, if you'd be so kind. I have to be able to see straight ahead." For another wonder, Sostratos moved aside without argument.

Arrows started thudding into the *Aphrodite*'s planking. The two ships were only about three plethra apart now, and closing fast. Menedemos wished he had a catapult up on the foredeck, not cages full of peafowl chicks. A few of those darts would give the Romans something to think about! Of course, the catapult would also make the akatos bow-heavy as could be; not even a trireme could afford the weight of such an engine. A rower howled with pain. He sprang up from his bench, an arrow transfixing his right arm. Another sailor took his place. The *Aphrodite* scarcely faltered. Menedemos let out a silent sigh of relief.

Each heartbeat felt as if it came about an hour after the one just past. Menedemos' gaze fixed on the Roman trireme's ram. He could read the other captain's mind. *If these mad merchants want a head-on collision. I'll give them one,* the barbarian had to be thinking. *My bigger ship will roll right over theirs and capsize it, sure as sure.*

Menedemos didn't want a head-on collision: that was, in fact, the last thing he wanted. But he had to make the Roman captain think he did up till the last possible instant, which was just about . . . now.

Another wounded rower screamed, and another. Menedemos ignored them. He ignored everything, in fact, but the onrushing bulk of the enemy trireme and the feel of the steering-oar tillers in his hands.

He tugged on the tillers ever so slightly, swinging the *Aphrodite* to port just before she and the trireme would have smashed together. At the same time, he cried out in a great voice: "Starboard oars—*in!*"

As smoothly as they had in practice farther south, the rowers brought their oars inboard. Instead of ramming the Roman trireme, the *Aphrodite* glided along beside her, close enough to spit from one ship to the other. And the merchant galley's hull rode over the trireme's starboard oars and broke them as a man's descending foot would break the twigs of a child's toy house.

Rowers aboard the Roman ship screamed as the butt ends of the oars, suddenly propelled by forces much greater than they could generate, belabored them. Menedemos heard two splashes in quick succession as Roman marines fell into the sea. Their armor would drag them down to a watery grave. His smile was fierce as a wolf's. He wanted to wave good-bye to them, but couldn't take his hands off the tillers.

The *Aphrodite* slid past the crippled trireme. "Starboard oars—*out!*" Menedemos shouted, and his ship, undamaged, pulled away from the Roman vessel. He looked east. The rest of the Roman fleet had headed up the Sarnos. He was all alone with this ship that had tried to sink him. Now he did turn and wave to the man at the trireme's steering oars. The fellow was staring back over his shoulder at the merchant galley, his eyes as wide as any man's Menedemos had ever seen.

"You can ease back on the stroke now, Diokles," Menedemos told the oarmaster. "Let us get a little distance between our ship and that polluted barbarian, and then . . ."

"Aye aye, skipper!" Diokles said. Menedemos had never heard so much respect in his voice. *And I earned it, too, by the gods,* he thought proudly.

"What are you going to do?" Sostratos asked.

"I'm going to ram that wide-arsed catamite, that's what." Menedemos' voice was savage as a maenad's. "Romans don't sail any too bloody well. Let's see how good they are at swimming."

"I wish you wouldn't," Sostratos said.

"What?" Menedemos stared. He wondered if he'd heard correctly. "Are you out of your mind? Why not? You treat your friends well and your enemies badly, and if these bastards aren't enemies, what are they?" He tugged on the steering-oar tillers to bring the akatos' bow around to bear on the trireme. The Romans were starting to shift oars from their undamaged port side to starboard. That would eventually let them limp away, but it wouldn't let them escape a vengeful *Aphrodite.*

"They're enemies, all right," Sostratos said. "But think—wasn't it wildest luck that we hurt them in the first place?"

"Luck and a good crew," Menedemos growled. He still hungered for revenge.

"Agreed. Agreed ten times over," Sostratos said. "But now that we've been lucky once, wouldn't another run at that cursed big ship be hubris? Suppose the ram stuck fast. All those marines—except for the ones we knocked into the drink, I mean—and all those rowers would swarm aboard, and that would be the end of that."

Menedemos grunted. He wanted to tell his cousin there wasn't a chance in the world of that happening. He wanted to, but he couldn't. Such mishaps were all too common; ramming could be as hard on the attacking ship as on the victim. And if that did happen here, it would be as deadly to the *Aphrodite* as Sostratos said. He took a deep breath and let it out, then blinked a couple of times almost in surprise, like a man suddenly lucid again after a ferocious fever broke.

"You're right," he said. "I hate to admit it—you have no idea how much I hate to admit it—but you're right. Let's get out of here while the getting's good."

"Thank you," Sostratos said softly.

"I'm not doing it for you," Menedemos said. "Believe me, I'm not doing it for myself, either. I'm doing it for the ship."

"This far from home, that's the best reason," Sostratos said. Menedemos only shrugged, despite watching Diokles dip his head. He'd made his decision. That didn't mean he had to like it.

The Romans on their trireme's deck gawked at the *Aphrodite* as she passed safely out of arrow range. Menedemos thought some rowers were gaping out through the oar ports, too. "Got a little lesson today, didn't you?" he shouted at them; though they were a long way off and probably didn't speak Greek anyhow. His rowers were much less restrained. They blistered the Romans with curses they'd picked up all over the Inner Sea.

"I don't suppose we're heading up to Neapolis any more," Sostratos remarked.

"What? Why not?" Menedemos said in surprise.

As if to an idiot child, his cousin answered, "Because how do we know that that's the only Roman fleet around? Suppose four triremes come after us the next time. What do we do then?"

"Oh." Menedemos blinked. He rubbed his chin as he thought. At last, he said, "Well, best one, you're right again. Twice in one day—I didn't think you had it in you." He grinned at Sostratos' splutters, then went on, "I hadn't thought it through. I was too busy dealing with that one bastard."

"And you did it splendidly," Sostrastos said. "I thought we were doomed."

So did I, Menedemos thought. Aloud, he answered, "If you've got only two chances—one bad, the other worse—you do the best you can with the bad one." He raised his voice to call out to the sailors: "Lower the sail from the yard. We're heading back down south, and the wind should be with us most of the way."

Men leaped to obey. They'd leaped ever since Aristeidas first spotted the Roman triremes. Then it had been out of fear. Now . . . *Now it's because they admire me,* Menedemos thought. *And after what I did, they should.*

One of the sailors said, "Pity we can't land and set up a trophy to remember this by."

That only made Menedemos prouder. He showed it in an offhand way: "The barbarians wouldn't know what it meant, anyhow, and they'd just plunder it. We have our trophy, perfect in memory forever."

"That's right, by the gods," Diokles said. "And we've got a story we can drink on in every wineshop from Karia to Carthage, too."

"Truth," Menedemos said.

But Sostratos tossed his head. "I don't think so."

"What? Why not?" Menedemos demanded.

"Wrecking a trireme with an akatos?" Sostratos said. "Be serious, O cousin of mine. Would you believe a story like that if you heard it?" Again, Menedemos thought for a moment. Then he too solemnly tossed his head.

SOSTRATOS WAS GLAD to sail south past the island of Kapreai. He doubted whether any Roman fleet, no matter how aggressive, would ever dare to come deep into Great Hellas. And, after beating a trireme, he didn't worry nearly so much about piratical pentekonters as he had before.

Two of the sailors the Roman arrows had hurt quickly began to heal. The third had taken a wound in the belly. Even though the injury didn't look too bad, he began to run a high fever. It soon became clear he wouldn't live.

The men began to mutter among themselves. Few ritual pollutions were worse than having a corpse on board. "What are we going to do?" Menedemos murmured to Sostratos, not wanting anyone else to hear. "It's as if they're forgetting we beat that trireme."

"Let's put him in the boat," Sostratos answered. "He's too far gone to care what happens to him, and that way the *Aphrodite* won't be polluted when he dies. We can either have a priest cleanse the boat when we put in at a polis or else, if we have to, just buy a new one."

Menedemos stared at him, then stood on tiptoe to kiss him on the cheek. "Those brains of yours are good for something after all—every once in a while, anyhow."

"Why did you add that last little bit?" Sostratos asked.

"To keep you from walking around with a swelled head," his cousin answered with a wicked grin.

"Thank you so much," Sostratos said, which only made Menedemos' grin wider. A couple of sailors eased the man with the belly wound down into the merchant galley's boat. Sure enough, he was so lost in his battles with demons only he could see, he hardly noticed being moved. They rigged an awning with sailcloth to keep the sun off him. Every so often, someone went down into the boat to give him watered wine from a dipper. He drank a little, but spilled more.

"Sail ho!" Aristeidas sang out. "Sail ho off the starboard bow!"

Everyone jumped. Sostratos' heart began to thud in his chest. The last time the lookout spied a sail, they'd been lucky to escape with their lives, let alone their freedom. Along with the whole crew—since they were moving under sail, they didn't have anyone facing backwards at the oars—he anxiously peered southward.

After only a few minutes, relief flowered in him. "That's a round ship's sail," he said. "It's bigger than anything a galley would carry."

One after another, the sailors dipped their heads. "If we have to run from a merchantman, we're really in trouble," Diokles said. The laughter the oarmaster got was louder than the feeble joke deserved. *Relief, nothing else but,* Sostratos thought. He certainly felt it himself.

"He's not running from us," Sostratos remarked after a while.

"No, he's not," Menedemos agreed. "He's tacking his way north— if he turns and runs before the wind, he'll take three or four times as long beating his way back as he would to flee. And, since we're really not pirates, he wins his gamble."

Sostratos wondered if he would have risked life and freedom against convenience. He hoped not. But then, after a longer look at the merchantman, he said, "I don't think he's gambling. I think he recognizes us, and I think I recognize him, too. Isn't that Leptines' ship?"

His cousin squinted to peer across the waters of the Tyrrhenian Sea. "By the gods, I believe it is," Menedemos said. "All that reading you do hasn't shortened your sight yet, anyhow. Maybe I'll put you up at the bow instead of Aristeidas."

"Don't!" Sostratos tossed his head. "He's a regular lynx—I know his eyes are better than mine. Most of the time, yours are, too, I think—you just weren't paying any attention." If his cousin gibed at him, he was going to return the favor.

Menedemos tugged on the steering-oar tillers, swinging the *Aphrodite*'s bow to starboard, toward Leptines' round ship. "I want to get within hailing distance and warn him off," Menedemos said.

"Wouldn't do to have him sail up the Sarnos to Pompaia and right into the jaws of those Roman wolves."

If that wasn't Leptines, and if he hadn't recognized the *Aphrodite,* then he was a prime fool to let the akatos approach his ship so closely. But, before long, Sostratos saw the tubby skipper with his hands on the steering-oar tillers for his tubby ship.

Leptines lifted one hand from a steering oar to wave. He shouted something Sostratos couldn't make out. Sostratos cupped a hand behind his ear to show as much. Out of the corner of his eye, he saw Menedemos doing the same thing.

Leptines tried again. This time, Sostratos understood him: "How was Pompaia?"

"Pompaia was fine," Menedemos yelled. "We did some good business. But you don't want to go there."

"What? What's that you say?" Leptines asked. "Why not?"

"Because there's a Roman fleet attacking the town and the countryside right now, that's why," Menedemos answered. "If you sail up there, you're just sticking your head in the wolf's mouth."

"Herakles!" Leptines exclaimed. "A barbarian fleet? Not pirates? Are you sure? How did you get away?"

He asked more questions than one man could conveniently answer. Sostratos said, "They were Romans, all right—they all had the Roman wolf on their sails," at the same time as Menedemos replied, "One of their triremes chased us, and we crippled it, that's how."

"What?" Leptines said, and he didn't mean he had trouble making sense of two voices at once. "How could you beat a trireme with that puny little akatos of yours? I don't believe a word of it."

"I told you so," Sostratos murmured to Menedemos. His cousin made a horrible face at him.

But the sailors wouldn't let Leptines get away with thinking Menedemos a liar. They still reckoned themselves heroes, and shouted out the details of what they'd done. If they'd been pirates and not the crew of a real, working merchant galley, it would have gone hard for the round ship's skipper and his sailors. For a moment, Sostratos wondered whether it would go hard for Leptines and his men anyway; the sailors from the *Aphrodite* were in no mood to be slighted.

Leptines didn't need long to figure that out for himself. "All right!

All right!" he called. "I do believe you!" By then, the two ships lay only ten or fifteen cubits apart. Had Menedemos or his crew chosen to turn pirate, the other captain could have done nothing to stop him. "Where will you go now?" he asked Menedemos.

"I'd had in mind heading up to Neapolis," Menedemos said. "You know about that—I told you when we were in port together. But who knows how many Roman ships are prowling that stretch of the Tyrrhenian Sea right now? Better to head back south, I figured, so that's what I'm doing."

"*You* figured?" Sostratos said under his breath. This time, Menedemos didn't hear him, which might have been just as well. By the way his cousin spoke, Menedemos was convinced coming south had been his own idea and no one else's. Sostratos knew better.

Or do I just remember differently? he wondered. After a moment, he tossed his head. He knew what had happened there after he talked Menedemos out of ramming the Roman trireme. But his cousin sang another song altogether.

If—no, when—I write my history, how will I be able to judge which of two conflicting stories is the true one? he thought. *Both men will be certain they have it right, and each will call the other a liar. How did Herodotos and Thoukydides and Xenophon decide who was right?* The next time he looked at their works, he would have to think about that.

Meanwhile, Leptines was saying, "That's smart, getting out of there. Polluted barbarians are everywhere these days. They might as well be cockroaches. We Hellenes should have squashed them before they got so strong." A few days before, he'd extolled the Pompaians. Would he remember that if Sostratos reminded him of it? Not likely, and Sostratos knew it full well.

"Pity you had to work so hard just to turn back," Menedemos said.

"Maybe so, but I thank you for your news," Leptines replied. "Going forward would have been a bigger pity."

"Have a safe trip south," Sostratos said. Leptines waved to him. So did a couple of the round ship's sailors. He waved back. Menedemos swung the *Aphrodite* to catch the wind once more. She began to glide over the waves. Leptines' ship wasn't nearly so handy. Sostratos looked back past the sternpost for some time before he saw the other ship also heading away from trouble instead of toward it.

Even though the round ship's sail was far bigger than the akatos', and even though the breeze filled it well, the *Aphrodite* easily pulled away. When Sostratos remarked on that, Menedemos said, "I should hope so, by the gods. If that pig outsailed us, I think I'd go home and drink hemlock."

"It still seems strange," Sostratos said.

"Nothing strange about it," Menedemos insisted. "War galleys are faster than we are, because we're beamier than they are. They cut the water like a sharp knife. We cut it like a dull one. And as for that polluted round ship—won't even a dull knife cut water better than a drinking cup?"

"Sokrates couldn't do better, O best one," Sostratos said. "I find no flaws in your logic."

"Thank you very much." Menedemos looked smug.

Sostratos wasn't about to let him get away with that. "Why do you only think so straight when you've got ships on your mind? Why do you start acting like a madman as soon as you smell perfume?"

"I don't know," Menedemos answered.

"Well, at least you don't deny it," Sostratos said.

"Ships aren't women, though," his cousin said. "Even if we give them feminine names, they *aren't*. Most of the time, a ship will do what you want. Oh, you can make a mistake, but you usually know what's what. But with women . . . My dear fellow! You can't know *what* a woman will do next, for she usually doesn't know herself. So what's the point to logic?"

Sostratos stared at him. "That's the most logical argument for illogic I've ever heard," he said at last.

"And I thank you again." Menedemos grinned. He'd won that round, and he knew it.

When they got down to the little town of Laos once more the following evening, a ship so like Leptines' was tied up at a quay, Sostratos wondered if the plump merchant skipper had somehow stolen a march on the *Aphrodite*. But the skipper of this round ship proved to be a scrawny fellow named Xenodokos. He said, "If you've got more greed than brains, you might want to think about getting down to Rhegion quick as you can."

Sostratos hoped he had more brains than greed. Because of that, a certain amount of horror went through him when he heard Menedemos ask, "Oh? Why?"

"Because Agathokles of Syracuse has men getting up a fleet of grain ships there," Xenodokos answered. "He's going to try and sneak 'em past the Carthaginian fleet so his polis doesn't starve. He'll pay gods only know how many times the going rate, even for a load from a skinny little ship like yours."

"And what will he pay if the Carthaginians catch us?" Sostratos asked.

"Syracuse," Xenodokos said.

Sostratos looked at his cousin. He didn't care for the gleam in Menedemos' eye. "The ship," he said pointedly.

"I know, the ship." Menedemos sounded impatient. "Remember, we have to go by Rhegion anyway." Sostratos remembered. His heart sank.

10

MENEDEMOS WAS LIKE A CHILD WITH A NEW TOY. "WE'LL make the family rich with this run!" he said. "We'll throw grain into the *Aphrodite* till we're down to about a digit's worth of freeboard, and we'll get paid for it as if we were that full of fine wine. What could be better?"

His cousin, predictably, was like a mother watching her son play with a sword he thought was a toy. "What could be better?" Sostratos said. "Not getting sunk could be better. So could not getting caught. Not getting killed. Not getting sold into slavery. Not getting gelded. If you give me a little while, I can probably think of some more things."

"Oh, nonsense." It wasn't altogether nonsense, as Menedemos knew. But he didn't want to dwell on that. Had he dwelt on it, he would have been just like Sostratos. He had trouble imagining a fate less appealing—or, for that matter, a fate less interesting.

As a brisk, hot breeze from out of the north pushed the *Aphrodite* ahead of it towards Rhegion, Sostratos scowled. Sostratos, in fact, did everything but stamp his foot on the timbers of the poop deck. "It isn't nonsense. What you want to do is senseless. We already have a profit. This is a needless risk."

"We'll be fine." Menedemos did his best to sound soothing. "From what Xenodokos said, there'll be a whole fleet down at Rhegion. The polluted Carthaginians can't nab everybody."

"Why not?" Sostratos retorted. "And you didn't see Xenodokos setting out for Syracuse, did you? Not likely! He went the other way. I wish we would, too."

"You worry too much," Menedemos said. "You were jumping up and down about putting in at Cape Tainaron, too, and that worked out fine. Why shouldn't this?"

"We weren't sailing into the middle of a war when we put in

at Cape Tainaron," his cousin answered. "You're just asking for trouble."

"The wind should be with us and against the Carthaginians," Menedemos said. "We'll just slide right into the harbor at Syracuse along with all the round ships—and if the barbarians do get after this fleet, they'll have an easier time catching round ships than they will with us."

Sostratos exhaled angrily. "All right. All right, by the gods. You're going to act like an idiot—I can see that. You lust for this the same way you lusted for that Tarentine's wife. But promise me one thing, at least."

"What is it?" Menedemos asked.

"This: if Xenodokos is wrong, if there is no fleet of merchantmen gathering at Rhegion, you won't load the *Aphrodite* up with grain and try to sneak into Syracuse all by your lonesome."

"We might have a better chance that way," Menedemos said. Then he saw just how furious Sostratos looked. He threw his hands in the air. "Oh, very well. If there is no grain fleet, we'll head for home. There! Are you satisfied now?"

"Satisfied? No," Sostratos said. "I won't be satisfied till we do sail for home. But that is a little better—a very little better—than nothing."

Menedemos didn't think it was anything of the sort. The more he thought of tiptoeing into Syracuse past the Carthaginian fleet, the better he liked it. A man could dine out on such stories for the rest of his life. But he'd gone and given his word, and he felt obliged to keep it.

I hope there's a fleet at Rhegion, he thought. *There'd better be a fleet at Rhegion, because I want to do this.* Sostratos was right, and Menedemos was honest enough with himself to admit it: he did lust after going to Syracuse the same way he lusted after some frisky young wife he'd chanced to see.

"Remember," Sostratos said, "whatever else you do, you're not supposed to risk the ship."

"I don't intend to risk the ship," Menedemos snapped, wishing Sostratos hadn't put it quite that way, "and I'm the one who judges when the ship's being risked and when it isn't. You aren't. Have you got that, O cousin of mine?"

"Yes, I have it." Sostratos looked as if he liked it about as much as a big mouthful of bad fish. He stormed down off the poop deck and up toward the bow. *Daft,* Menedemos thought. *Daft as Aias after he didn't get Akhilleus' armor. Anybody who'd rather deal with peafowl chicks than stand around and talk has to be daft.*

The peafowl chicks! Menedemos brightened. "*Oë!* Sostratos!" he called.

Reluctantly, Sostratos turned back toward him. "What is it?"

"How much do you think young peafowl will bring in Syracuse?"

"I don't know," Sostratos answered. "How much do you think they would bring in Carthage?" Having got the last word, he went on up to the little foredeck.

When Menedemos steered the *Aphrodite* into the harbor at Rhegion, he anxiously scanned the quays. If things looked no busier than usual, he would have to sail on toward Rhodes. He let out a whoop on seeing a couple of dozen large round ships all tied up together. If that wasn't a fleet in the making, he didn't know what was.

His cousin saw the ships, too, and also knew them for what they were. The look he gave Menedemos was baleful. Menedemos grinned back, which, by Sostratos' expression, only annoyed him more.

With a handful of men at the oars to put the merchant galley exactly where he wanted her, Menedemos guided her toward the quays alongside which the round ships floated. "Go somewhere else!" a man called from the stern of the nearest big, tubby merchantman. "We're all together here, loading up on grain for Agathokles."

"That's what I'm here for, too," Menedemos said as Diokles eased the *Aphrodite* up against the pier.

"You?" The fellow on the round ship laughed loud and long, displaying a couple of teeth gone black in the front of his mouth. "We can carry eight or ten times as much in the *Leuke* here as you can in that miserable little boat. Take your toy home and sail it in your hip-bath." He laughed again.

"Toy? Hip-bath?" Menedemos was tempted to yell, *Back oars!,* and then spurt forward to ram the round ship. How much grain would that sneering fellow carry then? But, unfortunately, no. It wouldn't do. Menedemos said, "However much or little we haul, Syracuse'll still get more with us than without us—and Agathokles'll pay us for it, too, same as he'll pay you."

"Well, all right. When you put it like that, I suppose you've got something," the other Hellene said. "And when the Carthaginians come after us, you can be the one who fights 'em off." He laughed again, louder than ever.

But he wasn't laughing by the time the *Aphrodite*'s crew finished screaming abuse and the details of their battle with the Roman trireme at him. He was white with fury, his fists clenched, his lips skinned back from his teeth. He had to stand there and take it, as did the other sailors on his ship. Had they chosen to answer back, the men from the akatos would have made them regret it—for, while the round ship held more cargo, the merchant galley held more crewmen.

A fellow wearing an unusually fine, unusually white wool chiton bustled up the pier toward the *Aphrodite*. "Are you here to carry grain to Syracuse?" he asked.

"We certainly are," Menedemos answered—this chap, unlike the man aboard the round ship, looked to have some clout. "Who are you, sir?"

"My name is Onasimos," replied the fellow with the fancy tunic. He also, Menedemos saw, had buckles on his sandals that looked like real gold. With a bow, he continued, "I have the honor to be the Syracusan proxenos here in Rhegion, and I'm doing what I can to help the polis I represent."

In normal times, a proxenos looked out for the interests of citizens of the polis he represented in the polis in which he dwelt. He was, necessarily, a man of some wealth and importance in his home town. He might aid in lawsuits. He might, at need, lend money. He got no pay for his services, only prestige and business connections. When the polis he represented was in danger, he might do extraordinary things, as Onasimos looked to be doing now.

"How do we get the grain?" Menedemos asked him.

"It's in the warehouses," Onasimos said. "Gods be praised, Great Hellas had a good harvest this past spring. I have plenty of slaves and free men ready to bring it aboard for you."

"Good." Menedemos dipped his head. "Now—about arrangements for payment."

"You've probably heard Agathokles is offering four times the going rate for grain delivered to Syracuse," Onasimos said.

Menedemos tossed his head. "I hadn't heard exactly how much he offered, as a matter of fact. But I have heard a lot of Agathokles himself—including the way he got rid of the Syracusans who weren't of his faction earlier this year. Anyone who could come up with that little scheme wouldn't think twice about going back on a promise to pay a merchant skipper."

The Syracusan proxenos looked pained. "I assure you, my dear fellow—"

But Menedemos tossed his head again. "Don't assure me, O best one. Let me ask some of the other captains and see what I find out."

Had Onasimos called his bluff and told him to go ahead, he might have believed the proxenos' protests. As things were, Onasimos sighed and said, "Oh, very well. I'll pay you the going rate now, and you can collect the rest on delivery."

"I'm sorry." Menedemos tossed his head for a third time. "The going rate isn't enough to make me want to risk the Carthaginian fleet. I know the Carthaginians are supposed to be splendid torturers, but I don't want to find out how they do what they do for myself."

He waited to see what Onasimos would say to that. The proxenos glared at him. He smiled his sweetest smile in return. Onasimos sighed again. "You're one of the canny ones, I see. All right, then— one and a half times the going rate in advance, but not an obolos more. If I give you everything promised ahead of time, you might just sail off with the grain and never go near Syracuse."

Menedemos thought about squeezing the proxenos some more. He glanced toward Sostratos. His cousin ignored him—Sostratos wanted no part of the Syracusan venture. Menedemos sent him a covert dirty look. He wanted to know what Sostratos thought, for his cousin was often better at haggling with these fancy types then he was himself. But Sostratos seemed determined to sulk.

That left it up to Menedemos. Onasimos had a point. Some men, with silver in their hands, *would* sail away from Syracuse. *Not me, of course,* Menedemos thought. But Onasimos didn't, couldn't, know that. "All right," Menedemos said. "One and a half times the going rate it is. Sostratos!"

His cousin jumped. "What?"

"You'll keep count of how many sacks of grain Onasimos' men bring aboard the *Aphrodite* here," Menedemos said. "As soon as we get paid our first installment for hauling them, we're off with the rest of the fleet."

"I'll have a man of my own doing the counting," Onasimos said.

"Good." Menedemos smiled that sweet smile at him. "I'm sure his count and Sostratos' will match very closely, then." The Syracusan proxenos' answering smile looked distinctly forced. *He was going to try to cheat me,* Menedemos thought. *Why am I not surprised?*

Muttering under his breath, Onasimos tramped back down the pier. About half an hour later, a line of men carrying leather sacks, each with a talent of grain, came out from the interior of Rhegion. "Where do you want these?" asked the man heading up the line. He carried no sack himself; he was obviously the fellow who would do the counting for Onasimos.

"Sostratos!" Menedemos called, and Sostratos, still seeming just this side of mutinous, went up onto the pier and stood beside Onasimos' man. For that worthy's benefit, Menedemos continued, "Now—I'll want you to start at the stern, just forward of the poop deck, and work toward the bow, one row of sacks at a time, till she holds as much grain as she can."

"Right," Onasimos' man said, and shouted orders at the men he was in charge of. They came down the gangplank and started loading the grain.

By the time they finished, the *Aphrodite* rode a great deal lower in the water. That worried Menedemos. Not only the extra weight but also the extra amount of hull now in the sea would slow the merchant galley. She didn't need to be slow, not when she might have to flee from Carthaginian warships. But he couldn't blame Onasimos for wanting to put as much grain into her as he could: the proxenos was doing his best to feed the people of the city he served.

"How many sacks of grain did we take on?" Menedemos asked once the last sweating hauler left the akatos.

"By my count, 797 sacks," Sostratos answered.

Onasimos' man sneered. "I reckoned it as 785." Sostratos bristled. Anyone who accused him of inaccuracy was asking for trouble.

Menedemos had no time for that kind of trouble. He said, "We'll split the difference. What does that come to?"

Sostratos counted on his fingers, his lips moving. "It would be 791," he said. "But I still think this fellow—"

"Never mind," Menedemos broke in. He nodded to Onasimos' man. "Tell your master we've got 791 sacks of grain aboard. As soon as we get paid, we're ready to go. Agreed?"

"Agreed," the other said. "Some of these round ships hold more than ten times as many sacks as that, you know."

"Every bit helps," Menedemos replied. Onasimos' man dipped his head and went back into Rhegion as his master had before him: to get money, Menedemos hoped.

Diokles said, "I hope the wind stays with us. The men'll break their backs and their hearts rowing with us laden like this, and she'll handle like a raft—if we're lucky, that is."

"If the wind fails, we're not going anywhere, not with all these round ships," Menedemos said. "They have to sail."

"Mm, that's so," the oarmaster agreed. He flashed Menedemos a sassy grin. "In that case, skipper, maybe we ought to hope for south winds for the next three months, so if Syracuse falls, we don't have to come close to all those Carthaginian war galleys, and we pick up a nice pile of silver anyway."

"You sounds like Sostratos," Menedemos said, and Diokles' grin got wider and even more provocative. Menedemos mimed throwing something at him and went on, "I wouldn't mind getting paid for doing nothing, either—who would? But if we don't get to deliver the grain, they'll just take it off and make us cough up the money again."

"If we were proper pirates, we'd sneak out of the harbor if that looked like happening," the keleustes said. "We're a galley, after all. We could do it."

"We *could,* sure enough." Menedemos wished Diokles hadn't put the idea in his mind. It was tempting. But he had no trouble finding reasons it wouldn't work. "You said it yourself—we'll be slow as a cart-ox with all this grain aboard. And my bet is, Rhegion would send her navy after us if we made off with the grain *and* the money. This Onasimos fellow looks to pull a lot of weight here."

"Well, so he does," Diokles said. "All right, then. I'd sooner pray for fair winds than foul, anyway."

"So would I," Menedemos said.

SOSTRATOS THOUGHT OF himself as a modern, rational man. He'd been embarrassed to spend the past couple of days praying for contrary winds. And he'd been embarrassed all over again to have his prayer fail so ignominiously, for a fine breeze blew from the north this morning. *So much for the gods,* he thought, *and a solid point for rationalism.*

Menedemos was up before dawn, too, smiling at the sky. *He'd* probably been praying for fair winds, so his belief in the gods was bound to be vindicated, too. That thought made Sostratos grumpier than ever. But, instead of gloating, Menedemos just pointed to the thin crescent moon rising a little ahead of the sun. "Another month almost done," he said.

"Sure enough." Sostratos peered into the brightening twilight between that little cheese-paring of a moon and the horizon. "And there's Aphrodite's wandering star."

"Why, so it is," Menedemos said. "Sure enough, your eyes aren't so bad if you can pick it out against the bright sky. The sun's almost up."

"I knew where to look," Sostratos answered with a shrug. "It's been sliding down the morning sky toward the sun for weeks now. Before too long, we'll see it in the evening instead. People used to think the evening appearance was a different star from the morning one—the same with Hermes' wandering star."

"What do you mean, used to?" Menedemos said. "Half our sailors probably still believe that."

"I meant educated people," Sostratos said. "The sailors are fine men but. . . ." Most of them thought of little save women (or, with a few, boys), wine, and tavern brawls. *How does one talk with such people?* he wondered.

"I like 'em fine," Menedemos said.

"I know." Sostratos did his best not to make that sound like a judgment. Still and all, what did it say about his cousin's taste?

Menedemos didn't seem to notice Sostratos' tone, which was just as well. He said, "We'll sail today."

"I know." Sostratos knew how unhappy he sounded, too, but he couldn't help it. "Do you think we'll make Syracuse by nightfall?"

"*We* would, if we weren't so overloaded," his cousin answered. "These fat scows we'll be keeping company with? Not a chance. We'll put in at one of the Sicilian towns tonight, or spend the night at sea, then go on in the morning."

"All right." Sostratos sighed. "One more night to spend worrying."

"Nothing to worry about," Menedemos said. "What could possibly go wrong?"

Sostratos started to answer. Then he started to splutter. And then he started to laugh. "Oh, no, you don't. You're not going to get me to turn purple and pitch a fit. I'm wise to you, Menedemos."

"A likely story," Menedemos said. They grinned at each other. For a moment, Sostratos forgot how much he wished the *Aphrodite* weren't sailing for Syracuse.

But he couldn't forget for long. All around the harbor, captains were waking up, tasting the breeze, and realizing it would be a good day to sail. They called orders to their crews and to the longshoremen who came down the wharves to cast off their mooring lines and bring them aboard once more. The sailors grunted and heaved at the sweeps even round ships carried, and slowly, a digit at a time, eased the ships away from their berths so they could make sail and head for Sicily.

Seeing their struggles to get started, Sostratos laughed again. "Our rowers may have to work hard, but not that hard."

"You're right." Menedemos waved to a couple of longshoremen. "Over here, too!"

"You're going to take this little thing to Syracuse?" one of the men said as he tossed a line down onto the sacks of grain in the *Aphrodite*'s waist. "Good idea—you can be a boat for all the real ships." He laughed at his own wit.

That sort of remark was as calculated to make Menedemos furious as Menedemos' crack had been to infuriate Sostratos. But Sostratos' cousin only shrugged, saying, "Onasimos likes us well enough to pay us to haul grain." The longshoreman turned away, disappointment on his face. Menedemos raised his voice: "Come on, boys, let's show these round-ship sailors how to row."

Diokles set the stroke. The men—all of them at the oars—pulled as hard as they had in the fight with the Roman trireme. And the *Aphrodite* . . . moved as if she were traveling through mud, not seawater. Diokles said, "I think this is about as much as we'll get from her, captain."

"Yes, I think you're right," Menedemos agreed. "I'd hoped for a little more, but. . . ." He shrugged.

"She feels different in the water," Sostratos said. "More solid, more as if we were on dry land. She doesn't shift so much underfoot."

"I should hope she doesn't," Menedemos said. "She's carrying twice as much as usual, so the waves don't seem to hit her so hard."

"That's true. We've never really felt what she's like fully laden before, have we?" Sostratos said, and Menedemos tossed his head. The merchant galley didn't have to travel full up to hope for profit, as a round ship did. She carried luxury goods, valuable for their rarity, instead of being a bulk hauler. Now Sostratos got a glimpse of what the usual sailor did on a usual voyage, and found he didn't much care for it.

One by one, the round ships lowered their great sails from their yards. One by one, the sails bellied out and filled with wind. The tubby ships began their southward journey, but not at a pace above a walk. The *Aphrodite*'s sail came down, too, and Menedemos called the rowers off the oars. Before very long, he had to order the men to brail up half the sail; otherwise, the akatos would have shot ahead of the other ships in the fleet despite her load.

When Sostratos let some peafowl chicks out of their cages to exercise, they ran around over the leather sacks of grain as happily as they had over the planking. They picked at spilled wheat as happily as they had at the cockroaches and other bugs that normally infested the *Aphrodite*—not that loading hundreds of sacks of grain onto the vermin had got rid of them.

Once the crew helped chivvy the chicks back into the cages, Sostratos could take a long look at the scenery. Indeed, he had little choice, unless he wanted to find a place to stand and brood. Considering where the *Aphrodite* was going and what she was liable to face when she got there, that didn't strike him as the worst idea in the world, but he refused to give in to it.

Because the merchant galley couldn't make anything close to her usual speed if she wanted to stay with the fleet of round ships, Sostratos had plenty of time to admire each bit of scenery as it passed. There was a great deal of Mount Aitne to admire. Now that Sostratos had seen both Aitne and Mount Ouesouion from fairly close range, he realized how much more massive the Sicilian volcano was than the one on the mainland of Italy. The soil on its slopes and around its base, though, had the same grayish, ashy look he'd seen near Pompaia. The Sicilian vineyards looked very rich, too, though the fields lay fallow under the hot summer sun.

Slowly, slowly, the fleet sailed past Taruomenion and Naxos and Akion. Sostratos looked longingly at each inviting little harbor, and sighed as the *Aphrodite* and the round ships crawled past each one. That summer sun seemed to speed across the sky. Before the fleet reached Katane—the largest polis on the east coast of Sicily except for Syracuse—it set behind the island. Anchors splashed into the water as the captains got ready to spend a night at sea.

"Unless I'm wrong, those merchant skippers wish they were tied up at a quay," Sostratos remarked to Menedemos.

"Well, when you get right down to it, so do I," his cousin answered. "If a storm were to blow up all of a sudden, we'd be in trouble, especially when we're heavy with grain."

"A storm, right now, is the least of our worries." To show what he meant, Sostratos pointed south.

Menedemos tossed his head. "A storm is never the *least* of your worries, not when you're at sea. If you want to worry about the Carthaginians more, I don't suppose I can stop you."

"I wonder how you say, 'Sail ho!' in the Phoenician language," Sostratos said. "Himilkon would know. I wish I were back in the harbor of Rhodes so I could ask him."

"After we deliver the grain and get paid, we'll be going home," Menedemos answered. "You can find out, if you still want to know by then."

He kept his tone light. If he didn't believe everything would go well when the fleet got to Syracuse, he didn't let on. Some of that, no doubt, was to keep the crew from fretting. The rest, Sostratos was convinced, sprang from his cousin's natural self-confidence—or was it arrogance? Menedemos had never yet found himself in a spot from which he couldn't wiggle out, and so seemed convinced he never would.

Sostratos hoped his cousin was right without believing it. That wasn't how things worked. Hoping Menedemos would prove right this particular time seemed a better bet . . . though not a very good one. *We'll know tomorrow,* Sostratos thought. He wrapped himself in his himation and lay down on the sacks of grain. They were a little more yielding than the planks of the poop deck, if lumpier.

He thought he would worry too much to find sleep, but exhaustion proved stronger. Next thing he knew, Menedemos announced the new day like a rooster. Several sailors let out groans and sleepy curses. Sostratos said, "If I were wearing shoes, I'd throw one at you."

"It's a day worth celebrating," Menedemos said, his voice full of the false heartiness some traders used to sell things that weren't worth buying. "Tonight we'll feast in Syracuse, a polis famed for its feasts wherever Hellenes live."

That made some of the sailors cheer up. It did nothing to raise Sostratos' spirits. For one thing, Syracuse was a city under siege. What kind of feast would the Syracusans be able to make? For another, weren't the *Aphrodite*'s crew and those of the rest of the fleet likelier to make opson for the eels and crabs than to feast off seafood themselves?

But all around the fleet captains were shouting their crews awake, even if none of the others chose to crow. There was Aphrodite's wandering star glowing through the twilight in the east, with the very thinnest sliver of moon not far from it. Were it not for the blazing beacon of the wandering star, Sostratos doubted he would have noticed the moon at all.

Menedemos wasn't worrying about either the moon or Aphrodite's wandering star. Like any captain worthy of the name, he was tasting the wind. "Out of the north, sure enough," he said. "As long as it holds, we can slide right into the northern harbor—the Little Harbor, they call it—at Syracuse."

Well, we could if it weren't for the Carthaginian war galleys, Sostratos thought. *They're between us and where we want to go, and with oars driving them they don't care which way the wind blows. Those are the things Menedemos conveniently forgets to mention.*

His cousin went right on not mentioning them, too. The crew raised the dripping anchors. They lowered the sail from the yard. The round ships' big sails were coming down, too, and filling with the fine breeze that would waft them in exactly the direction they were mad enough to choose to go.

Again, the *Aphrodite* felt much more solid, much more stable, in the water than usual. And again, she moved through the water much more slowly than usual. Sostratos went up onto the poop deck. "If we had to," he asked Menedemos, "could we have the men who aren't rowing throw sacks of grain overboard?"

"You mean, to lighten ship if the Carthaginians were chasing us?" Menedemos asked, and Sostratos dipped his head. His cousin shrugged. "We could have them do it. I doubt it would help much."

The answer struck Sostratos as honest if uninspiring. He watched Katane come into view and then disappear behind him. It *was* a good-sized town, bigger than Messene. He clicked his tongue between his teeth. He still thought it would be a good place to pause for, say, twenty or thirty years. But Menedemos didn't care what he thought, and Menedemos was in command. Sostratos wondered why more soldiers led by a bad general didn't simply run away.

He couldn't run away, not in a ship. Katane was too off away to swim to, and a lot of sailors couldn't swim at all. And Sostratos didn't *know* Menedemos was a bad captain. He did, however, have a strong opinion about that.

His cousin was doing all the little things he needed to do to succeed. He had sharp-eyed Aristeidas in the bow as lookout. And, some time past noon, Aristeidas called, "Ship ho! Ship ho dead ahead!" He pointed south, toward Syracuse. There was the city on the mainland. There was the small island of Ortygia, a few plethra offshore and also heavily built up. And there, worse luck, was the Carthaginian fleet blockading the Little Harbor north of Ortygia and the Great Harbor south of the island.

Aristeidas had spoken with the precision a good lookout needed: he'd called, *Ship ho!* and not, *Sail ho!* The Carthaginian war galleys had their masts down; as warships on active duty did, they moved with oars alone, ready to fight at any moment. Only specks in the distance now, they would look bigger all too soon. Sostratos knew that better than he wanted to.

"What do we do now?" he called to Menedemos.

"Hold our course," his cousin answered. "What else can we do?" *Run* sprang to Sostratos' mind again. But Menedemos went on, "I still think we've got a pretty good chance of sneaking into the Little Harbor. The Carthaginians will go after the round ships before they bother us."

"And how do you know that, O sage of age?" Sostratos demanded.

"For one thing, all the round ships carry a lot more grain than we do," Menedemos answered with surprising patience. "That's what the Carthaginians want to keep from getting into Syracuse. And, for another, we can fight a little bit, and the round ships can't. Why should the Carthaginians make things harder on themselves than they have to?"

All that made a certain amount of sense to Sostratos, but only a certain amount. He pointed toward the oncoming war galleys, which were closing with the fleet of grain carriers at a frightening clip—it certainly frightened him. "Do you really think we can fight *those* even a little bit?" Some of the galleys had two banks of oars—those would be fours. Others had three banks—those would be fives. All of them dwarfed the Roman trireme the *Aphrodite* had crippled. And Sostratos could see how smoothly the rowers handled the oars. These weren't half-trained crews, like the one in that trireme.

"Of course we can," Menedemos said, so heartily that Sostratos knew he was lying in his teeth.

Sostratos couldn't even call his cousin on it, not without disheartening the crew. The Carthaginian galleys scurried toward the round ships like so many scorpions. The sternposts that curved up and forward over their poops like upraised stings added to the resemblance. But the galleys carried their stings at the bow, in their rams. White water foamed from the three horizontal flukes of those rams. Sostratos could see it much more clearly than he would have liked.

But then Aristeidas proved he was indeed a first-rate lookout. "Ships ho!" he sang out. "Ships ho off the port bow!" He'd kept looking around while everyone else thought of nothing but the Carthaginian war galleys, and pointed southeast, where another fleet of warships was rounding Ortygia, heading north as fast as their rowers could take them.

"Are those the Carthaginians who'd been patrolling outside the Great Harbor?" Sostratos asked. "If they are, why aren't they coming after us?"

"How should I know?" Menedemos, for the first time, sounded harassed. He'd seemed ready to deal with one fleet. Two . . .

Sostratos hadn't been ready to deal with even one fleet. He didn't think his cousin had, either, no matter what Menedemos said. But, when he saw something strange, he wanted to find out about it.

And find out about it he did. The Carthaginians had come within three or four stadia before they noticed the compact formation of ships to the east. Then Sostratos heard cries in the harsh Phoenician language. The Carthaginian war galleys forgot all about the fleet of grain ships. They turned their prows to the east, ready to ward off the onslaught they expected from the other ships.

Menedemos whooped for joy. "Those aren't more Carthaginian galleys!" he exclaimed. "Those are Agathokles' ships, sailing out of Syracuse to save us!"

The sailors aboard the *Aphrodite* cheered. They couldn't have been any happier than Sostratos at the thought of those Carthaginian fours and fives bearing down on the akatos, and could know nothing but relief when the enemy fleet's rams turned in a new direction. But then Sostratos said, "If Agathokles aims to rescue us, why aren't his ships turning in on the Carthaginians?"

He'd expected Menedemos to have an answer ready for him. He wasn't ignorant of the sea himself—few Rhodians were—but his cousin knew as much as a man twice his age. All Menedemos said, though, was, "I don't know."

Diokles undoubtedly knew more about the sea than Menedemos. He too sounded baffled. "They're rowing north right on past us, fast as they can go. What *are* they doing?"

"I haven't the faintest notion," Sostratos said. Menedemos dipped his head to show he didn't know, either.

Agathokles' fleet kept on heading north, at the best speed the rowers could make. Again, Sostratos heard shouts from the closest couple of Carthaginian war galleys. He wished he understood the Phoenician tongue. Before long, though, the Carthaginians' actions showed what was in their minds: they began to row after the ships from Syracuse, forgetting about the round ships they'd been on the point of capturing or sinking.

"They're more worried about Agathokles than they are about us." Menedemos sounded affronted.

But Sostratos said, "Wouldn't you be? Those ships can fight back. This fleet can't."

He waited for Menedemos to tell him the *Aphrodite* certainly could fight back. His cousin only sighed, dipped his head again, and said, "But what's Agathokles *doing*? He's sailing out of the harbor where he's safe, he's sailing away from Carthage, not toward it. . . ." His voice trailed off.

What had to be the same thought struck Sostratos at the same time. "If they go along the north coast of Sicily . . ." His voiced faded away, too.

Menedemos took up the idea for him: "They can make for Carthage that way. If that's what Agathokles is doing, he's got balls ~~and~~ to spare." He let out an admiring whistle.

"Look at the way the Carthaginians are chasing him," Sostratos said. "They have to think that's what he's after."

"I do believe you young gentlemen are right," Diokles said. "At least, I can't think of anything else Agathokles'd be up to. And he's a son of a whore who's always up to something, if half the stories you hear about him are true."

"That's the truth," Sostratos said. "Look at how he let his enemies leave the polis and then got rid of them."

"He's ready for anything, sure enough," Menedemos said. "Now we've got to get ready to get into Syracuse ourselves."

"We've got to get ready for more than that," Sostratos said.

"How do you mean?" his cousin asked.

"We've got to get ready to see if we get paid."

"Yes, I suppose that does matter," Menedemos agreed.

"Matter?" Sostratos said. "Matter? Now that we've come all this way without getting killed or captured, making what we were promised would almost make up for the fear we went through getting here. Almost—though I can't think of anything else that would even come close."

Menedemos grinned at him and said, "You worry too much." He pulled back on one steering oar and forward on the other, guiding the *Aphrodite* toward the waiting, welcoming harbor ahead.

"YES, OF COURSE you'll be paid," the Syracusan official said—officiously—as slaves carried sacks of grain off the *Aphrodite* and down the quay into hungry Syracuse. "Come to the palace on Ortygia tomorrow, and you shall have every obolos owed you. So Agathokles promised, and so shall it be."

He spoke as if the sun wouldn't rise if Agathokles broke a promise. Menedemos wondered how the Syracusan tyrant's political enemies felt about that. A moment later, he stopped wondering: being dead, they doubtless felt nothing at all.

No matter how bold a front he'd put up for Sostratos and the akatos' crew, he knew he'd stuck his head in the lion's mouth by sailing down to Syracuse. Now he was going to have to put his head there again. If Agathokles—or rather, Agathokles' brother Antandros, who was in charge of the city while the tyrant led the fleet to Africa—didn't feel like living up to the bargain Onasimos the proxenos had made in Rhegion, what could anyone do about it? Not much, as Menedemos knew too mournfully well.

Some of the sweating slaves taking grain off the *Aphrodite* and the round ships were big, pale, fair-haired Kelts. Some were stocky Italians of one sort or another (Menedemos hoped there were plenty of Romans among them, but couldn't tell by looking). Most, though, had the swarthy, hook-nosed look of Carthaginians.

"Plenty of Hellenes enslaved in Carthage, too," Sostratos said when Menedemos remarked on that. "If you get captured instead of doing the capturing, that's what happens to you. We were lucky, you know."

"Maybe we were." Menedemos could admit it now that they were tied up in the Little Harbor. "But Tykhe is a strong goddess."

"Fortune is a fickle goddess, too," Sostratos said. "Remember what happened to the Athenians who came here a hundred years ago. Most of them would have been lucky with anything so light as lugging sacks of grain."

"I think I've heard you tell that story before," Menedemos said. "Me, I'm more worried about what will happen tomorrow than what happened a hundred years ago."

He'd hoped that would annoy his cousin. It did, but not quite enough to suit him. Instead of going off in a huff, Sostratos answered seriously: "What happens tomorrow will happen in part because of what happened a hundred years ago. How can you understand the present if you don't understand the past?"

"I don't know, and I don't much care," Menedemos said. That *did* affront Sostratos. He stalked toward the bow, dodging men with sacks of grain on their shoulders. Menedemos smiled behind his back.

The slaves weren't the only people on the pier. A tavern tout called, "First two cups of wine free for all the sailors who brought us grain when we needed it so bad. Come to Leosthenes' place, right off the harbor."

A cheer went up on the *Aphrodite.* The cheers that rose from the round ships were smaller—they carried fewer sailors. Menedemos said, "Diokles, I'm going to want half a dozen men on board through the night. Two days' bonus pay for anybody who's willing not to drink and screw himself blind tonight."

He hadn't tried to keep his voice down, on the contrary, he wanted the sailors to hear and to volunteer to pick up an extra three drakhmai. Along with the sailors, Sostratos also heard. He whirled in alarm: he hated spending extra silver. Menedemos thought he would protest out loud, which wouldn't have been good. But Sostratos proved to have sense enough not to do that. Menedemos beckoned him back to the stern as Diokles found volunteers.

"Don't worry," Menedemos told his cousin. "Once Antandros pays us, a few drakhmai won't matter one way or the other."

"They always matter," Sostratos said primly, "and I always worry. One of the things I'm worrying about now is, suppose Antandros doesn't pay us?"

"His man said he would," Menedemos said, that being the strongest reply he could make. He was worried, too, and doing his best not to show it. "And even if he doesn't, we still got half again the going rate up in Rhegion—and we're in *Syracuse,* by the dog of Egypt! We've got a fresh chance for top prices on peafowl chicks and silk and Ariousian—and a fresh chance to unload what's left of our papyrus and ink. If we can't sell 'em here, we can't sell 'em anywhere this side of Athens. And everybody takes them there, so nobody gets a good price for them."

He waited to see if his cousin would stay mulish. Most men would have. But Sostratos was uncommonly reasonable—sometimes, as far as Menedemos was concerned, too reasonable for his own good. Instead of growling, he stopped and thought. At last, grudgingly, he dipped his head. "Fair enough, I suppose. You were right about coming here, as things worked out. Maybe you'll be right again. I hope so."

"Me, too," Menedemos said. And then, because Sostratos had gone halfway toward healing the quarrel, he tried to do the same himself: "I'd have had more faith myself coming down here if I'd known ahead of time that Agathokles would pick that moment to sally forth. Good luck, like we said before."

Sostratos snapped his fingers in annoyance. "By the gods, I'm an idiot! Why didn't I see that before?"

"If you'd asked me, I could have told you you were an idiot," Menedemos said cheerfully. Sostratos glowered. Menedemos went on, "But what didn't you see?"

"It probably wasn't just good luck," Sostratos answered.

"What wasn't?" Menedemos hated it when his cousin got ahead of him. Sostratos thought too well of his thinking as things were.

"Agathokles' sally, of course," he said now. "It all fits together, don't you see? Agathokles had to use something to break the Carthaginians' blockade if he was going to get his own fleet loose. What would be more likely to make the Carthaginians move than a gaggle of nice, fat grain ships?"

Menedemos stared. It *did* fit together, provided.... "That Agathokles must be one sneaky rogue." He held up a hand; this time, he was running even with Sostratos. "We already know he is, from the way he treated his enemies."

"We can't prove any of this, you know," Sostratos said. "I wonder if Antandros would tell us."

"If you ask him, I'll hit you over the head with the biggest pot I can pick up," Menedemos said. "How can you be clever enough to see plots and schemes and foolish enough to want to get in trouble sticking your nose in where it doesn't belong, both at the same time?"

"Hmm." Sostratos pondered again. "Well, maybe you're right."

"I should hope so!" Menedemos said. "Are you going to stay aboard the *Aphrodite* tonight?"

"I think so," Sostratos replied. "Why?"

Menedemos grinned. That was the answer he'd wanted to hear. "Why? Because, O best one, I intend to go into Syracuse and celebrate getting here without getting sunk the way such things ought to be celebrated."

"You're going to have a couple of girls and you're going to get so drunk you won't remember having them," Sostratos said with distaste.

"Right!" Menedemos said. His cousin rolled his eyes. Menedemos couldn't have cared less about his cousin's opinion.

*   *   *

As THE OARSMEN rowed the *Aphrodite*'s boat across the narrow channel separating the Sicilian mainland from the island of Ortygia, Sostratos took a certain somber satisfaction in Menedemos' condition. His cousin's eyes were red, his face sallow. He shaded his eyes from the sun with the palm of his hand. Even though the sea in the Little Harbor was calm as could be, he kept gulping as if he were about to lean over the gunwale and feed the fish.

"I hope you had a good time last night," Sostratos said sweetly.

"I certainly did," Menedemos answered—not too loud. "This one girl—by the gods, she could suck the pit right out of an olive. But . . ." He grimaced. "Now I'm paying the price. If my head fell off, it'd do me a favor."

Sostratos hadn't had the pleasure, but he didn't have the pain, either. As he usually did, he thought that a good bargain. The boat slid up to one of the quays on Ortygia. The fellow standing on the quay looked more like a majordomo than the usual harborside roustabout, but he made the boat fast. As he did so, he asked, "And you are . . . ?"

"I'm Menedemos son of Philodemos, captain of the merchant galley *Aphrodite*," Menedemos told him, still speaking softly. He pointed to Sostratos. "This is my toikharkhos, Sostratos son of Lysistratos."

"You will be here for payment, I expect?" the Syracusan servitor said.

Menedemos dipped his head, then winced. Carefully not smiling, Sostratos said, "That's right."

"Come with me, then," the servitor said, and walked off toward a small, metal-faced gate in the frowning wall of gray stone that warded the rulers of Syracuse from their enemies. Over the past hundred years, those rulers had had a good many foes from whom they needed protection. Not only had the Athenians and Carthaginians besieged the city, but it had also gone through endless rounds of civil strife. *I don't always remember how lucky I am to live in a place like Rhodes,* Sostratos thought. *Coming to a polis that's seen the worst of what its own people can do to one another ought to remind me.*

Inside the grim wall, Ortygia proved surprisingly lush. Fruit trees grew on grassy swards that sheep cropped close. The shade was welcome. So were the perfumes of oleander and arbutus and lavender. Sostratos breathed deeply and sighed with pleasure.

So did Menedemos. "I'm glad to be here," he said. "The light doesn't hurt my eyes nearly so much as it did before."

"That's because you're in the shade now," Sostratos said: only tiny patches of sunlight dappled the path along which they were walking.

"No, I don't think so," Menedemos replied. "I guess my hangover is going away faster than I thought it would."

Sostratos scarcely heard him. He was staring at those little sun-dapples, the places where light slid through gaps in the leaves above. They should have been round. They should have been, but they weren't. They were so many narrow crescents, as if the early moon had broken into hundreds or thousands or myriads of pieces, each shaped like the original.

He looked into the morning sky. It did seem dimmer than it should have, and more so by the moment. Alarm and something greater than alarm, something he belatedly recognized as awe, prickled through him. "I don't think it's your hangover," he said in a voice hardly above a whisper. "I think it's an eclipse."

The sky kept getting darker, as if dusk were falling. The chatter of wagtails and chaffinches died away. The breeze caressing Sostratos' cheek felt cooler than it had. But his shiver when he peered up toward the sun had nothing to do with that. Like the shadows, it too had been pared to a skinny crescent.

"By the gods!" Menedemos was whispering, too. "You can see some of the brighter stars."

So Sostratos could. And seeing them, oddly, touched a chord of memory in him. Speaking a little louder than he had before, he said, " 'In the same summer, at the time of the new moon—since, indeed, it seems to be possible only then—the sun was eclipsed after noon and was restored to its former size once more: it became crescent-shaped, and certain stars appeared.' "

"It's not after noon," the Syracusan servitor said, his voice raucous in the sudden, uncanny gloom. "It's only about the third hour of the morning."

Menedemos knew his cousin far better than the stranger did. He asked, "What are you quoting from?"

"Thoukydides' history, the second book," Sostratos answered. "That eclipse happened the year the Peloponnesian War broke out, more than a hundred and twenty years ago. The world didn't end then, so I don't suppose it will now." He shivered, hoping he was right. In the face of something like this, rationality came hard, hard.

Screams—from women and men both—showed that a lot of people weren't making the least effort to stay rational. "A horrible monster is eating the sun!" someone howled in accented Greek.

"Is he right?" the servitor with Sostratos and Menedemos asked anxiously. "You fellows sound like you know something about it."

Sostratos tossed his head. "No, he's mistaken. It's a natural phenomenon. And look—it's one that doesn't last long. See? It's already getting lighter."

"Gods be praised!" the servitor said.

"I can't make out the stars any more." Menedemos sounded sad.

Birds started singing again. The clamor that had echoed through Ortygia—and, no doubt, through all of Syracuse—ebbed. The small speckles of sunlight on the ground and walls remained crescent-shaped rather than round, but the crescents seemed wider to Sostratos than they had when the eclipse was at its height.

"Well, *that's* something I can tell my grandchildren about, if I live to have any." Agathokles' man—Antandros' now—recovered his aplomb quickly.

So did Menedemos. "Lead on, if you would," he told the fellow.

Following them both, Sostratos thought, *I should be making notes, or at least standing still and remembering all I can. When will I see another eclipse? Never, probably.* But he kept on after his cousin and the servitor. With a sigh, he strode into the palace from which Agathokles had ruled Syracuse and in which his brother now held sway for him.

Before they came into Antandros' presence, more servitors patted them most thoroughly to make sure they carried to weapons. Sostratos thought himself more likely to want to kill someone after that sort of indignity than before it, but kept quiet.

Antandros sat on what wasn't quite a throne. He was older than Sostratos had expected; he'd lost much of his hair, and gray streaked what remained. When a steward murmured to him who Sostratos and Menedemos were, he leaned toward the man with a hand cupped behind his ear. "What was that?" he asked. The steward repeated himself, louder this time. "Oh," Antandros said. "The chaps from the akatos." He turned his gaze on the two Rhodians. "Well, young men, between the Carthaginians and the eclipse, I'd bet you've had more excitement the past couple of days than you really wanted."

We certainly have! Sostratos thought. But before he could speak, Menedemos said, "I always thought a quiet life was a boring life, sir."

Antandros held his hand behind his ear again. "What was that?" As the steward had, Menedemos repeated himself. Antandros said, "My little brother would agree with you. Me, I don't mind sleeping soft in my own bed with a full belly every now and again, and that's the truth."

I'm with you, Sostratos thought. But Antandros' homely desires went a long way toward explaining why Agathokles ruled Syracuse and his older brother served him.

"How many sacks of grain did you bring into the polis?" Antandros asked.

Menedemos looked to Sostratos, trusting him to have the number at his fingertips. And he did: "It was 791, sir," he replied, loud enough to let the man in charge of Syracuse hear him the first time.

Antandros' smile showed a missing front tooth. "Paying you won't even hurt. A merchant galley doesn't hold much next to a round ship, does she?"

"She wasn't built to haul grain, sir," Sostratos agreed, "but we were glad to help your polis as best we could." *Menedemos was, anyhow.*

Amusement sparked in Antandros' eyes. Sostratos got the feeling Agathokles' brother knew he was lying. But all Antandros said was, "You'll be glad to get paid, too, won't you?"

"Yes, sir." Sostratos wouldn't deny the obvious.

"You will be," Antandros said. "No, you aren't made for hauling grain, sure enough. What other cargo have you got aboard?"

"Rhodian perfume, Koan silk, Ariousian from Khios, papyrus and ink—and peafowl chicks," Sostratos answered.

"What was that last?" Hearing something unfamiliar, Antandros hadn't got it.

"Peafowl chicks," Sostratos said again. "We sold the grown pea-cock and peahens earlier, mostly in Taras."

"Can't let the polluted Tarentines get ahead of Syracuse," Antan-dros exclaimed. "Now we have plenty of grain to feed birds, too—plenty of grain to feed everyone. We went from hungry to fat in one fell swoop when the fleet got in. What do you want for these chicks? And how many have you got?"

"We have seven left, sir." Sostratos flicked a glance toward Me-nedemos. His cousin's lips silently shaped a word. Sostratos fought back the urge to whistle in astonishment. Menedemos didn't do things by halves. But Sostratos had, in a way, asked, and the gamble struck him as good, too. In a calm voice, he went on, "We want three minai apiece."

The steward looked horrified. Privately, Sostratos didn't blame him a bit. "I'll take all of them," Antandros said. "To the crows—no, to the peafowl—with the Tarentines. As soon as I get the chance, I'll send one on to my little brother in Africa."

"Ahh!" With the pleasure of curiosity satisfied and a guess confirmed, Sostratos forgot about the dismayed steward. "So that's what Agathokles was up to! He *is* sailing around the north side of Sicily, then?"

"That's right." Antandros dipped his head. "Up till now, all the fighting in this war has been here in Sicily. But my brother decided it was time for the Carthaginians to see how they like war among their wheatfields and olive trees. No one has ever invaded their home-land—till now."

"May he give them a good kick in the ballocks, then," Menedemos said. Sostratos thought the same thing. The Macedonian marshals littering the landscape in the east of the Hellenic world were bad enough. Having barbarians overrunning poleis in Great Hellas struck him as even worse.

A moment later, he wondered why. What could the Carthaginians have visited on Syracuse that Hellenes hadn't already inflicted on other Hellenes? The question struck him as no great compliment to Carthage, but rather a judgment on what Hellenes had visited on one another.

Antandros spoke to the steward: "Take them to the treasury. Pay them for the grain and for these birds."

"Yes, sir," the steward replied, though he looked as if he would have said something else had he dared. He turned to Sostratos and Menedemos. "Come with me, O best ones." He didn't sound as if he meant that, either.

Can it be this simple? Sostratos wondered as he followed the steward out of what would have been the throne room had Agathokles called himself a king. *Will Antandros really just pay us for the grain and the peafowl and send us on our way? Nothing this whole voyage has been that simple.*

Seeing the treasury did nothing to reassure him. Ortygia was a fortress. The rulers of Syracuse stored their silver and gold in a fortress within a fortress, behind massive stone walls, gates whose valves seemed to Sostratos as thick as his own body, and a veritable phalanx of soldiers: some Hellenes, others Italians and Kelts. Sostratos tried to imagine what those soldiers would have done had he and Menedemos approached them without the steward's protective company. He wasn't sorry to find himself failing.

But the steward, whatever he thought, did not dare disobey Antandros. The clerk to whom he spoke looked surprised, but asked no questions. How long would a man who asked questions last in Syracuse? Sostratos couldn't have gauged it by the water clock, but thought he knew the answer nonetheless: *not long.*

Instead of asking those dangerous questions, the clerk started bringing out leather sacks. When Sostratos hefted one, he asked the fellow, "A mina?" The clerk dipped his head and went back for more silver. By the time he was done, what seemed like a small mountain of sacks stood on the broad stone counter that separated him from the two Rhodians.

Solemnly, Menedemos said, "We have just made a profit."

"So we have," Sostratos said. "I ought to count the drakhmai in a few of these sacks." Cheating by one part in twenty, maybe even one part in ten, would be easy if the treasury clerk didn't offer the use of a set of scales to weight the silver, something he showed no sign of doing.

The silence that came crashing down was so very frigid, it put Sostratos in mind of snow: only a word to most Rhodians, since none had fallen on his island in all the days of his life, or, for that matter, his father's, but he'd seen the stuff in a hard winter in Athens. Now Menedemos spoke quickly: "I think we're all right."

"But—" Sostratos was the sort of man who liked to see everything pegged down tight, so there could be no possible doubt about where it lay.

"I said, I think we're all right." As if trying to get something across to Antandros, Menedemos spoke louder than he had to. He spoke so loud, in fact, that his voice echoed from the stone walls and ceiling of the treasury.

Hearing those echoes reminded Sostratos of exactly where he was. It also reminded him of his earlier thought about what happened to Syracusans who asked questions. That thought led to another: what would happen to a stranger who asked questions in Syracuse? Sostratos decided he didn't really want to find out the answer to that one.

"Well, I suppose we are, too," he said, with what he hoped wasn't too sheepish a smile. Menedemos' sigh of relief was loud enough to raise echoes, too. The steward and the treasury clerk relaxed.

Menedemos said, "Could we have two large leather sacks and a couple of guards to take us back to the *Aphrodite*'s boat? This is a *lot* of silver, and all of Ortygia knows by now that we're getting it."

When the steward hesitated, Sostratos said, "If you like, they could come across to the akatos with us, and bring the peafowl chicks and their cages back for Antandros."

"All right." The steward dipped his head. "That does make sense."

Sostratos felt like cheering. The peafowl had been a weight on his back like the world on Atlas' ever since he first heard the peacock screech in the Great Harbor at Rhodes. Now, at last, after spring and most of summer, he would be free of it. He hadn't known just how heavy it was till he faced the prospect of having it lifted from him.

And he gave a sigh of relief of his own when the guards the steward summoned proved to be Hellenes. Had he had a couple of tall, beefy Kelts for an escort, he would have worried that they might set on Menedemos and him. Of course, Hellenes could be light-fingered and murderous, too, but he chose not to dwell on that.

"How much money have you got there?" one of these fellows asked in interested tones.

"As much as Antandros wanted us to have," Menedemos answered before Sostratos could come up with a reply to a question with so many implications. He admired the one his cousin had found.

From somewhere or other, the rowers in the *Aphrodite*'s boat had got hold of a jar of wine. When they took the Syracusan soldiers across the narrow channel to the merchant galley's berth in the Little Harbor, their stroke suggested that this was the first time they'd ever handled oars in their lives. Sostratos was embarrassed. Menedemos, plainly, was mortified. He couldn't even yell at the men without making them all look even worse to the Syracusans than they did already.

Menedemos cursed in a low voice as he boarded the *Aphrodite*. But Sostratos' exasperation melted away as sailors loaded the peafowl chicks and their cages into the boat. He even tossed the two Syracusans a drakhma each, more in sympathy with them for having to deal with the birds than as a tip for getting him and Menedemos back to the akatos unrobbed.

"Thank you kindly, O best one," one soldier said. The other waved and grinned. The boat's crew took them back to Ortygia. The channel between mainland and island was narrow enough to let them escape misfortune.

As the crew returned—still rowing most erratically—Sostratos said, "It's a good thing they didn't have to do anything difficult."

"What's so good about it?" Menedemos growled. He screamed at the men in the boat: "You idiots! If you're on your own polluted time, I don't care what you do, you whipworthy rogues. I'll do it right alongside you, as a matter of fact. But you've got no business— none, not a dust speck's worth—getting drunk when you know you're going to have to do something important in a little while. Suppose Sostratos and I had been running for our lives. Could you have got us away safe? Not likely!"

The rowers wore wide, wine-filled, placating smiles, like so many dogs that had somehow angered the leader of their pack. One of them said, "Sorry, skipper. That eclipse knocked us for a loop, it did. And everything worked out all right." His grin got wider and more foolish.

Sostratos thought that a fair excuse, but not his cousin: "No, it didn't, the gods curse you." Menedemos' voice rose in both volume and pitch. It got so shrill, in fact, that Sostratos dug a finger in his ear. "You wide-arsed simpleton, you made the ship look bad. Nobody makes my ship look bad—nobody, do you hear me?"

Half of Syracuse heard him. By the way he was shrieking, Sostratos wouldn't have been surprised if Agathokles, somewhere off the north coast of Sicily, heard him. He tried to remember the last time he'd seen Menedemos so furious, tried and failed. *It's been a long time since anyone embarrassed him in public,* he thought.

If the sodden rowers had had tails, they would have wagged them. "Yes, skipper," said the one who felt like talking. "We *are* sorry, skipper—aren't we, lads?" All of them solemnly dipped their heads.

But Menedemos, like a Fury, remained unappeased. "Sorry? You aren't sorry yet!" He spun toward Sostratos. "Dock every one of those bastards three days' pay!"

"Three days?" Sostratos said—quietly. "Isn't that a bit much?"

"By the gods, no!" Menedemos didn't bother lowering his voice. "One day because they've wasted a day's work with their antics. And two more to remind them not to be such drunken donkeys again."

Instead of getting angry themselves, as they might have done, the men in the *Aphrodite*'s boat looked contrite, as if they were sacrificing their silver in place of a goat in expiation for their sins. That too was the wine working in them, Sostratos judged. "It'll never happen again, skipper," their spokesman said. "Never!" A tear rolled down his cheek.

Sostratos nudged Menedemos and spoke one word out of the side of his mouth: "Enough."

He wondered if his cousin would listen to him, or if Menedemos' anger, like that of Akhilleus in the *Iliad,* was so great and deep as to leave him beyond the reach of common sense. For a moment, he feared passion held complete sway over Menedemos. But at last, gruffly, Menedemos said, "Oh, very well. Come aboard, you clods."

The drunken sailors scurried away from him. Another Homeric comparison occurred to Sostratos. In a low voice, he asked, "How does it feel to be Zeus, father of both gods and men?"

Menedemos chuckled, the rage finally ebbing from him. "Not bad, now that you mention it. Not bad at all."

"I believe you," Sostratos said. "You don't often see anybody put men in fear like that."

"Every once in a while, a captain needs to be able to do that," Menedemos said seriously. "If the men don't *know* they have to obey, know it down deep, you won't get the most out of them. Sometimes you need to—when a trireme is coming after you, for instance."

"I suppose so," Sostratos said, "but wouldn't it be better if they obeyed you out of love? As the godlike Platon said, an army of lovers could conquer the world."

His cousin snorted. "Maybe it would be better, but it's not likely. Try to make your rowers love you, and they'll just think you're soft."

Sostratos sighed. Menedemos' words had the hard, clear ring of probability to them, like silver coins dropped on a stone counter. As for an army of lovers . . . The soldiers of Philip, Alexander the Great's father, had killed the Theban Sacred Band—made up of erastoi and their eromenoi—to the last man, after which Alexander went out and conquered the world without them. Platon hadn't lived to see any of that. Sostratos wondered what he would have had to say about it. Nothing good, he suspected.

Platon *had* come here to Syracuse, to try to make a philosopher out of the tyrant Dionysos' worthless son. That hadn't worked, either. Sostratos sighed again. People seemed harder to change than lovers of wisdom wished them to be.

Menedemos changed the subject like the captain of a round ship swinging the yard from one side of the mast to the other to go onto a new tack: "Now all we need to do is a little more business here, maybe, and then get our silver home. Even my father won't have much to complain about."

"It'll be a shorter trip, or it should," Sostratos said. "We won't have to stop at nearly so many places." He coughed delicately. "And we'd do better not to stop at Taras after all, wouldn't we?"

"What if we would?" Menedemos said. "We can visit Kroton again, and then sail across the gulf there to Kallipolis. Old what's-his-name in Taras won't hear about us till we're gone."

"You hope Gylippos won't," Sostratos said. "Was Phyllis worth it?"

"I thought so then," Menedemos answered, shrugging. "A little too late to worry about it now, wouldn't you say?"

"A lot too late." But Sostratos didn't sound amused or indulgent. "When *will* you grow up?"

Menedemos grinned at him. "Not soon, I hope."

11

MENEDEMOS SAT IN A TAVERN NOT FAR FROM THE LITTLE
Harbor, drinking wine of the best sort: wine he hadn't bought. Even
now, half a month after the grain fleet came into Syracuse, its sailors
had trouble buying their own drinks. The polis had been hungry;
now it had sitos and to spare. Menedemos wondered how long the
gratitude would last. He was a little surprised it had lasted this long.

He might have been able to get his wine free even if he hadn't
brought grain into Syracuse. Like a lot of wineshops, this one gave
sailors and merchants cups of the local vintage if they told what news
they'd heard and so drew customers into the place. His tales of the
wars of Alexander's generals could well have kept him as drunk as
he wanted for as long as he wanted.

He was going on about Polemaios' defection from his uncle, An-
tigonos, when a panting Syracusan dashed into the tavern and gasped,
"They've landed! They've burned their ships!" He looked around.
"Am I the first?" he asked anxiously.

"That you are," the tavernkeeper said, and handed him a large cup
of neat wine as the tavern exploded in excited chatter.

"Who's landed?" Menedemos asked.

"Why, Agathokles has, of course, not far from Carthage," the Syracusan replied. Menedemos started to ask, *How do you know that?*
It was, he realized, the kind of question likelier to come from his
cousin. Before it could pass his lips, the new arrival answered it: "My
uncle's cousin is a clerk on Ortygia, and he was bringing Antandros
some tax records when the messenger came in."

"Ahhh," went through the tavern. Men dipped their heads, ac-
cepting the authority of this source. Menedemos wondered what Sostratos would have thought of it. Less than most people here did, he
suspected.

Another question occurred to him. Again, someone else antici-
pated him, asking, "Burned the ships, you say?"

"That's right." The fellow with news dipped his head. "It was six days from here to Africa, a long, slow trip around the north coast of our island, made slower by bad winds. Our ships were getting close to land when they spied the Carthaginian fleet right behind them—and the Carthaginians spied *them*, too."

He could tell a story. Menedemos found himself leaning toward him. So did half the other people in the tavern. "What happened then?" somebody breathed.

"Well, the Carthaginians came on with a great sprint, rowing as if their hearts would burst," the Syracusan said. He held out his cup to the tavernkeeper, who filled it to the brim without a word of protest. After a sip, the fellow went on, "They got so close, their lead ships were shooting at Agathokles' rearmost just before our fleet beached itself."

"Our men must have thought their hopes were eclipsed," the taverner said. People hadn't stopped talking about the uncanny events of the day after the grain fleet's arrival.

But the man with news tossed his head. "My uncle's cousin said Antandros asked about that. The way Agathokles read the omen, he found out, was by saying it foretold ill for the enemy because it happened after our fleet sailed. He said it would have been bad if it had happened before."

Menedemos wondered what a priest of Phoibos Apollo would have had to say about that. He was sure a ready-for-aught like Agathokles wouldn't have asked a priest, but would have put forward the interpretation that served him best. And the local still hadn't answered the question. Menedemos asked it again: "What happened to Agathokles' ships?"

"Well, we outshot the Carthaginians, because we had so many soldiers aboard our ships. That, I gather, was how we beached, with the barbarians staying out of bowshot. Agathokles held an assembly once we were ashore."

"Just like Agamemnon, under the walls of Troy," someone murmured.

"He said he'd prayed to Demeter and Persephone, the goddesses who watch over Sicily, when the lookouts first spied the Carthaginians," the local went on. "He said he'd promised them the fleet as a burnt offering if they let it come ashore safely. And they had, so he burned his own flagship, and all the other captains set fire to their ships with torches. The trumpeters sounded the call to battle, the men raised a cheer, and they all prayed for more good fortune."

And they can't come back to Sicily again, or not easily, Menedemos thought. *If they don't win, they all die, as slowly and horribly as the Carthaginians can make them. Burning the fleet has to remind them of that, too. Sure enough, Agathokles knows how to make his men do what he wants of them.*

A man with a short gray beard asked, "How did Agathokles' messenger get here, if he burned all his ships?" That was a question the precise Sostratos might have found.

"In a captured fishing boat," the man with news replied. He had all the answers. Whether they were true or not, Menedemos couldn't have said. But they were plausible.

It soon became clear that the Syracusans were much more interested in Agathokles' doings than in those of the generals in the east. The latter might have been exciting to hear about, but didn't affect them personally. No one from out of the east had come to Sicily with conquest on his mind since the Athenians a century before. But war with Carthage was a matter of freedom or slavery, life or death. A Carthaginian army remained outside the walls. If it ever broke into Syracuse . . . Menedemos wasn't sorry he'd be sailing soon.

He grabbed a couple of olives from a red earthenware bowl on the counter in front of the tavernkeeper. The fellow didn't charge for them, and he quickly discovered why: they were perhaps the saltiest he'd ever tasted. The extra wine the taverner sold on account of them was bound to make up, and more than make up, for the few khalkoi they cost.

Fortunately, his own cup was half full. He gulped it down to water the new desert in his throat, then left the tavern for the harbor not far away. As he got back to the *Aphrodite,* he saw her boat making the short pull from Ortygia. The rowers' strokes were so perfectly smooth and regular, they might have been serving one of the Athenian processional galleys, not an akatos' boat.

Sostratos sat near the stern of the boat. "I've got news," he called when he saw Menedemos. "Agathokles has landed in Africa!"

That was news to most of the sailors aboard the merchant galley; they exclaimed in surprise. But Menedemos only grinned and answered, "Yes, and he burned all his ships once he did it, too."

The sailors exclaimed again, even louder this time. Sostratos blinked. "How did you know that?" he asked. "I just heard it myself."

"I was wasting my time in a tavern—or that's what you would call it," Menedemos said as his cousin and the rowers came aboard at the stern. "A fellow came across from Ortygia practically on fire with the word, and earned himself some free wine to put the fire out."

"Oh." Sostratos gave the impression of an air-filled pig's bladder that had sprung a leak. Then he snapped his fingers, plainly remembering something, and brightened. "Well, I've got some other news, too."

"Tell me, O best one," Menedemos heard. "I haven't heard it all."

"Only the best parts of it," Sostratos said unhappily. "But I managed to sell all the papyrus and ink we had left, and I got a good price for them, too."

"*Did* you?" Menedemos clapped him on the back, glad to give credit where it was due. "You were right about that, then."

His cousin dipped his head. "Thanks to the war with Carthage, Agathokles' chancery was almost out of papyrus altogether. They were scraping the ink off old sheets and writing on boards and potsherds, the way people did in the old days. One of the chief clerks kissed me when I told him how much we had."

"He *must* have been excited," Menedemos murmured. Sostratos dipped his head again. Then, a moment too late, he glared. As a youth, Menedemos had had more than his fair share of older men as admirers; he'd quite enjoyed playing the heartbreaker. Sostratos, on the other hand, had been tall and skinny and angular, all shanks and knees and elbows and pointy nose. So far as Menedemos knew, nobody'd bothered pursuing his cousin, either in Rhodes or, later, in Athens. Changing the subject looked like a good idea: "Just how much did you get?"

Sostratos told him. Menedemos whistled and clapped him on the back again. Sostratos said, "It's not so much when you set it against what we made for hauling the grain and for the last of the peacocks, but it's a lot more than we would have got in Athens. That's where everyone with papyrus and ink goes."

"Bad for prices," Menedemos agreed. "And that's one less stop we'll have to make on the way back to Rhodes."

"What's wrong with stopping in Athens?" Sostratos asked. "I like Athens fine."

"I like Athens fine, too, when we've got time for it," Menedemos said. "But we're a long way from home, and it's starting to get late in the sailing season: we're less than a month from the fall equinox. Things get murky when the days go short; you can't tell your landmarks the way you should. And there's always the chance of a storm, too. Why take the extra risk?"

"All right." Sostratos threw his hands in the air. "If it's enough to make *you* careful, that's plenty to convince me." Before Menedemos could reply, Sostratos added, "If there were a woman in Athens, you'd stop no matter whose wife she was."

"Not if she were yours," Menedemos said. Sostratos gave him an ironic bow. As Menedemos returned it, he wondered if he'd just told the truth.

SOSTRATOS HADN'T SEEN much of Syracuse during his time in the polis. He couldn't have gone up onto the wall to walk around the town, not unless he wanted an arrow in his ribs. And he couldn't have ridden out to see the countryside, as he had up at Pompaia; the next sight he would have seen was the inside of a Carthaginian slave pen.

I wonder when I'll come back to Sicily, he thought. *I wonder if I'll ever come back to Sicily.* He shrugged. No way to know the future.

Menedemos stood at the *Aphrodite*'s stern, his hands on the steering-oar tillers. He dipped his head to Diokles, saying, "Set the stroke."

"Right you are, skipper." The keletustes struck the bronze square with his mallet. To emphasize the rhythm as the merchant galley left port, he raised his voice, too: "Rhyppa*pai*! Rhyppa*pai*!"

For swank, Menedemos had every oar manned as the *Aphrodite* left the Little Harbor. The rowers did him proud, their oars rising and falling in smooth unison. *Of course,* Sostratos thought, *it's a lazy*

man's pace, nothing like what we did when we were running from that
Roman trireme—or when we turned back towards it! What an adven-
ture that was!

He paused in bemusement and some dismay. *I'll be telling the story
of that trireme for the rest of my life, and I'll sound more like a hero
every time I do.* He didn't care for men his father's age who bored
dinner parties with tales of their swashbuckling youth, but he suddenly saw how they came to be the way they were. *A historian is
supposed to understand causes,* he thought, but then he tossed his
head. This was one of which he would sooner have stayed ignorant.

As Syracuse receded behind the merchant galley, Menedemos took
more than half the sailors off the oars. The ship glided up the Sicilian
coast toward the mainland of Italy. Dolphins leaped. Terns splashed
into the sea, some only a few cubits from the *Aphrodite.* One came
out with a fish in its beak.

"You'll have an easy trip home," Menedemos called to him from
the stern. "No more peafowl to worry about."

"I'm *so* disappointed they're gone," Sostratos answered.

Not only his cousin but half the sailors laughed. Aristeidas the
lookout said, "The foredeck still smells like birdshit."

"You're right—it does," Sostratos agreed. "It probably will for a
while, too."

"So it will," Aristeidas said darkly. "Now that you don't have to
take care of peafowl any more, you can go wherever you like on the
ship. Me, I'm stuck up here most of the time."

You can go wherever you like. Aristeidas had said it without irony,
and Sostratos took it the same way. Then he thought about what a
landlubber would make of it. The *Aphrodite* was only forty or forty-
five cubits long, and perhaps seven cubits wide at her beamiest. From
the perspective of someone used to strolling through a polis or across
his fields, that didn't give a man much room. A sailor, though, had
a much more cramped view of what was roomy and what wasn't.

As if to prove as much, Sostratos went back to the poop deck,
which to him felt as far from the smelly foredeck as Athens was from
Rhodes. Menedemos asked him, "What have we got left to trade on
the way home?"

"A little wine," Sostratos answered. "Some perfume. I'd like to get rid of that, if we see the chance—taking it back to Rhodes would be a shame, when it came from there. And we still have some silk." He sighed.

Menedemos took a hand off the steering oar to poke him in the ribs. "I know what you're thinking of: that copper-haired Keltic girl you were screwing in Taras."

Sostratos' ears heated; he had indeed been thinking of Maibia, in and especially out of the Koan silk tunic she wore. "Well, what if I was?" he asked roughly.

"It's all right with me." As usual when the talk rolled around to women, Menedemos sounded disgustingly cheerful. "I've got plenty to think about myself."

"If you'd do some thinking beforehand . . ." Sostratos said.

"That takes away half the fun. More than half," he cousin answered.

"I don't see it that way," Sostratos said with a shrug.

"I know you don't." Menedemos leaned forward and spoke in a low voice: "Just exactly how much silver *are* we carrying? In the name of the gods, don't yell out the answer. The last thing we want to do is give the sailors ideas." In something close to a whisper, Sostratos told him. Menedemos whistled softly. "That's even more than I figured. It's almost enough for ballast."

"On a ship this size?" Sostratos made the automatic mental calculation, then tossed his head. "Don't be silly."

"Mm, I suppose not." By the look of concentration on his face, Menedemos was making the same calculation. "But I'll tell you this: it's more silver than my father expected us to bring back. And I'll rub his nose in it, too."

"Why bother?" Sostratos asked. "Uncle Philodemos will be glad to see you home safe, and he'll be glad of the profit. Isn't that enough?"

"No, by Zeus." A hot eagerness thrummed in Menedemos' voice, like a following wind in the rigging. "Ever since I started toddling around and stopped making messes on the floor, he's always gone on and on about what a great trader he is and how I don't measure up. Let's see him talk like that now."

"I didn't come out here thinking to outdo my father," Sostratos said.

"You're toikharkhos. I'm captain," Menedemos said, that hot eagerness turning to something cold and hard for a moment. But he went on, "Uncle Lysistratos doesn't go around bragging and carping all the time; I will say that. And the two of you get along better than Father and I do. Anyone who saw us would say *that*."

"I suppose so," Sostratos said. "We'd have a hard time getting along worse than the two of you, wouldn't we?"

"You're as comfortable together as a foot and an old sandal, and you know it," Menedemos said. "The two of you *fit* like that. Do you have any idea how jealous it makes me?"

"No, I didn't, not till you just mentioned it." Sostratos studied his cousin with an avid curiosity of a small boy seeing an unexpected lizard emerge from under a chunk of bark. "I'm usually the one who holds things inside, but you've kept that secret for years. Forever, really."

By Menedemos' expression, he wished he hadn't told it now. He said, "I'm not sorry to get away from Rhodes for months at a time, I'll tell you that."

"I can see as much," Sostratos said judiciously. He set a hand on Menedemos' shoulder. "We won't be back for a little while yet. Nothing happens in a hurry on the sea. Even when we were fighting that Roman trireme, we seemed to be moving as slowly as if we were in a dream."

"Not to me," Menedemos said. "It all happened very fast, as far as I was concerned. I needed to gauge just the right moment to tug at the steering oars, and it all felt like it happened in a heartbeat. That's the sweetest sound I ever heard—our hull riding up and over that polluted whoreson's oars."

"If you think I'll argue, you're mad," Sostratos said. "That sound meant we stayed free men, and what could be sweeter than that?" He pointed ahead. "There's Cape Leukopetra, with Cape Herakleion just off to the east."

"I know, my dear. I saw them quite a while ago." Now Menedemos sounded acidulous, perhaps because he'd shown more of himself to Sostratos a little while before than he'd wanted to. "I don't have to change the way the ship is heading this very instant, you know."

"So you don't," Sostratos agreed. "Proves my point—nothing happens in a hurry on the sea."

Menedemos stuck out his tongue. They both laughed. Laughter came easy when they'd made a profit, when they were sailing away from danger and not into it, and—for Sostratos, at least—when they were homeward bound.

"THAT SHOULD JUST about do it," Menedemos said as the *Aphrodite* eased into place alongside a quay in Kroton's harbor.

"I think so, too, skipper," Diokles said. "*Oöp!*" he called in a louder voice, and the rowers rested at their oars. A couple of sailors tossed lines to men on the quay, who made the merchant galley fast.

"You were here earlier this summer, weren't you?" one of the roustabouts called.

"That's right," Menedemos answered. "We went up the west coast of Italy, and then down to Syracuse with the grain fleet from Rhegion. You've heard how Agathokles landed not far from Carthage?"

"Sure have," the roustabout said. "That took balls, that did."

From the bow, Sostratos asked, "Do you know what happened when the Roman fleet attacked Pompaia? We were up that way, and almost got caught."

"It came to grief, or that's what I heard," the Krotonite said. Several sailors clapped their hands together in grim delight. The roustabout went on, "The sailors and soldiers aboard scattered to plunder, and the folk from all the towns thereabouts—not just Pompaia, but Nole and Noukeria and Akherrai, too—gathered together and drove 'em back to their ships with heavy losses." More sailors clapped. Some of them cheered. The local added, "Some people say one Roman ship got wrecked by a merchantman, but you won't get me to swallow that."

"I wouldn't either, if I were you," Menedemos said gravely. The sailors who heard him sniggered and brought their hands up to their mouths to keep from laughing out loud. The roustabout gave them curious looks, but nobody said another word, so he shrugged and started to turn away.

Before he left, Sostratos asked him, "How does the marvelous Hipparinos like his peafowl chicks?"

"You're those fellows!" The Krotonite snapped his fingers in excitement. "I thought you were those fellows, but I wasn't sure, and I didn't like to take the chance. Do you know what happened there? Do you?"

"If we did, would we be asking?" Menedemos did his best to seem the very image of sweet reason.

"That's right, how could you? You're just a pack of polluted foreigners," the Krotonite said. For Menedemos, sweet reason dissolved in anger. But before he could show it, the local went on, "Hipparinos, he has this Kastorian hunting hound—you know, brought here all the way from Sparta—he's as proud of as his son. Prouder, probably, on account of all his son wants to do is drink neat wine and screw." He paused. "What exactly was I talking about?"

"Peafowl chicks," Menedemos and Sostratos said together.

"That's right. I sure was." The roustabout snapped his fingers again. "Anyway, like I said, he has this hound named Taxis." Hipparinos, Menedemos thought, would be just the man to name a dog Order. The Krotonite continued, "And Taxis, he got his first look at these chicks and he ate one up before anybody could tell him not to or grab him to keep him from doing it. You could've heard old Hipparinos screaming from the agora all the way to the guard towers on the wall."

"I believe that," Menedemos said. "His precious hound is even more precious now—it ate up a mina and a half of silver at one gulp."

"A mina and a half? Is that all?" the local said.

"Is that *all*?" Sostratos echoed, as if he couldn't believe his ears.

"That's what I said, and that's what I meant," the Krotonite told him. "Hipparinos has been saying that miserable little bird cost him five minai."

Menedemos started to tell how Hipparinos had tried to cheat him on the price he'd paid for the two peafowl chicks. Just then, Sostratos had a coughing fit. Menedemos let the story go untold. For a Krotonite to disparage a rich fellow citizen was one thing. For him, a foreigner, to disparage that same man might prove something else again.

After a little more chat, the roustabout did leave. Sostratos hurried back toward the stern and climbed up onto the poop deck. "I don't think we ought to spend much time here at all," he said. "Hipparinos wasn't happy with us when we came here last. Now, thanks to that accursed dog, he'll like us even less."

"And thanks to our giving him the lie about the price he paid," Menedemos added.

"Yes, thanks to that, too," Sostratos agreed. "Besides, we did sell what we could when we were here last. I think we should push on straight to Kallipolis tomorrow morning."

"You're probably right," Menedemos said with a sigh. "The wind's out of the north, though. That means either tacking or rowing, and a two-day trip across the gulf either way."

"Things would be simpler if we could put in at Taras," Sostratos pointed out.

Menedemos glared. "Things would be simpler if you'd keep your mouth shut, too. I'm getting tired of hearing about that."

Had Sostratos pushed it any further, Menedemos would have given him all he wanted and then some. But his cousin just shrugged and said, "We both may be glad not to see each other for a while once we get back to Rhodes." Sostratos pointed north. "What do you make of those clouds?"

After studying them, Menedemos shrugged. "Maybe rain, maybe not. I don't think they look too bad. How about you?"

"They seem the same way to me, too," Sostratos answered, "but I know you've got the better weather eye."

That was true, but it was one more thing Menedemos wouldn't have admitted so casually. He tasted the wind, trying to read the secrets it held. "I think we will get rain if it stays steady. No more than a little rain, though. It's still early in the year for one of those equinoctial storms—a bit early, anyhow."

"Good," Sostratos said. "I was hoping you'd tell me something like that. Because you're so weatherwise, of course I believe you." Menedemos felt proud of that till he remembered how fond of irony his cousin was.

SOSTRATOS WOKE BEFORE sunrise. The eastern sky was just going from gray to pink. Dawn didn't become spectacularly red. That eased his mind; a red, red, sunrise often warned of bad weather ahead. His gaze swung to the north. The clouds covered more of the sky than they had the day before, but not a great deal more.

From behind him, Menedemos said, "I'd like the weather better if we weren't likely to have to spend a night at sea."

Sostratos started. "I didn't know you were awake."

"Well, I am." Menedemos looked up the pier toward the dark, jumbled mass of houses and shops and temples that made up Kroton.

"Expecting Hipparinos with an army of ruffians at his back?" Sostratos asked.

"An army of ruffians *and* a Kastorian hound with a taste for peafowl." Menedemos' tone was light, but Sostratos didn't think he he was joking. And, sure enough, he started shaking sailors awake. "Come on, boys," he said. "The sooner we're on the open sea again, the better."

"Says who?" a sleepy man asked around a yawn.

"Says your captain, that's who," Menedemos answered.

"And your toikharkhos," Sostratos added, throwing his obolos of authority after Menedemos' drakhma.

Diokles sat up straight on the rower's bench where he'd slept. "And your keleustes," he said. Formally, his rank was lower than Sostratos'. Among the sailors, though, his word carried more weight.

Hipparinos had not made an appearance, with or without bravos, by the time the *Aphrodite* left Kroton. "Many good-byes to the town, and to the crows with him and his hungry hound both," Menedemos said.

The wind kept backing and shifting, coming now from the north, now from the northwest. When it blew from the northwest, the *Aphrodite* could sail quite handily, but whenever it swung back toward the north Menedemos had to tack, zigzagging his course with the akatos taking the wind first on one bow and then swinging about to take it on the other. Grunting sailors heaved the yard round till it ran from bow to quarter and slanted toward the breeze. It was a slow business, and a miserably inexact one when it came to setting a course.

"Here's hoping we can find Kallipolis when we get in the neighborhood," Sostratos said.

"As long as I head northeast, I'll strike the mainland somewhere," Menedemos said. "Then we can feel our way along the coast till we come to the island."

"There ought to be a way to navigate more surely," Sostratos said. "The only trouble is, I don't know what it would be."

"If you did, you'd get rich enough to make Kroisos look like a piker," Menedemos said. "Every captain in the world would buy whatever you had."

"Buy it or try to steal it." Sostratos pointed north. "Here come those clouds."

"I think they're finally done fooling around," Menedemos said unhappily. "When they cover the sun, I'll have even less idea of just where we're going—one more drawback to sailing out of sight of land."

"That storm almost sank us the last time you did it," Sostratos said. "I wonder if you offended some god without knowing it."

He didn't mean it seriously. Even so, Menedemos spat into the bosom of his tunic. Diokles rubbed his apotropaic ring. "Shouldn't say things like that," he muttered, just loud enough for Sostratos to hear.

Perhaps a quarter of an hour later, rain started pattering down. When Sostratos looked in the direction he thought to be northeast, he couldn't see anything much. All of a sudden, he was glad to be well out of sight of land. Without much in the way of visibility, he had no desire to find land where he least expected it.

Menedemos must have had the same thought. He called, "Aristeidas, go forward. You've got the best eyes of anybody aboard."

"All right, skipper, but I don't think we're anywhere close to shore," the sailor said.

"I don't, either. But I don't care to get any nasty surprises," Menedemos answered. "Besides, you can look out for fishing boats, too, and merchantmen. In this weather, anything can loom up before we know it's there."

Aristeidas dipped his head. "Right you are." He headed up toward the foredeck.

Sostratos blinked as a raindrop got him right in the eye. For a moment, he couldn't see anything. Not seeing anything gave him an idea. "Shouldn't you have a man with the lead up there, too?" he asked Menedemos.

"You're right—I should," his cousin answered, and gave the necessary orders.

The lead splashed into the sea. A few minutes later, the sailor handling it called, "No bottom at a hundred cubits."

"We're still out in the middle of the gulf," Menedemos murmured. He raised his voice: "I thank you, Nikodromos." The sailor waved to show he'd heard and hauled in the line hand over hand.

Rain kept splashing down for the rest of the day. A sail that got a little wet worked better than a dry one: the water filled the spaces in the weave so the breeze couldn't sneak through. But a sail that got more than a little wet grew too heavy to belly and easily fill with air. It hung, almost limp, from the yard, as laundry did from olive branches ashore. Menedemos called men to the oars to keep the *Aphrodite* moving.

"Gauging your course by the breeze?" Sostratos asked.

"It's all I've got left right now," his cousin answered. "If I keep it on my left hand, not quite straight in my face, we can't go too far wrong."

"That seems to make sense," Sostratos said. But not everything that seemed to make sense was true. He wished he hadn't thought of that.

The sea never got more than a little choppy. This wasn't a real storm, only rain—an annoyance, and a reminder the sailing season wouldn't stretch too much longer. It was indeed time to be heading home.

Dusk fell rather earlier than Sostratos had expected it to. The rain kept falling, too, making the night even more miserable and uncomfortable than it would have been otherwise. "How are we supposed to sleep in this?" Sostratos said.

"Wrap yourself in your himation, as if you were an Egyptian mummy," Menedemos said. "Wrap your face up, too. That'll keep you dry."

"Of course it will—till the whole himation soaks through," Sostratos said.

"By then you'll be asleep, and you won't notice till morning." As Menedemos so often did, he spoke like a man with all the answers.

Since Sostratos had no answers of his own, he tried his cousin's. For a little while, he thought it would work: the thick wool of the himation did keep the rain off fairly well. He was just getting really sleepy when he noticed he was also getting really wet. That woke him up again, and he took a long, long time to fall asleep. From a couple of cubits away, Menedemos' snores effortlessly pierced the soft patter of the rain. That didn't help, either.

It was still raining when Sostratos woke up the next morning. He felt half suffocated in wet wool. He undid the mantle, sat up, and knuckled his eyes, trying to convince himself this was all some horrid dream. He couldn't do it, and resigned himself to a long day full of weariness.

Menedemos was already up and moving. Seeing Sostratos stir, he smile. "Good day. Isn't this a splendid morning?"

"No." Sostratos was often inclined to be grumpy before breakfast. A bad night and wet clothes didn't help.

His one-word answer made Menedemos' smile wider. "But just think, O best one—today you can drink watered wine without pouring in any water." Sostratos' suggestion as to what Menedemos could do with and to his wine only pulled a laugh from his cousin.

Wine, watered from a jar as well as by the rain, helped warm Sostratos and resign him to being awake. Olives were olives, whether eaten in the rain or under a bright, sunny sky. But he gulped down his bread in a hurry, before it could get soggy.

"Come on, boys," Menedemos called to the crew. "We'll have to put more work into it than I expected, and that's too bad, but if we do we'll sleep warm tonight." In a soft aside to Sostratos, he added, "If we make the mainland anywhere close to Kallipolis, that is."

For most of the day, Sostratos wondered if they would know they'd made the mainland before running aground. The rain kept splashing down, as if it were the middle of winter rather than a little before the equinox. A little past noon—or so Sostratos guessed, but he was too tired to have much confidence in the hour—a fishing boat came into sight. Menedemos hailed it: "Which way to Kallipolis from where we are?"

"That way, I think," the fisherman said, and pointed. "Wouldn't take oath to anything, though—not in this. Early in the year for so much rain."

"Isn't it?" Menedemos agreed. "Thanks, friend." To Sostratos, he said, "Unless my reckoning's off even more than I think, he pointed close to due east."

"Easy enough for us to come too far north with nothing much we could use to judge our course," Sostratos said.

"I suppose so." But Menedemos still sounded discontented. He took as much pride in his ship-handling as Sostratos did in his bits of historical lore. *Trust Menedemos to be the one who's proud of something from which he can actually get some use,* Sostratos thought.

Towards evening, the weather finally began to clear again. "Land ho!" Aristeidas sang out. "Land dead ahead, and also land to starboard."

Sostratos saw the land, too, as did everyone else aboard the *Aphrodite*. The akatos lay forty or fifty stadia offshore, in no danger of running aground. To Sostratos' surprise, the beach ahead and the curve of the coast looked familiar. He needed a moment to realize why. Then, turning to Menedemos, he said, "Isn't that where we got rid of Alexidamos after he tried to steal the peafowl eggs?"

"Why, I do believe you're right," Menedemos said after a little study of his own.

"I half expected to see him bearing down on us in Taras, spear in one hand, shield in the other, blazing for revenge because we threw him off the ship," Sostratos said.

"He must have fallen foul of the Samnites before he made it to the polis," Menedemos replied. "I can't say I'm sorry, either. The only thing worse than a thief on board is a man with a sickness that spreads."

"How far are we from Kallipolis?" Sostratos asked.

"A couple of hundred stadia, maybe a little more," his cousin answered. "If I have this stretch of coastline straight in my mind, it's about halfway between Taras and Kallipolis."

"Can we make Kallipolis by nightfall?"

"I doubt it." Menedemos didn't sound happy about having to doubt it. He swung his leg in a way that meant he would have kicked at the dirt had he not been aboard ship. "I hadn't planned on spending two nights in a row at sea, but I'm not going to beach the *Aphrodite* on this coast."

"I should hope not." Sostratos shuddered at the thought of losing all the silver they'd worked so long and hard to gather. Every crewman within earshot dipped his head to show he didn't want to ground the ship, either.

"It's the rain's fault," Menedemos said. "We'd have gone faster and I'd have navigated better without it."

"Maybe it'll work out for the best," Sostratos said. "We'll have a little chance to dry out, so we won't look like such ragamuffins when we do come into port."

"We haven't got much left to sell," his cousin said. "It isn't worth worrying about."

"We may come back there one of these days," Sostratos said. "People will remember. They always remember scandal." He didn't need to read any history to be sure of that, and was slightly scandalized when Menedemos only shrugged. *He has no sense of anything but the moment,* Sostratos thought sadly. *Maybe that's why he ends up in trouble over women so often.* It never occurred to him to wonder what Menedemos was thinking about him just then.

They didn't make Kallipolis before nightfall, and did anchor offshore. The men grumbled a little about that. Sostratos wondered at their logic. They'd just made it very clear that they didn't care to risk going ashore, but they still didn't want to stay at sea? What did that leave? He imagined the *Aphrodite* floating several hundred cubits up in the air. Daidalos and Ikaros might get to the ship then, but he didn't see how anyone else would.

Menedemos' imagination was of a more practical sort: "I hadn't planned to lay over a night in Kallipolis, but I think I'd better, to give the men a chance to drink and roister."

"Good idea, skipper," Diokles said. If the oarmaster thought it a good idea, Sostratos wouldn't argue with him.

When they reached Kallipolis the next morning, it proved to lie on an island just off the Italian mainland, as Ortygia lay just off the Sicilian coast. Kallipolis, though, had never expanded off its island the way Syracuse had. It remained what so many of the colonies of Great Hellas had been in their early days: a Hellenic outpost at the edge of a land full of barbarians.

Despite its name, it didn't strike Sostratos as a particularly beautiful city. When he said as much, Menedemos laughed at him. "What would you expect them to call it? Kakopolis?" his cousin asked. "They'd enjoy trying to lure settlers to a polis with a name like that, wouldn't they? Uglytown?"

"All right, I see your point," Sostratos said. "But if you found a land full of snow and ice, you wouldn't call it a green land, would you?"

"I would if I wanted to get anybody to live there with me," Menedemos replied. "But I'm a good Rhodian. I don't even want to think about snow and ice, let alone live with 'em."

"It did snow once when I was in Athens," Sostratos said. "It was beautiful, but Zeus! it was cold." He shivered at the memory.

"We won't need to worry about that here," Menedemos said. "We have some wine, and we have some silk. Let's see if we can unload them. And"—he wagged a finger at Sostratos—"we don't need to tell the Kallipolitans what we think of their polis."

"I understand," Sostratos said. "We'll tell them the land is green."

His cousin laughed. "Exactly. That's just what we'll do."

Seen from its narrow, winding streets, Kallipolis was even less prepossessing than when viewed from the ~~streets~~ *SEA*. Because the island wasn't very big and had been settled for centuries, the locals used every digit of space they could. Many of their buildings were two and three stories high. They leaned toward one another above the streets, making them even closer and darker and smellier than they would have been otherwise.

That was one of the first things that struck Sostratos about the place. The second didn't take much longer. "Do you notice how nobody's smiling?" he said. "Everybody has a frown on his face."

"What is there to smile about?" Menedemos returned. "If you lived in a miserable little town in the middle of nowhere, how happy would you be? They probably wonder whether the barbarians will snap them up tomorrow or the day after." Since he was bound to be right, Sostratos took that no further.

They had to ask their way to the agora. On their way there, they passed several parties of mercenary soldiers: some Hellenes, others Italians in ordinary enough helmets but wearing odd, almost triangular, cuirasses that, in Sostratos' view, didn't cover nearly enough of the chest. The mercenaries looked no more cheerful than the ordinary Kallipolitans.

Menedemos was never one to leave well enough alone. Pointed to the soldiers, he said, "You see?"

And Sostratos had to admit, "I see."

The market square looked as if it had been bigger than it was. Buildings encroached on it from all sides, like weeds growing at the edge of a field. People buying and selling huddled together in the shadows the buildings cast. By the way merchants and customers kept glancing over their shoulders, they might have thought more buildings would spring up while they weren't looking.

"Fine wine from Khios! Transparent silk from Kos! Fragrant Rhodian perfume!" Menedemos' voice rang through the agora, echoing from the buildings that seemed to lean toward him from all the edges of the square. People stared, as if wondering who this loud stranger was. He certainly made more noise than half a dozen locals. "By the dog of Egypt," he murmured, "I think they're all so many wraiths here, like the spirits of the dead in the *Odyssey*."

"Fine wine and transparent silk will liven anyone up, if he gives them half a chance," Sostratos observed.

Menedemos shot him a quizzical look. "You can say that, when you want to hit me over the head with something whenever I go out and have a good time?"

"Yes, I say that," Sostratos answered. "I also say there's a time and a place for everything, and you haven't got the faintest notion of when and where."

"I think you're just jealous and using fancy talk to hide it," Menedemos said, and went back to crying their wares before Sostratos could do anything but let out an indignant, incoherent protest. Sostratos spent the next little while wondering whether his cousin had slandered him. He thought so, but he wasn't sure, and that worried him.

He didn't have long to worry undisturbed. In that rather subdued agora, Menedemos' brash, raucous shouts drew people far more readily than they would have, say, back at Rhodes. A tailor and a brothelkeeper almost got into a brawl over the length of silk Sostratos had brought from the Aphrodite. Only when Sostratos said, "We have enough for both of you, best ones," did they leave off glaring and snarling at each other. The brothelkeeper ended up buying some perfume, too, as Sostratos had hoped he might.

When a man in a fine chiton said, "Will you let me taste some of this fine wine of yours?" both Sostratos and Menedemos paused in embarrassment. They hadn't hauled an amphora from the merchant galley to the market square. They'd talked about selling Ariousian in Kallipolis, but they hadn't really believed they would. And now their failure was hurting their chances.

Sostratos would have brushed off a ragged Kallipolitan, but this fellow looked as if he could afford the best. "If you'd be kind enough to stay here, sir, I'll bring a jar from the ship. I won't be long."

"You should have one ready to hand," the local said. Since that was true, Sostratos could only dip his head and hurry away.

Nobody aboard the *Aphrodite* looked enthusiastic about putting an amphora on a carrying pole and lugging it to the agora, but Aristeidas and Teleutas did. On the way to the market square, Teleutas stuck his foot in a hole in a muddy street. He stumbled. The pole slipped from his shoulder. Only a desperate grab by Sostratos kept the amphora from smashing.

"That was fast," Aristeidas said as Sostratos helped Teleutas reassume the burden.

"That was me thinking about what Menedemos would say if we got back to the agora with a few potsherds and told our customer there he was welcome to lick them," Sostratos replied. Aristeidas and Teleutas both laughed, but he hadn't been joking.

They stabbed the pointed end of the amphora down in the mud when they got to the square. Sostratos scraped the pitch away from the stopper and got it out. They had to borrow a cup from a potter in the agora. The same thing had happened in Pompaia. Sostratos made a mental note to do something about that, at the same time wondering if he would remember it when the *Aphrodite* sailed away from Kallipolis. The Kallipolitan sipped the wine. Try as he would, he couldn't keep his face straight. "This was worth waiting for, I must admit," he said. "How much for the jar?"

"Sixty drakhmai," Menedemos answered, as he had up in Pompaia.

This Hellene howled louder at that than any of the Pompaians had. He and Menedemos were throwing arguments back and forth when somebody yelled, "You whoresons! You wide-arsed, turd-eating bastards!" a good deal louder than Menedemos had called out the virtues of his silk and wine and perfume—loud enough to drown out every other sound in the agora, in other words.

"Uh-oh," Sostratos said—quietly, but with great sincerity. He and Menedemos had idly wondered what had happened to Alexidamos the larcenous mercenary. Now they'd found out. Sostratos, for once, could have done without the enlightenment.

"Throw me off your stinking ship, will you?" Alexidamos shouted, even louder than before. "Leave me to be barbarians' meat, will you?" He carried no spear, but drew his sword and trotted toward the men from the *Aphrodite*.

Sostratos wore no sword. Neither did Menedemos. Neither did the other two sailors from the akatos. Few men did wear swords in a polis. If a man wasn't safe among his fellow Hellenes, where would he be? *Nowhere,* went through Sostratos' mind.

"Stop him!" someone exclaimed. But nobody seemed eager to stop Alexidamos. Who would want to try, unarmed, to stop a man with a sword in his hand and murder in his eyes? *And, for all these people know, he really does have some good reason to want revenge against us.* There were times when Sostratos wished he weren't so good at seeing the other fellow's point of view.

"Good day," said the Kallipolitan who'd been haggling with Menedemos. His departure showed a turn of speed that wouldn't have disgraced a sprinter at Olympos or any of the other Panhellenic festivals. When Sostratos looked around to ask for help from Aristeidas and Teleutas, he didn't see the latter, either. He cursed under his breath. *He trips in the street and runs from trouble. Many good-byes to him!*

"Whoresons!" Alexidamos shouted again. "Abandoned catamites!"

Aristeidas looked ready to take to his heels as the furious mercenary charged across the agora. So, for that matter, did Menedemos. Sostratos' cousin was a formidable sprinter in his own right. *I wish I were,* Sostratos thought. *But if I run, he'll catch me from behind. What man wants his death-wound in the back?*

Sostratos didn't want his death-wound at all. Since running would do him no good, he stooped, plucked a stone from the mud, and flung it at Alexidamos with all his strength. Had he missed, things would have gone hard for him—something he paused to think about only later. But, by then, Alexidamos was only three or four strides away; Sostratos had nearly waited too long to do anything at all. The stone struck the mercenary right in the nose.

The wet splat made Sostratos' stomach lurch. Blood splashed as Alexidamos' nose, already kinked by a scar, flattened and smashed. Alexidamos gave a great bellow of pain. He kept coming, but his hands—including the one with the sword—went to his face.

Menedemos jumped on him. Sostratos grabbed at his right arm and twisted the blade away from him. Aristeidas added his weight to the struggle. The three of them quickly subdued the mercenary.

As Sostratos helped hold Alexidamos down, he listened to the chatter of the Kallipolitans all around. "Should we seize them?" somebody asked.

"I don't see what for," someone else said. "They were only defending themselves. He attacked them for no reason I could see." The mutter of agreement that rose relieved Sostratos in no small measure.

A third local said, "If the soldier thinks they wronged him, better he should take them to law than slice them up." That produced more mutters of agreement. The fellow added, "He must think he's an Italian or a wild Kelt, to act the way he did."

Menedemos distracted Sostratos, saying, "I didn't know you could throw so straight."

"Neither did I," Sostratos answered, which made Menedemos laugh. Sostratos went on, "I did what I had to do. Out of necessity, throwing"—a paraphrase of Homer's *out of necessity, fleeing*.

"I understand." By his smile, Menedemos caught the allusion as well as the truth behind it. "Grab this lovely fellow's sword, Aristeidas. We don't want him getting his hands on it again."

"We sure don't," the lookout agreed. "But he'll never be lovely again, not with his nose looking like a beet you just stepped on."

"Too bad." Sostratos and Menedemos spoke together. Menedemos added, "Where did that cowardly wretch of a Teleutas disappear to? By the gods, I ought to pitch him off the ship."

Before Sostratos could answer that, there was a commotion in a nearby street. Teleutas reappeared in the agora, at the head of a dozen sailors carrying assorted implements of mayhem. When he paused to look around and find out what had happened, the expression on his face would have done credit to a comic mask. "You didn't even need me," he said indignantly.

"Well, now that you mention it, no," Sostratos answered. "But thanks for bringing help anyway."

"I still think he just ran off," Menedemos muttered. But he did no more than mutter, for Teleutas *had* returned promptly, and the reinforcements he brought might have been useful.

"What do we do with Alexidamos here?" Aristeidas asked.

"One of the useful things you might do would be to pluck that dagger from the sheath on his belt," Sostratos told him. After Aristeidas had done that, Sostratos said, "Listen to me, Alexidamos."

"To the crows with you, you stinking son of a whore." Alexidamos' voice didn't sound right. He probably couldn't breathe very well through that ruined nose. "You've maimed me. May the gods curse you forever."

"This is what you get for being a thief," Sostratos replied. "I told you once, you'd better listen to me. If we let you go, will you leave us alone after this?"

A considerable silence followed, punctuated by wet snuffling noises as the mercenary struggled for air. At last, he said, "How can I say no?"

Menedemos spoke before Sostratos could: "You'd better mean it when you say yes. Otherwise, we might as well cut your throat and offer you up for fair winds, the way Agamemnon did with his daughter before he sailed off to Troy."

Considering the misfortunes that befell Agamemnon after he sacrificed Iphigeneia, that didn't strike Sostratos as the wisest threat to make. But Alexidamos was not inclined toward literary criticism. "You're more trouble than you're worth," he growled. "You've shown me that twice over now."

Menedemos looked a question at Sostratos. Sostratos was mildly surprised to find his opinion sought. He shrugged and said, "I don't think we'll get any better promise out of him. It's either let him go, kill him, or stay here and go to law against him."

"May that not come to pass!" Menedemos exclaimed. "We might be stuck forever, and we haven't got the time to waste." He relaxed his grip on the mercenary. Sostratos and Aristeidas followed his lead. Menedemos said, "All right, Alexidamos. Count yourself lucky."

Gingerly, Alexidamos felt of his nose. He hissed in pain at the slightest touch, and cursed at the blood on his fingertips. It was running down his face, too, but he couldn't see that. "Lucky?" he said. "I'm going to be ugly for the rest of my days on account of you—" Remembering he didn't have the advantage, he swallowed a couple of choice epithets.

"You *are* lucky," Sostratos said. "You still have the rest of your life." *Even though I did my best to knock your head right off your shoulders when I threw that stone.* "You were ready to rob us of ours, the same way you tried to rob us of our peafowl eggs."

Alexidamos didn't answer. He staggered away, still dripping blood. "May we never see him again," Menedemos said.

"I thought we were rid of him when we put him on the beach," Sostratos said, "and then especially when we didn't see him in Taras."

"So did I," his cousin said. "We'll be gone tomorrow. We can keep enough men here till then to make sure he doesn't try anything. If we hadn't spent two nights in a row at sea, and if this weren't the last chance before we sail back to Hellas to let the men get their share of wine and women, I'd leave port now."

"You say that?" Sostratos demanded. "You say that after risking everything on the trip to Syracuse?"

With a shrug, Menedemos replied, "We made a lot of money in Syracuse. I don't see much chance for profit here, do you?"

"Nobody could make much of a profit in Kallipolis, and that includes the Kallipolitans." Sostratos spoke with great conviction. He also spoke quietly, lest any of those Kallipolitans hear him and think he slandered their city. He intended to, but he didn't want them to know it.

A moment later, Menedemos donned a wide, artificial smile. "Hail, best one," he said to the local who'd been dickering for fine Khian when Alexidamos made his unexpected appearance. "Good to see you again."

"Have things, ah, settled down?" the Kallipolitan asked. Then he answered his own question: "Yes, I see they have. Well and good. Where were we?"

"We were right here," Menedemos replied. *And we stayed here, while you ran like a rabbit with a pack of Hipparinos' Kastorian hounds baying at your heels,* Sostratos thought. He exhaled noisily through his nose in lieu of sighing. Doing business with a man too often meant you couldn't tell him what you thought of him. Smoothly, Menedemos went on, "Here, why don't you have another taste of a wine Dionysos himself must have specially blessed? The genuine Ariousian of Khios doesn't come to Kallipolis every day, or every year, either."

The cup they'd borrowed had got broken in the scuffle with Alexidamos. They had to pay for it and get another from the potter. When the local tasted the sweet, golden wine for a second time, his eyes got big. Sostratos smiled to himself; he'd seen that before. The Kallipolitan had to work to keep eagerness from his voice as he said, "Now, you named some ridiculous price before the ruction started."

"Sixty drakhmai the amphora," Menedemos repeated calmly.

"Yes," the local said. "I mean, no. I thought that's what you said, and I won't pay it. I'll give you twenty, and not a drakhma more."

"Good day, sir." Menedemos politely inclined his head. "It's been pleasant talking with you."

"Are you mad?" the Kallipolitan said. "You had to open the jar to give me a sample. It won't keep—wine never does, not after you broach the amphora. How much will you get for vinegar? You'd better take what I offer, and be thankful you're getting that much."

His smug smile said he'd played this game with merchants before. He'd probably got away with it with a few of them, too. *Another small-town, small-time chiseler,* Sostratos thought. Aloud, he said, "Good day to you, sir, as my cousin said. And to the crows with you, too." He didn't have to waste politeness on a cheat.

The Kallipolitan's eyes widened again, this time with a different sort of astonishment. "But . . . But . . . ," he floundered. "You have to sell the stuff, and—"

Sostratos had enjoyed bedding some girls less than he enjoyed laughing in the local's face. "We don't *have* do do a cursed thing, O marvelous one." Not for the first time, he stole Sokrates' sardonic salutation. "We just ran the Carthaginians' blockade to get grain into Syracuse. We have more silver than we know what to do with, friend. If you don't want the Ariousian—and if you don't want to pay our price for it—we'll give the jar to our sailors to drink."

"I've never had a merchant speak to me that way in all my life," the Kallipolitan said. Sostratos believed it. All he did was shrug. Menedemos matched him. The Kallipolitan spluttered wordlessly, then caught his stride. "Oh, very well. If you insist on being unreasonable, I suppose I can go to thirty drakhmai."

Normally, that would have been the start of a dicker. A dicker *had* started before Alexidamos interrupted things. Now, Sostratos just tossed his head. He said, "No," and not another word.

"Thirty-five, then." The local turned red. Anger or embarrassment?

Embarrassment, Sostratos judged. "My cousin told you sixty," he said. "Sixty it will be." He had, for once, the freedom of not caring whether or not he sold the wine. It felt exhilarating, as if he'd had a couple of quick nips from the amphora himself.

"You're not being reasonable," the Kallipolitan protested. "Here, now—I'll give you forty drakhmai. That's more than your precious Khian is worth."

"No," Sostratos said again. "Our price is sixty. If you want the wine, you'll pay it."

And the man from Kallipolis did pay it. He took a while to talk himself into it, and tried to get the two Rhodians to agree to forty-five, fifty, and fifty-five drakhmai first. Sostratos yawned in his face. Menedemos, who could be the most engaging of men when he wanted to, turned his back. The Kallipolitan stomped away. When he returned, a slave behind him, he threw a leather sack full of drakhmai at Sostratos almost as hard as Sostratos had thrown the stone at Alexidamos. Sostratos carefully counted the coins before dipping his head to his cousin.

As the local had the slave carry the amphora back toward his house, Sostratos sighed and said, "Thus we bid farewell to our brief layover in Kallipolis, a small polis where nothing interesting ever happens."

Menedemos stared at him, then started to laugh. "If only it were so," he said.

"Now we just have to hope Alexidamos doesn't go after any of our tavern-crawling sailors tonight," Sostratos said.

"No." His cousin tossed his head. "If that gods-detested mercenary is in any shape to go after our boys tonight after what you did to his beak, he's tougher than Talos, the man made all of bronze."

Sostratos considered that. "Well, maybe you're right."

DIOKLES POUNDED HIS bronze square with his mallet hard enough to make a lot of the *Aphrodite*'s sailors wince as the merchant galley left the harbor of Kallipolis. Menedemos leaned forward toward his crapulous crew and favored them with the smile of a man who'd stayed sober. "Next stop, boys, is Hellas," he said.

He got a few answering smiles. He also got a few answering groans. Diokles said, "Some of 'em don't want to live long enough to get to Hellas."

"But they all will by this afternoon," Menedemos replied. "Hang-overs don't kill you. You just wish they would."

Sostratos mounted to the poop deck. "And how shall we go back to Rhodes?" he asked. "Around Cape Tainaron again, or by the diol-kos across the Isthmus of Corinth?"

"I don't know yet," Menedemos answered. "We have a good no-tion of the risks at Cape Tainaron. But who knows what's happened in and around Corinth while we've been out here in Great Hellas? How can we guess whether we should use the diolkos till we know who controls the polis?"

"Hmmm," Sostratos said, and then, "You've got something there, no doubt about it."

"Nice of you to admit it," Menedemos said. His cousin made a face at him. Ignoring it, he went on, "We can put in at Kerkyra and hear the news there before we decide what to do."

"You're not going to sail southeast toward Zakynthos and reverse the way we came?"

"No. It's getting late in the sailing season for me to want to chance so much time on the open sea," Menedemos answered. "The cranes will be flying south for the winter pretty soon, and not many people want to do much on the water after that. How did Aristophanes put it in the *Birds*?"

"I don't know. How *did* he put it?" Sostratos said. "If you re-member it, it was probably foul."

"That's not fair," Menedemos said indignantly. "Aristophanes could write lovely verses about anything at all."

"Or sometimes about nothing at all," Sostratos said.

"Not here," Menedemos said. "It goes something like this:

'Time to sow when the croaking crane migrates to Libya
Which tells the shipmaster to lie idle after hanging up his
    steering oar.' "

"Well, all right. That isn't bad," Sostratos allowed.

"Do you think you can stand being so generous?" Menedemos said. He loved Aristophanes both for his poetry and for his bawdy wit. Sostratos, he knew, admired some of the verse but wanted noth-ing to do with the lewdness that went hand in hand with it.

To his surprise, his cousin answered seriously: "Being generous to Aristophanes isn't easy for me, you know. If it weren't for the way he pictured Sokrates in the *Clouds,* the Athenians might not have decided to make him drink hemlock."

"He's been dead for a hundred years—" Menedemos began.

"Not quite ninety," Sostratos broke in.

"Not quite ninety, then. Fine. Why are you getting so exercised about it?"

"Because he was a great and good man," Sostratos answered. "That's reason enough—more than reason enough. They aren't so common that we can afford to lose them."

"From everything *I've* heard, he was an interfering old busybody," Menedemos said. "Even if Aristophanes hadn't said a word about him, plenty of people still would've wanted to get rid of him."

For a moment, Sostratos looked as shocked as if he'd said Zeus did not exist—more shocked than that, even, for some bright young men these days did dare doubt the gods. But his cousin, as usual, thought before he spoke. At last, he said, "There may be some truth to that. He never did worry much about what other people thought before he opened his mouth. Platon makes that very plain."

"There you are, then," Menedemos said. "If it was his own fault, why are you blaming Aristophanes?"

"I didn't say it was *all* his own fault."

"Ha! Now you're backing oars. You can go one way or the other, O best one, but you can't try to go both ways at once," Menedemos said.

"I think you're trying to be as difficult as you can," Sostratos said.

"I'd sooner talk philosophy—or gossip about philosophers, which isn't quite the same thing—than think about pirates," Menedemos said. "Since I don't usually care to do that, you'd best believe the pirates worry me."

"You could have decided to make for Zakynthos instead of taking the short way across the Ionian Sea," Sostratos said.

Menedemos tossed his head. "I told you, it's too close to crane-flying season. Too much chance of a storm's blowing up for me to make the long journey across the open sea. But the pirates will be out. They'll know what honest skippers are thinking, the gods-detested bastards."

For once, though, the usually cautious Sostratos was the bolder of the two of them. "I still think you're worrying too much," he said. "If a pirate sees our hull, what will he think? He'll think the same thing half the fishermen in Great Hellas—and over in the Aegean, too—have already thought: that we're pirates ourselves. We don't look anything like a round ship, after all. And he'll leave us alone."

"Here's hoping you're right." Menedemos looked back over his shoulder toward the rocks of Cape Iapygia, the southeasternmost point of Italy. Soon it would disappear from view, and the *Aphrodite* would be out of sight of land till Korkyra or the mainland of Hellas or Macedonia crawled up over the eastern horizon. "But dogs eat dogs. Why shouldn't pirates eat pirates?"

"You've said it yourself: we've got enough men aboard to put up a good fight," Sostratos said.

Menedemos' laugh was less cheerful than he would have liked. "Well, maybe we'll find out if I'm as smart as I think I am."

They got their chance to find out sooner than he would have liked. It wasn't Aristeidas who sang out, "Sail ho!" but a sailor who was pissing from the *Aphrodite*'s stern. Menedemos turned to look back over his shoulder, as he had for Cape Iapygia. He had to follow the sailor's pointing finger to spot the sail, which wasn't much different in color from the sky or the sea. Whoever captained that ship didn't want it seen.

"Fast," Diokles remarked as the sail got bigger and the hull came into view. It too was painted greenish blue, so as not to stand out against waves and sky. "Almost bound to be a pirate, with that turn of speed and that paint job."

"I was thinking the same thing." Menedemos raised his voice: "Take your weapons, men. We may have a fight on our hands."

The skipper of that other ship was bound to be making calculations about the *Aphrodite*. Yes, she was a galley, but she didn't try to disguise herself and she was on the beamy side for a rowed vessel. That made her an akatos, not a pentekonter or hemiolia—probably not a pirate ship herself, but still a vessel with a formidable crew, one not to be taken lightly.

When Menedemos got a better look at the pirate ship, he saw she wasn't quite so long and low as he'd expected. She carried two banks of oars, though the rowers' benches of the upper deck aft of the mast could be taken out in a hurry to stow the mast and yard and sail. "Hemiolia," Sostratos remarked, coming up onto the poop deck: he'd noted the same thing.

"Which would mark her for a pirate even without her paint job," Menedemos said. "Not much use for hemioliai except to steal from slow ships and run away from fast ones."

"They might make naval auxiliaries," said Sostratos, who sometimes showed himself altogether too good at looking at all sides of a question to suit Menedemos.

But the hemiolia coming up behind the *Aphrodite* was without a doubt, without argument even from Sostratos, a pirate. Menedemos, who couldn't conveniently take down his own mast, could and did order the sail brailed up to the yard and put a full complement on the oars. As he'd done twice before, he swung his ship toward the pirate, showing he was ready for a fight if her skipper wanted one.

That skipper didn't run, as the other two had done. But he didn't attack the merchant galley, either. Instead, he shouted across a couple of plethra of seawater: "Ahoy! You coming from Italy? What news?" His Greek held a peculiar accent, perhaps Macedonian, more likely Epeirote.

"You have news of Hellas?" Menedemos shouted back. The pirate captain nodded, which proved him an Epeirote or something of the sort—Macedonians dipped their heads like proper Hellenes. Menedemos went on, "I'll trade what what I know for what you do. I won't give it away."

"All right," the other captain called. "I tell you, Polyperkhon still has Corinth and the isthmus and Sikyon to the west, and he's made friends with the Aitolians north of the Gulf of Corinth."

That was worth knowing. Menedemos spoke of Agathokles' dash to Africa, with the Carthaginian fleet on his heels. "I don't know how long he'll be fighting there, but the war between Carthage and Syracuse won't be the same any more."

"You're right about that, trader," the pirate agreed. "I tell you, too, Polyperkhon has from Pergamon the youngster called Herakles, the son of Alexander the Great and Barsine. He says he will make the youth king of Macedonia."

"He's not really Alexander's son," Sostratos said quietly. "He's just a pretender Antigonos raised up . . . I think."

"I know that—I've heard the same stories you have," Menedemos answered. "But whoever he really is, he's plenty to make Kassandros pitch a fit in Macedonia."

"Well, yes," Sostratos said. "When you think about what Kassandros did to Alexandros and Roxane, you know he doesn't want any heirs to the Macedonian throne running around loose. They hurt his own position."

"What's Polemaios doing?" Menedemos called to the pirate.

"He's still down in the south of the Peloponnesos," the fellow answered. "If that was me, I wouldn't go anyplace Antigonos could get his hands on me. If Old One-Eye caught his nephew now, I bet he'd keep him alive for *months.*"

"You're probably right," Menedemos said. "Speaking of Antigonos, what do you know about the war between him and Ptolemaios?"

"Not a thing," the pirate said, shrugging. "Who gives a fart what happens way over in the east?" He seemed suddenly bored with talking instead of plundering, and shouted orders to his crew. The hemiolia glided south, looking for prey easier than the *Aphrodite.*

"Which way will you go?" Sostratos asked.

"Over in Corinth, Polyperkhon's got trouble with Kassandros and Polemaios both," Menedemos said. "That makes Cape Tainaron a better bet, I think." Sostratos clicked his tongue between his teeth, but didn't try to tell him he was wrong.

12

"TELOS BEHIND US AT LAST," SOSTRATOS SAID. HIS COUSIN made a face at him, for the Aegean island's name sounded nearly the same as the word for *at last*. Grinning at Menedemos, he pointed eastward. "And there's Rhodes ahead."

"A good thing, too," Menedemos said. "No guessing how much longer decent sailing weather will hold."

"You've been grumbling about that ever since we left Syracuse," Sostratos said. "The weather couldn't have been much better."

"That's true, but it didn't *have* to stay good," Menedemos replied. "And when have you ever known a sailor who didn't worry about the weather?"

Sostratos didn't answer that. He eyed the birds overhead flying south for the winter. Sure enough, there was a long, straggling line of cranes, bigger than any of the other birds he could see. Aristophanes had had it right. *But he was still wrong about Sokrates,* Sostratos thought.

If he said that, he would start a real quarrel, and he didn't feel like one now, not with the *Aphrodite* so close to home. Instead, he chose something he reckoned harmless. "It'll be good to get back to our family."

But his cousin only grunted. "Good for you, maybe," he said at last. "You wait. My father will say he could have done better and made more money."

He's probably right, Sostratos thought. *Uncle Philodemos is never satisfied.* Aloud, he said, "Why don't you just smile and dip your head and tell him he's bound to know best?"

"Ha!" Menedemos rolled his eyes. "For one thing, he cursed well *doesn't* know best. And for another, if I told him he did, he'd fall over dead from the shock. I don't want his blood on my hands even by accident, the way Oidipous had Laios'."

And you're just as stubborn as your father, and you won't yield to him even by a barleycorn's breadth. One more thing Sostratos thought it better not to say. He did say, "Whether the two of you argue or not, he'll be glad to see you. We've come back safe, we only lost one man, and we made money. What more could he ask?"

"More money, of course," Menedemos replied.

"Oh, foof!" Sostratos said. "Once we get into port, the family will throw a celebration the polis will buzz about all through the winter. Your father wouldn't do that if he didn't care about you, and you know it. My mother and sister will be green with envy because they aren't men and won't be able to come."

"Maybe." Menedemos did his best not to sound convinced. "I wonder if my father's second wife will even care."

"Of course she will," Sostratos said. "Baukis is young—I remember that from the wedding, though I doubt I've seen her since, naturally. She'll want something she can gossip about with her friends."

"Maybe," Menedemos said again. He turned away from Sostratos, plainly not wanting to discuss it further. Sostratos wondered if he was angry at his father for remarrying after his mother died. If Uncle Philodemos had a son by his new wife, that would complicate the family inheritance.

As the *Aphrodite* neared Rhodes, the island stretched across more and more of the horizon. "The vines look good," Sostratos said, even though he was too far away to make any real guess about how they looked. It let him talk about something besides the family, which Menedemos plainly didn't want to do. Trying his best to come up with the light chat that his cousin managed as if by nature, he went on, "Not that we'd ever get sixty drakhmai the amphora if we shipped Rhodian to Great Hellas."

"No," Menedemos said, and made a production out of steering the akatos. *So much for light chatter,* Sostratos thought mournfully.

The fishing boats that bobbed in the blue, blue Aegean didn't flee when their skippers spotted the *Aphrodite*—most of them didn't, anyhow. The fishermen knew few pirates dared venture into the well-patrolled waters near their island. "We can certainly be proud of our fleet," Sostratos offered.

"Yes. Certainly." Again, Menedemos spoke as if he were being charged for every word he uttered. Sostratos gave up until the merchant galley rounded Rhodes' northernmost promontory, passed the fleet's harbor, and sailed into the sheltered waters of the Great Harbor, from which it had set out that spring.

"It *is* good to be back," he said then.

"Well, so it is," Menedemos admitted—something of a relief to Sostratos, who'd begun to wonder if his cousin ever intended to speak more than a couple of words to him. Menedemos wasn't shy about talking to the rowers, of whom he had ten on a side at the oars: "Come on, boys—make it pretty. The whole polis will be watching you, and there's not a Rhodian man breathing who doesn't know what to do with an oar in his hands."

Thus encouraged, the rowers showed what a well ~~beaten in~~ BROKEN-IN crew could manage, following the stroke Diokles set with perfect precision as Menedemos guided the *Aphrodite* to an open berth. "Back oars!" the keleustes called, and the men did that as smoothly as everything else. As soon as they'd killed the merchant galley's momentum, he called, *"Oöp!"* and they rested at their oars.

Sailors heaved lines to men on the wharf, who made the akatos fast. Sostratos tossed an obolos to each roustabout, and another little silver coin to a fellow to whom he said, "Hail, Letodoros. Run to the houses of Lysistratos and Philodemos and let them know the *Aphrodite*'s home and safe. They'll have something more for you there, I expect."

"Thanks, best one. I'll do that." Letodoros popped the obolos into his mouth and went off at a ground-eating trot.

"Won't be long now," Sostratos said to Menedemos.

"So it won't." His cousin still stood between the steering oars, as he had throughout the voyage. Menedemos drummed the fingers of his right hand on the starboard tiller. "It won't be *so* bad," he said, as if trying to make himself believe it. "We *did* make a profit, after all, and a good one. Nobody can deny that."

"Nobody will even try to deny it," Sostratos said. "You'll see. And you're the one who claims I worry too much."

Menedemos fidgeted while they waited for their fathers to come down to the harbor. Sostratos paid the sailors what he owed them since he'd last given each of them silver, and wrote down the payments so no one could say he hadn't got his due. Watching Menedemos, he thought, *I wouldn't twitch like a man with fleas even if I didn't have anything to do. I might feel like it, but I wouldn't do it.*

After he paid off Diokles, he clasped the keleustes' hand and told him, "I hope you'll sail with us again next spring."

"I hope so, too, young sir," the oarmaster answered. "Never a dull moment, was there?"

"Too few of them, anyway," Sostratos said, which made Diokles laugh.

"Oh, by the gods," Menedemos said softly. "Here comes Father." He'd attacked a Roman trireme with no visible trace of fear, but quivered to see a middle-aged man approach the *Aphrodite.*

Sostratos waved. "Hail, Uncle Philodemos," he called. "We've come back with every man we started out with but one, and with a tidy profit."

"What happened to the one man?" Philodemos rapped out. He aimed the question not at Sostratos but at his own son.

"Hail, Father," Menedemos said. "He died of an arrow wound he took in a sea fight."

"Pirates?" Philodemos asked. "The Italian waters are lousy with 'em. Polluted bastards all ought to go up on crosses." His right hand folded into an angry fist.

"Yes, sir," Menedemos agreed. "But this wasn't a fight with pirates. The Romans sent a fleet of triremes to raid a Samnite town called Pompaia just as we were sailing away from it, and one of the triremes took after us."

Philodemos raised an eyebrow. "And you got away from it? That must have taken some fine sailing. I wasn't sure you had it in you."

Menedemos grappled with that, trying to decide whether it came out a compliment. Sostratos spoke up before his cousin could: "We didn't get away from it, Uncle. We wrecked it—used our hull to break its starboard oars. After we crippled it, then we got away."

"Really?" Philodemos said. Not only Sostratos and Menedemos but also a good many sailors amplified the story. Menedemos' father stroked his chin. "That does sound like a smart piece of work," he allowed.

"There," Sostratos hissed. "You see?" But Menedemos ignored him.

He was miffed, but only for a moment, for he saw his own father coming down the wharf toward the *Aphrodite.* He waved again. Lysistratos waved back. "Hail, son," he said. "Good to see you again. How did everything go?"

Uncle Philodemos didn't say it was good to see Menedemos, went through Sostratos' mind. *He may have thought it, but he didn't say it.* "Hail," he answered. "We're here. We made money. And we got rid of all the peafowl and all of their chicks." Relentless honesty made him add, "Well, almost all the peafowl. One peahen jumped into the sea. That was my fault."

"Many good-byes to them," Menedemos said. "They're gods-detested birds, no matter how pretty the peacock was. The Italiotes and barbarians who bought them are welcome to them, believe ~~you~~ me they are."

"They did make nuisances of themselves in our courtyards, didn't they?" Lysistratos said. "But I'm sure the two of you will be glad to come home and sleep in your own beds again. That was always one of the things I liked best about getting back from a trading run, anyhow."

"I don't know, Father," Sostratos said. "I've spent so much time on the planks of the poop deck, the mattress will probably feel strange the first few days. And then there was the night on the sacks of wheat when we were going down to Syracuse."

"Syracuse?" Lysistratos and Philodemos said together. Menedemos' father went on, "What's the news from Syracuse?" and Sostratos realized the *Aphrodite* was the first ship coming into Rhodes with word of everything that had happened in the west.

He and his cousin told the story together. Menedemos told more of it. Of the two of them, he'd always had the quicker tongue as well as the quicker feet. Sostratos got his chances to talk after Philodemos' frequent questions, for each one would throw Menedemos off his stride for a little while. Questions from Lysistratos didn't faze Menedemos at all, Sostratos noted.

When the two young men finished, Philodemos clicked his tongue between his teeth. "You took some long chances there, son," he said, his tone suggesting he might have other remarks when not so many people could hear them.

"I know, sir, but we got by with them, and they ended up paying off well," Menedemos replied, with something less than the cheeky brashness he'd shown through most of the journey.

"Just how much money did you make?" Philodemos asked. Menedemos looked toward Sostratos. Sostratos had told his cousin the answer, but Menedemos had no confidence in it. Here in his home port, Sostratos saw no point in keeping it a secret. He told his uncle, and had the satisfaction of watching the older man's jaw drop. "You're joking," Philodemos said.

"And five oboloi," Sostratos added. "No, I'm not joking at all."

"Euge!" his father said, and clapped his hands together to show just how well he thought it was done. "That's . . . splendid is the only word I can find." Lysistratos clapped again. "I'm proud of both of you."

"We also still have a little silk and a little Ariousian and some perfume on board," Sostratos said. "They won't bring so much here as they would have in Great Hellas, but they'll bring something."

Lysistratos beamed. Even Philodemos didn't look too unhappy. Sostratos waved to Himilkon the Phoenician, who was heading over to find out the news. *We did it,* he thought. *We really did it, and now, at last, we're back. It feels even better than I thought it would.*

MENEDEMOS SAT IN the andron in his house, sipping from a cup of wine and wishing he were somewhere, anywhere, else. Even the men's chamber itself left him disappointed. Here in Rhodes, it was pretty fine. Set it next to Gylippos' in Taras, though, and it wasn't so much of a much.

But he wouldn't have minded the andron so much if his father hadn't been sitting a couple of cubits away glaring at him. "You idiot," Philodemos said. "What on earth or under it were you thinking of?"

"Profit," Menedemos answered in a low voice. His father always managed to put him in the wrong. With a flash of defiance, he added, "We got it, too. We got a lot of it."

Philodemos waved that away, as of no account. "You came much too close to getting exactly—exactly, I tell you—what you deserved for such a piece of foolishness. What did your cousin think of it? Was he as mad to put on wax-glued wings and imitate Ikaros flying up toward the sun as you were?"

Menedemos thought about lying, but reckoned he was too likely to get caught. Reluctantly, he tossed his head. "Well, no. Not quite."

"Not quite?" Philodemos put a world of expression into his echo. "What does that mean? No, don't tell me. I can figure it out for myself. Sostratos has some sense, at least—more than I can say for my own flesh and blood."

To cover his feelings, Menedemos took a long pull at the wine. He wished he could get drunk right now, so he wouldn't have to pay his father any attention at all. But Philodemos wouldn't let him forget that, either, and they'd be living in the same house till spring. However much he wanted to, however insulted he felt, he couldn't storm away, either, not unless he wanted to create bad blood that might last till he could sail away again.

What can I do? he wondered. Changing the subject was the only thing that came to him. He said, "We heard on the way back here that the war between Ptolemaios and Antigonos got going for all it was worth. Nobody really expected the peace to last, but even so. . . ."

"It's going, all right," his father agreed with a certain gloomy satisfaction. Philodemos was willing to criticize the follies of others besides Menedemos. "Ptolemaios sent his general Leonides up to Kilikia to seize the cities on the coast from Antigonos."

"And he did it?" Menedemos asked.

His father dipped his head. "He did it, all right—till Antigonos heard what had happened. Then old One-Eye sent out his son Demetrios, and Demetrios ran Leonides out of Kilikia and all the way back to Egypt. Ptolemaios sent messages to Lysimakhos and Kassandros, too, they say, asking them for help to keep Antigonos from getting too strong, but he sure didn't get much."

"But Antigonos' nephew Polemaios turned on him," Menedemos said. "That has to be a heavy blow to Antigonos, losing the fellow who was his right-hand man."

" 'Was' is right," his father said. "That's Demetrios' place now, Demetrios' and his younger brother Philippos'. Antigonos sent Philippos up to the Hellespont to take on Polemaios' lieutenant Phoinix, and Philippos whipped him almost as hard as Demetrios whipped Leonides."

Menedemos whistled softly. "I hadn't heard that before. You have to admire Antigonos. He's never at a loss, no matter what happens to him."

"If you're a fat partridge in a bush, do you admire the wolf who wants to eat you?" Philodemos said. "That's how Rhodes looks to the marshals. And the thing about Antigonos is, he frightens all the others enough to make 'em band together to try to pull him down. You mark my words, son: those Macedonians will still be knocking heads together when you're as old as I am."

"Thirty years from now?" Menedemos tried not to sound scornful. He also tried to imagine what he would be like if he reached his father's years—tried and felt himself failing. "That's a long way off."

"You mark my words," Philodemos repeated. "The generals have been going at each other ever since Alexander died. Why should they stop? What would make them stop?"

"One man winning," Menedemos said at once.

His father looked thoughtful. "Yes, that might do it," he admitted. "But if one of them looks like winning, all the others gang up on him, the way everyone is against Antigonos now. That's how it's gone so far. Why should it change?"

"Panta rhei," Menedemos replied.

" 'Everything flows'?" Philodemos echoed. "Some philosopher or other, isn't it? I thought you left showing off how much you know to your cousin."

"I'm sorry. I usually do." Menedemos liked his father much better when he was slighting Sostratos than when he was praising him.

Philodemos grunted. "Well, that's not much of an apology, but I suppose it's better than nothing."

You always find fault, Menedemos thought. *If I cut my liver out for you, you'd complain that the priest didn't read good omens from it.*

But then his father said, "You beat a trireme? And you came home with that much silver? I suppose, all things considered, you could have done worse. Here, let me pour you some more wine." Menedemos was almost too startled to hold out his cup—almost, but not quite. But as Philodemos poured, he asked, "And how many husbands did you outrage in Great Hellas?" Even when he tried to praise, he couldn't do it unmixed with spite.

And Menedemos answered with quick truth when, again, he might have done better lying: "Only one."

His father muttered something under his breath, then sighed and asked, "Where was it this time? Will you ever be able to do business there again, or is it as bad as Halikarnassos?"

"Taras, Father," Menedemos said, and Philodemos grunted as if he'd been hit in the belly. Menedemos went on, "I don't think it's quite so bad as at Halikarnassos." He didn't think Gylippos' toughs had intended to kill him, but only to beat him up. The fellow in Halikarnassos had definitely wanted him dead.

"Not *quite* so bad." Philodemos looked as if he were sipping vinegar, not wine. "And Taras is an important polis, too, the first one you're likely to come to on the way west from Hellas. What *are* we going to do with you, son?" Menedemos found it expedient to stay mute. His father grunted again, then said, "Well, at least you don't do things like that here in Rhodes, the gods be praised."

Menedemos didn't answer that, either. His father, fortunately, took silence for agreement.

"I WAS HOPING I might hear my sister had been betrothed when I came home," Sostratos remarked to his father as they sat in the andron.

"And I was hoping I might be able to tell you Erinna was," Lysistratos replied. "I did have some discussions about it with—oh, never mind what his name was: what point to going into the details when these things don't work out?"

"What was wrong with him?" Sostratos asked.

"Not a thing," Lysistratos said. "But he made a match with another family for their daughter who's never been married. They aren't so well off as we are, but the girl's fourteen, not eighteen. He's more likely to breed sons on her than he is on Erinna. You can't blame him for having that uppermost in his thoughts. What are wives for but sons?"

"It's not Erinna's fault—" Sostratos began before checking himself.

"It's not anyone's fault that I can see," his father said. "It's just one of those things that make life difficult for mortals."

Gyges, the Lydian majordomo, stuck his head into the men's chamber. "Master, Xanthos is at the door. He wants to congratulate the young master on the *Aphrodite*'s safe return."

Sostratos rolled his eyes. "Speaking of the things that make life difficult for mortals . . ."

His father laughed, but told Gyges, "Bring him in. He can drink some wine with us. Sooner or later, he'll go away."

"Later," Sostratos predicted, but in a voice low enough to keep his father from giving him a reproving look. A moment later, when the majordomo brought Xanthos into the andron, Sostratos got to his feet and bowed to the older man. "Hail, O marvelous one. How are you today?"

"Hail, Sostratos," Xanthos said. "It's good of you to ask. To tell you the truth, I do marvel that I failed to go down to the house of Hades while you were off in the west. My piles have been torture— and all the worse because I've been so constipated. And my shoulder joints ache whenever the weather gets damp. I dread this winter season, I truly do. I haven't been sleeping well, either. Old age truly is a misery; never let anyone tell you otherwise."

"Here you are, Xanthos." Lysistratos gave the other merchant a cup of wine, no doubt hoping to slow the tide of words. "Drink with us. We have reason to be glad, with the boys home safe and with a tidy profit, too."

"That's good news, very good news, very good news indeed," Xanthos said, flicking a few drops out of the cup for a libation. "Pity your son here couldn't have heard me at the Assembly earlier in the month. I'm immodest enough to say I surpassed even my usual eloquence."

"What did you speak on?" Sostratos asked.

"On how we should conduct ourselves if the fighting between Antigonos and Ptolemaios gets worse," Xanthos replied.

"That *is* important," Sostratos agreed.

He didn't ask the plump merchant to summarize the speech. He knew better. And Xanthos didn't summarize it. He said, "I believe I can remember how it went," and launched into it, complete with gestures that looked as if they would have been more at home on the comic stage than in the Assembly. His main point was that, since Rhodes did so much business with Egypt, she should stay on Ptolemaios' side provided she could do so without making Antigonos attack her. That made good sense to Sostratos, but he mightily wished Xanthos hadn't taken half an hour to get where he was going.

"Stirring," Lysistratos said when Xanthos finally finished. He poured himself more wine, which showed just how much he'd been stirred. Sostratos held out his cup for a refill, too. His father didn't offer the oinokhoe to Xanthos.

"Tell me the news from Italy," Xanthos urged Sostratos.

"Up north of Great Hellas, the Samnites and the Romans are still fighting," Sostratos said. He started to tell the other Rhodian how the *Aphrodite* had wound up in the middle of that war, but decided not to. It would only have brought more questions, and maybe, the gods forbid, another speech. Instead, he went on, "And from Sicily, Agathokles has invaded Africa to pay the Carthaginians back for besieging Syracuse." He didn't say anything about how the *Aphrodite* had been involved there, either.

"Well, well, isn't that interesting?" Xanthos said. He sensed he was being thwarted, and cast about for an opening: "You sold all your peafowl?"

"All but one, which, uh, died before we got to Great Hellas." Again, he said not a word about peafowl eggs or peafowl chicks.

"Ah, too bad," Xanthos said. "That cost you some money, it did, it did." Sostratos gravely dipped his head. He didn't say anything. Much later than Xanthos should have, he began to suspect he'd outstayed his welcome. "Well, I guess I'll wander over and pay my respects to Menedemos and his father."

"Good to see you," Sostratos said. *Good to see you go,* he glossed silently. He was glad enough to clasp Xanthos' hand as the other merchant took his leave. So was Lysistratos. Son and father looked at each other. When they heard Gyges close the door behind Xanthos, they sighed in unison. "Is there any more wine left in the oinokhoe?" Sostratos asked. "He's windy without eating beans and cabbage."

When his father shook the jar, it sloshed. He poured some into Sostratos' cup, the rest into his own. "He means well," he said.

After hearing every word of Xanthos' speech before the Assembly, Sostratos was not inclined to be charitable. "So does a puppy that piddles on my feet," he said, and drank the wine his father had given him.

"I know what you're thinking," Lysistratos said. "I'll have you know, though, that I suffered worse than you. I've heard his speech twice now."

"Oh, poor father!" Sostratos exclaimed, and put an arm around Lysistratos' shoulder. They both started laughing. Once they started, they had a hard time stopping. *It's not the wine*, Sostratos thought. *We didn't drink that much. It had to be Xanthos' speech. That would have paralyzed a man who'd drunk nothing but water his whole life long.*

"We shall have to have a feast to welcome you back," Lysistratos said. "A couple of feasts, in fact: one for your sister and your mother, and the other a proper symposion where you and your cousin can speak at length of your adventures in Great Hellas. Did you truly beat a trireme in the *Aphrodite*?"

"We wrecked its starboard bank of oars, and that let us get away," Sostratos replied. "Menedemos was telling Uncle Philodemos about it just before you got down to the harbor. I'm sure, at the symposion, he'll make a much more exciting story of it than I ever could."

"Exciting stories are all very well after the wine's gone round a few times," his father said. "I'd also like to have some notion of what really happened, though." Lysistratos' smile was lopsided, the smile of a man who'd learned not to expect too much from the world. "It might even make the stories more exciting."

"I'll tell you everything, as best I remember it," Sostratos promised. "But you should also listen to Menedemos' version, and Diokles' as well. Then you can put them together for yourself and decide where the real truth lies." He laughed at himself. "Anyone would think I wanted to write a history one day. That's how Thoukydides says he went about figuring out just what happened in the Peloponnesian War."

"Seems a sensible way to try to learn things," Lysistratos said.

Sostratos snapped his fingers. "Diokles!" he exclaimed. "I do want to put in a good word for him. We couldn't have had a better oar-master. Honest, sensible, brave when he needs to be—I'd love to sail with him as keleustes again next spring, but he'd make a good captain, too."

"I've always thought well of him, ever since the days when he first started pulling an oar," Lysistratos said. "I'll tell you what I do. When we have our symposion here, I'll invite him. I'm sure he can tell some stories of his own, and that will also let him talk with some other men who might want to offer him command of a ship."

"That would be very good, Father." Sostratos enthusiastically dipped his head. "It might be our loss, but Diokles deserves the chance."

"I should say so," Lysistratos agreed. "Considering how much silver you brought home, anyone who helped you earn it deserves a hand up from us. A man should lift up his friends and put down his enemies as he can, eh?"

"So Hellenes have said since the days of Akhilleus and Agamemnon," Sostratos answered. *And so Hellas has seen endless factions and feuds, too,* he thought, and then, *I wonder if that would make sense to any of Alexander's marshals. Probably not, worse luck, or they wouldn't be at one another's throats.*

Lysistratos pointed. "There's your sister, watering the garden. She'll be glad to see you."

Sostratos had heard water splashing from a hydria, too, but sat with his back to the courtyard. He'd guessed the slave girl, Threissa, was doing the work. "I'm always glad to see her," he said, getting to his feet. He walked out of the andron and called, "Hail, Erinna."

His sister squeaked, put down the water jar, ran to him, and threw herself into his arms. "Hail, Sostratos!" she said, and kissed him on the cheek. "When that wharf rat came yelling with news the *Aphrodite* was back, I almost veiled myself up and ran down to the harbor myself to come get a look at you as soon as I could." She grinned wickedly. "Wouldn't that have been a scandal?"

"It's not something girls of a good family do very often," Sostratos said diplomatically.

"I'm not exactly a girl of good family any more," Erinna answered. "The rules are a little looser for a widow."

"I suppose so," Sostratos said. "Father tells me you almost had a match this summer."

"Almost," Erinna agreed bitterly. "But then they decided to wed their son to a maiden instead. Look at me, Sostratos!" His sister seized his hands and held them. "Is my back bent? Is my hair gray? Are my teeth turning black and falling out?"

"Of course not." Sostratos answer was automatic. "By Zeus, you're still my little sister, and I'm a long way from an old man."

"Well, that other family treated me like an old woman," Erinna said. "When the other match came along, they dropped me as if they thought I'd be a shade in the house of Hades day after tomorrow. How am I supposed to have a family if no one wants to marry me any more?"

"You're always part of our family," Sostratos said.

His sister impatiently tossed her head. "I know that, but it's not what I meant, and you know it isn't. I meant a family of my own."

"Don't worry," Sostratos said. "You'll have one." *If we have to make your dowry bigger, then we do, that's all. We can afford it better than we could have before this voyage. The silver we made in Syracuse* will *come in handy, no matter how much I wish Menedemos hadn't taken such a chance to get it.*

"I hope so," Erinna said. "Childlessness is a terrible thing." Her smile seemed to Sostratos a deliberate effort of will, one that sprang from purposely turning her back on her troubles. She made her voice bright and cheerful, too: "Tell me about the voyage. Even if I am a widow, I'm a respectable woman, so I hardly get out of the house except to festivals and such, but you—you get to go across the sea. You know I'm jealous."

"You have less to be jealous of than you think," Sostratos said. "If you feel crowded and closed in here, imagine spending a night at sea aboard an akatos, where most of the men don't even have room to lie down to sleep."

"But you see something new every day, every hour!" Erinna sighed. "I know every bump and scratch on the walls of the women's rooms upstairs, every knot in the planks of the roof beams. Even coming out here to the courtyard feels like a journey to me."

He wanted to laugh, but he didn't. Men and women lived different lives, and that was all there was to it. So he spoke of meeting Ptolemaios' five in the Aegean, of the little earthquake while they were at Cape Tainaron, of Herennius Egnatius' toga in Taras, of seeing Mount Aitne and Mount Ouesouion, of his muleback excursion from Pompaia toward Ouesouion, and of the eclipse of the sun at Syracuse. He couldn't have had a more attentive audience; his sister hung on his every word.

Erinna sighed again when he finished. "When you tell me about these things, I can almost see them in my mind. How marvelous it must be to see them in truth."

"I'm just glad I saw the volcanoes when they were quiet," Sostratos said.

"Well, yes," Erinna admitted. "But even so." Her gaze sharpened. "When the man came running up here from the harbor, he was shouting about sea fights. You didn't talk about any sea fights."

"We really had only one," he said, and told her the story of the clash with the Roman trireme.

This time, his sister clapped her hands when he was done. "That was exciting," she said. "Why didn't you tell me about it before?"

Sostratos chuckled sheepishly. "Because it wasn't exciting while it was going on, I suppose," he answered. "It was terrifying. And seeing the Carthaginian fleet coming at us outside of Syracuse was worse. If that had turned into a sea fight, we couldn't possibly have won."

"Why did you let Menedemos go on, then?" Erinna asked.

Sostratos' mouth twisted into a wry, lopsided smile. His laugh was similarly sour. "My dear, it wasn't a question of my *letting* him do any such thing. I'm toikharkhos. He's the captain. The choice was his. I tried to talk him out of it." *I thought he was a fool. I thought he was a reckless idiot.* "When he said we were heading for Syracuse, what could I do? Leave the ship and swim home? It turned out well."

"Luck," Erinna said, and then, "Why are you laughing now?"

"Because you sound just like me," he told her. "But it wasn't all luck. Menedemos turned out to be right about that. Agathokles used the grain fleet to lure the Carthaginian ships away from the harbor and give his own navy the chance to get out and make for Africa."

"Can he take Carthage?" Erinna asked.

"I don't know," Sostratos answered. "Nobody knows—including the Carthaginians, I'm sure. But I do know they can't be anxious to find out. No one's ever tried to take the wars in Sicily to their country before."

"Alexander conquered the barbarians in the east," his sister said. "Why shouldn't Agathokles conquer the barbarians in the west?"

"I can think of two reasons," Sostratos replied. Erinna raised a questioning eyebrow. He explained: "First, the Carthaginians are still strong. And second, Agathokles isn't Alexander, no matter how much he wishes he were."

"All right." Erinna hugged him again. "It's so good to have you home. No one else takes me seriously when I ask questions."

"Well, if your brother won't, who will?" Sostratos kissed her on the forehead. "I'll be home till spring, so you'll have plenty of chances to ask them. But now I'm going upstairs." With obvious reluctance, she dipped her head and let him go. As he headed for the stairway, she picked up the hydria and went back to watering.

He was halfway up the stairs when Threissa started down them. "Hail, young master," the redheaded slave girl said in her oddly accented Greek. "Welcome home."

"Hail. Thank you," he said, and went up another couple of steps. The Thracian slave wasn't so pretty as Maibia had been. But Maibia was back in Taras while Threissa was here—and Sostratos had gone without a long time. "Come to my room with me," he told her.

She sighed. She couldn't say no, not when she was as much property as the bed on which he intended to have her. But she said, "All right," in a way that promised she would give him as little enjoyment as she could.

He considered ways and means. "I'll let you have a couple of oboloi afterwards."

He didn't have to do that, not with a family slave. "All right," Threissa said, but this time in a different tone of voice. "Maybe even three?"

Slaves are mercenary creatures, Sostratos thought. *But then they have to be.* "Maybe," he answered. Threissa waited for him at the top of the stairs. They went down the hall together to his room. He closed the door behind them.

"COME ON," MENEDEMOS said as he and Sostratos made their way toward the gymnasion in the southwestern part of Rhodes, not far from the stadium and the temple dedicated to Apollo. "It'll do you good. We've been away too long."

His cousin accompanied him only reluctantly. "What you mean is, it'll do *you* good to show you can still outrun me and throw me when we wrestle. I don't know why you bother. We both know how that will come out."

"That's not the point," Menedemos said, which was at least partially true. "The point is, a proper Hellene doesn't let himself go to seed."

"I can think of quite a few things you do that a proper Hellene doesn't," Sostratos said tartly. "Why shouldn't I get to pick and choose, too?"

Since Menedemos knew he had no good comeback for that, he didn't bother trying to find one. Instead, he repeated, "Come on," adding, "No point in going back now. Look, you can already see the theater and the southern wall beyond it."

"And if I went back home, I could see Demeter's temple," Sostratos retorted. "Did you drag me out here to see the sights? I don't mind that so much. Going to the gymnasion is a different story."

"Quit complaining," Menedemos said, beginning to lose patience. "You can let yourself get all hunched-up and flabby, like a shoemaker stuck at his bench all the time or a barbarian who doesn't care what he looks like because he never takes off his clothes, or else you can try to be as much of a *kalos k'agathos* as you can."

"I have much more control over whether I'm good than I do over whether I'm good-looking," Sostratos said. Despite his grumbles, he accompanied Menedemos into the gymnasion. They stripped off their chitons—being seamen, they didn't bother with sandals—and gave an attendant an abolos to keep an eye on the clothes while they went out and exercised.

Some of the men running on the track or grappling with one another in the sandy wrestling pits plainly didn't get to the gymnasion often enough. But others . . . Menedemos pointed. "There's a pretty boy, fourteen or fifteen, and handsome enough to have his name scrawled on the walls." His own name had gone up on more than a few walls when he was that age; Sostratos', he remembered rather too late, hadn't.

All his cousin said now, though, was, "Yes, and doesn't he know it? If he sticks his nose any higher in the air, he'll get a crick in the neck."

"When you look like that, you can get away with a few airs," Menedemos said. Sostratos only grunted.

They ran a few sprints to loosen up. Menedemos savored the feel of the breeze against his skin, the grass at the verge of the track flying by as he strained to get every bit of speed from himself he could. He also savored leaving Sostratos in his wake, hearing his cousin's panting breath fade behind him time after time.

"You're a pentekonter, sure enough," Sostratos said. "Me, I'm just a round ship."

Menedemos' turn of speed drew the notice of a fellow a couple of years younger than he who also had the lean, muscular build of a runner. "Try yourself against me?" the younger man said. "I'm Amyntas son of Praxion."

"Pleased to meet you." Menedemos gave his own name, and introduced Sostratos, too. "I'd be pleased to run with you. My cousin will call the start."

"Good enough," Amyntas said. "Would you care to put a drakhma on the race, just to make it interesting?"

"Interesting, eh?" Menedemos raised an eyebrow. "All right, if it pleases you. Sostratos, turn us loose." He took his position on the track beside Amyntas.

"Ready?" Sostratos called. "Set." Both runners tensed. "Go!"

Amyntas went off like an arrow from a bow. Menedemos stayed shoulder to shoulder with him till they were within twenty-five or thirty cubits of the end of the stadion course, but Amyntas pulled away and won by five cubits or so. "I can do better than that," Menedemos said. "Try it again, double the stake to the winner?"

"Why not?" Amyntas said, not quite hiding a predatory smile as they walked back to the beginning of the course. Several men gathered to watch them now. Menedemos wondered if Sostratos would give him a fishy stare for gambling on his legs. But his cousin only shrugged and called the start again. *He's probably glad not to be running himself,* Menedemos thought, leaning forward to get the best start he could.

"Go!" Sostratos said, and Menedemos and Amyntas shot away once more. Again, Menedemos stayed close to the younger man till the race was almost over. Again, he couldn't quite keep up at the end. Again, he kicked at the dirt in frustration.

"That's two drakhmai you owe me," Amyntas said, not bothering to hide his grin now that he'd won.

"Let's double it one more time." Menedemos sounded like a man determined to win his way back to prosperity no matter how long it took—and no matter if it broke him first.

"Just as you say, best one," Amyntas replied as they walked back toward the starting line.

"Give us a start one more time," Menedemos called to Sostratos. "I'm going to whip this fellow yet, and I've doubled the bet to prove it." Some of the men who stood at the side of the track watching murmured among themselves. Amyntas' grin got wider; he had witnesses, in case Menedemos didn't feel like paying up.

They took their marks. "Ready?" Sostratos said. "Set . . . Go!"

Amyntas and Menedemos flew down the track side by side. As before, Menedemos hung at the younger man's shoulder till they were about thirty cubits from the end of the course. Then Amyntas, leaning forward for his final sprint, let out a startled grunt. Menedemos went past him as if his feet were suddenly nailed to the dirt, and won by three or four cubits.

"That's four drakhmai *you* owe *me,*" he said cheerfully. "Or would you like to double the bet again?"

"Oh, no." Amyntas tossed his head. "I know what I just saw. You held back the first two runs to draw me in, didn't you?"

"I don't know *what* you're talking about." Menedemos' voice was arch. "Besides, how can I be sure you weren't trying to fool me there?" But he knew. Amyntas had been running flat out, and he hadn't been good enough. Menedemos chuckled. If he'd been fast enough to go to Olympia a couple of years before, Amyntas would have remembered his name. Nobody recalled the also-rans, but a man nearly fast enough to represent his polis at the Olympic Games was plenty fast to beat a fellow who picked up a little extra silver betting on his legs now and then.

"Why haven't I seen you round the gymnasion more?" Amyntas asked sadly. "I would have known better than to take you on."

"I just got back from Great Hellas," Menedemos replied, and the other man rolled his eyes in sorrow and chagrin.

They walked back toward Sostratos by the start line. Amyntas peeled off toward the building where the men left their tunics. "I hope he's not going to get dressed and skip out without paying you,"

Sostratos said. To him, it was the principle of the thing more than the money.

"I doubt it," Menedemos said. "He couldn't show his face here again for shame if he did—too many people watching. Shall we throw javelins while we wait?"

"Something to that," his cousin allowed. "Javelins? Why not? I'm not hopeless with them, anyway." And he wasn't. With his long arms, he threw fairly well—as Alexidamos had painful cause to know—though he would never be graceful. He matched Menedemos for distance, and almost matched him in accuracy throwing at a bale of straw.

Amyntas did come back. He gave Menedemos a fat, massy tetradrakhm with Apollo on one side and the rose of Rhodes on the other. "That'll teach me," he said.

"You'll win it back." Menedemos was willing to let him down easy. "Who knows? You may even use the same trick yourself one of these days."

"Why, so I may." Amyntas sounded surprised, as if that hadn't crossed his mind. Maybe it hadn't. Menedemos sighed. Amyntas didn't notice, as he hadn't noticed Menedemos holding back. Sostratos did, and contrived to look amused without smiling.

Having paid what he owed, Amyntas hurried away, as if afraid Menedemos would inveigle him into some other contest he was bound to lose. Menedemos turned back to Sostratos. "Want to wrestle?"

"Not especially," Sostratos answered. Menedemos' face must have fallen, for his cousin went on, "But I will, at least for a little while."

They dusted their arms and torsos with sand, to aid in getting a grip. Then they stood face to face, waiting. "Ready?" Sostratos asked. Menedemos dipped his head. Sostratos sprang at him. They grappled, grunting and heaving, each straining to throw the other off his feet. Sostratos' height did him no good in wrestling. If anything, the compact Menedemos had the advantage there, being closer to the ground. He got Sostratos on his hip, twisted lithely, and threw him down.

"Oof!" Sostratos said; he'd landed pretty hard. He was rubbing his right buttock as he rose. "I'm going to be sore about sitting down for the next couple of days."

"You made me work for it," Menedemos said. He did mean it; he often won a fall from Sostratos much more easily than he had there. And he wanted to keep him wrestling, too.

Before he could ask for another fall, his cousin said, "Shall we try it again?"

"Yes, if you like." Menedemos tried to hide his surprise. He couldn't remember the last time Sostratos had proposed such a thing. They squared off and grabbed each other, as they had before. Indeed, the second bout went very much as the first one had, right up to Sostratos' mistake. As Menedemos slid in to take advantage of it, he wondered if his cousin would ever learn.

He got his answer sooner than he expected. Instead of going up on his hip and then down in the dirt, Sostratos kept one of his long legs on the ground. Before Menedemos quite realized what had happened, his cousin had got round behind him, slipped an ankle in front, and shoved hard. Next thing he knew, he sprawled in the dirt himself.

He spat some out of his mouth, then said, "Well, well," as he got to his feet. Sostratos' face wore a grin as wide as that of a child with a toy chariot or a hetaira with a new gold necklace. He didn't throw Menedemos very often. Menedemos bowed, giving him credit for it. "Very nice. I thought I had you again, but I was wrong."

"I was hoping you would make the same move twice," Sostratos said. "I tried to steer you into it, the way you held back with that fellow who thought he was fast."

"*Did* you?" Menedemos said, and Sostratos delightedly dipped his head. Menedemos clicked his tongue between his teeth. He tasted more dirt, and spat again. "I'm never going to be able to trust you any more, am I?"

"I hope not," Sostratos told him.

They wrestled twice more. Menedemos won both times, but neither win came easily. He felt himself slower than he should have been. Instead of just wrestling, he was thinking about his moves before he made them, wondering, *If I do this, what does Sostratos have waiting for me?* Against an opponent who was skilled as well as clever, he probably would have lost both falls.

Sostratos noticed. As they rubbed themselves down with olive oil and scraped if off with curved bronze strigils, he said, "I had you looking over your shoulder there, didn't I?"

"As a matter of fact, you did." Menedemos mimed sorrow verging on despair. "A terrible thing, when I can't trust my own cousin."

"Trust me to go down like a sacrifice after its throat is cut, you mean," Sostratos said. "Maybe I'll be able to give you a real contest now."

"Maybe," Menedemos said. "Or maybe I'll find more tricks of my own." To his relief, Sostratos didn't look so happy about that. They finished cleaning themselves off and went back to reclaim their chitons. Then they left the gymnasion and headed up toward their homes in the northern part of the city.

Sostratos said, "Remember, my father's symposion is evening after next."

"I'm not likely to forget." Menedemos rolled his eyes. "And even if I did, you don't suppose my father would?" He didn't bother trying to hide his annoyance.

"If you looked on your father a little more tolerantly, he might do the same for you, you know," Sostratos said.

"Ha! Not likely," Menedemos answered. "If he looked on me a little more tolerantly, *I* might do the same for him. I'm not saying I would, mind you, but I might." His cousin sighed and said no more about it. That suited Menedemos fine.

GARLANDED FOR A SYMPOSION, Sostratos always felt like something of an impostor. Most men donned gaiety with the wreaths and ribbons, as if it naturally accompanied them. He'd never been able to do that. And yet, a man who wasn't jolly at a symposion was an object of suspicion. There were times when he had to pretend to what he didn't feel, which did make him feel like a hypocrite.

Still, he might have been more at ease than Diokles. The oarmaster didn't come from a circle where symposia came along very often, if at all. His chiton and himation were good enough, but, a seaman to the core, he'd arrived at Sostratos' house barefoot. And he kept fidgeting on his couch, trying to find a comfortable position in which to recline.

To Sostratos' relief, the symposiasts had chosen his father as symposiarch. "Let it be five parts of water to two of wine," Lysistratos declared. No one could possibly complain about that, and no one did: it was the perfect mixture, not too strong, not too weak.

On the couch next to Sostratos and Menedemos reclined an olive farmer named Damophon. Like any prosperous landowner, he took symposia for granted. He didn't grumble at the mixture, but did chuckle and say, "I'll bet you boys drank stronger than that in Great Hellas. When the Italiotes put on a revel, they don't do it by halves. That's what everybody says, so I expect it must be true."

"Shall we talk of what people say and what is so?" Sostratos asked. But, at the same time, Menedemos also spoke up: "I'll say we did. This one affair in Taras"—the only symposion they'd been to in Great Hellas, but he didn't mention that—"it was one of wine to one of water till nobody could see straight."

Damophon paid no attention to Sostratos, but whistled at Menedemos' words. "One to one will do that, all right, and do it fast." Slaves passed out cups of the mixed wine. The olive grower sipped. He whistled again. "That's mighty fine stuff, that is—mighty fine."

Several other symposiasts were saying the same thing. Lysistratos smiled. He coughed a couple of times to draw men's eyes to him, then said, "That's Ariousian brought from Khios by my son and my nephew. We should thank the Italiotes and the Italian barbarians for being too ignorant to buy quite all of it, and for leaving this amphora for us to enjoy tonight."

The cheers that rose from the couches in the andron were louder and more fervent than might have been expected for so early in the evening and so mild a mixture. "*Euge,* Sostratos! *Euge,* Menedemos!" Xanthos called. "As I was saying in the Assembly the other day—"

Sostratos' father overrode the fat bore: "Since we've gathered together here to drink and to welcome Sostratos and Menedemos back to Rhodes after their safe and prosperous journey to the west"—more applause interrupted him—"my thought was that tonight we would speak of others who are on journeys or have returned from them, so that the long absent may be called to mind again."

Menedemos chuckled. "No dirty stories, not when your father's running things."

"If you need that sort of thing at *every* symposion, my dear, go off and live in Great Hellas," Sostratos answered. Neither spoke loud enough for Lysistratos to notice.

As was the custom, the guests began at the far end of the semicircle from the couches Sostratos and Menedemos and their fathers shared. Diokles, by then, had drunk enough wine to blunt his shyness at drinking with men more prominent than he. He told a fine tale of shipwreck and rescue on the Lykian coast. Another man spoke of a brother who'd set off with Alexander and come back years later short an eye and three fingers on his right hand. Xanthos gave forth with an endless story that seemed to have no point whatsoever. Damophon told of ransoming his father, who'd been captured on a trading voyage by pirates from Crete.

And then it was Sostratos' turn. He rose. Dipping his head to Damophon, he said, "I don't think any man here would shed a tear if Crete sank into the sea, as the divine Platon says the island of Atlantis did in days gone by." No one contradicted him. Several men clapped their hands. He went on, "You meet Rhodians all over the Inner Sea. Menedemos and I ran into one on our journey to Great Hellas. Instead of making a long speech"—Xanthos wouldn't get the point of that, worse luck—"I was wondering if anyone here could tell me more about a soldier named Alexidamos son of Alexion."

Menedemos started to say something, then checked himself. Sostratos had only named Alexidamos; he hadn't told anyone what the mercenary had done, or even that he'd done anything. After stopping to think, Menedemos whispered, "Sly."

Sostratos bent down and whispered back: "You know me—I always want to find out."

"Alexidamos son of Alexion?" Damophon said. "A good-sized fellow a little older than you are, Sostratos, with a scar across his nose?"

"That's the man," Sostratos agreed, and didn't say anything about how he'd drastically revised Alexidamos' nose in Kallipolis.

"Alexion died five or six years ago," Damophon said. "I used to buy fish from him. Instead of taking his father's boat out, Alexidamos sold it and used the silver he got to buy his weapons. He said soldiering had to be an easier way to make a living than fishing. Where did you meet him?"

"Cape Tainaron," Sostratos answered. "We took him across to

Italy. With all the wars in those parts, a soldier wouldn't have any trouble finding work."

From the couch Philodemos shared with Sostratos' father, he said, "With all the wars everywhere these days, a soldier has no trouble finding work."

"Wherever Alexidamos draws his drakhma a day and his rations, he'll likely lay his hands on more somehow or other," Damophon said. "His father was reliable, but I stopped buying from Alexidamos even before he sold the boat. He was the sort who'd drench yesterday's fish in seawater to make them look fresh. Any man can have that trick played on him once, but only a fool lets it happen twice." He glanced over to Sostratos. "Did he give you trouble?"

"Nothing we couldn't handle," Sostratos said, and Menedemos dipped his head.

When Sostratos reclined once more, Menedemos rose from the couch and said, "I'll give you the most famous return of all—Odysseus' return to Ithake, and to his own home town. Here's how Homer tells it:

'Then Odysseus of many wiles, answering him, said,
"I know. I understand. You order someone with discernment.
But let us go, and you lead all the way.
But give me, if you have one anywhere, a stick
On which to lean, since you said the road was rough."
·He spoke, and flung his shabby pouch, full of holes,
Around his shoulder with a strap.
Then Eumaios gave him a staff that suited him.
The pair went off, but dogs and herdsmen stayed behind
To protect the farmhouse. He led the king to the city
In the guise of a wretched old beggarman
Leaning on his staff, and pitiful were the clothes on his
      back. . . .' "

Menedemos recited from the *Odyssey* for some time. As always, the ancient tale drew in all who listened to it, no matter how well everyone knew it. Even Sostratos, sophisticate though he was, found himself falling under Homer's spell. *How does he do it?* Sostratos wondered. The same question occurred to him whenever he read

Herodotos or Thoukydides. They were all writers he, like most Hellenes, despaired of matching.

When Menedemos took his place on the couch once more, his father rose from the adjoining one. Sostratos hoped Philodemos might say something graceful about the return of the *Aphrodite,* but he didn't. Instead, he spoke of how the Rhodians had ousted the Macedonian garrison in the city after news of Alexander's death arrived, and "how we had our freedom restored to us, and nothing for a polis is more important than its freedom. May we keep it in the future as we regained it in the past."

He reclined again. The symposiasts clapped their hands, Sostratos among them—and Menedemos, too, he noted. Philodemos *had* struck an important chord, all the more important because Ptolemaios and Antigonos were fighting again. When giants clashed, how could a dwarf like Rhodes stay safe? That comparison made Sostratos smile.

Host and symposiarch, Lysistratos got to his feet last of all. "I'll be brief, for we've got people waiting in the courtyard," Sostratos' father said. "A voyage to Great Hellas is always a risk. I thank the gods that my son and my nephew and almost all the crew came home safe. That's the most important thing. You always have another chance if it's true, even if the business end of things didn't go so well. But when they not only sailed west but came back with one of the biggest profits an akatos ever brought home—well, my friends, all I can tell you is that I'm proud to be kin to both of them. *Euge,* Sostratos! *Euge,* Menedemos!"

"*Euge!*" the symposiasts shouted, and clapped their hands and raised their cups in salute. *"Euge! Euge!"*

"Thank you all," Sostratos said. "A man who deserves special praise is our bold keleustes Diokles there. You couldn't hope to find a better sailor. *Euge,* Diokles!"

"*Euge!*" the symposiasts echoed. Diokles' lined features wore the bashful, proud grin of a boy praised for his beauty for the first time.

"Now everybody here will try to hire him away from us," Menedemos said.

"Tell me he hasn't earned the chance," Sostratos said, and Menedemos only shrugged. He couldn't do it, and they both knew as much.

Lysistratos beckoned to Gyges. He spoke in the majordomo's ear. The Lydian slave hurried out into the dark courtyard. As Sostratos' father had said, the entertainers were waiting there. A moment later, a couple of flutegirls in chitons of thin, filmy Koan silk pranced into the andron and began to play. The symposiasts whooped and cheered. A couple of them reached out to try to grab the girls, but they had no luck. Only a very raw slave would have let herself become a plaything so soon.

And then the men in the andron stopped reaching for the girls. There would be plenty of time for that later, and they'd done it plenty of times before. They whooped again, on a different note this time, and howled laughter, for into the room behind the flute girls bounded a naked dancing dwarf. His head and genitals were the size of a normal man's, his body and limbs sadly shrunken.

"Think I'm pretty funny, don't you?" he said in a light, true tenor as he spun in time to the music. "I'll tell you something, friends—if everybody looked like me, *you'd* be the monsters."

That made most of the symposiasts laugh harder than ever. Menedemos choked on his wine, and all but drowned. Sostratos had been laughing, too. He'd known his father had hired the dwarf; that was what had touched off his thought about the large realms Antigonos and Ptolemaios held, with little Rhodes doing her best not to get crushed between them.

But, though the dancing dwarf had made his gibe to amuse the symposiasts, it also made Sostratos think. Most people reckoned dwarfs less intelligent than normal men, but this fellow sounded bright enough. How did he feel, when he was able to make his living only by showing himself off for others to laugh at?

Sostratos thought about asking the little man. He thought about it, but not even his own sharp curiosity gave him the nerve to do it. After all, what was he but one more fellow who reminded the dwarf of his freakishness?

Instead, he got very drunk, even with his father's well-watered wine and shallow drinking cups. Maybe some of the symposiasts did end up rumpling the flutegirls. If they did, Sostratos didn't see it. They might have taken the girls out into the dark courtyard, or the symposion might just have stayed on the decorous side. After a while, he was dozing on his half of the couch.

What roused him was Menedemos's talent for quoting Homer. His cousin started to recite the section from the *Iliad* where lame Hephaistos bustled around serving wine to the other gods, who laughed at him despite his labor. "No," Sostratos said. "Find some other lines. Leave the little man here alone."

Menedemos gaped. "That's why he's here: to be the butt of our jokes. Look at the silly capers he's cutting." Sure enough, the dwarf was waggling his backside like a coy courtesan, and he *was* funny.

But despite, or perhaps because of, the wine he'd drunk, Sostratos found the distinction he wanted to make: "Laugh at what he does, not at what he is."

"Why?" Menedemos said. "What he does isn't always worth laughing at. What he is, is."

Sostratos ran out of logical arguments. That *was* the wine. "If you can't find any other reason, don't mock him as a favor to me."

"All right, best one," Menedemos said, and kissed him on the cheek. "You're my cousin, and you're my host, and as a favor to you I will keep quiet. You see? I deny you nothing tonight."

"Thank you, my dear. You've made our homecoming perfect." Sostratos yawned. That was the last he remembered of the symposion, for he really did fall asleep then.

AFTER THE SYMPOSION at his uncle and cousin's house, several days of rain kept Menedemos close to home. What point to going to the gymnasion to try to run through mud or, worse, wrestle in it? What point to going to the agora when hardly anyone would be buying or selling or gossiping?

He wouldn't have minded so much being cooped up if he and his father could have walked past each other without growling. But they didn't get along, and being at close quarters only made things worse. Menedemos tried to stay out of Philodemos' way by taking one of the slave women into his bedroom and not coming out for most of a day, but that didn't work, either. When he and the slave did emerge, Philodemos grumbled, "She didn't do any work at all yesterday, thanks to you."

"Oh, I wouldn't say that, Father," Menedemos answered blandly. "She got very sweaty by the time we were through."

His father rolled his eyes. "I've got a cockhound for a son. Everything I've work so hard to get will end up in some hetaira's hands when I'm dead."

"With what I brought home from Great Hellas, I could keep three of the greediest hetairai in the world happy for a long time, and the family would still be ahead," Menedemos said.

"That's what you think," Philodemos said. "You have no idea how greedy and grasping a woman can be."

"What I have no idea of right now is why I bothered coming home," Menedemos snapped. "It seems everything I've ever done is wrong."

"You said it. I didn't." Philodemos stalked out of the andron, his spine stiff with triumph. Menedemos made a face at him behind his back. Then he headed off to the kitchen; satisfying one appetite in his room had left him with another unslaked.

He took some olives and cheese. The cook warned him, "If you touch one scale—even one scale, mind you—on the mullet I've got there for supper, I'll snatch you baldheaded. I mean it. This is *my* domain, by the gods."

Laughing, Menedemos said, "All right, Sikon. Till you work your magic on that mullet, I don't want it anyway. Maybe a starving man would eat a raw fish, but I wouldn't."

He stood in the doorway, out of the rain, while he ate his snack. Sikon kept railing at him with the license a skilled and privileged slave enjoyed. Menedemos laughed. With Sikon yelling, he could afford to laugh. The cook's barbs didn't get under his skin and rankle, the way his father's did. He spat an olive pit out into the courtyard. It landed in a puddle with a splash. He ate another olive and spat again, seeing if he could make this pit go farther than the one before. When he spat a third pit, he wanted it to go farther than either of the other two.

I wish Sostratos were here, he thought. *We could bet oboloi. I'd beat him, too, even if I had to make silly faces so he'd laugh and spit badly.* If he got into any kind of contest, he wanted to win it. Imagining how furious Sostratos would be if his antics ruined a spit made him smile. The next time they ate olives together . . .

His good mood quite restored, he looked across the courtyard. He could probably go back to his room without running into his father. Probably. He hung around in the kitchen, enduring Sikon's insults, for a while longer. He didn't want to risk that better mood, and it wouldn't survive another meeting with Philodemos.

What do I do when I get to my room? he wondered. *Play the lyre, maybe?* He shrugged. He was no marvelous musician. The lyre had hardly come off its pegs on the wall since his school days; the kitharist who'd taught him had been too free with the switch to give him any love for the instrument.

After a while, he squelched across the courtyard and started up the stairs. At the same time, someone else started down them. He cursed under his breath. If that was his father . . . But it wasn't; the voice that said, "Hail, Menedemos," was thin, light, and feminine.

"Oh," Menedemos said. "Good day, Baukis." He hoped his father's wife hadn't heard the curse; she might think it was aimed at her. He probably should have said, *Good day, stepmother,* but that seemed ridiculous when he was ten years older than she. He didn't have anything in particular against her. If she had children by his father, that might be a different story, for his own inheritance would shrink, but for now she was only a girl learning what being a wife was about.

Baukis came down the stairs towards him. She *was* young, her figure still almost boyish though she wore a woman's long chiton. She said, "It's not a *very* good day, is it?" Then she paused, as if waiting for him to contradict her. When he didn't, she went on in a rush: "I'm awfully tired of the rain."

"So am I," Menedemos answered. "I want to go out into the polis, to stroll in the agora, to exercise in the gymnasion, to see my friends and chat with them. . . ."

"I just want the sun to shine again, to lighten up the women's quarters and dry out the courtyard, and to let me see farther than Lysistratos' house from my window." As a proper wife, especially one wed to an older, more conservative man like Philodemos, Baukis wouldn't get out of the house much. Being a man, Menedemos could go where he would. This little space was Baukis' world.

He hadn't thought about that before complaining of being shut up here. He changed the subject in a hurry: "Sikon has a fine mullet in the kitchen."

Her expression sharpened. She wasn't particularly pretty—she had buck teeth like a hare's, and pimples splashed her cheeks—but no one who spoke with her for even a moment would ever have thought her a fool. "A mullet? What did he pay for it?" she asked.

"I don't know," Menedemos said. "I didn't even think to find out."

"I'll have to," Baukis said fretfully. "Too much, unless I miss my guess. Sikon spends silver as if it grew on trees."

"What with the profit the *Aphrodite* made, we have plenty," Menedemos said.

"We do *now*," she said. "But how long will it last if we throw it to the winds?"

"You sound like Sostratos." Menedemos didn't mean it altogether as a compliment. With luck, Baukis wouldn't know that.

She just sniffed. "I don't think any man really knows, really cares, about money." Menedemos let out an indignant yelp, but Baukis went on, "Men don't have to manage a household, but wives do. Money and children. We'd better be good with those. We don't get much chance to deal with anything else."

"Well, of course," Menedemos said, and didn't stop to wonder if it felt like *of course* to Baukis. He'd heard similar things from the bored wives he'd seduced. That was probably why some of them had let him bed them, in fact—to get something out of the cramped and ordinary into their lives.

"I'd better go talk to him," Baukis said. "A mullet? That can't have been cheap. Excuse me, Menedemos." She slipped down the stairs past him and walked across the courtyard, raising a hand to her face to keep the rain out of her eyes.

Menedemos turned to watch her go. Her breasts weren't much more than a maiden might have had, but her hips and her walk were a woman's after all. *What does she think about such things, being married to my sour graybeard of a father?* Menedemos wondered. *Is she bored already? I wouldn't be surprised.*

He went up the stairs in a hurry, taking most of them two at a time. He trotted down the hall to his room, then went inside and closed the door behind him. For good measure, he barred it, too, and he couldn't remember the last time he'd done that. But what he ran from was in the room with him.

So was a good deal of darkness. The slave girl had wanted the shutters kept closed, and he'd humored her. He opened them, which turned things gray. He stared blindly out at the rain. Now he had another reason to wish it would stop. He wanted to flee the house as he'd fled up the stairs to this refuge that wasn't. He wondered if going out would do any good. He doubted it. Wouldn't he take his troubles with him, as he'd brought them here?

And then he started to laugh. It wasn't really funny—not to him, though a comic poet might have disagreed—but he didn't know what else to do. *My father would kill me if he knew what went through my mind.* He laughed again, more bitterly than before. He'd had that thought many times, ever since he was a little boy, when things went wrong. His shiver had nothing to do with the chilly, nasty weather. This time, it might be literally true.

But oh, wouldn't that pay him back for everything?

"No," Menedemos said aloud. He kept talking, too, in a soft voice no one in the hall could have heard: "This once, my dear, you're going to have to be like your cousin and use your head. It's not always the best part of you, but it's the only one that will do right now."

Next spring, I'll sail away and not have to worry about it for half a year. Meanwhile, I've got plenty of silver. I can have as good a time as I please. Even my father won't complain too much more than he usually does. That should cure me. It has before, plenty of times.

He heard Baukis on the stairs. After she'd returned to the women's rooms, he went downstairs for some wine. Dionysos' gift brought ease from all cares.

Even so, Menedemos could hardly wait for spring.

HISTORICAL NOTE

Over the Wine-Dark Sea is set in 310 B.C. The Roman attack on Pompaia (the Greek spelling for Pompeii) is described in Book IX of Livy. The journey of the grain fleet from Rhegion to Syracuse, and Agathokles' use of the opportunity it gave him to escape from Syracuse and invade Africa, are told in Book XX of Diodorus Siculus. The solar eclipse described here took place on August 15, 310 B.C. Diodorus is also the main surviving source for the machinations of Alexander's marshals, which form much of the background for this novel.

Of the characters actually on stage, only Menedemos himself and Agathokles' brother, Antandros, are historical figures. Historical figures alluded to but not visible include Agathokles, Ptolemaios, Antigonos, his sons Demetrios and Philippos, his nephew Polemaios (also known as Ptolemaios, but given the former spelling here to distinguish him from Antigonos' rival), Kassandros, Lysimakhos, Polyperkhon, Seleukos, Alexander's son Alexandros, Alexandros' mother, Roxane, Alexander's son (or suppositious son) Herakles, and Herakles' mother, Barsine.

I have for the most part spelled names of places and people as a Greek would have: thus Rhegion, not Rhegium; Lysimakhos, not Lysimachus. Taras was known to the Romans as Tarentum, and is the modern Taranto. I have broken this rule for a few place names that have well-established English spellings: Rhodes, Athens, Syracuse, the Aegean Sea, and the like. I have also broken it for Alexander the Great, whose shadow dominates this period even though he had been dead for about thirteen years when the story opens.

All translations from the Greek are my own. I claim no particular literary merit for them, only that they convey what the original says.

F

Turteltaub, H. Ň.

Over the wine-dark
sea.

$25.95

DATE			